Hidden Manna

Alec John Dawson

HIDDEN MANNA

BY

A. J. DAWSON

Author of

"African Nights' Entertainments," Etc.

" To him that overcometh will I give to eat of the hidden manna, and will give him a white stone, and in the stone a new name written, which no man knoweth saving he that receiveth it."
—*The Revelation of St. John the Divine* ii. 17.

NEW YORK
A. S. BARNES & COMPANY
1902

90

COPYRIGHT 1902 BY

A. S. BARNES & COMPANY

Published October 1902.

ADVERTISEMENT

" DEAR READER,

" I cannot approach you with that elegant, hand-washing air of humility, of apology for my work and my existence, which is so frequently and so ably affected by the writers of prefatory notes. If I were ashamed of my work, be sure you would never know it—the work or my shame. No; I cannot belittle the story, because it represents whole working years of my life, and deals with a land and a people that I love. Rather would I speak of it to you with a little pride and with much enthusiasm, seeking, by praiseful speech of it, to predispose you in its favour. But there is a false something, I know not exactly what, which deters me. As I see the thing, it must be hard even for the most foolish parent to be-praise his offspring in cold print. If you would be indulgent, call the feeling that deters me modesty. I call it a sham of some sort by token that I am fondly, beamingly delighted to leave the way clear for a pen more eloquent, and far more authoritative, than my own. But, as it happens, the wielder of that pen bears a name that may be almost as well known to you as to me. And here again my damnable false pride—or the other thing, whichever you may be pleased to call it—rears its smirking face, and bids me ask the friend (whose recognised position in the world of literature comes only second to his personal attributes in my esteem and respectful regard) to withhold his too

authoritative name, lest that alone should be said to win your consideration for my story. 'Then why bother us with all this, anyhow?' you may say. Well, did we not agree that you were to be indulgent, and, for civility's sweet sake, dub the thing modesty? I wish I could.

"A. J. Dawson.

" *Tangier*, 1902."

PREFACE

ADDRESSED BY A FRIEND TO THE AUTHOR

ONE of the prizes of friendship is the pleasure of rejecting the unsolicited aid and advice it offers. In this case, *Poscimur,* we are asked for our humble services. Now there are literary friends of more direct use than those just adumbrated. We know the gentlemanly creatures who go about looking after each other's books, inserting civil paragraphs about these same masterpieces before they are offered even to a publisher, indulging in the charmingly direct reciprocity of service which characterised, I gather, the lower orders of ancient Rome. They are supposed, it would seem, to be Bohemians, though they are too busy to be gay, and a good deal too practical to be out-at-elbows or devil-may-care fellows. They resemble, in fact, the Saint Stylites in advertising, with the best of motives, at the top of a column. Such you and I neither admire nor envy; yet I would declare, as my passport to prose here, that I am not ignorant of bookish matters and methods. Fiction in abundance I have read for the purposes of publisher, reviewer, and pleasure, and—I speak as a fool—I have noted some things and not forgotten others. I have seen reviewers who were palpably not omniscient, and recall prefaces penned on the slenderest occasion, mere pieces of authorial superfetation, amply justified as such, but in no way illuminating.

Here, I think, a preface is your due, and my boldness might supply what your modesty refuses. Persius has said that "your knowledge is nothing unless another knows that you know it." I should like a few to know that this book is unique of its kind, because it represents Morocco the real, the Oriental, the esoteric. The high authority who has written a trilogy on the Moors has recognised as the only two serious attempts in fiction to represent them, your "Bismillah" and Hall Caine's "Scapegoat." But the first is a slight thing, a love idyll, half in Tangier, and the other is but Tangier seen, the specialist might think, largely through the refracting imagination of the author. Now, Tangier is to Morocco as Earl's Court is to London.

This book is the real thing, then, for the first time, representing places and things unknown to people of leisure, travellers male and female, great persons, and newspaper correspondents. You have, I dare swear, carried your life in your hand to satisfy yourself; for instance, as to the details of Shareefian feasts. You have, in brief, been a Moor, or you could not have seen much that is pictured here. That is immediate romance. Yours is the true spirit of adventure and the love of the open road which we share, and which so many town-bred, middle-aged youths wisely affect.

Further, I must speak of your untiring search for accuracy in the smallest detail, which is the scholar's penalty and pleasure and a rarity nowadays, and then I have done, though I have made but little of my brief. But I have ever shunned exaggeration, and men have called me austere because I am honest.

HIPPOCLIDES.

CONTENTS

x CONTENTS

HIDDEN MANNA

Chapter I

AT THE CITY GATE

NOW, if it should be during the day's prime that you come to look upon the hoary face of Ed-dár, then assuredly will your hand rise to lend your eyes eaves for their shelter withal. Indeed, the same might be said of quite early morning time, when the day's a lad, for the city gates are built to face toward holy Mekka. But in the middle afternoon, es-sáhil, when siestas are some time past, and shadows everywhere step forth, like wayfarers within sight of their camping-ground, then is the forefront of Ed-dár el Kebeer quite otherwise; a calm and restful picture for a traveller's eyes to rest on, its outline softened by age and infirmity, its tones subdued to match the sweet, chaste garb of sober evening. And, es-sáhil, that is the time of our story's opening; the limpid hour in which a man may see all things clearly, as with eyes new-washed; the time for reflection, entertainment, and desultory converse.

At noon "A handful of jewels," you had called it, "flung pell-mell on the plain." But that were to overlook the city's crenulated, flaky walls, as a plain story-teller with a history of happenings to recount may not do.

The vultures do it, though, in another sense—they and their friends the hawks and crows, and their lords the storks, when hovering over that unsavoury mountain, the city rubbish-heap.

A litter of uncut crystals, let us say, filling to its splintered edges a decaying, lichen-grown mortar. The great Kasbah [1] tower is the long-disused pestle of our mortar. And the whole lies a-crumbling in unending sunshine and moonlight, sluiced once a year, when es-shitwá [2] sows er-rabeeâ,[3] and gives to the faithful Allah's promise of continued life.

Of such is the city of Ed-dár el Kebeer—Ed-dár the great, that is. And great it seems beyond compare in the eyes of the many believers who have never journeyed more than a few days' march from its lichen-covered battlements. Intricate, mazy, picturesque, and compact of essential romance and assertive odours it must needs be in the eyes and nostrils of any man possessed of a thought beyond barter, not to speak of recollections of Scriptural story or the legends of mystery-cloaked Baghdad.

It has thirteen large mosques (putting aside shrines), and thrice thirteen dungeons, with cut-throat alleys and body-snatching cul-de-sacs past reckoning. Much of it is roofed in, all of it is decrepit and marvellous. The more part of it is garmented in an ancient dirtiness which comes near to being venerable, and, think of it as you will, or not at all, it remains Ed-dár of a truth and of our story, a day's journey from holy Mismoo, a stage on the highway to scholarly Fez, and no more than three days as a mule ambles from infidel-afflicted Tangier and the

[1] Citadel, containing prison, official residences, and the like.
[2] Winter; literally, rainy.
[3] Spring; literally, grass.

turquoise ribbon that divides blood-letting Africa from blood-sapping Europe.

There is a by-word of none too reverent a sort which says, "With a closed mouth and open ears ye shall learn more of affairs at a city's gates than in the courts of the Karueen [4] or at the tombs of the righteous." That is as it may be in general matters. Bearing upon the matter in hand, it fits the writer's present business as water fits the skin its carrier bears it in, or as a lined slipper from Rabat will fit the foot of him to whose order it was designed—exactly. We have to do here with the city gate and its little circle of loiterers in later afternoon on a day of the grass season.

The little crowd was notable because that two Christians lounged at one side of it, and Nazarenes, as you may guess, were never plentiful in Ed-dár. To the other sort of infidel (Yahûdi) there is no end, wheresoever you shall find Muslims gathered together. Greasy and gaberdined, hovering ever betwixt spittle-licking and tyrannical oppression, the salted [5] place of Ed-dár is full of the crafty children of El [6] Kuds, who, as in every other plain or valley town of Morocco, and even in some of the mountain fastnesses, do Mohammedans' trading for them, are the city's menials, and hold the great bulk of its wealth. But Christians, they are scarce in Ed-dár, despite its nearness to hybrid Tangier, and the two travellers of that breed who loitered by the gates upon this particular evening received to the full as many curious glances from assembled believers as they gave to the scene about them.

There was Ahmet, the blind story-teller, and he has to

[4] The University of Fez.

[5] In Moorish towns the Jews' quarter is called the Mellah—i. e., the salted place.

[6] Jerusalem, the Holy.

be named first by reason that he was fresh from Tangier
with a budget of entertaining gossip, quite apart from his
stock of narratives of the sort that have come to us from
the ancients.   Ahmet was the man of the hour in the gateway, and occupied the position of host toward all and
sundry who rested there.

Ranged about the story-teller, some standing or lounging beside the walls, and more squatting decently upon
bare earth, or upon sitting mats, each in his degree, were
Haj M. Barak, the busy-body who prospered no man
knew how (el-Mâllim, or the skilled one, flatterers called
him), M'amet the bleeder and head shaver, Salaam the
blacksmith, old Hamadi of the fandak, a weaver, two
water-carriers, a saddler, a brass-worker, two oven-boys,
a scribe, the principal dillál, or market auctioneer, and a
dozen or more of others.   These others included a rather
noted f. keeh, a scarred wight newly released from prison
and from the question (put with hot irons), holy Haj
Cassim, the pivot[7] or hermit, and his companion in holiness and repute, the White Beggar of Ed-dár, who for
more than two years now had sat silent upon his mat
beside the hermit's, an arrival from nowhere, whose
coming no man had witnessed, and whose silent indifference to all things about him had quickly earned for
him devoutly generous regard and some celebrity.

Then there were the two onlookers, the Nazarenes,
both of the English sort, or from London-country, as
Moors put it, one an old resident of Morocco, somewhat
coarse of feature, with a cynical, indifferent look in his
eyes; the other new to it all, a painter, bearing about him
indications not a few of that mental twist which folk who
are free of it call the artistic temperament, that cross
which causes its bearers to go farther and fare worse, to

[7] Kot'b.

rejoice and suffer more, to see deeper and so know more sorrow than do other mortals. Angels' favourites, the afflicted of Allah, hermits, saints, idiots, fanatics, those born blind and those endowed as was this painter man; Muslims docket them all in a bunch, alike fit subjects for charity, indulgent kindliness, and a curious mixture of reverence and contempt, in which only reverence is made visible.

Mordant Dogget was a brilliantly clever young artist of the impressionist school, and it may be said of him now, and plainly, that the reason he is named in this place is simply that his were the eyes that saw and his the tongue which told, of this particular evening scene at Ed-dár's great gate. Some affairs there be, and the matter leading to this story is one of them, in regard to which no definite categorical record can be unearthed. Remains, then, in such cases the gleaming of impressions, the which, without doubt, are sometimes cogent and illuminative enough.

Chapter II

SUN PICTURES

"IS he preaching a holy war, or merely telling one of the Arabian Nights stories, this blind fellow with the wand?" asked the painter of his friend, the old resident in Morocco.

"Neither," replied the man, who saw but uninteresting littleness in the scene which formed a rare Eastern picture for his friend, "though, to be sure, he's done both in his time. That's Ahmet, the story-teller. You've struck his usual business—telling stories from the Arabian Nights."

"Really?"

"Really, and of his father's before him. But just now he's displaying a new pack, quite a fresh line—'The Forty Days and Nights of Entertainment,' he calls it; a chapter from 'The Sacred Mystery of our Lord of Ain Araish, his marriage with the Rarest Pearl of the Christians, whom heaven transformed into a believer at sight of the Holy Shareef.' They're death on long titles. I heard some of it in the Sôk at Tangier. There was 'The Miraculous Journey of the Shareef of Ain Araish through the Lands of the Infidels,' and a lot more."

"Ah! it sounds very fascinating."

"M'ph!"

"What's it all about?"

"Why, that, to be sure—the marriage of the Shareef of Ain Araish. Surely you have heard something of Moulai Hassan's goings on—his trip to France, and his six weeks'

6

carnival at Trouville, ending with the wedding? He married an English girl, you know—Hassan, the holy Shareef of Ain Araish! Such a thing had never been heard or thought of. From what I can make out he's expected here with his party in a day or so, *en route* for his own stronghold in Ain Araish. Oh, but he's a picturesque sort of a ' Piece of Heaven ' is Moulai Hassan el Gharbi, I can assure you! The English girl must know something about that by this time."

" I say, Crane, I hate to interrupt you—you won't often supply me sketches like that—but I must ask you something. Who is that lithe fellow lying like a Greek in tatters, or like Hamlet in the murder scene, chin in hand? Look."

" Oh, that's the White Beggar of Ed-dár. Quite a recent acquisition, I believe; only been here two years, and hasn't spoken to anyone yet except Haj Cassim the hermit, the other beggar beside him. I fancy they reckon he's fallen out of Paradise, or something—turned up from nowhere, you know. They just found him there one morning, and by-and-by, since he never spoke, but only crooned, they judged him holy, gave him a mat, and laid food on it every day. That's the way a man's canonized in this country."

" H'm! I wish he would speak. He makes mere filling in of the rest of the picture. Don't you notice that? Do you see how he gives his colour to the whole group, yet never moves a muscle. Gad! there must be a story or two, a picture or so, back of those eyes. His tattered hood's the lattice he looks through. Wonderful, wonderful country!"

" Yes, just so; people find it so—at first." The old resident made his living mainly by manipulating the credulity of the subject, and the corrupt cruelty of the administration in Morocco, and that is a process which somewhat strains one's vision after a while. "And now you mention it, I have heard some queer stories about that White Beggar. But, Lord, there are queer stories about a good many folk in this country, where a city's governor pretty often ends his days as a beggar at that city's gate if he's not in prison."

" But what was the story about this man? "

" Oh, nothing exciting; only some little rock-scorp or another—a guide it was—swore he was a Christian, a half-caste—name of Joseph Khassan, I think; but I expect it's all a yarn. I spoke to him in English once, for the fun of the thing, but he only stared, and——"

" Heavens above, Crane, look at the man now! Keep so! oh, for pity's sake keep just so! Picture! It's a three volume romance! Ah'mm——"

A pencil stuck hurriedly between the excitable young painter's lips left him humming inarticulately. For some moments he had been fumbling in his pockets after sketch-book and pencils. Now of a sudden he was at work. One workman's methods are Greek to another, and things not to be explained. Mordant Dogget's were swift, large methods—unpardonably crude, some called them—but he generally reached his destination. And his soul seemed fighting in his fingers now to catch the inwardness of the figure whose exterior has seized his interest.

It seemed that something had stirred that usually imperturbable person, the White Beggar of Ed-dár. With chin on hand, among the looped raggedness of his djellab-hood, this man had listened indifferently to story-telling Ahmet's flowery periods, the which told graphically of the holy Shareef's nuptials with the English woman at Trouville. The White Beggar's far-sunken great black eyes had been apparently looking through voluble Armet and into distant spheres; the pavilion then being prepared for him in Paradise, it might have been. It was just that curious, sullenly-contemplative glow in the black eyes that told one they saw nothing near at hand, and that had laid hold upon English Dogget's impressionistic faculty.

Suddenly some curious wight (one of the baker's oven-boys it was; and, by that token, his daring had surely earned the lad a sore ear, but for the excitement caused among his elders by the upshot of his rudeness) interrupted blind Ahmet in the full tide of his narrative, crying:

"Oh, Si' Ahmet! and how called they, then, the Christian Pearl whom our Shareef made holy?"

Ahmet, checked, made answer, without thought of his dignity, and was for rushing on to the next tableau in his narrative. But a halt came quickly; for the blind story-teller's exquisite hearing told him on the instant almost that, by some means, his answer to the oven-boy had robbed him of all hold upon his audience

"The name, the name!" he had cried. "A twisted, Nazarene name—Margaret Wycombe, it was, to be sure. And so our lord the Shareef, mounting his——"

And then, even thus speedily, had come the halt, and the beginnings of Mordant Dogget's vigorous sketching of the White Beggar. And, mark you, the Beggar's was a figure for the brush or pencil at that moment. The pen baulks. A hundred written strokes do but confuse, where fewer, drawn—if rightly drawn—might limn you the man as Dogget saw him.

His hand left the beggar's chin, smiting the sun-dried earth, palm down, as it raised the man's body to sitting level. The black gaze, recalled from Paradise, riddled blind Ahmet as morning sun-rays pierce dying night. The beggar blazed out from dully-glowing coma into the full flame of passionate living. His matted beard shook, his lips parted; the very silence of the man was a shouted interrogation. Then he gave one stiff quiver like a thing that dies. His arm bent, and, "Called they her so?" came from him harshly, as his figure drooped earthward once more.

Mordant Dogget gritted his teeth from disappointment. He had been allowed not many seconds; but the thing had bitten right into his impressionable soul none the less, as it had done even into the mind of sightless Ahmet, the story-teller, and the whole careless circle of his audience. The Christian painter had his picture conceived though still to be born. The artist mind of him thirsted now for the details, accessories.

And as for the city-gate gathering it was broken up. Here was story, hot in the making, at their hand. Si' Ahmet, at his best, dealt with matters accomplished, events of months past. His audience, being Moors, never dreamed of interrogating their White Beggar. The holy man must be left to his croonings and his holiness; but here, at all events, was an end of story hearing for the time. And so, nodding and muttering among themselves, the men edged away through the gates for gossip and coffee in the little cabin within the walls. And blind Ahmet, shrugging, followed his fickle masters, he having a pretty taste of his own in coffee and kief when paid for, as such things should be—is not your entertaining labourer worthy of his hire?—from out the public purse.

Then, hugging his somewhat indifferent interpreter by the arm, Mordant Dogget, not being a Moor, but merely an artist full to the throat of his craft's curiosity, walked straight forward to the place of the White Beggar, and, addressing him obliquely across the other Christian, said:

"I want to know—I want the story, please."

Dogget, sketch-book in hand, had his picture still to paint, you see, and as to what he heard you must learn, if you will, from his own words as he subsequently wrote them down. The picture was his; his also the hearing. It would appear, from all accounts, that Crane's hearing was commonplace by comparison. As has been said, this man's vision was not over bright or cleanly. Here, at all events, are the picture's accessories as Mordant Dogget gleaned them:

"You have heard of things seen through a glass darkly? Yet that was not altogether how I saw and heard what should be plain to read in my picture, if the artistry is right. You know how, when the sun is at whitest noonday brilliancy, it will seem to you a thin, black disc—quite black if you try to fix your eyes on it? That sort of darkness, then, was more the murk through which I saw my picture. Colour! Man, in the North we don't know the word's meaning. Sparks were struck from my eyes; it was as though an archangel were to take and shake a bunch of rainbows in your face by the hour together.

"There was the White Beggar on his ham-bones before us, and there was I, drunk with the picture quickening in me, and mazed with the gorgeous story trumpetings I had been hearing of some wondrous Shareef's Baghdad doings in Trouville-sur-Mer—of all places on top of this earth!— drunk and heavy with it, I tell you, and lugging Crane by the arm to play interpreter. He had a dumb man to interpret, and he's by way of being a log, a mute, himself, outside trade; but it seemed there was to be no interpreting. You can't well interpret a tornado.

"'You want to know—you want to know!' echoes our White Beggar softly, slowly, in English, by your leave, and just as a child might speak who had laboriously gotten

the words by heart.   And as he spoke he rose, moving in
a quickening way to where the wall bends.   'And why
should you not know?   It is time.   You are the first.
Someone should know.   Why not you?   By God in
heaven, you shall hear things!'

" And by that his voice was almost a shout, yet not one.
to carry a distance; a booming, telling sort of voice, no
inflection wasted, and his words came easily now.   Such
words, too!   I would give something to be able to repeat
them.   They were the bunched rainbows I told you of.
You remember the fable—the father with his sons who
fenced above his head with such marvellous dexterity as
to hold him dry and spotless in a downpour of rain?   Just
so our beggar's rainbow phrases played about my head
like flame.   An actor!—oh, a born actor! reflection told
me that.   And when I was clear of his witchery I could
remember how each odd tag of dropped speech or stopped
breath told to a hair's weight, as it was meant to tell, in
just that place.   But the dramatic instinct must have been
a part of the beggar's very fibre; for no child could have
heard him and not known him for a man highly wrought
and in terrible earnest.

" I believe he told us the story of his life; I know at the
end he was weeping about my knees, imploring me to forget and speak to no man of what had passed between us.
I promised, and so did Crane; and I think we kept our
promise—until relieved of it.   For what he said I am
powerless to repeat; only it made me see pictures, in between those painted by the blind story-teller, of the great
Shareef's marriage with a Christian woman, the mention
of whose name galvanized the clay they called the White
Beggar into the strange, wild outcast, spawn of civilization
by savagery, spewed out upon the earth by both, that you
have seen in my picture.   In between the sun-pictures,

silhouettes, of the Eastern saint's carnival in France, the beggar's glancing words gave me pictures in which his was the prime figure—volatile, serpent-like, vivid, and strange.

" First I saw the child born of shame forgot; a Spanish Jewish mother, a Christian Turk of sorts for father; the birth in a side-alley of some Armenian vilayet. A gutter-nosing infancy—you know your Levantine half-caste—God help him! Then a large, clean wave from over sea; an English missionary, who was more—a man, and very white as well. Corruption's spawn was adopted, and reared as a white man by a white man who feared God and kept His commandments most loyally.

" I've heard of wolves brought up in kennels by a dog-lover, but I never heard that they grew into friends of man. The name the missionary gave this one was Joseph, I gathered—Joseph Khassan. And by-and-by the good man went the way of flesh, and the lithe young half-breed of his upbringing lived on with Miriam, the dead mission-ary's adopted daughter and housekeeper, himself bidding fair to take a missionary's place in the queer little world of Tangier. There was a devout, dramatic, proselitizing fervour about the young man's piety. He had a per-sonality.

" Then he made a friend of an English artist, and robbed that Englishman of the lady of his choice and suit; stealing so deftly, so piously withal, that the man he robbed forgave him perforce, and loyally played the ' old dog of love' when trouble came to the curiously ill-mated pair—the dove-like Devonshire girl and the the-atrically fervent half-caste—in England, for to England they went. Mary Whateley (Mary Khassan now) had money. The half-caste had relied on it as the means of realizing his ambition, the which he thought was the winning of souls in civilization's great centres by virtue of the gospel of 'Love ye one another.'

" Then—oh! but it was marvellous, the manner in which the White Beggar gave me flashlight pictures of his degeneration; of how his half-bred personality was broken on the great wheel of London's civilization. I saw him striding downward, pursued ever by the jeering cries of those who, fascinated at first by his surface qualities, had weighed the man in their modern Western scales and found him worse than wanting, from the ministry to school-keeping, very base marital infidelity, play-acting, unsavoury agency dealings, fraud, and swinishly selfish abandonment. Yet so much of the essentially dramatic was left in the man that, in giving me these vivid pictures, he in no way detracted from the ragged, picturesque dignity of his own, the White Beggar's present figure.

" I heard then of the end of the English days—an ugly, sordid picture that. I saw the half-caste bitterly realizing that the test of civilization had crumpled him, as a blotted sheet of note-paper is crumpled and tossed aside. Sitting alone in the den of his last and least savoury escapades— can you not see the hunched figure in a dramatic agency office near the Strand, the weight of thunderous London that had crushed him pressing hard now on the sloping shoulders?—he tried to commit suicide, and found he lacked the stamina and singleness of purpose. So his poor worshipful wife was robbed of her very trinkets, left alone and penniless in the great city, and the half-caste disappeared utterly from out the confines of that civilization which had tested and rejected him.

But the theatrical strain lived still in his blood. A realistic suicide in the Thames by night, all save the finding of the body, was duly reported, and Mary Khassan was announced a widow, free to marry, as she subsequently did marry, loyal Dick Dunn, her first and only true lover. And, so carefully had his part been played, it was not until after Kassan's reported death that the veil of sanctity through which his wife's adoring eyes had seen him (her's the loving hand that wove the veil) was splashed and rent about his memory.

"There came a victim of his, one Margaret Wycombe, one among many most cruelly betrayed by the healer of souls. And her story was as ugly as it was piteous. A child born in shame of Khassan's begetting, dying in want caused by his betrayal and broken pledges. Mary and Dick Dunn adopted Margaret Wycombe as their daughter. A sullen Junoesque mute the girl had been, with slow-moving, panther eyes; a sphinx to mankind, but ripe fruit to Khassan; a tamed, docile thing he made her, with parted lips, dog's eyes, and full breast a-tremble at the one man's footfall. Poor thing! she had had her lesson. She had trusted but the one, opened her heart but the once; and, here was the end of it. The man was dead in the Thames, they said. Ah well, his memory should be torn to ribbons, at least. Margaret saw to that, snapped her white teeth then, and kept her own counsel as the adopted daughter of Dick and Mary Dunn, living and travelling with them, even to Tangier, where fell out her portentous meeting with Moulai Hassan, the great Shareef of Ain Araish; as I had heard in flowery phrase from blind Ahmet, the story-teller.

"My gleaning was nearing its end now. Short, sharp thrusts of speech went far; each word heavy-laden, told much. I saw through misty, river darkness a dripping figure crouched in a dinghy, being sculled away with a muffled oar from the carefully-arranged scene of suicide. Later, on a steamer's deck at Plymouth the half-caste, sneering over a newspaper account of his own end. I saw the same figure in brilliant sunshine, slinking through the Waterport market at Gibraltar; holding muttered converse there with a Moorish pedlar of eggs, withdrawing to an upper room in a side-street, still Khassan the half-caste, issuing again from there—never. There the half-caste ended, and not in English Thames.

"This upper room was reached by way of a greasy, sparred wicket in a patio. Presently there appeared at that wicket the egg-pedlar, shading his eyes with one hand, in the other bearing a soft bundle wrapped in a fringed Tetouan cloth. Finding the coast clear the pedlar turned back to his wicket, and beckoned to one who waited there. A tall Moor stepped out then from the wicket into the sunlight, his djellab-hood thrust well forward, and showing little of the head it shielded, beyond a wedge of chin and lip coated by a week's growth of black beard. They parted at the patio's edge, the pedlar to his chaffering in the market, the other to the landing-stage from which one embarks for Tangier.

"' Sahhah-il-ik!'[1] quoth the tall Moor gravely, as they separated. 'I will thank thee to give this morning no place whatsoever in thy memory. In thy gossip, friend, use it, and thy speech will turn and rend thee. Seer!'[2]

"The pedlar grinned, and went his ways with the bundle containing the garb of civilization, as worn in the world of civilization by the man who had been Joseph Khassan.

"I saw the tall Moor squatting among, but slightly apart from Moors who had never worn other garments than those of the faithful, under the forecastle of a little Tangier-bound steamer. I saw him stalk through the

[1] Literally, "Strength to thee"; by usage, "Thank you!"
[2] Go!

pillared, littered place of shadow, where the lords of the Moorish customs sit at their work of appraisement, oppression, and fraud. I saw him toil up Tangier's cobbled main street, turn off by the little Sôk, question a water-carrier for a moment, and enter then, presently, a little hovel in an alley near the Kasbah.

"'Miriam,' quoth he, to the bare-footed, half-Moorish, half-Spanish clad woman, prematurely draggle-tailed and middle-aged in youth, who stood within cooking. 'Miriam, look on me!' And he thrust back his djellab-hood, composing his features smoothly.

"'Virgin Mother of Gesu! It is him, it is Yûsef!' So she called Joseph. It is strange to tell, but trué, that so broadly open had been the mind of the Protestant missionary who, throughout her girlhood had given a home to this woman, that she had remained of the faith to which her parents had been born in Spain. She had but one oath, even in these later, bare-foot days of her descent from the point at which Khassan had deserted her and Tangier.

"'It is even myself—Yûsef,' replied the tall Moor, submitting indifferently to sallow Miriam's mumbling embrace of his right arm.

"'As a Moor, Yûsef?' cried she, returning self-possession opening her eyes to small matters.

"'A Moor, Miriam, and no other thing. Haj Yûsef, say, from afar, from by Mekkas.' The woman nodded, wondering comprehension. 'Are you quite alone here, Miriam?'

"She smiled a faintly bitter smile. 'Didst think, then, that Tangier's streets could yield me a husband, Yûsef?'

"'H'm! good. And here is a bed, and peace. Good. See, Miriam! Take this money, go out into the Sôk;

bring food and tea and kief, and, bring some hachsheesh, Miriam. Then come here again—to Yûsef. And speak thou to no man of this.'

" Slave-like, the woman turned and went out silently. ' At last ! ' said the gleam in her eyes it seemed.

" It was a week later. Think of Miriam's week in her kief-clouded, hachsheesh-scented hovel ! Then he went forth alone, in the violet dawn light. That was my next picture. The woman peering anxiously after him, from under the beetling lintel of whitened walnut wood; the man, Moor to his finger-tips, black-avised, opium-dazed, muttering of the one God, his Prophet, and the Faith. So on he climbed in the dawning out through the new-opened city gates, across the strewn, still drowsy Sôk, past the legation of the English, and the praying field, on by bamboo-walled lanes to open country and the great Fez road.

" Now, at length the man was afoot upon the naked earth. Ten months long he journeyed afoot, and my pictures of his journeyings are a mist, for he gave but half a dozen short sentences to their painting. He remained quite alone during all that while, and must have journeyed like a very wandering Jew; for Tetouan saw him, Wazdan, Fez, Mequinez, Beni Zemmour, Beni Madan, Aït Aïssa, Tafilet, and far Atlas villages. Men, women, and children may be found to whom he gave in money and food. Men there were toward the end of whom he begged food. One man only was there to whom he spoke. And to that man he said: ' Seer fii-hálak-um ! ' (Get thee hence.) ' I am unclean ! '

" And at the last of it his words showed me the man, gaunt, weary, harder than the earth he trod, halting at dead of night beside the mat of holy Haj Cassim the hermit, before the shut gates of Ed-dár el Kebeer. ' Peace, good man,' he cried. 'Give me of thy food, for I am near to starving and greatly weary.' And the hermit gave him food and the half of his mat. Afterwards they spoke together a little, and Haj Cassim bade the weary stranger rest there where he had eaten. So the man rested, shrouded in his ruin of a dejellab, and as day followed day he continued to rest, heeding nothing, speaking little, and that only by night to Haj Cassim; rocking his gaunt body idly, and crooning to himself by day, nourishing a frame worn by ten months of unceasing exertion, upon idleness in sunshine and the food scraps set before him by the pious.

" ' And comes then the story-teller with words that were air to me of the holy Shareef's marriage with a Christian. Some idler's question, and—I hear a voice from behind the grave of Joseph Khassan name—her—the Shareef's bride—Margaret Wycombe. The woman that I—— And coming here, a Moorish shareefa!'

" And that was the end of his speech as a man. The hard-knotted, earth-bound fibres of him seemed to give then; and in a moment the White Beggar was clinging about our knees, incontinently praying for secrecy, a very naked creature, showing many scars."

And with this comes the end of Mordant Dogget's impressions. In the morning he rode away from Ed-dár with Crane and their little caravan, leaving the White Beggar upon his mat, the same man in every outward detail that for two years had held the pious respect of all good citizens in Ed-dár.

Mordant Dogget protested angrily against leaving the city. He wanted to remain and witness the arrival of the great Shareef of Ain Araish, with his bride and retinue. But Crane had business elsewhere, and was an ill man to turn where his interests were involved. And so, the artist being helpless alone in that place, had perforce to accompany his guide.

Dogget saluted the White Beggar as they cleared the gates, but, with eyes staring fixedly upon the sun-baked earth, the beggar ignored his challenge, and cried aloud: " Ashahadu la ilaha il Allah! " (I testify that there is no god but God!)

Chapter III

SCHOOLING BY MOONLIGHT

WHEN the moon rides clear above Ed-dár (and, as though pitifully mindful of the bloody tyranny which obtains through the most part of that realm, the moon is wont to lighten Morocco by night with the most pellucid aspect of her loveliness) the city no longer sparkles as by day; it is no longer a litter of raggedly-set jewels, but an ordered array of softly-gleaming terraces in mother-of-pearl.

" An ill-smelling, cut-throat city enough by day, both in fact and by outward seeming," writes Haj Ben Ezra of Ed-dár, " but by night it hath a special friendliness with the moon, one fancies, and by her is decked most tenderly in garments of liquid beauty and soft radiance, the regard of which will bring tears to the eyes of a seeing man though his heart be glad within him. So much for outward seeming. Beyond regard of it, a wise man, having knowledge of the place, will not venture by night unless well armed."

But as yet we have still to do with outward seemings, for the story lingers still without Ed-dár's gates. On the night following that evening of the White Beggar's converse with an English painter the beggar roamed at large till the first false daybreak, Subhi Kázib, among the saints' graves and in the valley beyond. During the day he rocked, crooning, upon his mat, giving no word to holy Haj Cassim, his neighbour. The evening of that

day fell wondrous white and still, and the moon, almost
at the full of her regnant splendour, rose early and shone
far most radiantly.   Toward the hour of the night call
from the city manáráts, Haj Cassim, the hermit, turned
slowly upon his mat and addressed the White Beggar,
who was crouched, silent, in the shadow of that flaky
great buttress of the wall which sheltered the pair.

"Brother," he began quietly.

"Haj," answered the White Beggar, his voice coming
queerly from out the depths of his djellab.

"Hath the fever left thee?   Art in any way purged,
brother?"

"I have no fever, Haj.   Allah knows I see myself but
as a worm before him."

"H'm!   A poor creature, a worm, brother?   Poor
tribute, too, thy thought, to Allah who made thee in man's
likeness."

"Of what account is the body, and if the soul in it's a
worm's?"

"Nay, brother, but the shell's of vast account, I tell
thee, for it is no less than the ladder by which mortals
may ascend to Jinnah.   It is the tether. 'Thy possibilities,' it says to the soul, 'are thus and thus, that ye
see in me; these thy limitations.   Mount, soul!'   And,
scorning apparent token, ye bid your soul content itself
as a worm.   But take heart, brother; I see thy fever hath
departed, and so the purged flesh bleeds humility. 'Sahhah!'   That is 'Strength!'   Good luck!"

You are to remember that holy Haj Cassim believed
he knew the White Beggar.   There had been talk, naked
revealings, one may assume, between the twain on that
night, two years since, when Cassim's comrade first
descended upon him from out Morocco's ancient silence.
There had been quiet, moon-lighted communings a-many

since then, and to the Haj had come with these convictions that his should be the task of schooling into a hermit's passive philosophy, his neighbour, the White Beggar, with his black-streaked past.

The schooling had proceeded smoothly as a charm's work, and by all appearances it had not been easy to discover in all Morocco a thing at once human and yet so like to a piece of the earth on which he rested, as was the White Beggar. Judged by Haj Cassim's standards, this was as it should be—a notable achievement.

Then had come the evening of the story-telling and of the White Beggar's passionate outpouring into Christian ears.

"His blood is not of the truly chosen," Haj Cassim had sighed to himself. "The works of Allah are greatly cunning and very wonderful. I, in my nothingness, have hit upon a means unsuited. Mine the task, then, of putting it aside to make way for a better. It is in my mind that I am to lose my still devil-ridden brother. It would seem his road to Firdaôs must needs be a busy one. Well, well, by Mohammed's sword! but the blade, as well as the begging-bowl, has led men blissward before to-day. Bism 'Illah! Brother," he said aloud, "art still my brother? Have ye faith yet, and trust to be guided withal by the hermit who gave ye meat and rest?"

"Ihyeh, more than before," answered the beggar, thrusting back his djellab-hood and leaning forward to give the eyes' endorsement to the lips' assurance. Hollow, deep-sunk eyes they were, set in a face grown sallow from lack of exposure, yet gaunt and hard-drawn as that of any ill-fed, over-worked field slave.

"'Bárakah!' that is 'Enough,'" said the hermit, as an expounder pleased by a pupil's aptness in rendering an intricate passage from Al Koran. "That faith will

never serve ye ill. And now, tell me, of what spake ye so
cunningly with the Christians? Nay, but Cassim knows.
Tell me, however."

And the White Beggar told him, low and hurriedly.

"Even so, even so, as I knew. Brother, have ye forgot the period ye told me of, when ye strutted among
the infidels, an actor in plays?"

"I remember it, Haj."

"Ihyeh. Well, brother, that strutting beast is alive
and lusty in thee yet. Thy bitterest enemy in life, the
thou who needs must play-act, study the set o' thy hood,
the swing o' thy hand, and eke the folds the rags about
thee hang in. Brother, such matters may be well enough
as part of the story-teller's working pack. They are a
snare and an abomination in a free man journeying toward Paradise. Many are thus afflicted and carry the
tawdry burden to their graves; but the whole men,
brother, the chosen, Mother Earth will generally suck the
poison out of them. But, and if the earth absorb it not,
then must we look elsewhere for cleansing; be assured the
thing's a foul stain."

"Haj, I doubt it not. I have cause to know. But, by
the hairs of the prophet, his beard, Haj, there is no grain
of play-actor left in me now. This day hath purged me
fiercely enough."

"Brother, be not so assured. The creature spake but
now in thine oath, and again in thy 'I have cause to
know.'"

"Before God, the one God, you do me wrong, Haj."

"Do I that, brother? Then that is wrong well done.
But peace, brother; I would not harry thee, rather aid
thee with the staff that helps myself. Listen. This
hermit's life, the highest, as many commentators have
said, is not for thee, not thy shortest road, brother. For

thee a fight more strenuous, greater odds, heavier blows, more striving, and at the last of it, it may be, a richer and more spacious pavilion in Paradise, watered by ever-running streams, walled about by sweetest flowers, tended by maidens the most sumptuously lovely."

"Haj, let us speak of the road. The way is long enough, methinks, for thought and talk of what like its end might be."

"And that is well and truly said, brother, though a good half from the actor thing within thee."

"By the faith, no!"

"Ah! as thou sayest, brother, we are God's, and unto Him shall surely return, man and actor, brother, good and bad, the admitted and the hidden or denied. Bísm 'Illah! As to the way, then, listen! The day after to-morrow cometh our lord, Moulai Hassan, Shareef of Ain Araish, with all his people."

"Ihyeh, he comes, Haj." The White Beggar's right arm, on which his body's weight rested, quivered a little.

"The coming will be a great affair. Doubtless something bloody and fine by way of celebration will be looked for from us, the hermits of the gate—a little knife-throwing, head-chipping, or the like. None of this is for thee, brother. 'Twere ill so to feed the actor beast. Instead ye will fare forth at dawn to where the three great stones lie beside the Tanjah road, and there, occupying thy mind with thoughts of the one Faith, thou'lt sit and wait the coming of our lord and his people, seeing what things ye shall see, acting as it shall become ye—not the play-actor—to act. Do this, brother, and trust Haj Cassim."

Then a silence fell between the two, what time the hermit, Haj Cassim smiled thoughtfully to himself, and pearly-terraced Ed-dár slept on in the sheen of the moon.

You are to remember that Haj Cassim knew as much

as you know about the holy Shareef's bride and her connection with the life of the man the White Beggar had
been.

"How say ye?"

"Haj, thy counsel is mysterious as God to me, but I
will follow it."

"Bárakah! Well and wisely chosen, brother. And
now let us sleep."

And with that the hermit hunched him on his side, his
hood well forward, and came quickly upon sleep. Presently, when the hermit had once or twice snored:

"Haj, thou wert right: the truth was not in me; it was
the actor-beast spoke, as thou saidst," quoth the White
Beggar, softly as a woman. The Haj snored on, serenely
oblivious, as was to be expected. "But I am quit of him
now, God knows," added the beggar, murmuring, as he
composed himself to sleep.

Within five minutes the beggar slept, man, play-actor,
hermit and all. From which one may deduce that a con-
fessor need not necessarily listen to comfort his penitent;
that the beggar was not so surely quit of certain qualities
as he fancied, or any other trifling conclusion one may
incline towards. The fact is, the pair slept.

Chapter IV

ENTRA PER ME

DAY broke with gaudy and upstarting brilliancy upon the morning during which the great Shareef of Ain Araish was expected to reach Ed-dár. The townsfolk were early astir, on tiptoe for a holiday— a function—as Believers are ever. The Shareef's high holiness was the more keenly and piously felt in Ed-dár by token that he owned a deal of property in the city. Thus, for five days previous to this one of the event, slaves and leg-chained prisoners from the Kasbah had been at work under Basha's orders, in smoothing out and clearing the hundred yards wide ribbon of beaten hoof-prints which forms the road to Ed-dár's main gate, and in screening by a spread of grass and green boughs the great rubbish mountain that towers above the city wall, and casts its shadow (the very shadow hath a most distinctive odour of its own) athwart the arched gateway.

Shortly after es-sbáh, the first call to prayer, women in new washed haiiks began to range themselves like huge snowballs along those roofs which overlooked the walls, upon the walls themselves, and at every other point of vantage. For, if the Prophet's wisdom has ruled that women should not often be seen, there is yet no law against their seeing; and, further, no function were complete lacking the curious, jodelling cries of congregated womenkind.

At about this time it was noticed that the White Beg-

gar's place beside the city gate was vacant. Men nodded
significantly, and women, coyly biting their face-cloths,
muttered one to another as they passed the vacant niche.
Something notable and brave was anticipated from the
holy man, in honour of this great occasion. Any Sòk idler
with a few floos to spend upon powder may twirl and
fire a gun. No great learning is required to bring forth
a stunning noise from a *shibbábah* or *ghaïtah*, given that
one's lungs be sound. But for throwing knives and axes
aloft to catch the same upon a newly-shaven pate, for
eating burning straw or live sheep, for chanting and dancing till one falls prostrate, convulsed and foaming at the
mouth; for such contributions to festivity as these and
their like it may well be that a certain degree of saintliness, if not of actual magic, is an essential qualification.

As a fact, however, and one known to Haj Cassim, at
least, the White Beggar was engaged in no such mysterious preparation as Ed-dár folk fancied. On the contrary,
having left his mat before true daylight came, he had
wandered out along the Tangier track to where the three
lichen-covered boulders stand, beyond the fourth saint's
grave. And there he sate him upon the rock and waited,
his djellab-hood outthrust, a tattered eave to his forehead,
his earth-stained hands mechanically raising and lowering
his staff.

And now the sky-line across the farthest ridge of undulating plain began to yield a token which set eager minds
at rest, and whetted holiday anticipations about the city
walls. A cloud had risen betwixt green earth (the grass
season was young yet) and cloudless sky; and waiting
Ed-dár pictured the prancing of stallions, which had
churned that cloud from out the dust of the beaten trail.
A road in Morocco, you must know, means a strip vary-
ing in width from a dozen to 200 yards, beaten out of

the earth by the tramping feet of many generations of mules and camels, donkeys, horses and cattle, in a land which knows no vehicles.

Then, gradually came sound from under the advancing cloud, an answering blare to that which was growing in volume among the waiting multitudes of the city. The state by which the ordinary movements of an European monarch are attended, is as nothing compared with the pomp in which a great Moorish Shareef travels. And Moulai Hassan was the greatest of them all. The earth shook when Moulai Hassan went a-journeying. Eight hundred men and seven hundred beasts attended this saint upon his travels. His camp made a biggish village each night (as the permanent villages in its neighbour-hood knew to their cost, in solid tribute of money, food and labour) with its own fandak, or corral for beasts, its outer and inner sôks or market-places, its cordon of armed guards, and its temporary mosque or praying-house.

A great roar of welcome from the city walls marked the first clear view obtained of the Shareef's advance guard of a hundred mounted men—a four-deep line of twenty-five riding abreast, waving their long guns as the stage Irishman twirls his blackthorn, their horses champing and foaming at a hard-held, ambling walk, the sunshine glori-fying their bravery of crimson saddle-peaks, triangular silver stirrups, and silver and coral-studded dagger-hilts. At their heels were a score of drummers and reed-players, banging and blaring as for dear life.

Then came the twelve upstanding Ain Araish slaves who bore the Shareef's magnificent litter, a Sultan's gift of three generations back. From out this gorgeous frame of gold-trapped, prophet's green, Moulai Hassan el Gharbi beamed upon all men, says an irreverent commentator, "With a benign complacence born of hach-sheesh and attributed to saintliness."

Next, the holy Shareef's son and heir, Moulai Ben Hassan el Gharbi, twisting a miniature gun of rare workmanship above the ears of a venomous-looking, grey Barb, whose thoroughbred head was carried almost as high as its rider's; Ben Hassan, the adored tyrant of his sacred father's following, a divinely handsome boy in his tenth year now, well-grown, a perfect horseman, and one having in him a deal more of the young prince than the young saint, despite his sacred ancestry.

Ben Hassan had never known fear as yet, and had never been seriously thwarted. No Moor had ever dared so far to cross the Shareef, his father. As to what an unbeliever, and a woman at that, might dare in this direction, the young saint had yet to learn. Camp rumour had it that the new shareefa would shortly become a mother. Ben Hassan, for his part, had once or twice caught a queer, cold gleam in her eyes when he had surprised her regard of him. And that had struck the boy with a chill as being probably one of the misfortunes of her heathen origin, even as a toad's slime is a part of the creature from birth. The young saint had his life before him— a long lesson.

Immediately behind the Shareef's son rode the Shareef's bride in a gorgeously-caparisoned litter, borne by six long-limbed, Guinea coast slaves, curtained in trailing silks, and securely veiled from the vulgar gaze. Not a doubt but Shareefa Margaret had hit already upon a policy which placed her lord's will in the hollow of her two hands. The state with which she travelled suggested so much. By night the shareefa occupied her own separate pavilion, a little place in canvas, and about this was erected each evening a brush fence enclosing a circle of six paces in depth. Four armed soldiers rode before and behind her litter by day. Three long-tailed, daintily-mincing Barbs were led behind her litter, one always saddled in anticipation of her wish to ride.

In the rear of the shareefa's led horses came Ahmet Ben Hamet Arâf, Moulai Hassan's counsellor and man of affairs. The counsellor rode alone, as befitted his grave renown; a massive figure of hauteur enveloped in cream cashmere, he bestrode a bay mule of surprising height, smooth gait, and balloon-like girth. A notable personage, who looked the part, and knew it.

The Shareef's two scribes crouched with scholarly humility over their saddles' front peaks at a decent distance from the bay mule's heels. Their outstanding modesty disarmed criticism of their deplorable assmanship. Behind the scribes came the various officers of the saint's household, well-mounted, richly-armed, and carrying with them all that mixture of dignity, braggadocio and full-fed ruffianism, which distinguishes the servants of great men in other corners of this earth beside Sunset Land.

Then, mounted and afoot, marched a mixed body of Moulai Hassan's dependent followers, in every sort and grade—slaves, workmen, couriers, grooms and the like, leading from three to four hundred pack-animals, who again were followed by a second score of music-makers. Then came the rear-guard; four mounted lines of five-and-twenty picked men, armed to the teeth, and loving all other states before those of peace and quietness.

A brave procession, and one that glittered from front to rear with pride of place, and pomp, wealth, strength, and the habit of receiving applause. Yet this brave, proud gathering was within a few paces of confusion of the sort which hangs upon the skirts of catastrophe; and this (the age we live in should attach a special value to truisms), when one thinks of it, made it resemble very intimately that other procession which we call life.

Word of the happening in question has been given to the world with tolerable accuracy, saving in one singular confusion of names, in the "Annals of a Saintly House," the which were compiled from the translation of a certain folio written by Ahmet Ben Hamet Arâf.

One point in the episode remains a moot one, regarding which nothing is definitely known. Who loosed those camels from the fandak behind the great rubbish-hill, in which they had been securely penned? Among believers no shadow of suspicion ever fell upon Haj Cassim in this connection; and, for myself, I think the expression of any opinion in the matter uncalled for.

Lord Mohammed's youngest scion, Ben Hassan, stirred to excitement by the sheen of the occasion and by the antics of his grey Barb, grew restive and aweary of the sober, processional pace which kept his mount for the more part of the time upon its hind legs.

"Have I thy leave, my father?" he whispered behind the green curtains of the Shareef's litter. A nod toward the front lent point to the request, and a narcoticized smile from the Shareef supplied consent. So, with a flourish of his gun Ben Hassan gave rein to the grey, and raced past the advance guard's flank to the open plain beyond. A great shout arose from among the saint's following, to find its echo in a dull roar from the hiving thousands clustered about Ed-dár's walls.

"Sidi Ben Hassan. Ohé! Child of God's anointed saint!"

Partially veiled in a dust-cloud of his own begetting, Ben Hassan performed an extempore powder-play before the guard. Two hundred yards away upon his left hand, and toward the city, a man on a wayside rock stood shouting and gesticulating at circus-riding Ben Hassan. This was the White Beggar of Ed-dár. At about the same distance ahead and upon his right were three camels, advancing and retiring, but chiefly advancing, with a fine display of that open-mouthed, frothy and bucking abandon which, in a camel betokens ever but one thing, and that the madness of the grass-season. The camel madness is not pretty at any time; but when it comes early in the season and to a beast usually tethered, it is a thing to flee before, more horrible than the revolt of a sheep and more dangerous than the Nazarene's madness, which arises from the drinking of forbidden liquors. These camels (the which Ben Hassan ignored, some thousands of other pairs of eyes failed to note, and only the White Beggar appeared to recognize as an imminent source of peril) were very potently under the spell of the devil of their kind.

Now, the White Beggar on his rock was murmuringly quoting to himself the schooling words of Haj Cassim, " the pivot," who had pointed out to him his taríkat, or mystic path to heaven: " ' There ye will sit and wait the coming of our Lord and His people, seeing what things ye shall see, acting as it shall become *thee*—not the play-actor—to act.' I must act," he muttered, " not play-act, by the faith!"

" Seeing that his cries and gestures remained unnoticed," say the " Annals," " the White Beggar left his rock, and began running at speed in the direction of the young saint and his caracoling steed. But the maddest of the three camels was fleeter of foot; the White Beggar was a little too late.

" The camel gurgled triumphantly and emitted a sound like that of steam escaping from a safety valve when he charged Ben Hassan from the rear. The boy left his saddle as a nine-pin leaves its stand what time the ball hits it squarely. For three seconds he hung in one stirrup, head and arms down, while the grey Barb jumped, its four feet clear of the ground. Then his small foot cleared the silver trap, and the camel paused to gaze down at the human, bleeding, and prostrate, before proceeding to trample his life out. The Barb, by the way, reached Ed-dár within the minute.

"The mad camel sniffed inquiringly at Ben Hassan's sainted head. Half a hundred horsemen were thundering down from the Shareef's cortège, not daring to shoot, too terrified to shout. The holy Shareef of Ain Araish had leapt from his litter, his eyes flaming forth passion's triumph over hachsheesh, and was absolutely charging toward his son upon his own silk-clad and slipperless feet. But the camel held the situation's key, and he was a singularly mad camel.

"A kind of moan, half-choked, went up from the Shareef's following when the camel's jaws were seen to close above Ben Hassan's girdle, and the boy was raised in mid-air, dangling and helpless.

"'Now comes the crushing, then—Paradise!' gasped one of the bearers of Shareefa Margaret's litter, coming to a halt from sheer stress of excitement.

"The shareefa, standing in her litter and gazing over the bearers' heads, drew a long sigh, of sorts. The light in her dark eyes was hardly womanly, not very pleasant, and a far remove from pity or sympathetic fear."

It has been said that the gossip of the camp suggested that the shareefa would ere long become a mother. At present, you see, she was no more than a stepmother, and of an alien race.

"Twice the bundle which contained a great Shareef's only son was swung outward at the end of a mad camel's

wrinkled nose. Then the White Beggar arrived, and that
was the loss of the camel by token that the crushing had
not begun. It was, further, the camel's loss, for, that, an
instant later, the iron-shod point of the White Beggar's
staff entered the beast's right eye, leaving no room there
for the further existence of any seeing organ.

"The boy was dropped on the instant, as though he
burned, and the infuriated camel wheeled in response to
a sharp stab in the flank nearest his blind eye. The
beggar leapt four paces backward, and received the
camel's open-mouthed charge on the point of his staff.
'Twas dexterously managed and very effective, though a
desperate measure, because it disarmed the man. The
iron entered the brute's palate; but, his massive jaws
closing upon it, the staff was wrenched from its owner's
hands, and himself flung to the ground six paces distant by a sidelong buffet of the camel's nose.

"But the White Beggar's famous task was accomplished. He had drawn off the camel. Ben Hassan was
surrounded by a score of guards, whose horses were left
to follow out their own plans. No one looked at the
fallen White Beggar. There was but one heir to Ain
Araish its Shareef. The camel's right fore-foot pawed
air. Its aim was uncertain now; the human cause of that
uncertainty had to be mangled. This particular mad
camel regarded itself as the camel for the work.

"At that moment, the Shareef of Ain Araish, panting
and trailing cambric, arrived upon the scene afoot. One
glance at his still prostrate son satisfied the great man.
The boy's eyes were open; his hurt a trifle. A back-
handed blow across the mouth from Moulai Hassan sent
a stooping soldier to earth, gabbling incoherently. His
gun, it seemed, leapt to the Shareef's shoulder, and an
instant later the mad camel came to his knees not six

inches from the beggar, humped itself spasmodically on all fours, and fell sideways, dead as Moosà, and cleanly shot through the brain by Moulai Hassan's own sacred hand.

" The kaid of the guard sprang forward at this, and botched his master's work by slashing the dead brute's throat into ribbons with his curved dagger. The fellow was mostly savage at bottom, and flustered savage to boot just now, for the reason that he had witnessed the back-handed felling to earth of one of his subordinates, and felt uncertain as to the Shareef's immediate intentions. He had seen men bastinadoed almost to death upon lesser occasions, had Kaid Absalaam, and he desired to live to see more of the same sort of thing.

" Just then the Shareef's great litter came up with the party about the dead camel, and, at the Shareef's order, Ben Hassan was placed therein by half a dozen pairs of hands that sprang to the command. The boy laughed in his bearers' faces, saying:

" ' But that was a fine to do,[1] my men. That camel's nose would serve thy women to grind their wheat on, and, b'Allah! but it found my ribs where they are softest.'

" Ahmet Ben Hamet Arâf, the counsellor, rode up at a moment inopportune for his dignity when his sacred master was fuming over the White Beggar where he lay, bruised and stunned, near the dead camel.

" ' Down, thou, from thy bay mule!' roared the saint. 'Am I a Hûdi that ye ride into my presence? Down, I say, and lift this man into thy place. By Allah! but the Shareef of Ain Araish is surrounded by women and mules—and asses that ride upon mules!' The counsellor reached earth smartly. 'This man here saves the life

---

[1] As the " Annals " truthfully add, the original word used here does not lend itself to translation.

of my son, and a herd of gaping heads of mud stand about and leave him food for mad camels. Ho, there! Abdullah! Salaam! Cassim! Hamed! Aji! and tend my guest who saved my son. Bear ye him tenderly, hollow-heads! or presently, by holy Mekka! but he shall bear thy hands and ears—everyone, at his stirrups! I have sworn it, by Mekka! Stand aside thou, Hamet Arâf!'

"Then," say the "Annals," "the procession moved on, and the city of Ed-dár was entered while the heavens echoed gun-firing, drum-beating, shibbábah-blowing, the shouts of men, and the rhythmic crooning of a thousand high-voiced women. But the event of the day was Ben Hassan's affray with the mad camel, and the hero of the day, despite the fact that he had tossed no naked blades upon his pate, was none other than the White Beggar of Ed-dár, who entered the city gates behind the shareefa, and mounted upon no less a beast than the great bay mule of Ahmet Hamet Arâf, the Shareef's own right-hand man. As to what things happened within the city walls, there is no room to tell of them here; but this was the way of the Shareef's first meeting with Ed-dár's White Beggar."

And so, to be done with the "Annals," a useful record and truthful as histories go, yet somewhat narrow in the reach, and of necessity (by reason of the material to hand in the making) far from exhaustive.

Ben Hassan's adventure, the event of the day, for example; it was no less to the soldiers of the guard, let us say. The shareefa's first glimpse of the White Beggar was no event to be marked by a soldier. It was natheless a markworthy event, however; a thing for the student of the human animal to marvel over.

The thing happened in this wise: The White Beggar, open-eyed and conscious then, was being assisted to the counsellor's bay mule when the shareefa's litter drew up abreast of that beast, and its occupant looked out between her curtains to see the man whose timely daring had saved the life of her lord's son.

Now an end had been made of the half-caste Khassan within a certain wicket-gate in Gibraltar, just upon three years before this day. The Moor who had risen from that ending had spent the three years upon the earth. It was to be expected that the White Beggar should be master of his countenance. Moreover, he had been schooling himself for this very meeting. He knew well that his appearance in Moorish rags, with a face untouched by razor's blade for several years, and a skin first tanned and worn by exposure, and then sallowed by inaction, was in no least line reminiscent of the handsome, theatrical-looking Rev. Joseph Khassan of Margaret's bitter foreknowledge. It was not astonishing, then, that no flicker of emotion should have been permitted to betray him.

But with Shareefa Margaret, a woman, and one at a physically sensitive stage of her womanhood, the matter was far otherwise. Yet hear her own words upon that meeting, written long afterward and in cool blood:

" His eyes met my eyes, and it seemed to me that every pulse in me stopped its beating. My body shook and stood still under a physical shock which I could not understand. I did not reach the stage of telling myself that this man was Joseph Khassan; but I found myself nervously assuring myself that he could not be. ' Joseph Khassan is dead; this man is a Moor of the Moors,' I was telling myself. And again: ' He is not in the least like Joseph Khassan.' And that was true, in a way; and yet—and yet, somehow, as I have said, the meeting was a terrible shock to me, and for a moment I could not look calmly upon the man. I raised a handkerchief to my face, and, as it were, laid hold upon my feelings. And then I stared at the man, as though calmly curious; and that, for the time at all events, put an end to my doubts, for his face remained absolutely impassive and expressionless under my stare."

And so the White Beggar rode into Ed-dár, feeling vaguely pleased with his morning's work, as a man might be, and satisfied that there had been no hint of recognition. Shrewd Margaret, for her part, thought the same thing; the shrewdest must needs occasionally be at fault.

And Haj Cassim, spread-eagled in the dust as his lord passed, with the White Beggar not many yards behind, the Haj, calling upon Mohammed in Paradise to bless Moulai Hassan his right hand upon earth, smiled secretly, bidding the dust to witness that there was something of the prophet and his seer about himself.

Chapter V

A SAINT AT SUPPER

THE Shareef of Ain Araish had been mightily put about in connection with his son's escapade before the city gates; but Ed-dár hospitality is generous, and all the world knew Moulai Hassan for a saint more readily moved to laughter or to any other state than that of cherished anger.

There was for Moulai Hassan first a sleep during the afternoon's heat to the inner patio of his castle, then with the enjoyment of green tea, made syrupy with mint and sugar, came the receiving of many and various presents, the emptying of three pipes of kief, and the frank adulation of several dancing-girls. These matters served finally to remove all traces of Moulai Hassan's morning outburst of wrath, and to wreath him in smiles of sensuous good humour before the hour of the evening feast arrived.

The shareefa's evening meal was, of course, served in her own quarters. El mra Sidi (the wife of our lord) was full of questions upon this and that, and, through the Pearl Tender, gave her women a busy time. The Pearl Tender, as the woman called her, was the shareefa's own attendant, a Moorish woman who had spent some years in Constantinople, and was said to be the only English-speaking woman of her race living. As yet, Margaret's command of her lord's language was something faulty and laboured.

Many had kissed the shareefa's litter that day, and not
a few had pressed their lips to the garments of her
bearers, but none the less the fact that the holy descend-
ant of the Prophet had so far outraged tradition as to
take a Nazarene to wife had rankled and was rankling in
the minds of all Believers. Faith made it impossible to
believe evil of the Shareef of Ain Araish. Piety enforced
reverence for his wife, as for one holy beyond other living
women; but her actual presence in their midst, a known
infidel, had stirred up in many breasts resentment, the
more keenly felt by token that it must needs be harmless
and had no possible vent.

In her own ambitious mind Shareefa Margaret was perfectly conscious of all this, and, before entering Ed-dár,
she had smiled contemptuously behind her curtains at the
pious who had kissed her litter. But whatever she may
have been as a girl, this saint by marriage showed no lack
of politic circumspection as wife and shareefa, for on the
evening of this her first entry into a Moorish city of importance (Tangier is infidel-afflicted and without the
pale), she appeared in the great hall or patio when the
feast was in full progress (robed splendidly in scarlet silk
trousers and a flowing kaftan of green silk, veiled in lace
and muslin, jewelled superbly, and cloaked in white cashmere), and there made humble reverence to her sainted
lord at his own raised table. Then, accepting some sweet-
meat at his hands, and allowing several of the most
honoured guests to kiss the hem of her haiik, she withdrew
in silence to her own quarters. As has been said, gossip
announced that the saint's new wife would soon present
him with an heir.

The act was deeply appreciated, for a shareefa is not as
other women, and though infinitely more sacred than
others, or perhaps because of that, is looked to to play a

more public part than are the women of a temporal potentate's household.   Whether or no Shareefa Margaret would have so far deigned in Christian-influenced Tangier is another matter and beside the mark.   She did it here.   And ten camel-loads of dollars could not have bought for her in Ed-dár the favour that she won by this simple action.

" Allah hath gifted her with the grace of all the houris," quoth Hamet Arâf the counsellor from his place below the Shareef.   He bowed as he spoke, adding in his beard then, below breath, " and the cunning of the Pit."

" The holy shareefa wins the worship of every he in Ed-dár," opined the city's basha oilily, earning thereby the Shareef's forefinger to kiss, and a dish which had been set before the holy man to eat. Eyes of pious envy followed the basha's fingers to his lips, devout ejaculations anent the shareefa became general, and thoughtful men docketed in their already kief-clouded minds this hint as to a new method of angling for the Shareef's favour.

Mention of " kief-clouded minds " makes it necessary to add here, in justice to the men of Ed-dár, that they, in common with most respectable Believers in Sunset Land, were far too orthodox to be in the habit of " drinking the shameful " (Anglicè smoking) in public.   The presence among them of a great pillar of the Faith, their devotion to which debarred them from the use of all intoxicants, had the paradoxical effect of putting aside these and other religious scruples, and permitting conduct that at any other time had been deemed beyond description shameful. This incongruity may sound preposterous to Christian ears, and even in Morocco was exceptional, just as in many respects Moulai Hassan was a very exceptional Shareef; but it should be remembered that many of the social and moral features of Christendom appear at least equally absurd in the eyes of believers.[1]

It should be stated that the patio in which the Shareef and his guests were supping (the saint was host by virtue of his position, but his castle and every article in it, down to the bread and meat, were merely an accumulation of offerings from the people of Ed-dár to the ruling house of Ain Araish) was a spacious sexangular hall, into which opened all the ground-floor rooms of the castle. It was a lofty place, inasmuch as that its roof was the building's roof. Midway up its walls a solidly built gallery skirted the patio, and upon this the upper rooms opened.

But, fairly to limn for you the place as it appeared upon such an occasion, a Rembrandt with his brush, and not a plain story-teller with his pen, is the craftsman required. Here were high lights and deep shadows; the essence of the mystery and the romance that filled blood-stained Morocco; humanity's patriarchal days of the earth's youth, and dagger blades forged in Sheffield, and, alas! even in Birmingham; a feast presided over by " a piece of heaven " and attended by slaves bought and sold in open market among the camels and the grain.

To be sure, there is nothing incongruous in the juxtaposition of slaves and slavery, and a saint of Al-Islam, since slavery has always been a legitimate and respectable institution in the Mohammedan world, and one stained by none of the hideous abuses with which Christians loaded it in their lands. The contrast here indicated lies between

---

[1] Standing in Rotten Row with a Moor, one sunshiny May morning, I was interrogated regarding the custom of the docking of horses tails. In the interest of my Moorish friend I made some inquiries, and was informed that the practice was illegal; the operation was prohibited by law. A few minutes earlier I had pointed out to the Moor the carriage of the Lord Chief Justice, with its high stepping, thoroughly-docked horses.—A. J. D.

slavery and the influences of Europe, separated from Ed-dár by less than a hundred miles.

The whole centre of the patio was occupied by very low, round tables, so arranged among carpets and cushions, that when in use no gap showed between them, save in the midst of them where one, raised a few inches above its neighbours, was used by the Shareef alone. These tables resembled sieves, save that solid wood took the place of a sieve's net-work. Battens four inches in depth raised these structures from the floor and their rims measured from three to four feet in diameter.

Little twisted ropes afloat in oil flared out from curiously carved brazen dishes, hung in chains from each of the six arches which made cloisters about the patio. Every table had beside it a Rabat carpet of price, woven in the days when simple Moulai Ismail maintained perfect order in Morocco by a rule of sheer butchery. Europe possesses at the most two or three such. The pavement was of marble, in large, irregular slabs. The cloisters were thronged by slaves, attendants, and the hangers-on of great men—companions of the right hand, as their like are called, yet the occasion was deemed one of privacy, the general public having no entry there.

Neither forks, knives, or any substitute for these other than a man's ten fingers were in use at this feast. Napery there was none, but hand-towels were passed to and fro, and at intervals slaves bearing brass bowls of orange and rose-water marched round the divans, in order that the fastidious might lave their fingers, and others might have perfume sprinkled upon their heads. For the latter purpose an instrument resembling a pepper-cruet, but with a long spout in place of a perforated lid, was in use.

Huge vessels of thick, crudely-coloured porcelain, surrounded by flat Moorish loaves, occupied the tables, one to every four or five guests. Dishes and tables both were changed with every course in the meal, and were dipped into haphazard for what they might contain by every member of the party. Betwen courses, sweet tea and coffee thicker than syrup were served in tiny and highly ornamented cups, and pipes and kief were handed round on Fez-made trays of brass. Who would be extra courteous to his neighbour plucked choice tit-bits of meat from out the messes, rolled them very deftly betwixt thumb and finger, and presented them then to the favoured one's lips. For deftness and delicacy a well-bred Moor's manipulation of his food is something a Christian might envy, but could scarcely hope to emulate, without years of training and practice.

To any infidel or stranger from a foreign land, the meal had seemed interminable. But what would you have? The Shareef and his party were not feeding, but feasting, a vastly different matter. Then, too, at times no food appeared for the half of an hour, and dancing girls and boys sued for applause instead. The girls were, of course, slaves, and in this case were of purely negroid origin. They gained applause, and earned it, too, if consistent sensuality and provocation incarnate in rythmical motion be deserving of praise. In this, as in the matter of the " drinking of the shameful," the great Shareef's presence meant something like license to orthodox believers.

Of a sudden the Shareef looked up dreamily from his first pipe of kief and spoke to Hamet Arâf.

" Is the saint my son here, Hamet? " he asked.

" My lord, he is with the women in the upper rooms."

" Send for him."

And presently the boy stood before his father, and bowed low as in duty bound. The Shareef struggled with an urgent hiccough—he was the one man present who

had so far outraged the laws of his faith as to taste
spirits at that meal—and smiled largely at the favourite.

"Ho, son," he cried, "where is he who saved thy life
this day?"

"I know not, Sidi; but it was not written that a camel
should kill my father's son, or that I should die this
day."

"Sayest thou so? But natheless thou hadst died. this
day but for one man. H'm! Or if not died—since, as
thou sayest, art thy father's son, and the Prophet's
through him—then been sorely wounded, but for this
same man I speak of. Small things such as wounds—
great enough, ugh! to suffer, my son—are not always
written of in heaven; and, by thy father's beard, it be-
seemeth not my son to allow one who saved him to go
thankless. See to it, Ben Hassan, and presently."

A murmur of worshipful applause skirted the divans,
what time the Shareef leaned backward and spilt snuff on
the fork of his thumb from an ebony and pearl inlaid
snuff-tube. Ben Hassan turned half round toward the
guests, one little hand resting on the jewelled haft of
his dagger, where it gleamed at the open waist of his
violet kaftan, the other hanging, a curled autumnal leaf,
at his side.

"Ohé!" he cried aloud. "Ho! thou who helped the
Shareef's son this day, stand out, come forth!"

"The very Shareef, in every vein—a miracle!" murmured the basha of Ed-dár, mellifluously tuning his voice
to reach Moulai Hassan's ear.

There arose from a bench among the slaves and cloister
idlers a figure familiar to many of the Shareef's guests
as that of the White Beggar. Slowly he moved forward,
thridding the divans of the lounging feasters, and finally
coming to a standstill before the edge of the four-inch dais

upon which Ben Hassan stood beside his father's table. He bowed low to the Shareef, and then, raising his dark eyes till they met the boy's fairly and truly, he said:

" Sidi, I am here," and waited then, silent and grave.

This " sidi," by the way, is something more than the English " sir "—something it is betwixt " sire " and " saint," not easily to be rendered into English. A richly-tasselled djellab, soft of texture and cream-coloured, had been flung over his rags by some officer of the household, and his head was thickly bandaged, because that an ugly contusion was there to bear witness to the truth of the young saint's laughing comment upon the stony hardness of a mad camel's nose.

" Ask of me something that I may give thee, friend," said Ben Hassan in his most princely tone, " for they tell me that thou hast this day done service to my father's son."

" It was a free man's service, Sidi, neither a slave's or a hired servant's, and no great work when all is said."

The White Beggar had spoken, and all the Ed-dár men present were on tiptoe to hear more from him. It seemed to them that he had spoken creditably. In any other than the worshipped favourite of all believers, Moulai Hassan's one son, the boy's cavalier method of addressing one who had served him, and who was deemed a holy man in Ed-dár, would have earned resentment.

" A free man may accept reward at the hands of my father's son, and no shame be thought," said the lad, his voice breaking a little from its first confident C major of princeliness.

" Thanks fall hollow if the stomach be ill at ease, son of mine," murmured the Shareef of Ain Araish, where he reclined on his cushions. " Ask thy friend if he hath supped well."

"Hast eaten well this night, friend?" asked Ben Hassan, somewhat abashed now.

"I broke bread this morning, Sidi."

"Ho, Hamet Arâf, what is this?" shouted the Shareef, rising to a sitting position on his cushions. "How many lessons am I to give thee this day? Is the Shareef of Ain Araish a schooler of servants and waiting men? Thy mule and thy belly will bring thee to sore disgrace yet, friend Arâf. This is, ugh! by the Prophet's toes, it is to cast mud upon the name of my fathers. Rise, rise, thou, b'Allah! Why was this man not bidden to my tables?"

The counsellor glanced hurriedly about him for some slave or subordinate upon whom he might lay this his fresh disgrace. Someone should suffer, that he mentally vowed. Meantime, louting very low before the Shareef's table, he murmured:

"Lord, the word was given, the order passed from me. I am in the dust at thy feet, but—the word left me. Some dog, son of a dog, is at fault, and shall be dealt with, holy Sidi. The word left me, and, hastening to be near thee this night, I did think it carried out."

But the Shareef's wrath was already subsiding in thunderous mutterings over his kief-pipe. At that stage of the night his surcharged body could not hold anger.

"Sidi," said the White Beggar, "here is surely much smoke for very little fire. By thy good leave, I had no desire to feast this night, having many matters to think upon. Not being gifted of Allah as a shareef, my poor mind is baffled by trifles, and if lent to feasting, then— then can no other thing, Sidi. Therefore, I pray thee, let not thine anger consume any good servant of thine for me, who am but a pariah and outcast, im sha'Allah!" (by God's grace).

Ben Hamet Arâf looked grateful. The Shareef smiled drowsy acquiescence. His son peered respectfully into the White Beggar's djellab-hood with an expression of growing interest. The men of Ed-dár looked upon their beggar with increasing approval, and waited for his further speech with keen curiosity. The question of his origin, the whereabouts of the place from whence he came, had always been a mystery. Now, at all events, they heard his tongue, and knew him for a man of sense a man of wisdom and learning many thought—whilst noticing that his speech, though slightly foreign-sounding to Ed-dár born ears, was yet Arabic, and of the more polished, semi-literary sort.

"Friend," began Ben Hassan, bending forward now with a very pretty gesture of humility and regard, "for an outcast and pariah, as thou sayest, thy speech hath to mine ignorance a most wise and learned flavour, and, also, a something of reproach."

A low murmur, half denial, half approval, made circuit of the tables. Reproach is not for the sons of the Shareefs of Ain Araish. But the White Beggar only smiled gravely at Ben Hassan, bowing slightly, as though in good-humoured, half-ironical acceptance of youthful praise, and remaining silent, waiting.

"Truly a most worshipful outcast!" muttered the Shareef.

A more or less pious ecstasy was stealing over the saint's replete senses. His last eaten course had been a tiny embossed cupful of honey and potent hachsheesh. There were but two quite unclouded minds in the assembly— little Ben Hassan's and the beggar's. The former, half angered to find that his advances met with no encouragement, somewhat abashed, as has been said, and moved and interested, for why he knew not, in the grave man who was so difficult to thank; Ben Hassan began again to speak in a low voice and with proud deference, one slim-fingered small hand outstretched toward the beggar's shoulder, the other resting still upon his dagger's hilt.

"And if my father's son deserves reproach and hath offended thee," he said, "then I would ask thee wherefore and in what manner, since my will was warm to thee. We who be of the Prophet's blood have ever proffered reward to those who serve us. I had my holy father's word."

The divans offered up applause now, no more than a murmur, but applause. A slight upward movement of the White Beggar's left hand seemed to suggest that he heard and understood the applause, and besought a free conduct of his own affairs.

"Sidi," he said, as gravely as before, "I bow before the child of Mohammed. To the young man Moulai Ben Hassan el Gharbi, I would say that it is possible for a man—even a pariah and outcast—to serve another for the sake only of that other's welfare. Let rewards be. How, Sidi, if I served thee this day that thou mightest be served and saved, for love of thee, whom I had never seen, because, though the child of Mohammed, whose name be blessed art also a man, like me, or will be."

Once more the assembled guests signified approval. The White Beggar had touched upon the note of all others most calculated to appeal to that singular mixture of the democrat and conservative, communist and aristocrat, republican and ancestry-worshipping Tory, which goes to the making of the average Moor.

"Of all pariahs the most redoubtable in my experience," came from the Shareef, with a thick chuckle.

Pride born of upbringing seemed to struggle with and

yield the mastery to a stronger, better something in the expression of the saint's son.

"How then?" he echoed, touching the beggar's shoulder gently. "Why, then, am I rightly reproved friend, for not judging better of thy quality. Prythee! forget not that I am but—but a youth; and, indeed, I had no thought of offending thee, and now do thank thee fittingly as—as equal and teacher. Kiss thou my hand, friend. My father's son is wiser and nearer to a man this night for having speech with thee. Of rewards let there be no more talk, but—but I would not lose thee neither."

Ben Hassan bent toward his recumbent father and whispered to him briefly. Hachsheesh and his princely habit would have made of his right hand a gift not hard to win from Moulai Hassan just then.

"Art thy father's son, Sidi," he murmured. "Who should deny thee?"

The boy turned again to the beggar.

"I have said it, friend: we speak not at all of rewards; yet would I profit by thy goodness and wisdom. I like not the thought of losing one who did serve me for—for me, for mine own sake. I would have thee about me always, near to the person of my father's son." The divans rustled. "How sayest thou, friend: wilt remain with me, my guide and counsellor, companion of the son of the Shareef of Ain Araish?"

Even kief fumes and hachsheesh were powerless to deaden the eager expectancy of those who sat about the tables. A sibilant murmur spurred the White Beggar on the path of destiny. But it seemed that he was one of those to whom spurs are all unnecessary, for, with hardly a pause, and with traces of a fleeting smile about his weather-worn cheeks, he said:

" Gladly will I stay with thee, Sidi, true friend and guide, if it may be, to—Moulai Ben Hassan el Gharbi."

The change of wording was almost ostentatious; but, even if sober, the Shareef had never for an instant given credence to the suggestion that any man would liefer serve his son as Ben Hassan than as the son of the Shareef of Ain Araish.

Chapter VI

MORNING

"EH, eh! my fair dames and noble cavaliers, is there in the whole universe, or in holy Church, any miracle more miraculous than this that I show you now?"

In this portentous manner the writer once heard a Spanish juggler, with a greasy pack of cards in his hands, address an audience of loungers on the neutral strip at Gibraltar.

"Si, señor! I saw the dawn this morning," quoth a Spanish-speaking Moor, who stood near by, with fine Eastern scorn. The roadside idlers laughed; the Moor, his point made, stalked off; the writer burned his fingers over the lighting of a morning cigarette, for the reason that he thought instead of puffing. In an age of careless hurry the Moor's little lesson to the Spaniard was worth a thought, however; even a scorched finger, it may be.

The most marvellous of each day's many mysteries penetrated Moulai Hassan's great castle at the same moment that it dominated the rest of Morocco, and assuredly not in a less mysterious manner. Men who supped with the holy Shareef of Ain Araish were never early risers. Dawn discovered in the castle's patio no preparations for this day, but only the stark and bedraggled remains of yesterday. Indeed, had dawn come earlier by, say, three hours, it had surprised the Prophet's Right Hand in the process of being assisted to an upper chamber by Hamet, the portly counsellor, and two elaborately stained and painted slave-girls.

The Shareef of Ain Araish, you must understand, not merely can do no wrong, but cannot even be suspected of an impropriety. Not for nothing is a man born with the prophet's blood in his veins.

There were as yet no rays, no fingers of light, in the patio, but only a general filtering away of the darkness; a nacreous and opaque radiance full of promise and of mystery. One rose from among many slumbrous figures about the edges of the patio, and in this dim forecast of daylight threaded his way carefully to the great barred door which opened upon the castle courtyard. This was the man whom his fellows had known as the White Beggar of Ed-dár; the newly-made wazeer and henchman to a great Shareef's son, and one accustomed, be it said, to morning awakenings in surroundings something sweeter and more wholesome than he found in the littered place of last night's feasting.

Along the narrow and as yet silent street of grocers, across the alley of the cloth-makers, and so, by way of Ed-dár's principal thoroughfare, the eight-feet wide street of haberdashers, the White Beggar, his rags cloaked by the fine djellab provided by the Shareef's officers, wended his way to that gate in the shadow of which he had reposed through two years.

" Sbáh el khair,[1] brother! What news of thee? What is thy condition? " cried Haj Cassim the hermit to his erstwhile companion of the gate, giving salutation, as the Moorish custom is, in the form of a shower of small questions, but prefacing the same with " The morning prosperity! "

[1] The morning prosperity, or, " Good morning."

"Lá bás, lá bás; el hamdu 'l I'llah!"[1] (*No wrong, no wrong; the praise to God!*) came the reply· in orthodox fashion. And then, as though quitting formalities for business, the White Beggar squatted down upon his old mat, and said earnestly: " But I would have thy counsel, Haj. In the beginning—and as I live, Haj, it doth appear to me that some ages have elapsed since yestermorn —I followed thy word as one blind followeth whosoever serveth Allah by leading him aright. Out of that sowing hath come already a standing crop. Direct me now, therefore, Haj, for the crop is indeed of thy sowing."

Even years spent as a naked hermit upon the earth do not entirely cut a man off from the influences of place and consequence as understood by mankind. There was a note of something approaching authority in the White Beggar's tone in this pearly morning-tide of his new-found wazeerate.

" Ihyeh, so sets the wind, brother. ' We are God's, and unto Him we shall surely return.' But tell me, then, of thy doings, or shall Cassim tell thee? Art a man of note and standing to-day, brother—is it not so? Art entering now upon—— But thine the tale; tell it, brother."

So the White Beggar told him.

' " And she knew me not, Haj—she knew me not at all; but b'llah! the burnt soul of me knew her."

" Friend, beware the actor-beast!"

" Tsh! thou'rt more censorious than any kadi, Haj."

" Sho! does even that bit irk thy jaw this morning, brother?"

The White Beggar waved his hand lightly, a gesture once familiar to him, but one very foreign to his life upon the earth in these last years.

" But having gone thus far, Haj," he said, " I would

[1] No wrong, no wrong; the praise to God!

have your counsel. Have I done well? Who am I to be
guide and counsellor to a young Shareef? Have I done
well?"

"Ihyeh, and wisely, friend. Go on, I say, as thou hast
begun. Who leadeth the blind so safely as the lame?
Go on, I say, and Allah's blessing with thee. It is marked
clearly thy tarikat, brother; but beware of pitfalls.
'Tis thy tarikat, the right road for thee, friend; but
look not upon the face of the woman—upon forbidden
liquors or into the mouth of a gun, rather!"

"Nay, Haj, have no fear of me there."

"Natheless, I say again, look not upon the face of the
woman; heed ye not the jingle of her ornaments (that
dance ends in hell), and stand ever with heels hard down
on the play-actor in thee. There, there! scowl not at
Cassim. Say the beast is dead. Bury him, then, and
stand upon his grave. And now, friend, get ye hence
to the new place—the new life—the true way of thy salvation. It should be shining plain to thee; for thou
hast seen clearly enough the stain upon the old life of
which you have told me. So to the cleansing; I say; serve
the woman to the death, if need be—but look not upon
her face. Go, and may Allah and his prophet go with
thee! Give me thy hand!"

The two clasped hands, each then raising his own
fingers to his lips. And so, in the blaze of a sunrise, they
parted, and the White Beggar returned to the castle
and his young lord, pausing by the way to offer up his
prayers in the mosque of Abd er Rahman.

"Ho, Sidi!" cried a groom in the courtyard at sight
of the beggar. "Here is honour come thy way by the
hand of a poor man whose virtues are but lightly rewarded in this world. It seems the holy shareefa would
stand well with one who is at the right hand of the

Shareef's son. See else, in the fandak here. I am bidden give ye this barb, black as Eblis, with greeting from the wife of our lord. Its saddle-trappings are velvet, as thou seest, worshipful sir; this breast-plate, woven of the true gold, a comely gift methinks."

"And food for thought—ground for circumspection. Eh'm'm! My grateful thanks and lowly greeting to our lord's wife, rajil.[1] And for thyself—patience! Ye must know that hermits and those that sit in thought at city gates bear no purse. Patience awhile, therefore."

"Nay, Allah's blessing upon thee, Sidi; I meant nought with my clatter about my virtues. See what it is to serve the veiled side of a house. My tongue's become a female."

[1] Man. The customary method of address to one of this class.

Chapter VII

WAYSIDE MIRACLES

THROUGH four days and nights were the men of Ed-dár honoured by the presence among them of the Shareef of Ain Araish and his retinue. The poor of Ed-dár (and they were never few in number) might have fared bounteously for many moons had they been given the cous-cousoo alone, not to mention the three years' kept meat, the fatted lamb, the countless sweetmeats, and other delicacies consumed during the daily feasts in our lord's castle.

It was a new power in the land that put an end to the Shareef's entertainment in Ed-dár—his new wife, to wit, Shareefa Margaret. For Moulai Hassan himself, he appreciated the loyal piety of Ed-dár's wealthy folk, and desired no happier illustration of it than was given in the daily and nightly feasting of the castle. Shareefa Margaret, however, had a woman's eye for the solid, practical tangibilities of life.

"Lord," said she, in behind the curtain morning converse with the saint; "it is clear that there must be limits to the amount of tribute that can be paid thee by thy people here. For every hour of feasting, so many dollars must be deducted from the coffered tribute taken before we leave the city. This is surely worth consideration. And there be other matters amany of which ye wot —something. My condition—a wearisome journey—thy child's life——"

"Ehyeh, show me not wet eyes, Margaret. Shalt have thy way, child. Oh, wonder of miracles, that eyes so keen for affairs should be so instant in weeping!"

"Nay, Lord, 'tis nothing. I am but a woman, and pleased now that I have thy promise for to-morrow's start."

"Nay; said I so soon?"

"Methinks to-morrow was the day, Lord."

"'M'm! Well, well; that which is written. Bid thy women prepare; I must see my counsellor."

It will be seen, then, that Shareefa Margaret's methods thus far were in this sort, clinging, womanly. At least, she was no prude; it was not as Puritan that she eyed askance the midnight carousings of her Lord. She had nicely weighed the saint's thraldom to those practices which had come to him through intercourse with Christians. Her own position as new-made shareefa was very clear to Margaret. She could not stand alone as yet, she told herself. A few more nights in Ed-dár, and she could not hope to manage or guide her lord by morning light. Hence the "wet eyes" and wifely guile, which gave the signal for departure. In praise of motives or methods one cannot perhaps advance much. The attainment was well enough, however. There is a decency to be observed in this dissecting-table work of judgment.

Believers have been warned of Allah for all time by the mouth of His Prophet, and in the Book of His Word, that dealings with infidels and unbelievers would not leave them void of harm or uncontaminate. Proof of Allah's all-knowing wisdom lieth, to look no further, in the experiences of those who have not heeded this injunction. Moulai Hassan el Gharbi, Shareef of Ain Araish, was one of these; though, since the shareef cannot err, believers, never admitted the fact. And as others had fared before him, so had Moulai Hassan fared; but, bringing a notably reckless, pliable and sanguine carnal nature to the test, he had reaped a fuller harvest than most.

When a man of the Shareef's full-blooded habit and more than half savage nature, betakes him to brandy drinking, he is apt to drink a great deal and often. Linked generously with the kief and hachsheesh habits, high feeding, complaisance toward dancing girls, and life in a subtropical climate, excess in the direction named will sooner or later undermine the constitution of even a shareef of Ain Araish.

Sad reflections for a bride, these; and there were large-looming side issues. As has been said Shareefa Margaret's personal prestige was still to make. The instincts of her sex and condition made her forethoughtful in securing to herself support and protection. She felt young life stirring within her, and anger was uppermost in her mind a dozen times a day, when she heard young Ben Hassan addressed as " Shareef " or " Saint," and saw believers kiss his garments with the air of men devoutly assured that they saluted the future ruler of Ain Araish. The shareefa's plans for the future embraced the enlightening of Moorish minds upon this and many similar points.

Every owner of a gun in Ed-dár (and who had not gun and dagger was poor indeed) turned out to take part in escorting the great Shareef over the first mile of his journey toward his own far territory of Ain Araish. The scene was one of some impressiveness, and thunderously noisy. Half a dozen parties of musicians warred crudely one against another, and the sunny air was befogged by the smoke of constant discharges from thousand muzzle-loading Moorish guns. Hardly a member of the Shareef's party but carried Ed-dár men's kisses upon his fingers and

Ed-dár men's gifts in his djellab-hood. The shareef's
money paniers, too, required a deal more carrying now
than before they had reached Ed-dár. The city had been
generous, and its inhabitants knelt in serried hundreds in
the dust of the plains, when at length the final benedic-
tions and farewells had been spoken.

The White Beggar, worthily clad now in decent, all-
covering white, rode beside his young lord, mounted upon
his gift from the shareefa. He was followed by three
slaves, who had been told off to tend him, and were leading two laden pack-mules and three saddle-horses, presents from devout men in Ed-dár, and the residue of six
times the number of gifts, the which, in all courtliness
and gratitude, the beggar had declined. To be taken
under the protection of a great Shareef's son, particularly
if one is already of holy repute, is no small matter in
Morocco.

" Some day, good friends," the beggar had said to those
whose gifts modesty had induced him to decline; " some
day, so surely as I now speak to thee, will I remind thee,
true men all and kindly, of this, and ask of thee bread
or a friendly hand at honest need. And maybe even then,
good friends, I will not supplicate thee altogether for
myself and mine own needs. Yet, if for another, then
only—be sure of that—for one who stands high in thine
eyes, and Allah's whose Name be blessed! Peace be with
thee!"

" And upon thee peace, holy man!" they had cried.

The kindly declining of gifts is rare in the Sultan's
dominions, and so when found is the more keenly appreciated. The White Beggar left a fine reputation behind
him in Ed-dár, and cordial thoughts of him lingered in
the minds of more than than a few, when he and his lord,
Ben Hassan, were far enough away, scaling the Atlas,

fording mountain torrents, or ambling on sun-scorched
plains, in the holy Shareef's train, and in the course of
the forty odd days of processional journeying which were
occupied in reaching the far south-westerly country between Tarudant and Tintazart, where Ain Araish saints
have had their stronghold since the Exodus, when the
Prophet's foot-prints were still fresh upon the earth, and
the true faith fared gloriously forward at the sword's
point—nowhere more forcibly than in Ain Araish, where
Moulai Hassan's greatest forbear was said to have laid
the fountains of his kasbah upon the bones of slaughtered
Berbers, and where he remained the only Arab chieftain
who succeeded in dominating the " noble people " in their
own mountain homes.

The journey was a triumphal procession, and, but for
the unceasing vigilance of Shareefa Margaret, had doubtless occupied as many weeks as it did days.   Whenever
—and it happened upon most fore-noons—the Shareef protested good-humouredly against making a " courier's jog "
of his saintly. progress to Ain Araish, Margaret brought
forward the weapons of her sex and prospective motherhood, and peace could be purchased only by surrender.

But comparatively steady as was the rate of travel
maintained, the journey was, in despite of that, processional.   The inhabitants of every village passed followed in the Shareef's train to the outskirts of the next
settlement.   Couriers and advance riders prepared the
way, the number of the Shareef's unladen or lightly laden
pack-animals grew fewer with every village left behind,
the money-bearers finished the journey with more, by a
year of the saint's expenses in solid Moorish half-dollar
pieces, than they had carried at starting, music and gun-
firing surrounded the party from dawn till dark, and

more than one miraculous cure of sickness was reported among those of the faithful who had been fortunate enough to reach and kiss one of the Shareef's yellow and crimson riding-boots, or to find, and, as a matter of course, treasure, some fragment that the sacred hand had touched.

Another sort of miracle occurred at the village of Beni Hudra, and of that the fame went far and wide, echoing to the holy renown of Moulai Hassan. The Basha of Beni Hudra hailed before the Shareef, where he sat receiving homage in a pavilion erected for the noonday halt beside the village well, a miserable rag of a man, a fanatic beggar, who had been three days in Beni Hudra's haboos (prison) as a caution against the practice of ribald blasphemy, vagrant incenting to riot, and insolent, gabbling comment upon the practices of Mohammed's holy descendants and Allah's chosen saints. The wretch stood quaking, an invitation to commiseration, too grotesque to win much beyond scorn.

" And what said the dog, good Basha?" asked the saint pleasantly.

The Basha bent low.

" Holy Sidi," he said, " I dare not to repeat the utterances of so swinish a dog. Lord, he did revile thy sacred person! His foul tongue handled the food and drink which is made holy by thy use of it."

" Aha, Iyeh! did he that?" chuckled the saint, enlightened now. " Good Basha, my command upon thee, he did accuse me in the matter of forbidden liquors?"

The Basha bowed to the earth.

" Such, holy Sidi, was his pig-begotten, blasphemous insolence. But thou, lord, knowest; what need for me to speak?"

Miracle number one. The holy Shareef was aware by

divine wisdom, and before a name had been lain upon it, of the exact nature of the wretch's blasphemy.

"Ha! he said that I, the Shareef of Ain Araish, drank the brandy of the infidels?"

"Lord, thou sayest that which this dog, son of a dog, hath spoken, and I dare not repeat. Verily, Sidi, thou art a piece of heaven and very holy."

"Ho, Cassim!" shouted the Shareef to one of his body-servants. "Bring to me here a bottle of the Christian liquor—bidgeree!"

The man brought an ordinary bottle of brandy bearing upon it the name of a well-known European firm, and drew its cork. The Shareef poured out the half of a tumblerful whilst the Basha and all assembled stared open-mouthed. He of the blaspheming reputation quaked in his filth-sodden slippers. Three days of the haboos had removed any trace of spirit which might ever have been his, and, further, he was assured now of being presently beaten with many stripes. Life seemed a dreary sort of foolery to this straggler in it. The Shareef, like many another reckless man, was not lacking in the sort of shrewdness which mother-wit supplies. There was cunning in his blood as well as saintliness.

"Look on me, good Basha!" he cried aloud, raising the half-filled tumbler of brandy shoulder high. "And look, thou, loose-tongued head of mud!"—this to the incendiary oaf of blasphemous habit—"the Shareef of Ain Araish is Allah's hand upon earth, the lineal child of Mohammed. Goes, then, without the saying that he is not as other men. Huh!"

"A glimpse of heaven to the devout on earth," chimed the Basha.

The teeth of the "head of mud" chattered over an abject murmur.

"Not as other men, I say; most surely not as blaspheming sôk-dogs, town-gate idlers, and prison-sweepings!"

"Now the holy prophet of Allah forfend!" prayed the Basha unctuously.

"On a day," continued the holy man, "there came to this Shareef of Ain Araish, who, mind ye, is not as other men, certain infidels, Christians to wit, with a desire to entrap Allah's anointed."

"For these kaffirs, sons of kaffirs, hungry fires await in Jihennam," murmured the Basha.

"They did work upon my courtesy to take food with them, and passed to me, calling it a fruit-juice, a vessel of this same brandy, such as I hold here, and the use of which Al-Koran forbids to all believers. God's voice spake in me then, warning me, and I knew the liquor for what it was, despite the craft of the infidels in mis-naming it. But look ye, Basha, and listen thou, tongue of dirt, the Shareef of Ain Araish is not a common man to be made a fool by kaffirs. Knowing what I knew I did raise the glass thus, and drink the half of it thus, and in drinking turn the forbidden liquor, by the grace of Allah in me, into good tea, such as the prophet's holy lips might have touched, *as I do now*, good Basha—*as I do now*, thou tongue-wagging son of sôk-rats there! And thus were the infidels humbled by Allah's anointed of Ain Araish, and thus have I humbled them ever since that day. The Shareef of Ain Araish is not as other men. Basha, taste thou this liquor—my command—and pass it then to the babbling one, and thence to—who will follow him."

The Basha sipped respectfully.

"Cold tea!" he cried. "By Allah's prophet's beard! cold tea and lacking sugar!"

"Thou hast seen from whence it came. Taste thou now that. Ho, Cassim! Ah, ill-luck! Another bottle of the brandy, then, Cassim."

By a sweep of his kaftan's flowing sleeve the saint had knocked over upon the stones and broken the bottle from which he had drunken. Another similar looking bottle was drawn. The Basha tasted its contents. Others did the same; it was veritable brandy. Many touched their lips to the contents of the glass from which the shareef had drunken; it was veritable and unsweetened cold tea. Now to a Moor unsweetened tea belongs to the state of fasting, prayer, and mortification of the flesh. A small matter, truly, yet, upon reflection, one which added lustre to the saintly nature of the episode.

The "head of mud" was given his liberty, and spent the remainder of his not very respectable life in chanting of the Shareef Ain Araish, his miraculous holiness. As has been said, the fame of this miracle travelled far and wide, and materially added to the loyalty of the reverence in which the great saint was held by the people. As for the shareefa, when the story was told her, she said to her lord laughingly and in English: "So you gave them of your entertaining bottle, did you?" An observant woman was the shareefa; but, as was natural, less distinguished by saintliness than was Moulai Hassan.

Chapter VIII

THE SAINT AT AIN ARAISH

BY the time the outskirts of Ain Araish were reached there were no two among all the Shareef's following more frankly on good terms, one with the other, than were Ben Hassan, the ten-year-old saint, and his guide and counsellor, the erstwhile White Beggar of Ed-dár. Many and wonderful were the tales with which the beggar beguiled time for Ben Hassan as they rode together during the day's march, and as they rested together at a tent's mouth after the evening meal. The most of these tales went to prove that the White Beggar had travelled far and wide, sojourned in many strange lands, and grown familiar with men and women of all sorts and conditions, so that now at the last of it he did appear a very storehouse of adventurous recollection and wisdom, able to speak, and speak knowingly, as well of infidels and rascals as of true men and believers.

"Friend," said Ben Hassan, when their friendship was not many days old, "it is in my mind that the days of thy life in the living must have been not unlike to 'The Thousand Nights and a Night,' thou knowest, of which our story-tellers in the sôks never tire talking, and the people never tire hearing."

The beggar smiled in his queer, grave way, and said thoughtfully:

"The more moving a story in the hearing, O Ben Hassan, the less pleasant, believe thou me, in the living."

"Sayest thou so truly? Ah! but that is hard for me to feel; for to me, indeed, it would seem that, and the hearing is so fine, the living would be most glorious—a kind of Firdaos here upon earth. Yet without doubt thou knowest, who, having lived, now also tell the tales. Friend?"

"Sidi."

"It is in my mind that during all our talk together I have heard no name by which men have called thee, and myself have called thee ever 'friend.'"

"A name very pleasant in the hearing, Sidi, of one who hath been long outcast and a man of solitude."

"True, yet would I know thy name—a name by which to speak of thee; for thou art not 'friend,' surely, to all men?"

"Nay, indeed; that were to change one's djellab too often. Call be, then, Haj Yûsef; but the same will sound ever unfamiliar to thee, coming, as myself did, from nearer to holy Madinah than to Ain Araish. Therefore, I pray thee, oh Ben Hassan, trouble not thy tongue with my poor name; but, so long as thou trusteth me and I deserve the same, call thou me as heretofore, 'Friend.'"

And so it happened that the White Beggar remained "Friend" to his young lord, and was more often spoken of by others as "Sidi Ben Hassan's friend" than as Haj Yûsef, or than by any other title. The Shareef of Ain Araish had ever a smile and a friendly word for his son's new henchman, and the shareefa showed some disposition to make a favourite of him. But, whereas the man frequently remained an hour or more in converse with his lord's father, diverting him with informing talk of other lands, he was sedulous in avoiding the proximity of Shareefa Margaret, and when called into her presence showed himself always pedantically mindful of the true

Faith's traditions by never under any pretext raising his eyes or looking upon her face, whether veiled or un-veiled.

At somewhat less than one hour distant, as a horse walks, from the city of Ain Araish, which is the centre of the province bearing that name, the Shareef was met and welcomed home by the great Sheikh Abn Mohamet Tor, hereditary prince (so far as any official in Morocco may be so described; his fathers before him for many gen-erations had ruled where tradition said he ruled) and temporal ruler of Ain Araish. The sheikh was an elderly man, gentle of heart, and of bookish disposition. He was the last of his line, a widower, childless save for one little daughter, and a man more fitted for the recluse's life than the ruler's; just as, some ventured to say, Moulai Hassan was liker to a sheikh than a saint in the most of his habits and inclinations. Be that as it may, there were few in Ain Araish who feared Sheikh Mohamet Tor, and fewer who knew the old man well enough to speak of loving him. There were many who loved the Shareef, more who spoke of loving him, and those who did not fear him were very, very few.

In a tiny litter of embroidered Fez leather and velvet, borne by two women slaves at six paces distant from the nose of her father's great black charger—a venerable Barb whose deportment was that of an eminent ex-pounder of Al-Koran grown stout in age and honour—came Fatimah, the eight-year-old daughter of the sheikh, robed resplendently in stiff gold and silver-embroidered drapery, and brimming over with childish curiosity to see and speak with the new shareefa. In her lap was a chased silver box of bon-bons, richly jewelled at its four corners, Fatimah's gift to the bride. A blithe little lady was the sheikh's one child, and the only tyrant in Morocco who could harry the old man from his studies and meditations.

The sheikh's following on this occasion consisted of the bulk of his mounted soldiery, the Basha of the city, and most of its principal inhabitants, with a mixed rabble some four or five hundred strong at their heels. They came most obviously rather to greet their jovial and potent spiritual lord than to follow their kindly but weak-willed prince. There was a fine thunder of drums and a most piercing conflict of reetas as the musicians of the two forces came together. The grey-bearded sheikh dismounted to do reverence to the saint, and afterwards prostrated himself stiffly before Shareefa Margaret in her litter. Quite solemnly then, and without a gleam of playfulness, the sheikh's one child was presented to the shareefa, after being permitted to kiss the hand of Moulai Hassan. Shareefa Margaret won a roar of applause from the huge gathering by lifting Fatimah in her two hands and swinging the little maid bodily into her litter, rustling broideries, bon-bon box, anklets, armlets, earrings and all. Later on in the day the holy shareefa was understood graciously to inform the venerable sheikh that she would be a mother to the small princess. Mohamet Tor protested courteously that a tenth part of such honour would make him the shareefa's slave in this world and humble attendant in the next.

But, putting aside its elaborate speeches, gun-firing, and ceremonial, the really interesting feature of the Shareef's welcome was little Fatimah's sudden awakening to a sense of loyalty in childish friendship. Her old and well-beloved playmate, Ben Hassan, had remained throughout the ceremony seated on his gray Barb beside Haj Yûsef and behind his sacred father's litter. Etiquette demanded so much. The Princess Fatimah had dreamed for days and nights past of her favourite's return, yet now, in her excitement at meeting the new shareefa and being seated in the sacred litter, she had been made to forget for the time the very existence of Ben Hassan. Suddenly loyal recollection awoke in her, and with scant regard for the holy place in which she had been permitted to rest, Fatimah scrambled from the shareefa's lap, over the litter's edge, and out upon the ground, lisping aloud as she descended:

" Woe's me! my heart's a stone; I had forgot! O my father, I have kissed a piece of heaven, and—never seen Sidi Ben Hassan! O my father! O Sidi Ben Hassan! Oh, I should be whipped! "

The rumble of bass laughter among the notabilities, subdued out of respect for the high personages involved, but none the less hearty and spontaneous, was good to hear. At a nod of permission from his father, Ben Hassan rode out before the litters and dismounted at Fatimah's feet. Ben Hassan's Friend followed at his lord's heels.

The little lady knelt to kiss the fingers of the saint's son, as in piety obliged, and rising then she flung her small arms about his crimson-capped head, and two children embraced. It was pretty to see, and some hundreds of eyes, set in rough, sun-darkened faces, were moistened by the sight of it. Drawing himself up once more then, as Sidi Ben Hassan, the boy led his Friend forward, and Haj Yûsef, bowing lower than any had seen him bow to saint or sheikh, was made known to the Princess Fatimah.

Shareefa Margaret was a proud woman when she entered her new home that day; for as yet the charm which accompanies mere strangeness, and the novelty of receiving homage was still with her, and had not worn

thin. She had some ground to base her pride upon; for
the holy Shareef's castle in Ain Araish was one of the
most imposing buildings in Morocco, and, unlike the
great dwelling-places of Marrakish, was built to stand
ten centuries, rather than ten decades, of wear and tear.
Beside it the sheikh's palace, though considerable, appeared a flimsy edifice.

The rear wall of Moulai Hassan's castle was a portion,
and by far the strongest portion, of the outer wall of Ain
Araish. Beyond was a moat of unknown depth and
stagnant foulness. Over this a seldom-used and cumber-
some drawbridge gave the holy Shareef a separate entrance to the city, free of espionage and beyond the province of the town guards. Skirting the wall within, and
overlooked by an outstanding wing of the castle, Moulai
Hassan's garden stretched its lush and tangled length
over a good eighth part of the city's circumference, and
to a width of perhaps six hundred feet. At its end rose
the yellow, rain-stained walls of the sheikh's palace, flaky
and lichen-streaked, and surmounted by a ruinous balus-
trade patchily decorated in tile-work.

The shareefa's pride of possession received something
of a shock when, turning to Hamet Arâf, the secretary,
she inquired to what purpose the wing of her lord's
castle overlooking his garden might be devoted.

" That, oh M'ra Sidi " (wife of our lord) " is the
holy Shareef's harem," replied the counsellor, inwardly
enjoying the hot flush of anger which swept over the
new saint's face.

By his own dispensation, duly attested by the kadi,
Moulai Hassan had put away as wives the two Moorish
ladies who had occupied that position before Margaret,
and Margaret was not sufficiently versed in Mohammedan
tradition to know that shareefas differed from all other

wives in that for them no divorce was valid. The question of concubinage had not occurred to Shareefa Margaret in Europe, and had but vaguely been thought of by her in Tangier. Now she was to live under a roof which covered her husband's harem, and a pretty extensive one at that from all appearances.

"An iron rod for you," she muttered in English, and the expression of her face boded discomfort in the near future for the sweet-eating, childish-minded women behind the jalousies, whose offence against Margaret had been hard to discover. But the shareefa was drawing near to motherhood.

These same jalousies, by the way, had cost Moulai Hassan more than such things are wont to cost. They covered slot-like windows of real glass of which, outside the Shareef's castle, there was not another pane in that countryside. The Shareef had brought these luxuries from Tangier to please one of his women. Very fortunately for himself he had brought the whole of them in duplicate; for, upon the evening of the day they were fitted, an angry mob of Believers had smashed every window visible from the courtyard and streets with a shower of stones and other missiles.

That had been a bad night for Ain Araish. Unarmed and alone, the Shareef had rushed among his people before the great gate. There he had cursed them with curses too lengthy and horrible for quotation. At the last he told them a plague should descend upon them before another night was passed. Twelve men he called upon by name, and they grovelled before him. Next day they grovelled again, but lacking their ears and with slit palms. This they had suffered in el haboos, whither they had gone at the Shareef's command, unguarded, on the evening of the window-breaking. Their plight at-

tracted the less notice, however, for that when daylight
came it discovered Ain Araish a moving yellow sea of
locusts, a province blotted out, its atmosphere so dense
that mules lay down in it, to become in three minutes
yellow hillocks, too burdened to rise.

For seven days Ain Araish battled against the most
virulent plague of locusts ever seen in El Maghreb, and
during that time men knelt in hundreds kissing the outer
walls of Moulai Hassan's castle and calling out to him
to spit upon them and forgive. On the eighth evening
Moulai Hassan strode over prostrate believers through
the still raging yellow storm to the principal mosque of
Ain Araish. There he besought Allah, through his own
holy forbear Mohammed, to remove the curse and save
Ain Araish. Before morning the plague began to di-
minish; before sunset upon the following day there was
not a live locust in the city, and no more than a few in
the province. There were some thousand of tons of
dead locusts, however, and many were the men, women,
and beasts that summer who lived on starvation's extreme
edge, that the Shareef's castle might not be short of
barley, wheat, and other food-stuffs. Such happenings
as these are not easy to forget. As Moulai Hassan said,
" The Shareef of Ain Araish is not as other men." Meantime, the castle had its windows and jalousies, and no
man hinted that they were infidel innovations or an out-
rage upon the Shareef's descent.

But Shareefa Margaret recked nothing of all this.
Enough for her that the jalousies of the great garden wing
sheltered an unknown number of curious women folk,
possibly beautiful, who, upon an orthodox footing of
some sort, enjoyed intimate relations with the great
Shareef. It falls to be noted here, by the way that the
Shareef's dalliance with an hundred women whose rela-

tion toward him was illicit, would not have disturbed his English wife for one moment. After mature consideration the shareefa started life in Ain Araish with two hard and fast domestic stipulations. She would never meet or know any lady of the harem; no inmate of the harem should ever enter any other portion of the castle.

Moulai Hassan had tasted no brandy for several days when his bride faced him with these stipulations. He was feeling kindly toward the ladies of his harem, his heart being of that sort which is always made fonder by absence.

"Shareefs of Ain Araish," he began, and there was trouble in his eye, "are not wont to take their inner lives in meted out bundles packed by their women—by any woman. Ain Araish is not Trouville. Order thou thine own affairs, O Margaret; seek not the ordering of the Shareef's."

"I spoke in English," snapped Margaret, in the terser tongue.

"And I in the prophet's Arabic, being the Shareef, and in Ain Araish. Watch thy feet whither they lead thee, Margaret."

The warning was unneeded. Margaret was eyeing the situation and her lord up and down and comprehendingly. Her scrutiny ended, she chose her weapons deliberately and sat her down to weep noisily, and in an attitude which displayed her figure to the full. The Shareef passed a trying quarter of an hour, and heard his outlook as a prospective parent seriously threatened. Then he yielded with the best grace he could assume, which was not very good, for neither habit or education had shown him any virtue or art in giving way, and dispatched a slave to announce his intention of paying the harem a visit. He was at least sure of his ruffled plumage being decently smoothed there.

Meantime, Sidi Ben Hassan was introducing Haj Yûsef, to his own quarters in the castle. Up till now the youthful saint had been an important personage in his father's household. His quarters were in keeping with his footing, then, and spacious. Their outer wall was the city's, their windows overlooked the moat, if six-inch wide, fan-shaped embrasures might be said to over-look anything.

"Here sit the slaves, and any who wish to see me," explained Ben Hassan, with childish pomp, as he led his Friend through a lofty ante-chamber. They passed a heavy Berber rug, hung portiere-wise across an archway. "Here I live in the day." They entered an arched and vaulted apartment, dimly lighted from narrow, high win-dows, big as a barn, and furnished exclusively with rugs, carpets, three or four low divans, tapestries, and some scores of daggers and guns. Beyond this were three smaller rooms. As to the central one, "There I live at night," quoth Ben Hassan. That on the right hand was occupied by a medley of boy's treasures and belongings—riding-boots, soft as stockings and coloured scarlet and yellow, richly embroidered saddles, musical instruments, and the like, all of the finest, and all suited to their owner in point of size. The other small room, that of the three which overlooked the moat, was placed at the disposal of Ben Hassan's Friend for a sleeping apart-ment.

"Now let us call the slaves into the big room and hear all news."

The young saint's oddly-chosen companion complied with one of those grave smiles which had of late become frequent with him, and they took to themselves seats upon the cushions in Ben Hassan's great living room. There, some eight days after their arrival in Ain Araish, news of some note to the pair was brought them by Boaz and Marzuk, two of Ben Hassan's slaves.

"Allah hath sent a second son to the Shareef. The shareefa hath borne a man child, saint and son of saints, and liveth yet, and is well. La ilâha illa 'llaho!"

"Ohé!" cried Ben Hassan, "now I shall have a brother."

"Ah!" muttered the Friend in Christian English, "here begins trouble, I suppose."

"What sayest thou, Friend, in that curious tongue? It hath a sound like the shareefa's—English surely. My father hath some knowledge of it, but not I, though my father, too, is of the Prophet. But what hast thou said?"

"Nothing Sidi—a very little thing. Only that, brother or no, methinks there can be but one Shareef of Ain Araish."

"Why, what else?" cried Ben Hassan, round-eyed. "My father is Shareef, and I, his son, come after him."

"Ah!"

"Wherefore 'ah,' Friend?"

"It is even as thou sayest, Sidi."

"Ih-yeh, im sha' Allah!" (Why, yes, by God's grace! that is.)

Chapter IX

BEN HASSAN'S FRIEND

THERE was by no means the same element of incongruity in the companionship of youthful Ben Hassan and his Friend that there might have been between a man and a child similarly divided by years in a western and modern community. The White Beggar of Ed-dár had been looked upon as an aged man by the same token and on much the same grounds that he had earned his reputation for holiness. His solitude, silence, and manifest indifference to creature comforts had been data enough for Ed-dár to found its conclusions upon.

But now that he was finely turbaned and clothed decently in a djellab, the hood of which was seldom raised, and never worn in such a way as to hide his face, it did appear that he was by no means a bad-looking man, and one still under middle age. He wore his beard and moustache very full, and this, whilst hiding altogether the lower part of his face, served also to soften and modify the haggard look which his sunken cheeks, lined forehead, and deep-set eyes had otherwise given him. The ample turban he wore reached his eyebrows. The small patch of skin which his beard left exposed over each high cheek-bone was rather unusually dark for an Arabian born man, which was what men called the Friend. His hands, however, as is frequently the case, were lighter in hue, white as to their palms, and delicately formed.

All this did not prevent his being a matured man, and one of notably serious bent, whilst Ben Hassan had scarcely passed the age of childhood to enter that of youth. But amongst true believers, even in so comparatively temperate a clime as that of Morocco, the years of childhood in the sense in which Europeans understand that word are very few indeed. The characteristics of Northern childhood are many of them unknown at any age among Moors, and those that do exist disappear with the term of infancy. In Ain Araish a boy of six would be deemed a poor sort of weakling if he could not manage a horse or drive a herd of cattle. Soon after that he takes to the use of his elders' kief-pipes, and, when he can, their guns. At nine or ten he adopts an air of authority toward women and children, in a land where the existence of souls in women is an open question, which lends itself to recondite discussion. During all this time, if he be the son of a Shareef of Ain Araish, he has grown used to the humble and devout homage of his seniors in every grade of the community, his person and his will have been openly and alike held sacred, and his words welcomed respectfully under all circumstances.

Says the unbeliever, " But this is to manufacture a prig most inconceivably priggish."

Among unbelievers the conclusion would be safe. Among Arab peoples the prig is very, very rare, though arrogance, insolence, and violence of temper are common enough, allied almost invariably to a kind of dignity and repose which in most cases is solid enough to correct and purify the blemishes named, so far, at all events, as they are visible. And for that priggishness which is not discernible, one is not sure that it is a blemish at all.

It were a task of much difficulty to analyze, or even to

describe, the nature of that influence upon the young saint's adolescence which came from his intimacy with Haj Yûsef. The man's teaching, though it never bore upon religious matters, was markedly the teaching of a Believer, inasmuch as it contained much explicit insistence upon racial exclusiveness, the aristocracy of pure Mohammedan breeding, and the dangers involved in carelessness as to the laws of blood, and caste, and faith.

" But, O Friend, there is my holy father, whose wife——"

" Is like himself, 'a piece of heaven,' and no subject for discussion, they or their doings."

" And my new brother; the blood of——"

" Hush, Ben Hassan! I pray thee not to peer into these matters as yet, but rather to accept thy Friend's true word, and render to Allah thy thanks that thou'rt born, apart from sainthood, of one blood, one race, unmixed and undefiled."

And again in some respects the teaching of Ben Hassan's friend smacked somewhat of Christendom and western civilization, but only in its essence, and without consciousness upon Haj Yûsef's part of its foreign element. In a hundred different ways he impressed upon the boy the evil of lying and all forms of deceit in any cause whatsoever. No Believer could well have contradicted such teaching, but most would have smiled at it, and few indeed would have been at any pains to teach it. It was distinctly foreign in origin, and it supplied Ben Hassan with some foreign born ideals of a kind which sent the ladies of his sacred father's harem into fits of laughter when, ruffling it swaggeringly among them, as the boy often did, he aired his lofty judgment upon a point of honour. Oriental morality makes a very venial fault, if fault at all, of many forms of deceit. In no other corner of an Oriental community is deceit so rampant as it is among the denizens of a great man's harem.

A curious personage was Ben Hassan's Friend, and one who did appear to be altogether devoid of craft or subtlety. But for a certain sombre immobility, a habit of meditative silence, the man would have seemed but little removed from the boy, so much there was in him which suggested the beginning of a life, the youth's preparation for the affairs of manhood. And, remembering the nature of his life as the White Beggar of Ed-dár, its hermit-like isolation, one could easily imagine that his meeting with the Shareef's son had meant a beginning for this man from nowhere. As for what had been before this beginning, and before the White Beggar came to Ed-dár, that was so absolutely dead and remote, that Ben Hassan's friend was able to draw upon it for stories wherewith to interest his young lord, and that with never a suggestion of reference to anything connected with the living man, Haj Yûsef.

It was at about this period, and before the shareefa's little son was many months old, that Ben Hassan made one of the famous remarks of his boyhood, a remark which filtered from mouth to mouth among the slaves of the household, hummed for an afternoon in the Sôk and about the gates of Ain Araish, and then was carried up and down the highways of Morocco on the lips of devout and other travellers. Said the holy Shareef to his son when they met one sunshiny morning in the castle courtyard:

"God's peace be with thee, Sidi Ben Hassan. Thy father is grateful for a sight of thee. Since thou hast gotten this 'Friend o' Ben Hassan' I am not often privileged to meet with thee."

"Nay, my father," murmured the lad, dropping on one knee to kiss the Shareef's hand; "my friend is before all things a modest man, and mindful ever of the saying, 'Sultan and beggar alike must give unto Allah that which is Allah's.' Therefore, lord, and if in these days thou hast been seldom troubled by meeting with thy little son, I pray thee credit not his friend unjustly, but give the glory unto the holy shareefa, O my father!"

The Shareef laughed long and lustily, but not before an upward glance in the direction of Shareefa Margaret's windows had assured him that her holiness was out of hearing. Then he called his son a monkey, a monkey with the solemnity of a kadi; and the monkey, seizing opportunity by the forelock, obtained a promise of three new saddles for his men while yet the saint's merriment gurgled in his throat. There is no other thing for which a Moor, of whatsoever degree, will pay so readily as for a laugh; and Ben Hassan's little shaft struck well home for the reason that its barb and feathers were truth.

The Shareef himself was the first to quote his son's remark to Margaret, and she received it with a broad smile, a smile which was made the more pronounced by its contrast with a lowering brow and eyes, into which flashed a light of something quite other than amusement.

"The young rascal!" she exclaimed, speeding her smile with a little laugh. "Heaven forbid that I should ever keep him from his father, except, to my great regret, when he is in one of his unmanageable tantrums. I don't like you to be troubled by him then, and, indeed, I think he would be ashamed to see you."

"I pray thee, Margaret," said the Shareef in Arabic, "speak not to me in the cold tongue of the North. I like it not at all, and it is not good for thy learning of be-

liever's speech. But, speaking of Sidi Ben Hassan, my
son " (this with a good deal of dignity), " this talk of
temper is new to me. He hath ever been beloved of all
my people, O Margaret."

" Slaves do not find fault with their master's son,
Shareef." When Margaret spoke in Arabic to her lord,
she managed for some reason of her own to use the
phraseology and grammar of her own tongue, though
her words were Moorish. When she spoke to other Believers this was not so. " Be sure," she continued, " that
I, who am no slave, am anxious to see and show all that
is best in him. But mine would be a poor care of Ben
Hassan if I could not see the faults as well. There
is not a grain of real harm in him as yet, but it is not
good for the boy to be always idling here in the castle;
he should be learning."

And there the subject was allowed to drop for the time
being, and for many subsequent months, and even years,
the Shareef being called upon to discuss a more important matter, bearing upon the health of his younger son,
and to express an opinion upon the growth of that interesting infant's hair. But, without doubt, Shareefa
Margaret bore in mind the remark of Ben Hassan, and
was made the more determined thereby in certain plans
for his welfare which she had pondered over for some
time. Ben Hassan missed two of his slaves that afternoon, and, upon inquiry, found that for the future their
attendance was required by the shareefa.

" Trouble not thy head for that, Ben Hassan," said Haj
Yûsef, when the boy dejectedly gave the news to his
friend. " I will see that ye lack nothing. Indeed, there
was little enough for them to do."

" Nay, Friend, I grieve not for myself. Ben Hassan
can find slaves in any sôk. 'Twas for the two men, for

Hamet and Boaz, I grieved; to leave me for—for the shareefa!"

"Ah, they were better off with us, Sidi; but ' We are God's, and unto Him we shall surely return.' "

Haj Yûsef, despite his reputation for holiness, rarely quoted the Koran. When he did, it was generally in this last sentence, or else from one of the many passages in which Mohammed has given to the world Allah's word that "That which is written is to be, and that which is not written cannot be."

Chapter X

KADI MARGARET

MOULAI MOHAMMED EL GHARBI was the name which, with a great deal of christening-bath and sheep-slaughtering ceremony,[1] had been bestowed upon Shareefa Margaret's little son. But the name was rarely heard in Ain Araish, and never in the Shareef's own household, and for this the child's own mother was responsible.

On the very day upon which her son's name had been given him, the shareefa had soundly whipped a slave for uttering that name in her hearing.

"Saint's names are no playthings for slaves," she had assured the bewildered victim of her wrath. "Speak thou of my son, if at all, as 'the Shareef's son,' and then with reverence."

A couple of days later, the Shareef's m.koddem, his major-domo, that is, or man of affairs, Ben Hamet Arâf, received a similar lesson without the whipping. So, for

[1] In Morocco the christening takes place upon the eighth day after birth, when, for the first time, the child is washed (generally in water to which salt and fennel-seed have been added) and dressed in new clothes. The water thus used is then passed among the spectators upon a tray, in which visitors place coins for the nurse's benefit. On the christening morning the father slaughters a sheep, saying: "In the name of the mighty God, for the naming of," so and so. In the case of the Shareef's son, scores of other sheep had been killed, and feasting was kept up from the day of birth till the day of naming.

the future, it was Ben Hassan and Ben Hassan's Friend, on the one hand—and every passing month, whilst seeming to lessen their importance in the household, made them the less talked of—and " the Shareef's son," as though he had but one, on the other hand.

This little circumstance, and others not so small ensampled by it, did not altogether escape the Shareef's notice. At intervals, and for the most part during early morning fits of depression, Moulai Hassan el Gharbi was moved to sour reflection, and even to spoken words of vague complaining, anent the changes, the new rule which seemed to be growing up in his household and dominating it. The chiefest among the Shareef's vices was creeping upward and over him, sapping his manhood and dissipating his old masterful authority, as the air of each new day's dawning, fresh and wholesome, dissipated the fumes of brandy which night brought to the saint's banqueting-hall.

Margaret, her desire for power as yet unslaked, her ambition still fresh and virile, was not the woman to stand aside and watch the reins of government slipping from hands she could rule and control into the grasp of adventurers or seekers after place. For every inch of authority which the easy-going Shareef allowed dissipation and his fibre-sapping indulgencies to steal from him, his wife made it her business, her smoothly-arranged, tactfully-managed business, to take unto herself a good two inches of influence, sway, and prestige in Ain Araish. All the suggested light of pomp, of coming dominance and power, which could be shed upon an infant was made to play about the figure of Moulai Mohammed, " The Shareef's son," as Ain Araish had learned to call him.

Once the woman's curious aloneness in a world of pure Orientalism rose up in her, took her by the throat, and insisted on recognition. Margaret sent for Ben Hassan's Friend.

"Friend," she said, "my women tell me thou'rt a man of learning and a great traveller to boot, one who knoweth the lands and lives alike of Christians and believers. Tell me of the Christian lands thou knowest. Hast ever been in England?" Then, with a gust of urgency, she added in English: "For pity's sake talk English! Have you ever been in the Strand? Don't stare, man! I'm certain you know English. Swear if you like, so it's in English!"

"The wife of our lord does me too much honour," murmured Ben Hassan's friend in Arabic. "My travels and my learning are alike small matters. I have no more——"

"There, drat the man! Seer fi-hálak-um!" (Get away!) "Eh, eh-yeh-b'is-salámah!" (Go in peace!) "Er—er—Tabká âla khair!" (Good be with ye!)

When next her loneliness fell upon her the holy shareefa wrestled with it in private, and when Ben Hassan questioned his friend as to the nature of the shareefa's business with him, the man said:

"A small matter, O Ben Hassan; the shareefa had forgotten something."

"What?" persisted the boy.

"Her position," said Haj Yûsef sharply. "Where do we ride this afternoon?"

But later on in the same day the man who had been called the White Beggar of Ed-dár asked Ben Hassan a question in a tone of careful carelessness:

"Who is it that hath spread a report in the castle that I have knowledge of the English tongue and of Christian countries?"

"Nay, I know of no one who hath spread such a report, Friend—not to say spread a report. Myself have spoken of thy learning and knowledge of strange lands. Also I have heard words on thy lips of that same English tongue which is the shareefa's. I, too, have travelled a little, friend, and so can judge somewhat of thy greater knowledge. I have lived awhile in Fransawi " (France) " with the Shareef my father."

The child recorded his achievement with something of an air.

" Eyeh," hummed the friend, and to himself he added: " I might have known she could never suspect and keep suspicion from her eyes. H'm! And I, who should help her, *must* help her where I can—and her ' Shareef's son '—I—yet, by Allah! one blood, one faith; race should be respected—I—I am ' Ben Hassan's Friend.' Bism' Illah! and yet my path's plain: I *must* serve her!"

Among the many circumstances which, during the infancy of her little son, tended to strengthen Shareefa Margaret's hold upon the people and affairs of Moulai Hassan's own territory, the weightiest and most important had its root in the Shareef himself, his life, and conduct. A month or two spent in the Ain Araish castle seemed in these latter days to fill the holy man with an overpowering desire for change and movement. Tafilet, Fás, Marrakish, Meknás, in turn he visited them all, and, tiring of these purely Moorish cities, he journeyed overland to Es-Sooerah, or Mogador, as its infidel inhabitants call it, and there took ship for Tanjah (Tangier), the Christian-ridden, where caste is forgotten of all, Babel is outdone, the faith is befouled, and forbidden liquors and forbidden habits are a part of the daily life.

From such trips the Shareef would return to Ain Araish aged and coarsened, weakened in body and still more weakened in his standing as Shareef, to find a quiet, self-contained, masterful woman watching over his interests at the castle; guiding his people on a steady, hardheld rein; obtaining more and more deference and homage from them as they grew to realize her power more clearly; the mistress of the town and district, Shareefa of Ain Araish, and mother of the Shareef's son.

It was during the few days of clumsy, unrestful dissipation which Margaret was accustomed to regard as the immediate precursor of one of Moulai Hassan's expeditions, that the shareefa made her first notable move in the way of disassociating Ben Hassan from the position of heir-apparent to the Shareef of Ain Araish. Her own son was at this time making weakly progress in a delicate boyhood. For five years the mother had been deftly paring here and padding there, in pursuance of her policy of shareef-making. She had by no means gained her own way in all things. In Ben Hassan's Friend she had found one who served her with rare loyalty and machine-like tireless precision. Yet, though he obeyed her in all things, even (and this with obvious pain) when her command robbed Ben Hassan, her stepson; yet it was a fact that in some curious way he stood between her and the lad she strove to belittle. If he stripped Ben Hassan at the shareefa's orders, he managed at the same time to rob the stripping of all humiliation. Margaret's orders were carried out; yet their purpose was, in some measure, defeated. But Margaret was the shareefa, and Haj Yûsef a dependant.

When the Shareef first heard that, since he contemplated a visit to Fás, he must take his son, Ben Hassan, to that centre of scholarship and learning, there to establish the boy for a few years to be educated, he laughed at the notion, shrank from the trouble it involved, and said that the lad was the son of his loins.

"The blood in him of Allah's anointed is sufficient education for a Shareef of Ain Araish, good Margaret," said the holy man. And in his innocence he fancied the question to have been closed by this remark.

Margaret folded her hands, palms uppermost, and, gathering together her carefully organized forces of persuasion, settled down to the carrying of her point. It was like a well-drilled body of English infantry closing in upon a camp of twenty or thirty predatory Bedouins. A tenth part of her ammunition served Margaret.

"There, there; brow-beat me not, Kadi Margaret. One God, the Shareef of Ain Araish, is a driven sheep these days, and needs protection more than do those who seek it at his hands! Bid my son prepare for the road, and—and if ye love me give me no more words this day."

Two days later, the Shareef, with a small following of fifty men, set out from Ain Araish for the royal city of Fás, which even to-day retains some store of Moorish culture and learning. In his train were Ben Hassan, his friend, and the one slave whom Fate and the shareefa had left the Shareef's first-born son.

Seeing tears in the eyes of his young lord, Haj Yûsef proffered cheerful conversation as the party filed out through the city gates. His instructions to prepare for several years of absence from Ain Araish had been something in the nature of a shock to Ben Hassan. There had been partings with friends, four-footed and human. Little Fatimah, the sheikh's daughter, had wept on her playmate's neck.

"But Fás is a great city," said Ben Hassan's Friend. "There are fine horses, fine houses, guns, books, and other treasures in Fás, O Ben Hassan."

"Ye—es, Friend," assented the Shareef's son, manfully,

and spurring his horse the while into a series of restrained antics; " and there—there is no shareefa—too—neither ! "

" True," said Haj Yûsef, with grave thoughtfulness; " Fás lacketh any such great shareefa as ours of Ain Araish, but, but—the bread and the sweet cakes of Fás are most excellent."

" La, la, la," hummed the boy, smiling through his dejection.

There was perfect understanding between the two; but Ben Hassan had learned that no word disrespectful to his step-mother might be pronounced within the hearing of his friend.

Chapter XI

IN THE CITY OF THE HOE [1]

ITT was, perhaps, as well for Ben Hassan and his friend
that their establishment in the city of industry and
learning should have been personally supervised by
the Shareef himself. The footing thus given to the pair
in Fás was a happier one than had been theirs if Shareefa Margaret had filled her lord's place. Moulai Hassan's prestige was still high in the north-eastern capital.
His princely style of living and open-handed generosity
were appreciated to the full as much as his exalted spiritual rank was reverenced. Fás is a conservative city, and
remains finely impervious to the influences of change and
movement in lesser towns.

As was fitting where the son of a Shareef of Ain Araish
was concerned, the key of a madarsah, or student's cell,
in el Sherrátin, the most aristocratic of all quarters of
the Karueen University, was purchased, at a stiff figure,
for Ben Hassan from the retiring son of a wealthy Tafilet
sheikh.[2] But it was not to be expected that a great

[1] Fás (Fez) in Arabic means a hoe; the hoe is the spade of
Morocco. Tradition hath it that the great Idrees, founder of this
most venerable capital of El Maghrib, turned the first sod of the
city with a hoe, saying: "Here I plant this my fás," on the first
Thursday of the holy month, Rabi'a el Awal, in the year 192 A. H.

[2] There are no college fees of any sort. either at the Karueen
University of Fez or at any similar institution in Morocco; but
the incoming student must purchase the key of his cell or study

Shareef's son should actually live in a Karueen cell, or require the daily dole of bread. An entire house in al Attarin, within a short distance of the great mosque of Moulai Idrees, was rented and fittingly furnished for the use of Ben Hassan, his friend, and those of the learned who were to instruct him privately. A slave of the Shareef's was told off to do duty with Cassim, the single one of his body servants that Margaret had left to Ben Hassan. Money was placed in Haj Yûsef's hands, and credit arranged for with a merchant of the Attarin. And then, leaving a saintly blessing with his son, the holy Shareef took his departure for Tangier, feeling, it may be, somewhat restricted and hampered in his conduct whilst under the enquiring eye of Ben Hassan.

Before Fás had known the pair a month, Ben Hassan, for his part, was well pleased with the acquaintance, and had ceased to bewail his enforced departure from Ain Araish. Haj Yûsef forbore to point a homely moral as to obedience and resignation, he being occupied in the teaching of a good many other lessons to Ben Hassan.

For lessons, as the same would be understood by an European school-boy, Ben Hassan had none. His studies were, for the greater part, theological, the most of his learning having Al-Koran for its base. To acquire any form of bookish lore, however, is something of an undertaking, if before knuckling down to it you have mastered horsemanship, the use of guns, and the open-air daily life of a great Shareef's son, with a body-guard to manage and pious homage to receive. Also, if Al-Koran be but one book, it should be remembered that learned men's

(at a price which varies from twenty to one hundred dollars or more), and this he sells again when leaving the University, the authorities of which supply him with one loaf of bread per day and one new djellab per annum.

commentaries upon it form a desirable, nay, a necessary study, and represent the fill of many and many a rusty tome. Something, too, about other lands (a few of them), secular history and planet lore, were branches of scholarship in which Haj Yûsef and certain worthy lecturers and f.keehs of the Karueen sought to interest the Shareef of Ain Araish, his son.

The Nazarenes' idea that no real education is imparted to students in Morocco is on a par with their peculiar habit of believing only their own stories and laughing to scorn the legends and traditions of Believers. As a fact, any other pupil than the son of a great Shareef would have found it impossible to enter the Karueen University as did Ben Hassan without first mastering the whole of Al-Koran, and obtaining some knowledge of Arabic grammar and rhetoric. In the case of a son of Moulai Hassan's no searching inquiries were made, but Ben Hassan had none the less to conform with the customs of the Karueen to the extent of following the usual course of tuition. His day's work would commence after the morning prayers, with an hour's study of Al-Koran and its commentaries. Then, accompanying his fellow-students, he would go to another professor for a course of law which would last till about eight or nine o'clock. Astrology, astronomy and kindred subjects would likely occupy him then till close on noon, and in the afternoon grammar and rhetoric, taken in a rather more leisurely manner than the morning courses, would be the young man's task. In all cases a pupil would be chosen to read a passage bearing upon the study in hand; then the learned professor would proceed to expound, and lastly students would ask questions and seek further explanation. Further, Ben Hassan was expected to devote some time in his own house to the reading of geography,

poetry, history, and the like. His Wednesdays were half
holidays. Thursdays and Fridays were whole holidays.

But, withal, there was little fear of Ben Hassan or
any other student in all the vast Karueen deteriorating
into a mere bookworm after the manner of many Nazarenes and other infidels. In Fás the wise words of the
alchemist (El Ûfráni) are not likely to be forgotten:

"The number of radicals in the word kimiah" (al-
chemy) "is five, as also is that of the fingers. If, my
friend, you wish to practice that science, undertake agri-
culture and toil, for they are the true kimiah of man, not
that which works with copper and lead."

Ben Hassan made neither a very promising nor yet
altogether a disappointing pupil. But it was not the
fascination of any form of study which made Fás seem
a pleasant place to the youth. He was happy in his
life there by token that he was a healthy lad, under no
other than healthy restraints. He had learned to love his
staid counsellor and friend, and, here in Fás, was no
alien in authority, no strange, steely-eyed woman to come
between the pair with resentment, distress, and humiliation in her gift.

And the henchman, too, Haj Yûsef, found life in Fás
to his taste, and did appear to progress toward youth
rather than age as time wore on. Put into words, as
himself certainly never put them, the main causes of the
Friend's content appeared vaguely in his mind in this
wise: "My part, my business in life, is atonement, working clear, the serving of Shareefa Margaret. At her
bidding I am here with Ben Hassan. That is so far
good. Further, it is here with Ben Hassan that I would
be, if inclination were the only guide; therefore, it is
altogether good."

So Haj Yûsef went his ways smoothly and told him-

self the " actor-beast " in him was long since dead. ·And
he believed it, too; albeit a short-lived murmur of truth
in him more than once suggested that, on his own showing, and according to his own theory of his work in
life, his true place just now was not the smooth, con-
genial round of days spent in Fás with Ben Hassan, but
rather back in Ain Araish among constant pricks of em-
barrassment and discomfort within sight of the shareefa.
" What does she know of the nature of the material
she works upon? " murmured Truth. " You should be
there to guard her in despite of herself." It was but
the faintest of murmurs. " Herself sent me here," pro-
claimed the man aloud, and—and stayed, well content.

Meanwhile, in Ain Araish happenings were all of a
colour. The shareefa pursued the direct path of her
ambition, and no man could have denied that this her
path was illumined by consistency, strenuousness and
ingenuity—three good and serviceable lamps, which may
be burned alike to good or evil purpose. Margaret was
shareefa by right of wifehood, through the rule of a
rapidly ageing and weakening man. She was preparing
to be shareefa by right of motherhood, through a rapidly
growing and developing child, her son, Moulai Mohammed. And hers were the sort of preparations which
generally spell achievement.

To be born in Ain Araish is to hurry through childhood to quickly attained youth and manhood. When the
boy was seven, Margaret decided that Moulai Mohammed
must go to Europe to be taught. This was a natural
decision enough, yet, as a part of her policy, an error
of Margaret's—one of few.

The mistake was not carried so far as to involve the
shareefa's leaving Morocco. That were too obviously to
neglect a half-grown crop. The shareefa wrote at length

to her adopted parents in England. Dick and Mary Dunn, welcoming an excuse for visiting scenes they loved, journeyed south to Tangier, and there met Margaret, who accompanied her boy so far from his sacred father's territory, and no farther.

In these good and kind hands the future great Shareef (the first of that race to be born a half-caste) was confidently left and willingly received, while Margaret hastened back to Ain Araish, as shrewd observers remarked, "to keep the young saint's place warm." The rebellious, the scurrilous, and the many Moors in Christian-ridden Tangiers, whom intercourse with the infidel has made irreverent, said "bastard" instead of "saint," though, to be sure, themselves living in one of the most racially corrupt cities on earth, were in no position to rail at Moulai Mohammed's mixed blood. Yet they did it none the less, and a few even made ostentatious pilgrimages to the Karueen at Fás for the purpose of paying tribute to young Ben Hassan "of the true blood of the Prophet." But these insurrectionaries were few. In Ain Araish itself the danger surrounding such heterdoxy made it even more rare. There the shareefa was a very real power; and now, with years before her, free of motherly cares, she meant to be a greater power.

Chapter XII

HOME-COMING

ON a morning in February, during an interlude of that singularly joyous, gladsome weather which, in sunset-land, most generally precedes the final rain of winter, a spreading troop of young men, mostly of the richer, if not the better class of Fâs society, streamed out from El Fatûh gate of that historic city in the immediate wake of a tiny caravan. Ben Hassan, upon an aged grey Barb, still mettlesome, and Haj Yûsef, upon a tall, raw-boned blue stallion; Cassim and another slave behind them, riding laden mules and driving two other mules, whose shwarries also loomed bulky, pendulous against the sky-line. This was the caravan.

The following represented the cream of the tolbah or scholarly community of Fás, and included the sons of the city's Basha, Kadi, Khaleefah, Kaid, and other leading residents gathered together on this jewel-eyed, glad-voiced morning of the year's childhood, for the purpose of bidding Allah's speed and blessing upon his journey to the son of Morocco's chiefest saint, now leaving Fás after five years of study there for his hereditary home in Ain Araish.

A deal of gunpowder was noisily dissipated by the youths of the city, and discordant *éclat* was lent the occasion by a dozen purple-cheeked reed-players and as many drummers, hired for the purpose by admirers of the young saint.

Half a mile from the gates they parted, little caravan and big escort, beside the stream called Running Gladness. The tolbah had no desire to wet their gleamingly new yellow slippers donned for this occasion.

"Little from a friend is much!" shouted a lusty young Moor, fair as a Norwegian, as, kilting up his spotless djellab, he ran forward to Ben Hassan's side to kiss his hand and press some little token therein.

"May God take thee through! God cause thee to arrive in safety! God make thy way easy!"

These and such-like phrases, a dozen or more, echoing in that pellucid morning air, followed the little caravan across Running Gladness and well over the green slope on the southern side thereof till, the ridge crossed, Ben Hassan and his party dipped into the vast plain beyond, specks in a boundless sea of asphodel, cactii, and scrub, in which rare olive-trees and occasional great aloe-spears rose like the top-hamper of sunken craft, overtaken there by disaster while tacking through endless sunshine to the remote, mysterious Atlas. A rich, a marvellous country, a beautiful and fascinating—albeit in some way benumbing and awful—land; teeming, men say, and one believes, with unexploited wealth, stained from end to end by centuries of bloody cruelty and oppression, only to be endured and survived by men whose breath is sweetened and whose muscles are hardened by the time-honoured, patriarchal life of the nomad, itself pulsing with life in every patch, yet impregnated weirdly, stamped in some indelible, inexplicable manner, as by a reflection of the dry, wasting decay which would appear to be eating up and destroying the race which roams its surface.

"Lord," said the favoured Cassim, the one slave still with him who had been Ben Hassan's since Ben Hassan left swaddling clothes. The man had pricked his mule forward beside the flank of the young saint's Barb.

"Ih-yeh, Cassim; and hast bade farewell to busy Fás?"

"Yea, lord. But I would ask of thee, lord: is it fitting that we ride thus to Ain Araish?"

Haj Yûsef looked up sharply from his horse's ears, and Ben Hassan, too, turned with some surprise toward his questioning slave.

"How? Why, what would ye, then, Cassim—that we should go afoot, like couriers?"

"Nay, lord, but with less of the courtier's humble way. Lord, thou hast seen the great press of men who thronged the road to bid Ben Hassan good speed from Fás. Think, lord, in thine own place, where thy father, Allah's right hand upon earth, reigneth, for every one who pressed to bid thee farewell to day will be an hundred clamouring to welcome thee home. And we ride even as small traders journey, but three men and six animals, with the son of the Shareef of Ain Araish!" Cassim paused, humiliated by the picture he evoked. "Lord, may we not gather a score or so of horsemen from some villages by the way, and so do justice to thy station?"

Ben Hassan laughed aloud, and then grew thoughtful, as who should say, "But, to be sure, the idea is worth consideration." The friend of Ben Hassan looked serious and thoughtful, and then laughed, as who should say, "But the matter really requires no consideration."

"It is as thou sayest, Cassim, we cut but a poor figure," said the young saint.

"Methinks thou hast yet to learn the emptiness of vain shows, O Cassim. Those who wish to welcome thy lord will not come to witness a powder-play," said the friend.

Now, as a fact, its journey done, this unimportant little caravan filed through the hoary old gates of Ain Araish city just at the sunset hour, when the town Jews were being locked in their quarters, the salted place, with never one word of welcome or so much as a cry from the city gate beggars, though a courier from Fás had borne word as to the day of their probable arrival.

Ben Hassan was a little chilled; at least, he had no chance to augment his impression by speaking of it. His friend talked loudly and without pause, a thing strikingly foreign to the man's grave habit, till the courtyard of the Shareef's great castle was reached, and the real business of arriving began. The arriving at the end of real journeys—journeys as they are made in Morocco, and were made in most other lands a thousand years ago—is something of a business; an agreeable, deliberate ceremony, the accompaniment to which is a running fire of questions and answers, the clatter of iron-shod hoofs upon rough cobbles, and the whinnying of fed and stalled beasts, who thus greet their jaded companions, from the open road of travel.

"Ye came not far to meet me, O M'amet," quoth the young saint to one in the quadrangle, who, years before, had been his own slave and who now, after louting low to mumble over Ben Hassan's finger-tips, was busying himself about the unloading of animals.

The Friend frowned expectantly. He had hoped to avoid that which he now anticipated. His warning glance failed to catch the slave's eye.

"Lord, none dared. It was an order from the wife of our lord."

"La, la! What do we weary ones here, gossiping?" hummed the Friend, with a worried smile. "Sidi Ben Hassan, let us to thy rooms for tea and good rest."

But the young saint was staring straightly before him.

" Sayest thou so, truly, M'amet? God's Prophet! This smelleth to my nostrils of evil days to come. 'Tis a poor business to be Ben Hassan. Ih-yeh, we have come—home! M'amet, is my father within doors?"

" Lord, he hath not been seen without doors these four days and nights."

" And where——"

The slave raised a hand to his great mouth, lowered his rolling eyes, and murmured below breath, as slaves will in such a case: " In the harem, lord."

" So. Then, Friend, Ben Hassan will take tea with thee. By Allah's mercy the Shareef's son shall see his father—some day."

" Nay, nay, lord," began his Friend soothingly.

" Yea, yea, Haj Yûsef, but Ben Hassan hath eyes in his head, though ye strive ever so to make him doubt them," snapped the youth impatiently, and giving his Friend a formal name as men had never heard him give it before.

But over the mint-scented steam of a great tea-pot the young man softened, was moved almost to tears, and touched his Friend's hand silently—a gracious, heart-reaching way he had—and there was peace.

Ben Hassan slept for an hour after drinking tea. The Christian habit of settling down to a good meal as soon as may be after a day's journeying seems a poor sort of grossness to a Moor; equal, say, to choosing a moment of great bodily fatigue, heat and thirst, for the drinking of a rare and delicate wine. First tea, then quiet chat or a doze, and then, when the body has recovered tone and is rested, the meal at ease. Such is the Moorish habit, as your hungry Christian traveller learns to his aching inconvenience, when chance brings him Moorish hospitality and entertainment upon the evening of a long day's march.

While the young saint slept, one harvest-coloured arm curved under his crimson-capped small head, one shapely leg extended across its fellow's foot, his Friend sat eyeing him gravely through the gray smoke of a curiously inlaid kief-pipe, two feet long and good for, say, ten puffs, no more.

Into the Friend's life had crept, soon after his first arrival in Ain Araish, a complication. In most men's lives are scores, you say. And that may well be. But it is possible that complications resemble, within limits, tasks or occupations, and weigh the less the greater their number. Who so bare of leisure as the man with no occupation. The Friend's life had been simplicity itself. Its single complication was an ever-present, rarely-slackening strain. The keynote of it was Shareefa Margaret's policy and attitude toward her step-son. Three rising streams fed it; the Friend's love of his young lord; the shareefa's increasing devotion to her policy; Ben Hassan's ripening manhood, and accompanying growth of insight and personality. As years count in Morocco the young saint's age entitled him now to the claim of having entered upon his manhood.

" Serve ye the woman; serve her to the death; and look not upon her face as ye hope for Paradise." The masterful words of the hermit of Ed-dár's gate rose this evening in Haj Yûsef's mind, with undeniable insistence. And he knew them for wisdom and sooth, or believed he did; which comes to the same thing, you know, in a matter of conscience. Honestly he had striven to obey the injunction, was striving and meant to strive. Great and thorough (greater far than the wise hermit had hoped) was the moral and spiritual purification already wrought in Haj Yûsef by the mere consistent loyalty of adherence to the moral obligation, voluntarily accepted with the hermit's injunction. And in that, if you will consider it a moment, was nothing surprising; nor would have been, had the hermit's instructions involved any other sort of obligation, such as the worship of a tree or the sacrifice of clothing. For how else would you define the essence of all religion than as the voluntary acceptance of, and loyal devotion to a moral obligation? And the ages have taught that that way lieth moral and spiritual purification.

But (and though a person theoretically die in Gibraltar and be born again after years spent upon the naked, all-cleansing earth, yet the essential fibre of him remains, the spring of his individuality) Haj Yûsef was still a half-caste; remained in him yet the radical enmity of two strains. He could do much with his life. Somewhat had been done therewith before ever it became his. And such early writings, though a man may revise them, he may not eradicate nor wipe out. There lies life's pathos —life's virtue, a nobler thing, you may find in the revising. But, and if mixed blood be his ink it shall ever be ill for the revisor. His destiny's a see-saw, his task that of Sisyphus, his reward such as Tantalus knew, and the upshot of it all—to the cynic a Dead Sea fruit, but in truth far otherwise.

"Friend," said Ben Hassan, waking with a yawn, as from thoughtful dreams; "it is Ben Hassan and his Friend against the shareefa; that is clear to my father's son—hey?"

"Nay, Sidi; but Ben Hassan and his Friend for the shareefa; ay, and even though it be also the shareefa against us."

And with that they clapped their hands, as sign to Cassim without, that the time for supper had arrived, and that water was therefore required for ablution.

Chapter XIII

DEVOUT PILGRIMS TO A SHRINE

THE two faced one another amicably across a fragrant bowl of cous-coosou, into which they dipped at intervals two fingers and a thumb. When either happened upon a particularly choice morsel, (your rightly conceived cous-coosou is rich but not lavish in such tit-bits) he fingered it, connoisseur-like, and placed it then upon the bowl's opposite edge with matter-of-course altruism.

Ben Hassan laved his fingers reflectively in a little brazen dish of orange-water, and whilst so occupied, said casually:

"Friend, have ye never the desire of women?" as who should say: "Do you not occasionally feel the need of tobacco?"

And, indeed, Ben Hassan meant something rather like that; but the question came with somewhat of a shock to Haj Yûsef, stirring depths in him, and reaching the man he had been through the ears of the man he was.

"Why—why ask ye that, Sidi?" asked the Friend, while collecting his thoughts."

"Eyeh, but I thought it, Friend, and so did ask."

"And why should thy Friend desire women?"

"Nay; why should he not? For what did Allah send women upon earth? Do not all men desire and possess women?"

Then the Friend make a mistake. Thinking only of the two wives which that dignitary had buried whilst still a comparatively young man, he instanced the Prince and Sheikh of Ain Araish.

"Does Abn Mohamet Tor desire women, then? His wives died, men say, before thou wert born."

Ben Hassan smiled.

"The sheikh is an aged and venerable man, O Friend; and, besides, behold the wall of his harem. It shutteth out the city, and if you would see it from any chamber here. To be sure, I have been told—his daughter hath told me—that the sheikh is never seen to enter it, but the sheikh is an ancient, and—and somewhat shrivelled, friend. May Allah's peace be upon him!"

"Ah! h'm! Well, it may be, Ben Hassan, that the least desirable thing about women is the possession of them. And for me, what have I to do with women? Have I not my lord and his affairs to busy me withal?"

"Art thy lord's most excellent and beloved Friend, truly; but, Friend, is not the love of a—of women—something far otherwise and apart? Supposing that I, Ben Hassan, did love a woman, I should not love my Friend the less. Rather the more, for—for he would help me in this as in other affairs—or—how—say—ye— Friend?"

So now the murder was pretty nearly out. Haj Yûsef sighed. He had been thinking, and now was making guesses. He liked it little; the prospect seemed to him to bode no good to anyone.

"Sidi, that is no more than my duty, to help thee in all things for thy good; and ye know, besides, that—— But I must hear more."

"Friend, thou knowest that, since I was a child "—the

young man's hand rested now lordly-wise upon his dagger's haft—"that Fatimah hath—that—Friend, thou knowest there hath been—Fatimah!"

The confidence had not advanced to the stage of begetting eloquence, but the main fact, like murder, would out.

"Ah!" said the Friend, with that vague utterance which suggests that words are no more than the droppings of a mind full to the lip, "it is Fatimah, then, the sheikh's daughter?"

"Why, who else?" cried Ben Hassan, with a young lover's superb narrowness of vision.

"Oh, there be others, there be others; but——"

"But not Fatimahs, O Friend, and not for Ben Hassan. Why, Friend, I tell thee the sheen of her great eyes lighteth the earth about her as the moon lighteth El Maghreb. Her——"

And he said many other extravagant and natural things, equally near or wide of the truth, whilst his Friend pondered deeply, giving thanks for that he had not repeated the gossip a slave had given him below, to the effect that the shareefa had gone so far as announcing her intention of marrying her young son, who sojourned now in infidel lands, to the daughter of Sheikh Abn Mohamet Tor.

"But," he said at length, "how comes it that all this is fresh in thy mind, lord? Years have passed since thine eyes saw these earth-brightening orbs of the Princess."

"Ah, Friend, what are years or miles? Such eyes, too! I have a heart, Friend; Allah gave me a mind. Therein Fatimah hath dwelt since ever I knew to lift a gun or ride a horse; and, though I told thee not, it was to see her ride with her father when they passed within two days of Fás on a journey that I left thee to go shooting with the basha's son last year."

" Ah, Sidi, and so deceived thy Friend!"

" O Friend, the thought of her passing was like hachsheesh in my veins. I could see her on the tall red mule, her little feet in the great silver stirrups, her one hand on the green embroidered pommel, the other slipping, soft, woman-like, between the crimson reins, where they are held together by that bangle, thou knowest; the veil to keep her little face from dust of the plain and eyes of travellers, the very saddle she bestrode.[1] Name of the Prophet, Friend, I could see it all, feel it in the very bones of me, there in Fás! I had to go. Not all the soldiers of the Sultan could have stayed me."

Now, in the beginning of this talk Haj Yûsef had told himself his course was clear enough. The shareefa's will had already been conveyed to him, perchance—her son was to wed the only daughter of the Sheikh of Ain Araish. Haj Yûsef's clear duty, then, was to discourage Ben Hassan; yet, before the evening was ended, his view of his duty was thrust aside by the dictates of dramatic fitness, inclination, and his love for his young lord. The Friend lent his aid to the composition of a letter to the dazzling Fatimah, and thus gave his countenance to the beginning of what in infidel lands had been a courtship, and among the Faithful was of necessity by way of being an intrigue. Ben Hassan could write (it was to him a severe and hated form of labour), but his confidence in himself boggled at the single-handed composition of an important epistle. However, he contributed his share. The hyperbole, the flowery, intricate compliments, the gorgeous similes, the phrases of perfervid adoration—

[1] In Morocco no woman is called upon to face the dangers of the side-saddle.

these were exclusively inspired by the young saint. The practical information—that he would frequent a certain lonely shrine without the city walls each afternoon, and such-like—this was wrapped in polite Maghrebbin by Haj Yûsef. The time was the night of Thursday, eve of Muslim Sabbath.

"To-morrow she will go with her women to the cemetery,[1] below the cloth-merchant's gate. Cassim shall find me a woman who will lay this in her little hand for —for money. Have we money, Friend?"

Haj Yûsef looked grave.

"Not one bilyûn," he said. "The last was that ye bade me give the groom who took thy horse to-day."

"Ah!" The young saint swallowed a yawn. His literary efforts had brought the desire of bed. "No matter; to-morrow I will see our lord, my father, and get money. Friend, mine eyelids are leaden; let us sleep."

Chance directed that Ben Hassan should see his father on the following day. Soon after sunrise the chiefest saint in Morocco reeled out from the forbidden door, his private entrance to the harem, and faced daylight for the first time that week. The pupils of his large eyes were reduced to vanishing point by the use of kief and hachsheesh, his whole being was wrenched out of balance by a violent access of dissipation. The great Shareef was playing sad havoc with his life.

"By God! I have a wife outside, thou seest," he had growled, in response to the half-frightened remonstrance of one of the ladies of his harem when, several days

---

[1] There is but one day in the year on which Moorish women make a practice of attending the mosques, but on Fridays they are given to the visiting of shrines and to the laying of myrtle boughs upon the graves of departed relatives.

prior to this morning of his awakening, he had plunged recklessly and with frenzied avidity into excess.

Sight of his son struck into and shook the unstrung man as wind shakes the luff of a boat's sail. He loved Ben Hassan, and was ashamed. He extended a tremulous brown hand with maudlin intent, then withdrew it upon a stronger impulse.

"Sidi Ben Hassan," he cried, "son of my loins, is all well with thee?"

Ben Hassan dropped upon one knee to kiss his father's hand.

"Lord, my father, I am well enough; but I desire a little money to meet affairs of mine withal. But another time, my father, I—I would not——"

"Peace, my son, peace. It is useless to come to thy father for money. I have seen no money in these many moons. Go to the shareefa, Ben Hassan, and—and if ye succeed, get money also for thy father, who, like thee, hath a need of it in his affairs withal. Go, my son. God guard thy ways. I would rest a little alone here."

Ben Hassan did visit Shareefa Margaret, but he did not get money. And this incident, like the shareefa's comments, was typical of life in the Ain Araish castle as Ben Hassan found it after his return from Fás. Fatimah received her love-letter, however—her first, it was—and as yet there were many in Ain Araish ready and willing to serve Ben Hassan without pay; but his inability to pay was none the less a humiliation to the young man, a blow at his dignity, as it was meant to be, one among many struck by the same hand.

Week after week and month following month found Ben Hassan in the same poor case. No chance was small enough to escape Shareefa Margaret, it seemed, no single opportunity among the many which came her

way of belittling Ben Hassan in the eyes of the Faithful
of Ain Araish, of lowering his standing in this his
father's stronghold, did the shareefa allow to pass her
without first yielding up its sting under her deft, in-
exorable manipulation of events.

Ben Hassan drooped and was cramped by daily chills;
but there was a fire at which the young man warmed
himself, if not quite every day, then certainly at intervals
sufficiently frequent to prevent any serious congealment
of his young blood. Your lover in his first love develops
wonderful capacity for the storage of warmth. Biting
winds leave him snugly unscathed, and upon a diet of
bread and fruit he shall face you with the roseate sleek-
ness of the daily feasted. There was little enough of the
vampire about Ben Hassan, but if he waited his lady at
their rendezvous a young man chastened in spirit and
mentally chilled, he left her mettlesome as the stalled
Barb, warm, elate, and gladly ruddy, so princely and
complete in youth is the dominance of the master passion.

You are to remember, also, that in these meetings with
Fatimah there was never by any chance a suggestion of
that saccharine alloy, that burden of too great and too
easy a sweetness, which lovers sometimes know in Christian lands. Married life among Believers may be what
you will. It has, as a fact, a good deal more of dignity
than is to be found in many Christian homes. But in
those rare cases where courtship is attained by an Oriental, circumstances effectually bar the way to any chance
approach of monotony, and the love-making story never
lapses into mere languid gossip. Sacred though his
birth made Ben Hassan to all men in Sunset-land, and
doubly sacred in Ain Araish, it yet had gone hardly with
him if any slaves or dependants of Sheikh Abn Mohamet
Tor's household had come upon him during one of his

meetings with Fatimah at the shrine beyond the city walls. Ain Araish is not Christian-influenced Tangier, by your leave; and if in the city sôk there a man would buy fruit from a woman's pack he must select the same and pay for it from behind the woman, and not before her, and that though her spine be curved and her cheeks shrivelled by the wear and tear of three generations.

Fatimah, you may be sure, attended these meetings finely swathed and voluminously enwrapped in the most generous of haiiks. Ben Hassan's great travelling djellab, too, gave you little hint as to his age, rank, or identity when its hood was thrust well forward. A capacious hood it had, this Wazzani djellab of his, as Fatimah's dainty self had cause to know, for it had held and covered more than once or twice her head in addition to its wearer's own what time lip had silenced lip in hot heart converse, or Ben Hassan babbled flowery nothings in the little pearl-shell ear of a face too warmly blushing for unprotected contact with the outer air.

"Oh, Sidi, but if any of my father's people should learn of this!" murmured Fatimah one sweltering noon-tide, when all in Ain Araish lay asleep, and the persons of these two cooing creatures formed one shapeless, white-swathed outline in the deep shadow of their trysting shrine.

The male dove cooed reassurance, adding then:

"But that were a lighter matter far, my Pearl, than if some creature of the wife of our lord did come upon us. The sheikh is the sheikh, O moon of my happy nights, but the shareefa, body o' the prophet! what a woman is that!"

"To me, O Ben Hassan, she hath ever shown great kindness."

"Ah!"

The young saint had heard ere this the common gossip regarding the shareefa's determination to marry her own son to Fatimah, the spiritual ruler's heir—so in her own mind Margaret undoubtedly thought of her son—to the daughter of the temporal chief.

"Indeed, I have been ashamed for that no love of her grew in my heart, lord, she being the shareefa, and so courtly kind and more than kind to my father's daughter. Lord, she hath said it in public that she desired to be a mother to me—she, the shareefa!"

"And well might she desire it. Fire of my heart, though she had been one of the Perfect Four,[1] instead of—ah'm'm——"

"O Ben Hassan, is she not el m'ra sidi?" (the wife of our lord.)

"Thus, delight of me, my Friend rebuketh me; just thus, and often."

"Lord, Fatimah would never dare to rebuke her——"

"Her true lover; the slave whose heart is under the hollow of her little feet when she goeth abroad. Say after me, heart's life, 'Hassan is the slave of my littlest finger, loving me with the last least drop in his veins, worshipping the earth beneath me if I tread upon it, because—because that I love Hassan, my dear slave!' Say after me, starshine."

"Lord—love—I dare not."

And then she said it, mouthing the words with tender slowness, and bringing to the task a confusion most sweetly moving to Hassan.

[1] Legend hath it that Mohammed named four perfect women.

Chapter XIV

TO COVER HIS NAKEDNESS WITHAL

"FRIEND," said Ben Hassan thoughtfully, as he sat one evening-time with Haj Yûsef upon a terrace overlooking the castle gate, "there is a saying I heard in Fás: 'The friend of mine enemy hath a place at my table and in my counsels, but none in my heart.'"

The Haj looked up uneasily.

"And so?"

"Nay, that is the whole of the saying."

"Ah! a smooth saying enough, lord, and one having meat in it, withal; but—well——"

"Well, has Ben Hassan no enemy, Friend?"

"Nay, I would not say that. It were hard to find one man of so little worth or note in the world that he had no single enemy. But there is no enemy that Ben Hassan need fear."

"Oh, fear, that is for women and children. But what if one's friend is the friend also of one's enemy? Not to speak of fear; that were cause for sorrow, Friend, hey?"

"But who, then, are these friends and enemies, lord?" asked the Haj, hating the question and dreading its answer.

"The wife of our lord is mine enemy, Friend, and—and all men of position are her friends, even—even thyself, Friend. Eh-yeh?"

115

"Lord," began the Friend, inclining by habit to the roundabout Moorish method, and meaning to evade the point by playing about it. And then he stopped short, a light of very real affection shining in the eyes which looked upon Ben Hassan. "Lord, trust thou thy Friend —thou mayest trust—and press him no farther in this matter. Doubt not, probe not, lord, but, whatever may be, trust thou thy Friend, who loves thee."

Ben Hassan touched his Friend's hand in his own caressing manner.

"Forgive me, Friend; I do trust ye."

And then they fell to thinking. But it was the first time Haj Yûsef had ever tacitly admitted the shareefa's enmity in speaking with Ben Hassan. The fact was the thing had become too transparently obvious to bear denial. Shareefa Margaret was no longer at any pains to cloak her policy where her lord's son was concerned.

"Is the wife of our lord wise?" Haj Yûsef had ventured to murmur, with eyes rigidly downcast, when the shareefa had brusquely refused him money required for new clothes and other small needs of Ben Hassan's. "Would our lord be quite pleased with this? Would he not be angered to find his son, his first-born, clad like a city gate beggar?"

"Like his Friend, eh!" snapped Margaret, her dark eyes angrily a-glitter. "And what think ye that I care who is pleased or displeased Who am I that I should fear displeasure, sir cub leader? The Shareefa of Ain Araish——"

"Is the wife of our lord of Ain Araish," interposed the cub leader quietly.

"Ay; and men with eyes have learned ere this that that is to rule in Ain Araish. Get hence, schooling-man;

keep thine eyes open, and thou'lt learn better which side
o' thy cous-coosou the meat lies."

"The wife of our lord mistakes. I care not for meat
for myself; I thought but of her own welfare, and—and
the young man's. But be it is as thou sayest. Haj Yûsef
is thy servant in all things, seeking only thy good."

"Come, that's better. Only learn to change thy djellab
to serve thy interests, and all may yet be well with ye in
Ain Araish, Haj Yûsef; but never seek gifts at my hands
for Ben Hassan."

"But covering for his nakedness."

"Let him beg it or go uncovered."

"The Shareef——"

"*I am* the Shareef and shareefa both. Go and learn
that lesson well if thou wouldst prosper in Ain Araish,
good man."

Haj Yûsef had gone, sighing, penniless as when he had
entered the presence.

And in a sense, grieve over it as he might, he knew
that what the shareefa had said was truth. She was
shareef and sheikh too in Ain Araish; by token that her
husband found the one thing upon earth worth respect-
ing, the thing he could not choose but fear, was the rough
side of his white wife's tongue. As for Sheikh Abn
Mohamet Tor, "I desire peace, nothing else," he had
been heard to affirm, when warned that the temporal rule
was slipping from his scholarly old hands into the white
fingers which held the reins in the castle of the Shareef
of Ain Araish.

But it is true that the Shareef had by no means been
wont to rate peace higher than all other earthly things, or,
indeed, to permit much opposition to his own will from
high or low. But the Shareef had found his master at
the last of it, and that without knowing it, which is a

woman's way in obtaining mastery. To be sure, the Shareef's own vices had done more towards enslaving him or fitting him for his present subordinate estate than had Margaret's self. But it had been hard to say in just what degree their growth had been spontaneous, and to what extent they were the engines of Margaret's will. It is in any case a fact that, whatever else he lacked, however much the mistress of the castle denied him, the great saint never lacked kief, hachsheesh, the attentions of dancing-girls, or even the replenishment of his secret stores of the strong waters of the Nazarenes.

It was not often that father and son met. Ben Hassan was not encouraged to frequent other portions of the castle than his own apartments. Indeed, the shareefa's especial creatures, personal attendants, and the like had been taught openly to flout the young man and forbid him access to the inner chambers. When by chance the saint did meet his son, there was that in the gist of the sire's words which suggested an old prisoner's condolence with a new-comer, with one less inured to oppression.

Now and again the old imperious nature of the saint would blaze forth fitfully as a pinch of damp gunpowder among smouldering embers. Then something would be done. That way came Ben Hassan's long-needed new clothing. He happened by good luck upon Shareef and shareefa together. He made jocular play with a torn and patched kaftan, seeking funds from the shareefa to replace the garment withal. The great lady accepted the jest as jest, but declined further treaty. The Shareef had tasted no hachsheesh that day.

" By the withers of the mare of Allah's holy Prophet, stir thyself, woman, and get money! Body of a dog, is the holy Shareef of Ain Araish, his son, to go naked

before men while thy slaves are fat, and thy brat among
the infidels spends a prince's fortune? Get money quickly,
Margaret, or, by Allah's thunder, thy women shall be
sold in the sôk o' market day! Get money, I say—eh—
I—get money! Ho Abdullah! Bring kief and pipes
here. I—eyeh, eyeh; let us have a little peace. What
would ye here, my son? For why make ye trouble, Ben
Hassan o' me? Eh? What? Ah! Well, well, money
ye shall have, my son—surely, surely. What else?"

And as the green kief-smoke began to rise, and the last
fitful jets of the holy man's wrath to subside, he forgot
utterly the cause of the explosion, and presently lurched
off toward the forbidden door, upon narcoticized philan-
dering intent.

But Ben Hassan waited there in the full blaze of morning sunlight. He had faith in the Shareefa Margaret's
perspicacity. She was too shrewd to allow smouldering to
lead to a second explosion. In the fulness of time an
impudent slave brought a bag of money " for the young
man to cover his nakedness withal." It was rash of the
slave to bear his mistress's message so literally and with
such gusto in the carrying. Ben Hassan's eyes blazed as
his father's had been wont to do. His brown left hand
swung out and forward, and the slave stretched his length
with a mouth full of blood and loose teeth among the
young orange and oleander shrubs. But a moment before
and the fellow's thick lips had been insolently curled in
the enjoyment of what he had deemed his license to insult
a fallen lord. Now his blood moistened the roots and
shrubs, and Ben Hassan, money-bag firmly grasped in
his hand (the young saint had a thought to spare for
affairs, you see, as well as for the wiping out of insults),
stood over him, darkling, one foot upon his chest.

" When thy foul mouth is somewhat cleansed and

healed, dog, son of a dog, it may be thou'lt set a guard upon it. It will surely bring thee fresh trouble else from some true man's forehead,[1] though the foot were fitter weapon for thee. Get up and hence, dog, quickly!"

The fellow seemed to melt away among the shrubs, so unobtrusively and swiftly he departed, who had come forth with slow and mincing gait humming a gimbri measure. The flunkey nature is not peculiar to any one clime or community.

But though in his son's interests the Shareef was once or twice roused to an old-time assertion of authority, his sympathy was for the more part weak and quite ineffectual—maudlin almost, and certainly not sufficient to hinder appreciably Shareefa Margaret's consistent policy of humiliating and belittling her step-son. And, in view of this unwaveringly pursued policy of the shareefa's, Ben Hassan found it difficult to understand how it came about that his Friend remained her devotedly loyal subject, her trusty and apparently trusted adherent. But the young man had promised to trust Haj Yûsef, and, whether or no, he did instinctively trust his grave, sober henchman, whose counsels were all for dutiful orthodoxy and respectful submission to el M'ra Sidi, whilst his actions and unspoken devotion all pointed to love and solicitude for Ben Hassan himself.

It was in no way surprising that the attitude of his Friend should be puzzling to Ben Hassan, for the man's life was a puzzling business to himself. His policy was at daggers drawn with his inclinations, his chosen line of conduct was diametrically at variance with his natural instincts; in him conscience warred unceasingly with affection, making his life a complicated and wearying game

[1] In a personal affray among Moors the forehead plays a more prominent and effective part than the fist.

of cross purposes, the which a careless observer had called futile, whilst a deeper-seeing student, and more especially one having knowledge of the half-caste temperament, had recognized in it an infallible process for the strengthening and feeding of moral fibre.

Meanwhile, if puzzled by him, Ben Hassan, as has been said, trusted his Friend, and—and courted Fatimah beside the old shrine which lies to the westward of the southern gate of Ain Araish. The crumbling old tomb had suffered a long period of neglect as a shrine, but Ben Hassan made up for all that now. Above the bones of a forgotten warrior saint of the far south-west, this now barely acknowledged but intensely alive young saint of the south-west worshipped and made his daily plaint of adoration before a maid who, though distinctly of the earth, was as fair and radiant to look upon as any she who maketh glad the days and nights of saints in Paradise. And Fatimah was none the less a woman in the making, in the bud, by reason that, growing up without a mother, she had seen less of the inside of a harem and more of her gentle father than is customary among daughters of the Faithful.

" Thou'rt all the world to me, my morning and evening star," Ben Hassan whispered beside the shrine.

" And thou'rt all this and the next world to me, my— man, thou being a man," quoth she, blushing, and pleased to outdo her lover in the old, old pastime which lovers have made classic.

So they feasted upon, and at the same time stored and nourished, their happiness, these twain. And Shareefa Margaret, at a window in her lord's castle, hearing Ben Hassan's voice blithely trolling a song beneath her in the courtyard, compressed her straight lips and told herself some further and more effectual step must be taken toward chilling the heart that inspired that song and reducing to more lowly insignificance the singer. Had she but guessed his business of an afternoon, the source and spring of his music, the course of true love had been prettily disturbed. But Margaret could not see all things, and so went confidently enough to work in paving the way both to Fatimah and to her father, the sheikh, for Moulai Mohammed, her son.

Chapter XV

A POINT OF ETIQUETTE

"AND so the great day is at hand, and by this time to-morrow will be ending."

"Ye-es, as much as ye will; but I pray ye, Friend, let me hear no more of my orders. Repeat them not again, as ye love me, for Ben Hassan is a poor creature, it may be, in these days, but not the Prophet's self could force him in this thing. There is a limit. A Hûdi will sometimes turn and snarl when spat upon. Thy lord, if somewhat ragged, and very poor, is no Hûdi, b'Allah, but the son of the Shareef of Ain Araish—the son, look ye, friend, first-born of his loins."

They were silent through a full minute or more, and then the Friend looked up slowly, as one who forced himself for duty's sake along a road he had no inclination to travel.

"Lord," he said softly, "It is surely a very little matter."

"A very little matter, Friend, was that last date thou knowest that brought the Tafilalt camel to earth, legs splayed, food for the driver's knife and belly, but never more to be the bearer of dates. A very little matter that, to pleasure the shareefa, I, the Shareef's son who am not of her blood, should dismount from my horse before assembled Ain Araish, to bow my knee and kiss the fingers of—of him that is her flesh and blood, new curled and washed from the Nazarenes! By the One, His

Prophet! Little or big, 'tis the last date; but it shall not bring my father's son to earth. So I pray thee say no more, Friend, and have no fear. There shall be neither shame for me nor blame for thee."

" Nay; as to blame, believe thou me, I——"

" Oh, I have said it, Friend; I have sworn to trust thee. Have no fear, I trust. But—but talk of these things hath a savour of sickness for me. Let me tell thee rather of the most beauteous, the rare, the lovely——"

The friend sighed. He had heard a good deal of Fatimah of late.

While the next morning was still young, there came signs to Ben Hassan and his Friend, in their high quarters, that the hour of the day's great event, the welcoming home of Moulai Mohammed, son of the Shareef and shareefa, was at hand. The castle court-yard was full of pent noises, the stamping of mettlesome beasts, and the cries and clatter of men. Presently came urgent word for Ben Hassan by a slave of the shareefa's. The Lord of Ain Araish waited Ben Hassan's coming, it seemed. All was ready below; only Ben Hassan's place in the procession was vacant. Lest their lord be angered, he must hasten. Ben Hassan listened and turned idly upon his cushions.

" Tell thou our lord, my father, that I have but one horse, and that is lame. My saddle is no better than a burda " (pack-saddle). " I cannot ride behind my father, or men would say the companions of our lord's right hand were beggars."

" But the wife of our lord sayeth——" began the slave.

" Thou hast heard the son of our lord, his message. Bear thou that. Get hence! "

The slave backed out from the apartment, cursing his errand. Three minutes passed, and the Shareef's portly councillor appeared in the entrance-arch breathing heavily, his draperies held clear of his knees by both his hands.

"Lord," quoth he—to one of the counsellor's rank and learning, the Shareef's flesh and blood, humiliated by the shareefa or no, was a being apart; true Shareef, whatever his position—"Lord, thy father waxeth impatient. Saddle not us who serve him with the Shareef's wrath. Animals await thee and thy—thy m.koddem here."

"Pack-mules belike?"

"Two of our lord's choicest Barbs, lord, fittingly trapped. I pray thee delay not."

Ben Hassan rose slowly, reaching for his silver-sheathed, curved dagger, where it hung by a green rope of silk above his cushions.

"Come, Friend; it is to be," said he to Haj Yûsef.

And so, together, they preceded the Shareef's man of affairs to the court-yard below, where the company, mounted and fretting, waited at the heels of the saint's famous white stallion, an imposing array. Ben Hassan bent one knee and lightly touched with his lips the hanging right hand of Allah's anointed.

"It is not well that thy father should wait thee, Ben Hassan," growled the saint, brusquely raising and kissing the fingers his son had saluted.

"Forgive me, father! I did fear to shame thee with my one lame beast and shabbiness."

"Pha! Who is master here, then? Are not thy father's beasts thine?"

"Nay; but, like my father, the shareefa's," thought the young man; but he did not speak.

"Come, mount thee here beside me, my son, and let us be done with this—er—with this our business."

So Ben Hassan mounted and rode out beside his father at the head of that company, every man of which was muttering some comment upon this last order of the Shareef's. His Friend, upon a great black horse, kept close upon Ben Hassan's heels.

"Beside him, too! Our lord's Shareef and the wife of our lord's Shareef are not the same then?" murmured one officer of the household to another.

"In the Name, no; but step-brothers!" came the reply, with a low chuckle. "But we know who ruleth in Ain Araish. Who ruleth chooseth who shall rule, methinks. I have it from Hamadi the eunuch that Ben Hassan will kneel to kiss the young one's stirrup this day."

"Iyeh! We know who ruleth, 'sh'Allah! But, yet there he rideth, sure enough, at the very right hand of our lord."

And so the snowy-garbed party ambled on, clattering in the narrow city way, stirring up a dust-cloud beyond the city gate, and debouching at length, followed now by half Ain Araish, upon the little scorched plateau where, a dozen years and more before, Shareefa Margaret had greeted little Fatimah from her litter, herself the new arrival in that sacred countryside. The new-comer to be welcomed this day, Moulai Mohammed, son of the shareefa, was to reap much sown by the mother that bore him. An organized reception was to be his, that thing most rare in Morocco, and hitherto quite unknown in Ain Araish, where events were wont to fall out upon such occasions, as Fate willed and the spontaneous impulses of the people directed, rather than as any administrator among them chose.

"Here must be great love and reverence," murmured

Ben Hassan, " for powder may not be found upon the earth in Ain Araish."

His reflection was occasioned by the discharge of scores of guns among the men of Ain Araish, who were reloading their weapons and firing again as fast as their fingers would let them and as recklessly as though gunpowder might be had for the asking. As a fact, in their case the powder had been even more easily come by. They had not asked for it, but had it brought to them by slaves of the shareefa, with handfuls of battered coins and orders to make merry on the occasion of the " young Shareef's home-coming." Margaret by no means cared to trust to spontaneous ebullitions of gladness.

Like hotly outflung arms two files of horsemen streaked, galloping and shouting, across the plain, one from either flank of the Shareef's following. Nose to tail, the plunging horses sped on like gulls in a semicircular course, converging upon the approaching caravan, in the midst of which rode the shareefa's young son. It was as though the leader of the Ain Araish party swung two long ribbons bearing weights at their ends. Immediately in front of the oncoming caravan the ends of the two ribbons met, deflected, and swept on, each skimming the inner side of the track just traversed by its fellow. And so they met again in the rear of the Ain Araish company, only to sweep on and out again, as though drawing forward Moulai Mohammed's caravan. Each rider's spurs were bloody (plain spikes three inches long), but their horses felt nothing in the heat of that wild, circling stampede. And in the midst of their flying progress these riders loaded and reloaded guns nearly six feet in length, kneeling on their saddles, hanging as low as their horses' bellies, or turning to face the beasts' tails while firing their salutes.

It was a gallant show, and one that both Ben Hassan and the horse he rode itched to take part in, till the young man remembered what had in no wise affected his Barb's excitement, that this powder play was a token of fealty and welcome to the home-coming son of Shareefa Margaret.

But a few moments more and the two bodies of men, the great crowd from Ain Araish and the little road-worn caravan from Tangier, were face to face, halted upon the sun-browned plateau. It was a strange meeting. Triangular silver stirrups chafed English riding-boots from Regent Street below the haiik of the shareefa's son. The hand in which he held three yards of crimson Moorish bridle-reins was covered by a tan driving-glove with a name upon its buttons familiar to the coaching clubs of London. Half sulkily, and not without audible promptings from his attendants, the lad dismounted, and awkwardly louted his head over the great Shareef's brown right hand.

"Welcome, son!" cried the lord of Ain Araish with formal heartiness.

And at that moment the Shareef's counsellor (this astute man had for some years now held great sway in Ain Araish by reason of his politic devotion to the shareefa), pricked forward a few paces and murmured in Ben Hassan's ear:

"Sidi, this is the time for thee to dismount and salute the wife of our lord's son before we and the lesser folk approach him. See, he is mounting again. The wife of our lord earnestly expects this friendly attention from thee. The others wait to come after thee, as is fitting."

Ben Hassan nodded as in acquiescence, sitting his horse the while like a figure in bronze. The counsellor drew back to his place beside Ben Hassan's Friend. Meanwhile, Moulai Mohammed's attendants, duly instructed in their part, had led their young chief back to his horse and assisted him into the saddle. And now the companies stolidly faced one another; the Shareef of Ain Araish yawned; the dignitaries of Ain Araish waited to follow Ben Hassan in saluting the new-comer. Ben Hassan sat beside the saint, his father, staring into space. The Shareef, accustomed for his part to have the details of all ceremonies carried out for him by others, yawned a second time, and glanced from right to left for developments.

"Sidi," murmured the counsellor behind Ben Hassan pleadingly.

"Peace," observed the young man, moving only his lips.

"Well, what make we here?" said the Shareef at length.

"On thine own rash head be it, then," muttered the counsellor. And then, edging his beast forward to the Shareef's side, he said: "Lord, thy people await Ben Hassan's greeting of his brother before themselves saluting thy son."

"Ay, verily. How, then, O Ben Hassan! Where are thy manners? Hast never a word for thy brother?"

"Father, thy first-born awaits greeting from his younger—step-brother."

"Eyeh, and that is true; thou'rt the elder. Come, Moulai Mohammed, thou hast overlooked thy brother in saluting me."

"Nay, he is to dismount and kiss my stirrup, they said," replied the lad from Tangier crossly.

"The first-born of the Shareef of Ain Araish kisses no other stirrup than his father's, and, not being afflicted of Allah with idiocy, is little likely to kiss any stirrup holding a Nazarene boot."

Ben Hassan addressed vacancy, an oracle in deep abstraction.

The Shareef laughed uproariously, whereat Moulai Mohammed's men smiled foolishly, and voices among the Ain Araish party murmured a hesitant backing of Ben Hassan. It was as well to laugh with the Shareef, but in Ain Araish, or near it, one had to reckon with the shareefa. Meantime the sun shone hotly upon Allah's anointed, making him sharply aware of a desire for shade, repose, and his usual morning refreshments.

"Well," quoth he, turning his horse's head homeward, "these be matters for the discussion of the 'Ulama'" (of the learned, that is) "within doors. 'Tis a poor greeting that keeps the traveller waiting without the gates. Ride we homeward."

And so, wheeling his horse sharply, the Lord of Ain Araish set out for the city, Ben Hassan close beside him, and the newly arrived caravan taking perforce a place quite in the rear of the saint's companions and attendants. And so they entered the city amid gun-firing and the blowing of horns, Ben Hassan smiling, and Moulai Mohammed angrily chewing a finger of his Christian-wrought handcovering.

The shareefa heard of it before the company reached the walls of Ain Araish. Her gossips were obsequious and fleet of foot. Sitting behind an upper window in the castle, she grimly watched the procession as it flowed into the great courtyard beneath her, headed by her lord and Ben Hassan—Ben Hassan, from whom every dignity had been stripped at her behest.

"A triumph for you, nigger brat!" said she, speaking in her own tongue, and with extraordinary bitterness.

"Make the most of it; it's the last you'll ever know, or
I know nothing. Miserable—Moor!"

And then she composed herself gracefully to receive
her son in state. Her face became smoothly radiant,
authority, calm dignity, and motherly fondness in every
line of it. Had you seen and heard the venomous re-
crimination in those last muttered English words of hers,
and judged the shareefa upon that, you had assuredly
rated her among the baser sort, a vulgar scold, vitriolic
as an angry fish-wife. But in the perfect self-command,
which wrought an instant change to dignity and repose,
Shareefa Margaret proved herself more than a mere
virago. It is something—not much, perhaps, but something—to be an actress, and the shareefa's swift assump-
tion of dignity and affection was good acting, because
there was more than mere personal spite at the root of her
venomous exclamation regarding Ben Hassan. There
was the broad, underlying bitterness of racial enmity.
"Moor" she had called him, lacking any name more
scathing, though it was a word unknown to Ben Hassan
and his fellows, a name invented by the Europeans for
their conquerors centuries before Shareefa Margaret was
born. "Nigger" she had flung at this gold-skinned
scion of the sacred essence of the aristocracy of Islam,
upon an impulse belonging not simply to her wrath, but
to the blood in her veins, to the race which had given
her birth, lowly and insignificant birth enough, yet withal
far above that of her own son, whom she would have
men revere, by reason that it had outraged no law of
nature, and given to the world no bastard fruit of mixed
race and caste forgotten.

"Did I well?" asked Ben Hassan of his Friend vain-
gloriously.

"Im sha Allah!" (that is, By God's grace).

" And now methinks the shareefa may change somewhat to my father's son."

" Ih-yeh, b'Allah; that is so, lord, that is so."

But there was no vain glory about the friend's aspirations. His meaning was not at all Ben Hassan's. His vision went farther and fared worse, or, at least, less brightly.

Chapter XVI

"THIS IS CLEARLY NO PLACE FOR MY FATHER'S SON"

"SIDI, art thou the Friend of Shareef Ben Hassan?"

The speaker was a truculent-looking Berber, gaunt as the pack-mare he drove before him, and as strong. His curiously broidered and thridded Berber djellab, or akhnif, was very much the worse for wear, and even his long curved dagger was less ornamental than worn and murderously serviceable in appearance.

Haj Yûsef halted in a niche of the wall he was skirting when the Berber's hoarse voice reached his ears.

"Ihyeh; so am I honoured. And what would ye, man, with Ben Hassan's Friend?"

"I would show him how to save his lord from danger, and if he cared to follow me to the gate here."

Haj Yûsef nodded gravely, and fell into line behind the hardy, cave-born barbarian with the pack-mare. Beside the first of the saints' graves that one passes after leaving this gate of Ain Araish, the stranger came to a standstill, and his mare began to nose dismally among burnt blades of grass and yellowed palmetto.

"You do not know me, Sidi?" he asked.

Haj Yûsef shook his head.

"And there is no need. Not that I fear thee, nor any other in Ain Araish; but—there is no need. I have a brother in Fás. Three years ago he was to be beaten by the Basha's men, he having—but there is no need to speak of that neither. The lord Ben Hassan did win him freedom, whom he had never seen before that day; paid money and laughed with the Basha; won freedom for my brother out of the goodness of his heart—a true Shareef, b'Allah!"

Haj Yûsef nodded agreement. He knew of many such episodes in Ben Hassan's life, particularly in that part of it which came before his hands were tied and his estate reduced to that of the common people by Shareefa Margaret.

" Now, hear thou me," continued the Berber. " I have no other family; my kin have all died fighting or in prison. But I have a partner who is a true man to me, albeit he hath a heart that is harder than the stones we grind our wheat between. Him the wife of our lord hath seen and spoken with, her meaning being an evil one for thy lord Ben Hassan. If ye would win me a speedy end, go straight and speak of this, and so thank me for my warning. If ye mean me well, yet would save thy lord, let him ride no more alone without the city walls here, as now he rideth each afternoon. This day he is safe, to-morrow and the next day he will not be safe, *in passing the hollow by the Sfraa road yonder, where the great stones lie beside an aloe clump*."

" Good man, I——"

" Nay, Sidi, seek not words from me, for they will lead me into the way of betrayal. Do but keep hold upon that I have said, which is sooth, and so act. And remember that my partner is a true man, though hard withal. He will do a true man's endeavour to earn that which hath reached him from the purse of the wife of our lord. Yet he hath no gun of his own, but only a dagger, and so it were easy for one coming behind him, knowing the place, to save thy lord, defeat my partner, and withal slay no man. The good deed done in Fás liveth in my heart, and so I needs must give Ben Hassan the warning through thee. Yet am I most loath to betray the partner of my right hand, and, should he fall, must ever count his death upon mine own head, and so God go with thee, Sidi."

"And with thee, and with thee, true man."

Thus they parted, and the Friend of Ben Hassan walked slowly back into the city to look for his lord.

Haj Yûsef's conviction that his salvation and atonement lay in unswerving adherence to the service of Shareefa Margaret partook of the nature of an obsession. It represented his sheet anchor of regeneration, his hold upon the new life into which he, a scarcely sentient creature, had been born outside the walls of Ed-dár el Kebeer. But it was an obsession of the moral and mental side of the man, and not a vital portion of the emotional fibres of him, as his love and devotion to Ben Hassan had grown to be. The conviction was a matter of principle. (With its ethical aspect the writer has here no concern. Right or wrong, it was principle, the basis of right, his one means of moral regeneration—by this man's way of it.) The loyal devotion to Ben Hassan was a matter of feeling, a piece of the living man, which is to say that the second must needs overcome the first if they should come to grips in a Haj Yûsef. To anticipate anything else were to presuppose a degree of civilization unattainable by this man, and foreign quite to his mixed blood and the setting of his birth. The instinctive desire would over-ride the mental and moral determination, but not without struggles, and in the struggles the theatre, the man himself would be finely harassed.

Thus it fell out that the Friend found no rest during

the night following his conversation with the Berber whose partner was under engagement to put away Ben Hassan. His conception of his life's scheme, his duty, forbade the making of any disclosures. He could take counsel with no man in this matter. Indeed, that same new conscience forbade any step in the direction of opposition to the shareefa. But there was yet that in the man's heart which made it impossible that he should deliberately stand aside whilst danger threatened Ben Hassan. Daylight discovered in him a henchman weary, ill at ease, and without plans, yet definitely clear upon two points: Ben Hassan was to be saved, and the shareefa was not to be betrayed or held at fault; hence it was obvious that whatever was to be done must be done by Ben Hassan's Friend, and by him alone.

When the hour of Ben Hassan's customary out-going arrived, his Friend engaged him weakly in conversation, seeking simply to postpone a situation he could not cope with. At the end of several singularly vapid passages between them Ben Hassan laughingly smote his Friend upon the shoulder and turned to leave him.

" Friend," he cried, " there is no kernel to the nut of thy speech to-day. I, who have a feast awaiting me, cannot in these our hungry days bide trifling with date-stones. We will talk in the evening hour. Strength to thee! "

And so he was gone—" To his death," muttered Shareefa Margaret from her post beside the slot of a window from which she overlooked the great courtyard. The Friend had recognized the impossibility of offering to bear his lord company, for the object of these afternoon excursions was no secret between the two. And now the Friend sweated in impotent dread and indecision behind the curtain of Ben Hassan's inner chamber.

"By God!" he suddenly exclaimed in English; and then, thinking swiftly, as his wont was, in Arabic, the friend snatched a light English-made gun from Ben Hassan's rack, loaded both barrels from a leathern pouch of cartridges, slipped the handy weapon under his djellab, and stepped out to the stairway.

The Sfraa road junction with the main way into Ain Araish is one of Nature's ambuscades. A handful of well-armed men judiciously placed there might decimate an army approaching Ain Araish by this pass. When Ben Hassan's friend took cover here among the oleander, the aloes, and the palmetto, he was shudderingly reflecting upon two circumstances of shrewd import to him. He had never in his life fired a gun. The man whose murderous scheme he came to thwart might have arrived before him, might even at that moment be taking stock of him from behind a gun in some sheltered nook among the boulders of that hillside. These were reasonable but not exhilarating thoughts, and little calculated to steady the aim of an unpractised marksman. The friend crawled on hands and knees into a position overlooking the junction of the two wide-spreading roads, and crouched there beside a boulder eighty feet above the track. Right and left he peered among the rocks and scrub, but never a sign could he discern of any other mortal's presence in that natural ambuscade.

So an hour passed, an aching, eager, nerve-shaking hour of watchfulness, and then in one moment breath left the friend's body, and he subsided, as it were—caved in upon himself—as close to earth as might be. The sound of a human voice had risen to his ears, and that from a point not fifty feet below his hiding-place.

"Ho-ah!" yawned the voice. "B'Allah, but I have slept, and the time is come."

And Ben Hassan's friend saw rising between two aloe-clumps an ill-shaven head encircled by a cord of camel-hair, and then a broad pair of shoulders, clad, Berber-wise, in goat-skin, and then two sinewy arms, bare from the elbow, swaying outward to give the yawn free passage. One of the thin hands displayed, gripped firmly, the middle of a battered silver inlaid Berber gun. The partner of the man who gave the friend warning had doubtless spent the day at his post, and, as Moors say, " Empty belly or full, all is one to him that sleepeth."

To Ben Hassan's friend, prone among the palmetto blades, it seemed that considerable time elapsed before he ventured to draw breath. Then, with infinite care, he raised his face inch by inch from the ground till the Berber below was brought within range of his vision. The man was sedulously priming his gun—"his borrowed gun," thought Haj Yûsef. Gingerly, and with elaborate precaution, the friend eased his recumbent body by three inches down the slope and nearer to the Berber, then another three inches, then six, then a foot. When ten feet had been covered in this way, the Berber tossed his head aloft with a sudden threatening, eager gesture, like a hound winding its quarry. The friend's face pressed earth. The Berber glanced piercingly up wind, then made a clicking sound with his tongue, and resumed the careful handling of his gun.

Using even more delicate care than before, the friend recommenced after a few minutes his snail-like progress down the hill's face, until at length he reached the gnarled gray trunk of a withered olive, barely ten feet above the crouching figure of the Berber. And at that point came sounds which gave pause to the friend's crawlings, and put a fine edge on the Berber's watchful expectancy. A horseman was rounding the bend of the ridge from which the Sfraa road dipped to the gully below the watchers. The friend heard and saw the cocking of the silver inlaid gun below him, and for the first time in half an hour gave thought to his own weapon. He had left it lying in his first hiding-place fifty feet away!

And now the horseman was in full view of both watchers. Ben Hassan rode idly, with hanging rein, and a muttered song on his lips. Another few seconds and he would pass immediately below the two who watched him. The Berber's gun rose slowly to his shoulder as the kneeling man took aim. Some horrible species of fascination held the friend, as one whose veins had been emptied, whose muscles had been drawn. Phlegm choked him, moisture started from his every pore. A prescient instinct seized Ben Hassan, and he raised his eyes toward the hillside, a signal for his execution, it seemed. But it was more than that. It brought life leaping and bounding to the dead limbs of his friend, and with a yell that sounded purely savage, that friend sprang through space upon the kneeling man beneath with clutching hands and the strength of frenzy in his muscles.

The silver inlaid gun discharged itself harmlessly in mid-air, and down the slope toward the astonished Ben Hassan came bounding and ricochetting the linked and knotted figures of two men. But when the rolling pair brought up beside a boulder a dozen yards from where Ben Hassan sat upon his horse there was no doubt as to which of them had gained the mastery. The friend, scratched and bloody as to his face and hands, knelt astride the wiry Berber, whose arms he held pinned firmly to earth.

" One God, Friend! " cried Ben Hassan, dismounting and running forward. " In Allah's name what make ye here? Get thee to thy feet, Friend. This dog will never

bite again, and I desire of all things to hear it bark.
Come, bark, scurvy dog! What shaitán thought bade
ye raise thy gun to the son o' thy lord?"

Released, the man rose and sullenly faced his questioner.

"Thy father is no lord o' mine. I speak the speech of
the nobles." (The Shillah or Berber tongue is thus called
by those who use it.)

"Ay, with thy tongue; but this that thy hands would
be at. Come, if ye would a little longer stay to foul
the earth, tell me quickly whose work ye do. Such a
market-sweeper can have no direct concern with my
father's son, 'm sh'Allah!"

"Nay, I'll tell thee nothing, Sidi, so now bind me if
ye will; 'tis but a little way to the prison."

"Lord," whispered the friend, one hand upon the
young man's sleeve, "there is no need here of questions.
He is in the shareefa's pay; not an ill man altogether,
I am told, but a poor one, and, being a Berber, no lover
of thy house. It was the shareefa's order. I tell you
this—Allah pardon me!—because—that—that ye may—
that ye may know it and take warning. But I would beg
thee to let there be no case here for the Basha—for inquiry and the hearing of evidence."

"Have no fear of me, friend; I want not to shame the
—thy shareefa. Nay, forgive me; I meant not to hurt
thee—and thou all bloody for my sake!" He turned
to the Berber. "Now that I know who paid ye, man,
I wonder not at all. What should it profit me to have
thee rotting in prison? Nay, I care not even to take thy
gun, for, by Allah and His holy Prophet, it is in my
mind thou'rt a true man in thine own fashion, when all's
said, and, having earned some money in a sorry cause,
will never again raise hand to my father's son; so go

thy ways, man, and peace with thee.   But—a second time
—a second time, man, hell would have thee very surely.
Go!"

The man strode forward and lifted his gun from where
it lay on the hillside.   Then back he slouched, and, pausing a moment, grasped the sleeve of Ben Hassan's djellab,
put his fingers to his lips then, and walked off with never
a word.

"So! Get we within, Friend. Here be matters upon
which I must have speech with thee."

And so, slowly, Ben Hassan and his friend made their
way homeward. As they entered the castle courtyard,
Ben Hassan touched his companion's shoulder with one
knee.

"Look up, Friend," he muttered, reining in his horse.

As the friend's gaze shot upward it showed him, in the
act of passing from the shareefa's narrow window, a face
all pallid and drawn betwixt fear, anger, disappointment,
and bitter hatred.

"So are we welcomed Friend, to my father's house. By
the Prophet, but the time for calling it home has passed.
My mind is made up. This is clearly no place for my
father's son—and his wife. El m'ra Sidi is little likely
to make way. Remains then—— But methinks the inside of four walls were a more wholesome place for our
talk."

"Eyeh! Harden not thy heart, lord," murmured the
friend across the stallion's withers. He had stooped to
hold Ben Hassan's stirrup what time the young man dismounted from his loose-girthed, high-peaked saddle.

"Nay, but rather my hide thou would'st say, Friend,
eh? It were doubtless safer."

Chapter XVII

"LORD, IT IS FINISHED"

BUT their talk, these two, when the shelter of Ben Hassan's quarters was reached, touched no more than the fringe of the matter between them, and that but briefly, for the friend proved all for deliberation, moderation, hesitation, and other natural outcomes of his peculiar state of mind. His lord safe and sound before him, the man's convictions began to assert their sway and to torment him. He had pitted himself against the shareefa, he, whose whole life scheme entailed loyal, even slavish devotion to this woman; also, danger at an end, he found himself overcome by a faint, sick weariness, and pleading this as his excuse, begged Ben Hassan to postpone discussion till both had slept.

This plea made Ben Hassan look closely at his friend, and served to remind him of the rough handling to which his elder had in his service been submitted. With his own hands then the Shareef's son bathed the scratches and bruises which starred his henchman's arms and face, and presently both were stretched and sleeping soundly on the divans of their joint living-room.

There was no sleeping done in Shareefa Margaret's quarters that afternoon. A bitterly angered and more than a little fearful woman was Margaret that day, and her attendants had cause to know and to rue the circumstance. But toward evening, and after an hour's absence unattended from the castle, the shareefa appeared to have

recovered, to have gained rather more than her usual
share of good humour. The atmosphere of her apartments cleared at once, and something like gaiety became
the order of the day there. Our lord's wife announced
that this was her birthday, and cooks were set to work
to make ready some sort of a small feast. Moulai Mohammed, the shareefa's puny and well-beloved son, was
formally escorted to his mother's chamber, and by her
informed of the occasion to be celebrated. Our lord
himself was somewhat unwell, it seemed, and not to be
tempted from the quarters of his ladies. But the Shareef's presence or absence had of late been accounted a
matter of small moment in the affairs of the Shareef's
house. Even the Shareef's son, Ben Hassan, was in
some way to share the light of the shareefa's favour
upon this auspicious occasion, it appeared, for messengers
were despatched to his quarters. But the young man
was not himself bidden to the shareefa's feast. That
were perhaps too much to look for, too great an honour,
even by way of marking such an occasion as this
was.

"But natheless 'twill be no small change, methinks, for
Ben Hassan to finger meat in his cous-coosou this night,
if I am any judge," opined one of the shareefa's chosen
creatures upon his return from an errand which had taken
him to the bare room which served Ben Hassan for
kitchen, and where, as a fact, the young saint's servants
had not of late had much to occupy their skill in cooking
withal. Times there had been when any hungry wight
might feed full for the asking by day or night did he but
look in at Ben Hassan's kitchen; but those times were
passed, and belonged to a period in which shareefas had
counted for little in Ain Araish.

The evening call to prayer had passed unheeded by the

sleeper, and the supper hour was gone by when Ben
Hassan brought himself to rouse his friend. The younger
man had been awake and abroad two hours before, and
now, but for the emptiness in him, made more apparent
by the presence in his quarters of certain savoury and
rare odours, would yet have delayed waking the man
who slumbered so still and peacefully before him. But
young blood is eager. The great porcelain dish with its
cous-coosou of unaccustomed richness and fragrance had
stood cooling for ten minutes on its sieve-like table under
the saint's very nose. Help himself he would not, but,
as though in protest against losing the food's first dainti-
ness, he had tossed a rich morsel to his favourite hunt-
ing dog, Libyah (Lioness), a lean, loving hound that
crouched expectant in the entrance archway.

The friend, new-wakened, turned briskly to perform
his ablutions before food in a great brass bowl which
stood on a tripod in one corner of that shadowy room; and
then, with a devoutly murmured " Bism 'Illah," the two
sat them down upon leathern cushions facing one another over the cous-coosou.

" Eyeh, lord, but thy friend hath slept, and this our
supper hath a most pleasing—— Body o' the Prophet,
but what ails the dog there? Ho, Libyah! So then—
there! Here cometh death in an evil guise, lord. What
foul thing hath the poor creature eaten?"

" Nay, b'Allah, I know not. Nought that I know of,
save that the bone of which thou seest beside her, good
leg of hajab[1] from out our cous-coosou here."

And even as he spoke the poor beast stiffened its
limbs, turning in agony almost on to its back, its fast-
glazing eyes fixed upon Ben Hassan, and full of that in-
tolerable expression of reproach with which dying crea-

[1] Partridge.

tures of the domestic sort so often visit the superior animals responsible for their welfare.

"Allah forgive me, old Libyah—look not so! I have not hurt thee. I—— She's gone, poor bitch! Poor bitch! Yá waili,[1] she's dead!"

There was no doubting the fact, nor yet that the poor stiffened thing had passed in great suffering.

"Lord, lord," cried Cassim the slave, who, having entered at Ben Hassan's first cry, had knelt beside the hound and now held between thumb and finger the remains of the portion of partridge that had fallen from its frothy jaws, "lord, thou knowest this was none of our doing. Mercy, lord; thou knowest this was brought hither from the kitchen of el m'ra Sidi. Lord, they who poison thee are——"

"Peace, man, hold thy prating tongue!" snapped the friend in the tone of one who waked on a sudden to a new and deadly serious aspect of the affair in hand.

"The shareefa, by Allah's holy Prophet!" exclaimed Ben Hassan, wheeling round to glare upon the untasted dish of cous-coosou as though the thing might speak and defend itself.

"Patience, Ben Hassan, I pray of thee; we are not alone," murmured the friend. And he turned to where Cassim stood in the archway, a-tremble and fearful. "Get thee to thy kitchen," he said. "No man hath blamed thee. Thoughts leap blindly in thy mind. Learn to keep them from thy tongue, and thou'lt have nought to fear. Go, now, and let no one pass thee."

And as the man withdrew, with lowered head, Ben Hassan followed his friend to one of the divans. As they seated themselves the friend laid its great sugar-loaf lid upon the dish of food, and sighed heavily.

[1] Alas!

" Now, lord," said he, " what of this ugly thing? "

" What of it? Nay, Friend, I know not what to tell
thee. It seems my life is not a moment safe in mine own
father's house, for that this, this stone-faced, black-
hearted woman, of whom thou'd have me speak ever with
'bated breath and lowering eyes, would murder me—
sweep me aside like carrion, b'Allah—to make clear the
path of her knock-kneed, puling brat, with the mongrel
blood in his veins and the shifty blue of the Nazarenes
in his eyes. Eyeh, by Allah, but I am aweary and sickened of it all; weary am I and sick at heart, Friend, and
—and most of all sick because that my friend is here—
in some way—not friend of mine, but—but of hers—the
creeping panther thing that dogs me with death in her
foul white hand. Yá waili! "

The friend's head was bowed, his thin face in his two
hands. No need of questioning here. He felt the truth
in the very bones of him. The food was sent by the
shareefa for them to eat. The dog had eaten and died
in agony. Only desperate hatred, spiced with fear born
of the failure of her first attempt, could have spurred the
woman to so daring a crime.

" And in Ain Araish who is to stay her hand? What is
to thwart her next effort? " reflected the friend, and he
came near to groaning aloud at this thought.

He who was bound to her by destiny, his chosen fate,
what power had he? And now he was like to lose his
lord's love and trust it seemed, and little wonder, when
he urged the courting, by submission, of insult, injury,
and death itself. Truly a pretty sort of friend! And yet,
and yet——

" Lord, lord! " he cried at length, showing a face all
puckered by thought and distress when he lowered one
hand and stretched it forth to the shoulder of Ben Hassan,

" have faith yet once more in thy friend, lord! Believe thou him, there be matters belonging to an old, bad time that is dead; matters of which thou canst not judge; matters whose shades, cold and dark, have cramped and chilled thy friend. Lord, this day thou wert nigh to—— Lord, take not thy loving trust yet from thy friend!"

" Nay, nay, dear Friend," began Ben Hassan, moved deeply; " fear it not. Indeed, I have not even asked yet as to thy knowledge of that other matter, by the hillside yonder. I——"

" Lord, it is finished. Thy friend claimeth no more indulgence; seeketh no longer to hold thee back. I admit all. Thy life—dear to me, lord, dearer far, God wot! than mine—is truly in danger. There can be no more half measures, no more of submission, no more disguising of the most bitter truth. Do thou speak, lord; do thou command, and I, thy servant—friend, still, dear lord—I will obey. I am with thee to the last—to the end; body and soul, lord, thine—body and soul!"

There was a reflective ring of almost passionate regret in the echoing repetition of these last words. Instinct and feeling had thrust out the mere ingrafted sprigs—principle and conviction. For the present the friend felt that he had entirely thrust aside duty and outraged principle to follow the dictates of feeling. Later on, the supple mind which had made so devious and crooked a track of his life's path from the beginning would put a quite different colour upon the episode, and he would grow gradually assured that the course he had chosen was in reality but part of his devoted service to the interests of the shareefa—a means of protecting her from herself. Yet he had been a fool who had doubted the genuine earnestness of the friend's pledge; and Ben Hassan was no fool. He drew a deep breath of satisfaction, laid one hand heavily, warmly on his friend's shoulder, and:

" Sahhah lik " (That is, strength to thee), he said. " I do not think I ever could have doubted—not to say have doubted thee, Friend. But, sahhah! And now, as man to man, and friend with friend, we may talk of these our affairs—of our poor plight, Friend, and of how best we may brighten it. But first let us call poor Cassim here— he left us mightily afraid, though innocent as any child of harm to us—he can take this mess away, and bring us some sort of food, if it be only bread; for, by the faith! but my belly is as empty as my purse.

So Cassim was called, and his peace of mind, at all events, partially restored to the quaking wight that he was, though as true a man as any in Ain Araish, and his lord's very devoted humble servant. Food was brought, and though in itself poor cheer and cold, and none too plenteous at that, the young saint and his friend made much of it, and at the same time made nothing of it, in the warmth and energy of the talk that passed between them, of the wide world outside Ain Araish; of how best they might fare forth into it (since hiding in Ain Araish seemed like to prove the death of them); and of what steps must be taken in the meanwhile.

And while Ben Hassan and his friend grew warm over their broken scraps of cold food in Hassan's poor quarters, Shareefa Margaret waxed hot and cold by comfortless turns over her feast in the sumptuous apartments of el M'ra Sidi, where half a dozen fawning, servile attendants ministered to the wants of an anxious, bitter, scheming woman and her weedy, pampered son. To satisfy her longing for definite news of the success of her scheme by sending a messenger on some errand to Ben Hassan's rooms would be too open a courting of suspicion. A slave would enter to her stepson and his friend in the early morning, she told herself, and then the looked-for news would reach her quickly and naturally enough. Then would come a burying, not of corpses alone, but of the sole remaining obstacles in the path of Shareefa Margaret's ambition, and, once that were over and done with, there would be found no person of weight in Ain Araish to listen to any Berber brigand's scandalous story, of silver offered for the roadside shooting of Ben Hassan.

The shareefa was safe, her desire within reach of her hands, and yet her eyes were not once closed that night, and daybreak found her a woman haggard and fevered, a thing a-tremble, as it were, on wires of nervous expectancy. And if the first light of day discovered her in this plight, then end of prayers, an hour later, brought no change, no improvement in her case for the shareefa. Now the great house was all astir; its comings and goings of the day had set in, and still no word came from those rooms in which the shareefa's hot fancy saw two drawn, contorted figures of pain lying dead and cold on their divans. The morning sun rode high, and the day's business advanced. Shareefa Margaret, at her loophole of observation, saw no sign of life or movement in the dark entrance arch by which one approached Ben Hassan's quarters from the courtyard.

The noon prayers were said, and still the aching woman sat at her post, lacking any word or sign of relief. Suddenly the thought came to her (born it may be of suspense no longer to be endured) that she would leave the castle and pay a visit. That would be politic, she told herself. Let the discovery be made in the shareefa's absence. She would take her litter, and visit the daughter of Sheikh Mohamet Tor, there to sow seed for her son's gleaning, who should presently unite temporal and spiritual authority in Ain Araish by marrying Fatimah, the sheikh's only daughter.

Margaret found relief in movement, and soon was swaying forward in her litter toward the sheikh's great ramshackle, flaky-walled house. But the visit proved a wasted one, for the " wise woman " of the old sheikh's harem explained that Fatimah had set out with her own woman, as was her wont at that hour.

" Her wont? " echoed the shareefa. " And whither goes she, then, in the ' hours of fire ' ? "

" Nay, 'tis to the tomb of Abd er Rahman belike, or to some shrine without the walls. I know not. Our Fatimah comes and goes as she may list. It is the will of our lord the sheikh, from whom she gat wisdom beyond the share of most of us that be women."

The shareefa sniffed at the " us," but could not take offence. The " wise woman " had humbly and piously kissed the hem of her robe before speaking. And in any case there were days in plenty yet for the schooling of Fatimah.

" She would find little enough to her fancy in Ben Hassan in any case if she saw the body of him now," thought the shareefa, with a twitching, nervous smile as she re-entered her litter for the return to the castle. " And so this slip of a girl is devout, a very orthodox believer, and a lover of shrines ! "

Even the shareefa could not know all things, and now she did not suspect for an instant that Ben Hassan had given a certain shrine its power of attraction to this young pilgrim of love.

Stepping from her litter in the castle courtyard, the shareefa lingered a minute near the inevitable group of idlers—the men who wait in every Moorish courtyard of any importance; folk whose business and aims apparently do not go beyond this waiting—her every sense alert and eager to seize upon some hint of the expected news—the gruesome discovery. But the idlers were gossiping list-lessly enough of men and horses, food and roads; the elemental topics which occupy most men of Arab blood, and are superior to the topics of more polite and sophisti-cated peoples inasmuch as that they are not to be ex-hausted—their state is one of perpetual virginity, even the guests at a harem tea-party cannot deflower them. And when they had stepped forward, these simple philoso-phers, and bent their lips, as piety demanded, to the robes of el M'ra Sidi, they fell back and resumed their browsing converse with the air of men in whose way no news had come these several moons past.

A hot access of impatience overcame the shareefa, and she beckoned a slave to her, turning her veiled face from him while she spoke, as befitted her rank and its faith.

" Go ye to Ben Hassan, man, and tell him the wife of thy lord would speak with him in thy lord's audience chamber. Go quickly."

And as the slave made off at the run, Shareefa Mar-garet swept on toward the main entrance, a commanding figure in her flowing, snowy draperies, the like of which lend even to a slight form a spacious dignity not to be attained in the trim garments of Western civilization. And so the thing was done, the train was fired, the point of culmination and achievement reached. Margaret sat alone in the Shareef's long hall of audience awaiting the news which should spread consternation and excitement throughout Ain Araish.

A patter of naked feet in the gallery leading to this upper room was the signal in obedience to which the shareefa braced herself for the scene. Her two women admitted the breathless slave, who ran forward to kiss her haiik before discharging his news as a rent water-skin pours out its load.

" Lalla,[1] our lord's son is not there; Ben Hassan's friend is not there; Cassim, slave of our lord's son, is not there. Lalla, no man is there, and since daybreak I have been without and seen no man from—— Lalla! our lord cometh!"

The fellow's voice was hushed to a reverential whisper; he cringed to one side, falling into a half-devotional attitude as the entrance curtains of the chamber were tossed apart, and the Shareef of Ain Araish, attended by his counsellor, a boy bearing his mat, and two followers came ruffling and swelling to the couch of the shareefa. At that moment Shareefa Margaret was perhaps the most thoroughly frightened woman in Al Maghreb. An idiot could hardly have looked upon the face of Moulai Hassan and not seen anger written there in blackest lettering.

" What shameless thing is this?" he thundered, shaking a foot-long manuscript before him, and addressing Margaret in a voice that rang through every passage and gallery in the castle. " What shaitán business is this thou'st set thy white hand to, woman? Is the Shareef of Ain Araish to be a mock for the children of the illegitimate?" (Oulad el Haram.) " Is the son of my loins an outcast of no note among men that he may be swept aside like a strange dog and nothing said? By the beard of the Prophet thou'st gone a step too far, woman! There be prison-holes in Ain Araish. Speak, woman! if Allah hath not struck thee dumb for thy sins. What of my son? Where is Ben Hassan?"

Here, then, was food and to spare for the tongues of slaves; but the shareefa had no thought of scandal. She was in worse case than that, and more desperately afraid

[1] Lady.

than ever in her life before. The thing of it was she knew not how much her lord knew nor how much there was to know. Using great self-control, then, she spoke accordingly, and somewhat as Cain answered his father in not altogether dissimilar circumstances.

"Nay, lord, I know not. Thy Ben Hassan is no infant that I—that he should acquaint me of his comings and goings."

The Shareef swore a most unsaintly oath.

"'Nay, lord, I know not,' is it?" he mocked. "And what mean these words, then?" Words jostled one another in the Shareef's throat as, with one menacing forefinger he tapped the long, heavily sealed letter that rustled in his right hand. "'Ask thou the shareefa, my father, for my pen halts, and, indeed, I would not write aught that seemed lacking in respect to thy house.[1] The wife of our lord can explain why the son of our lord hath come to feel that there is no longer any place for him in this, his father's house.' What say ye to that, O stone-faced 'wife of our lord?' Thou canst explain, says the lad— the Shareef, by Allah! flesh of my flesh, dost hear me? The Shareef, my son, whom thou hast driven forth, a wanderer and a beggar, from out my gates. By my fathers, 'tis not to be borne! What have ye to say, woman?"

The shareefa was rapidly recovering her shaken control. Her striving mind was piecing this and that into the truth, with results composing to her nerves.

"Lord, I have to say but very little—in the presence of men and slaves. When the Shareef forgets it, the shareefa of Ain Araish must have a care of his dignity, whatever slanders ill-tempered lads may put to paper."

[1] The most polite manner of referring to a believer's womenkind.

" Allah intended her for a man and a ruler," thought portly Hamet Arâf, the Shareef's counsellor.

And the pause that followed her words gave Shareefa Margaret the measure of her success. But still the Shareef stormed, if with less confidence.

" Iyeh, art all for modesty and dignity, when't suits thee," he said. " But I demand thy answer. Because of thee and thy shaïtán tricks, my son hath fared forth from this my house into the world, like the son of a water-carrier. What say ye to that? Or to this, his own word: ' Believe not, lord, that thy first-born is lacking in loving duty to thee, for, indeed, if he could think it thy will that he should fill a beggar's state in thy house, he would be fain to endure therein, lord. But he believes it not. There be others. Times have altered in Ain Araish. And so, lord, by thy leave I go hence, to give the new order freer play. But this, my seal, O father, I set here in all loving duty to thee. Ben Hassan.' And he is gone—my son, Ben Hassan, seed of my loins. Heard ever Shareef of Ain Araish the like? And we stand gaping here at a—pha!—at a woman! Ho, Hamet Arâf, art catching flies? Get thee about my affairs, man, and quickly! Send horsemen from each gate. A hundred dollars to the man who brings my son to my table this night. But gently, Hamet, let no man forget that 'tis the Shareef, my son, he brings to my house. Get ye gone! "

And, as the dependants melted away, the Shareef turned again upon his white wife. But the sting of his wrath was drawn, and Margaret knew it. The rest was no more than a matter of words—a little firmness here, a caress there, and hachsheesh and the strong waters of the Christians would do the rest; for, the shareefa told herself with relief, the matter at issue was so trivial. Her standard of comparison made it appear no more than trivial.

Yet, if all went well, she reflected, this exceedingly simple happening would serve her turn as well as the vastly more serious event she had looked to face this day.

The shareefa was well pleased, and as Ben Hassan, his friend and his slave, had a friend at court in the person of one of those horsemen who were despatched in their pursuit, the shareefa was fairly accurate in the conclusions which led to her complaisance.

Chapter XVIII

THE OPEN ROAD

IN a sheltered cup-like hollow, densely screened by flowering oleander, with a maze of prickly-pear and aloe clumps, and formed by the junction of two mountain water-courses, the beds of which were dry now as the inside of a date-stone, Ben Hassan's Friend and Cassim—the cheery, dog-like slave of Ben Hassan—were engaged in cooking fragments of mutton, skewered on a ramrod and held over the short, hot flames of a fire of olive wood and dung. The hollow lay no more than eleven miles distant from the principal gate of Ain Araish city, but it was half a mile from any track, and by no means sufficiently accessible to offer any attractions to the casual wayfarer. It is probable that its occupants might have lived, and died and become bleached skeletons in that particular spot without any human creature casting an eye upon their shelter.

" If our lord is to be here by sundown, as he thought," said Cassim, " he must——"

" Hush! Put thy foot on that spluttering twig. So! Listen now," whispered the Friend. " Is there not a tap, tap, up yonder to the right? Someone has left the road and is making this way, I think."

They listened in absolute silence, but no further sound reached them. Yet the Friend's ears had not misled him, for a few minutes later there were unmistakable footfalls among the undergrowth, telling of a rider close at hand. Doubtless the first sounds heard had been made by a shod animal scrambling among the loose stones and rocks beside the track half a mile away.

"The peace of Allah be with thee; a friend cometh!" cried a voice not fifty yards from the hollow.

And in another minute Ben Hassan, mounted upon a big flea-bitten grey mule, pushed his way through the living walls of the encampment and dismounted beside the fire.

"Good friends," said he heartily, "I smell meat in the cooking; a most grateful smell to my father's son, after a fasting day of three journeys, hither and back again, and yet again hither. And now my soles are clear of Ain Araish dust, if my heart is left to keep the dust company —'tis in loyal keeping, im sha'Allah!—my face is set toward the open road, and, by the Faith, my stomach acheth for very emptiness. Good Cassim, tether thou the mule, and—let us to the feast, Friend!"

"Wert seen by any Ain Araish folk?" asked the Friend, speaking with that peculiar caricature of distinctness which a man uses whose mouth holds food too hot for it. Cassim, had served the first skewerful of sizzling mutton upon a broad palmetto leaf.

"I saw but the one, Friend, unless ye reckon her faithful Ayesha, the tail of whose haiik I caught one glimpse of before my beloved swallowed up the light of mine eyes. Ah, Friend, there is a loving heart and true, methinks, in the fairest envelope withal God ever made. No idle reproaches, nor idle chatter of desertion. Only: 'Go, my true love, and win me for thine own in men's eyes, as Allah knoweth I am in His already.' Do not think shame of me for speaking thus openly to a man. Thou—somehow thou'rt——"

" Old enough to be thy father, and withal thy duteous and—and trusty Friend, lord. That is so—that is so."

" Thou had almost said ' loving Friend,' but some queer old djinn of formality that lives in thee jerked thy tongue."

" Maybe, lord—maybe; he did not touch the heart of me, lord; no djinn hath entry there."

It had warmed the heart in you and the more so if you had chanced to be feeling somewhat weary of cities and their ways) to see the kindly light in their eyes, these two, as they chatted affectionately over their simple meal, as, among Believers, only the very intimate will chat, since, to speak by the book, it is not good manners to talk over one's food in Morocco. The magic of the open road—that charm which has been as nectar to the palates of Arabs since time was, and which must needs appeal to any man of discernment in such wild strips of the earth as Sunset Land—was in the veins of both this evening, and it stirred them strangely.

" I feel a free man to-night, who have been enslaved in Ain Araish this long while," quoth Ben Hassan. " And ——"

" Ihyeh, lord, 'tis in me also; for which praise be to the One ! "

" Have I thy leave, lord? " asked Cassim, from the fire's far side, where he crouched with a watchful eye upon the sputtering stick of collops intended for his own delectation.

" Ihyeh, and if 'tis needed, O Cassim. We be here in the open three wayfarers, my man, no longer dependent upon any other person's good pleasure than our own. So eat, O Cassim, and to Allah the praise ! "

" Bism 'Illah ! " quoth the slave devoutly. And thenceforward for the half of an hour the world heard no sound from swart Cassim other than the steady munching of his massive jaws. The ramrod skewer needed no scouring when Cassim wiped his mouth, preparatory to his enunciation of the final " Bism̄ 'Illah ! "

Lying prone at the mouth of the tiny khosánah (in this case a simple and primitive kind of travelling tent), Ben Hassan and his friend discussed the step they had taken and whither it was likely to lead them, before finally curling down for the night in the long barbarically-coloured blankets, thick as carpets, with which they were provided. Cassim's mat and blanket lay under the lee of the khosánah. The whole impedimenta of the little caravan had been stowed in the shwarri, or panniers, of their one animal, and atop of all was comfortable space for either of the three to take a spell of riding should that be desired. Horses were not scarce in Ain Araish, but he who would travel with them must travel also with supplies of barley, the which is weighty stuff, and none too easily come by in some parts. Travelling over South American pampas, or through the bush in Australia, one looks to Mother Earth for the support, in every sense, of one's animals. But in Morocco such a course is not possible. And that is perhaps as well, for if South American methods were feasible here, no man would ever stay at home. Even as things are, and despite the country's bareness alike of " feed " and of roads, one half the days of most able-bodied men in Al Maghreb are spent in the saddle, a-journeying, with little other end in view than just the journeying. " The Nazarene is always stationary and never still; the true Believer is never stationary and always still," writes El Fareeyeh, the story-teller, whose wisdom hath ever some salt in it.

Now, these things being so, it will readily be understood that the question between Ben Hassan and his Friend was not " To what place shall we go ? " but merely

"Which way shall we take?" Not "What shall we do when we reach our destination?" but rather "What like will our fortune be on the road?" And the first question was one easily answered, since to the southward lay the desert, to the westward the sea, and to the eastward a scarce accessible, uninhabitable, and hungry spur of the great Atlas. North, or north and by east, was the course for our pilgrims, and they knew it, having journeyed that way before. And as for the second question, of fortune by the way, among believers it is only put in idleness, and never with any serious thought, for all save the infidel are aware that the books of Fate are locked, and writ in cypher not to be comprehended by mortal mind. No man may foresee the happenings of his Tarìkat, or path to heaven. That which is written will be, and God is merciful, as He is mighty, and alone.

So Ben Hassan and his Friend slept soundly in their sheltered dell, with no care for the morrow, with gladness in that they had won clear of Ain Araish, and with the peacefulness of good Mohammedans who have eaten and praised the One therefor.

Chapter XIX

WAYSIDE HAPPENINGS

THE river Tensift is a stream of note, having many important tributaries ministering to its greatness, one of which waters Morocco City, as the Christians call Marrakish, and all of which have their beginnings in the Atlas—the Great Atlas—that rugged chain of hills upon which some of our forbears maintained the whole world was based. Some claim that the river that is called the Father of Wells is also the parent of the Tensift, its beginning. Others, again, call the Father of Wells the Tensift's most easterly tributary. All men of sense agree in praising Allah for the Father of Wells, and acknowledging that it is good to look upon, sweet to drink of, invincibly strong to resist drought, beneficial to those who live near by its rocky walls, and deathly hard to ford. The great Kaid Abd es Selam of Tazigah is one of those who most should praise the Father of Wells, for he lives beside it, is guarded by its rushing torrent as no wall could guard his kasbah, and can journey to Marrakish, if he be so minded, without ever laying horse's hoof to water, so far as the river is concerned.

Tazigah is no mere village, but a district—a wild, rich countryside, very fertile where it is not rock-bound, and lying high in the very shadow of the great Atlas. But the Kaid's great kasbah (it is really a village, fortified, and within one wall) is also called Tazigah—as is the Kaid himself, for that matter, by many who know of him as

Kaid rather than as man. It is said that Abd es Selam (the Slave of the Peaceful) would never leave it alive should he visit the Court at Marrakish. This is as it may be, and, to be sure, however great may wax the girth of other men, our lord the Sultan is lord of all the Faithful. But, meanwhile, the Kaid goes not to Court himself, choosing rather to send relatives or dependents periodically, laden with rich presents. And, after all, a regular giver of presents is of more use to our Lord of the Parasol than a dead Kaid could be, even though in death that Kaid yielded one very rich haul of treasure. In any case, Kaid Abd es Selam remains in his great yellow castle of Tazigah, and his girth increases steadily with his wealth, his flocks and herds, the submissiveness of the subjects of his rule, the weight of his hand as ruler, the fierceness of his resentment, and the brightness of his favour to them that fear and please him.

Probably no more than four Christians have set eyes upon Tazigah kasbah in the last three hundred years, and of these two are Corony [1] Maclean, whom men call half a Muslim, and who is in the pay of our lord the Sultan; and Walter Harris, who can pass as a Moor wherever a Moor may pass, and who walked with his life in his hand into far Tafilalt. Now, it is a known fact, upon which Western civilization must put what construction it will, that the happiest, most prosperous, and in every way best places in Sunset Land are those of which the Nazarene knows least, just as the most decadent of Moors are those with whom Europeans have come into close contact. The men of Tazigah have, for the most part, never set eyes upon a Nazarene. A wild, hard, fierce race of men are the Tazigs, instant in wrath, slow to forget or forgive, un-

---

[1] Colonel, the title sometimes given to Kaid (now Sir) Harry Maclean.

derstanding not at all either fear in fight or freedom from what Europe would call tyranny in rule; a people who do not rate pillage and brigandage as sins, yet have a keen sense of honour among them, and keep it bright; a community very much nearer in dress, manners, feeling, and life generally, to the age of Moses than to the twentieth-century civilization of Europe.

Picture to yourself a very large castle, built of a sort of yellow concrete or tapia, having crenulated walls, a flat roof, and no windows, but only vertical slots and fanwise embrasures. The castle has two floors, and is surrounded by innumerable dependents in the shape of tapia-built offices, tradesmen's shops, dwelling-huts, and the like. Eighty odd horses live in a space hollowed out of the earth beneath the castle's front. Fifty mules, and as many head of cattle, with a score of camels and a herd of sheep and goats, spend each night in cloister-like shelters among the out-buildings. The whole is encircled by a great yellow wall, which in parts is the wall of the castle itself, and elsewhere stands a hundred yards from the main building, and nearly as high as its roof. The background of the picture rises in sharp relief and immediately behind it—one of the rudest, wildest, most inaccessible spurs among the foot-hills of the Great Atlas. The castle itself stands upon a spur, the whole width of which it covers. One approaches the castle entrance, slowly of necessity, on a steep, short rise. A moufflon, or wild sheep of the Atlas, would be puzzled to approach the castle from its rear, for on that side is the sheer, craggy face of the mountain. On either side the rocky earth falls so steeply from the spur to the hollow beneath that only birds may reach Tazigah that way. And the hollow on the eastern side has for moat and impregnable defence the full torrent of the Father of Wells perpetually expelled with rushing fury, through a gut, rock-bound, in which no creature needing breath could live. So you will understand the saying in the country-side which affirms that " Shaïtán " (that is, the devil) " himself cannot stab Tazigah in the back."

In the valley before Tazigah stretches, for the half of a mile east and west, and for the half of that by north and south, a strip of pasture level as the back of a fat mule. This is the maidan, upon which powder-plays are held, horses are exercised, visitors and petitioners make their camps, and the Kaid's three sons, with the other young men of Tazigah, play the Moorish equivalent to English football.

Across this plain, toward the end of a baking summer's day, three foot-sore travellers, a laden mule between them, approached the Kaid's stronghold, just as the white-bearded old muedhin, Mohammed Marrakshi, was in the act of mounting the little mosque manarat within the walls, to send forth among the echoing crags and hills his declaration of faith and call to evening prayer. The cry came as the strangers approached, and every crannied pinnacle in the bleak Atlas seemed to echo and acclaim the name of Allah. The travellers reverently halted, turning their backs upon the setting sun, and falling to their knees upon the scant, sun-dried herbage of the plain.

" God is most great! I testify that there is no god but God—no god but God! "

The veriest dog among the infidels had surely felt the Presence, the truth of the Faith, could he have stood, a speck among the shadows of those mighty peaks, and heard them echo Tazigah's evening salutation of Heaven.

But there were no infidels within a day's march of Tazigah, no strangers of any degree, as it chanced, save those of the insignificant caravan afore-mentioned, who now hastened forward, their devotions performed; to claim the castle's hospitality ere its great outer gate should clang to, and be locked with its foot-long key by Hamadi Eshé, the m.koddem of the Kaid.

"Lord," remarked that one among the approaching three who was evidently the slave or servant of the others, addressing the younger of his companions, "if that the pedlar said be true, and Tazigah giveth no shelter to strangers in these days, what in Allah's name is to become of us?"

"The answer is with Him in whose name ye ask," said the oldest of the trio.

"Why, Cassim," said the young man who had been addressed by the slave, "hast lost heart, man—hast lost heart, surely?"

"Nay, lord, but the belly of me's lost its last thin lining."

"So; then must we the more surely proceed to line it again, Cassim. But quavering and a long face will never do it, my man. 'The Kaid he dearly loveth a laugh and one who maketh laughter,' said the pedlar, who should know, look ye, having waxed fat here while two moons grew thin and died."

"Lord, 'tis hard laughing on an empty stomach."

"Then hold thy peace—and bide empty, O chicken-liver; but, b'Allah! hide thy head, show not thy hanging jaw to the detriment o' thy betters. Y'are but half a traveller yet, Cassim. Trust me; the poorest sort of fool can laugh on a full belly. By the beard! but I'll make the Kaid laugh if I have to show him the gaping looseness o' my sash—all shall be well."

"Lord, for thee 'tis easy. Thou'rt son to the Shareef of Ain Araish, and——"

"Hath an apprenticeship served to scanty feeding, ye would say? Ihyeh—but should have said stepson to the shareefa! And, again, ye should have said naught. Have we not agreed that I am but Ben Hassan, a poor man, as in very truth I am. I would not have our lord, my father, shamed by men pointing at our poor caravan as the sort of state in which young shareefs of Ain Araish must travel."

" Nay, lord, I spoke privily to thee."

" ' What is whispered at sunset is shouted at sunrise.' But come, brighten thy dull face, Cassim; we draw near, and methinks I see the m.koddem, or some officer of the house, going his rounds with the keys."

Cassim shook his weary frame as a dog will, having won through a stream, covertly prodded the gaunt, hammer-headed mule above its hocks with the spear-head of an aloe which he carried for that purpose, and applied, as his kind will, to the chafed sore below the palmetto breeching which stayed the burda, or pack-saddle, from sagging over its bearer's head when shuffling down hillsides. Yet Cassim had cheerfully fought and well-nigh battered in the face (with his forehead) of a burly Sûssi horse-dealer who, in a country sôk,[1] had ventured to heap added praise upon his sale beasts by jeering at the Ain Araish mule as a thing fit only for crows' food. Ben Hassan, his Friend, his slave, and his mule put their best feet forward then, and mounted, almost jauntily, to the great olive-wood gate, massively studded over with copper, which guards the way into Tazigah. They met Hamadi Eshê, the white-robed and dignified, face to face, and in the very act of swinging to the right-hand gate.

" Shelter, Sidi, shelter in Allah's name, for two weary travellers and their poor slave," began Cassim, " crying

---

[1] This kind of market is frequently held upon some convenient plain in the open country.

at the gate," plaintively and as training and instinct bade him.

" Good m.koddem," put in the Friend with dignity, " I beg you to seek the Kaid your master's hospitality for travellers overtaken by night in a strange place. 'Tis for one here of saintly blood——"

" La, la! " hummed Ben Hassan, touching his friend's djellab sleeve. " We be from a far country, m.koddem, and weary. Prithee, take us in, as we will thee one day, im sha Allah, and if ye come to our gate."

This persuasively, yet carelessly enough, and with a suggestion in the tone of one addressing his inferior in rank.

The m.koddem eyed the travel-stained three and their light pack with some disdain. So much he owed to his dignity. It is a way m.koddems have in most lands. But he was touched, impressed a little, and that neither by the slave's plaint or the Friend's courtesy, but by the indefinable something, which was not appeal and was rather brusque than deferential, which gave a ring of superiority and authority to Ben Hassan's voice. And that also is the way of m.koddems. The courtesy of your man of parts begets no civility in the menial, and nothing quells the arrogant rudeness of the flunkey like the arrogant rudeness of the young aristocrat. The original transgressor was probably the master.

" The night is fine without," suggested the m.koddem, caressing one knee with the point of his great key.

" But finer within," replied Ben Hassan with a chuckle.

" But travellers are wont to lie in tents. My lord the Kaid was robbed by travellers last month, since when ——" He glanced along his black nose at the listening, weary trio. There was a deal of negro blood in his veins, as in those of the stewards and companions of most great men. "And withal," he continued, "my lord is afflicted with a sadness. Now, if ye came bringing music and laughter that were another matter. I would freely welcome any who could bring smiles to my lord's face; but ye "—his nose turned skyward, followed by the gaze of his rolling eyes—" ye seem nearer unto tears."

Cassim grunted, muttering in his beard:

"And if thy fat paunch were as empty as mine—or as thy head—thou'd scare the cattle with thy wailing!"

But for Ben Hassan, he laughed long and loud, and that with less of artifice than inclination.

"Ih-yeh," quoth he, "'twas ever thus with merry men, good m.koddem. That's the salt they savour their quips withal. It's a poor jester grins at his own jokes. Come, say no more, friend, but show us the inside o' thy guest-room, and, by the beards of all the saints of Ain Araish! but if, when we have supped, I cannot make thy master laugh—why, his heart's dead within him. Man, man! heard ye ever—er "—for a moment Ben Hassan was at a loss for some hint of a charm to laughter—"heard ye ever the story of Ben Shudan and the forty pieces of money? Come, and if 'tis laughter ye need here lead us in—lead us in, m.koddem, and ye've laughter home-grown, so to say, in your own court-yard."

And Ben Hassan moved forward, as though never dreaming of further question being raised. Better tactics no man could have used in dealing with such a one as Hamadi Eshé.

"Ah well," and "Ihyeh," he muttered, falling back with his nearest approach to graciousness. "A night's shelter and food is no great matter to the lord of Tazi-gah."

"And much, very much, to tired travellers," said Ben

Hassan's friend. To which Cassim in the rear added a devout " Y'Allah!" And the three passed in with their gaunt beast, each heaving a sigh of relief at the sound of the great gates clanging to behind them. That sound had been so widely different in their ears had they heard it from the other side; for this was the eighteenth day of their wanderings, and differed from its predecessors somewhat in that it had brought no break whatever in the fast of the three men of Ain Araish.

So far, then, fortune had favoured the strangers; they had gained admittance. But the best was yet to be; and that was as well, since of food, either for man or beast, there was no crumb in the dust-encrusted pack of the hammer-headed grey mule. Cassim (good soul that he was, the slave had no other than physical concerns to occupy his mind withal, and so the man's hollow stomach was naturally a magnet to his thoughts) was thinking dubiously upon this very matter of the foodless pack when a slave, black as to cuticle but snowy white as to the garments which fluttered above his scaly, skinny legs, came running toward M.koddem Hamadi from out the castle.

" Ya wâili!" he cried; "but our lord is nigh to madness with the pain in his eye. Allah have us in his keeping, but poor Abs'l'm lies bleeding like a stuck sheep. Our lord drew dagger and smote him woundily in the upper arm, for naught but that the poor afflicted one had failed to find the Shaitán-sent grit, whatever it be, in our lord's eye. Three times Absalam hath sought it most cunningly, and now—and now lies a-bleeding—ya wâili!"

" Eh," muttered Cassim, " what bloody-minded father of sin is this we've come to for lodgment?"

Ben Hassan pricked up his ears, recollection coming to him of a happily ended day of torment spent by him in

Fás, when a fragment of olive-bark had lodged like a leech in his eye.

"What, then, has thy lord in his eye?" he asked of the wailing slave.

"Eh, eh, Sidi," replied the slave, uncertain as to the position of his questioner, and willing to stand safely, "that is what no man knoweth; but only some misbegotten djinn, who hath our lord afflicted these ten long hours—and we that be with him also, b'Allah! and we that be with him, ya wâili!"

"H'm! Take me to thy lord the Kaid, good m.koddem; I—I have some skill in these matters, and—— Take me to him, I beg."

The Friend stared in amazement at Ben Hassan, though he had already cause to know that the last two weeks had taught the Shareef's son more than had his years of ordered study in Fás.

"Lord," he whispered, "thy blood is not known here. He is like to be an ill man to anger, this Tazigah."

But Ben Hassan only smiled, as, in a grim sort, did the m.koddem, whilst turning upon the young man with:

"Well, sir doctor and story-teller, thou'rt quick to promise, but 'twere no more than just to warn thee. Thou'st heard the man here. One who came, as thou would'st, with proffer of aid, failed, and pays with his blood. Would ye follow him?"

"Ay, that would I," returned Ben Hassan, still with his confident smile, "for my cure cannot fail. So come, take me to the Kaid, and let us end his pain before—before we sup on his food."

"H'm! 'Tis my lord for the getting home of a point; but, by the beard, 'tis a long price for our supper, an' if our lord must pay in blood like t'other fellow."

"On thy head be it, then," said the m.koddem grimly,

and, with a most elegant sweep of his spotless silham,[1] he turned and led the way toward his lord's quarters.

In a T-shaped apartment (the stem of the T was long and narrow, its top cross being no more than a great divan, amply cushioned and raised a few inches from the level of the rest of the room) hung with heavy Berber rugs, and decorated plentifully with arms of various sorts, and with a half-crown German silver teapot on a very valuable nacre-inlaid ebony stool, Ben Hassan and his guide found the great man nursing his afflicted eye, plunging up and down his divan like a heavy-laden felucca in a sea-way, and cursing in a low continuous growl. A fine figure of a man was Kaid Abd es Selam, swart, richly dressed in the softest of white stuffs, and having at ordinary times a most commanding mien. Two small boys cowered in far corners of the apartment, eyeing their master as whipped spaniels might, and suggesting by their attitude that their present position had been reached in some swift, violent manner—possibly from the toe of the irate Kaid, one might have fancied, but for the fact that his feet had only white woolen stockings for shield and covering.

"Lord," murmured the m.koddem most humbly, "here is one claiming skill to relieve thee—a stranger, saintly, his companion sayeth, having skill in these matters by his own account."

The Kaid grunted, without lowering his hand from the eye which rained tears below it.

"Show him, Absalam," snarled the afflicted ruler.

"Lord," cried Ben Hassan, stepping forward, "I have heard of that poor bungler's blood-letting."

"H'm! Here be plenty daggers keen in the edge."

[1] A kind of burnous or outer garment, open in front, and affected only by the well dressed.

"I have no fear of them, lord. I pray you to be seated near by the lanthorn there and give me my chance."

The Kaid growled, but did as he was bid.

"Come, then," he said, "and, by the One, clear thou my eye, and ask what ye will for it. Fail me, and Allah pity thee; thou'rt better dead, my doctor saint!"

Ben Hassan bent over the badgered, grumbling man.

"Keep thy distance, m.koddem," said he, "and turn those boys out; I would not be flustered."

"'Twere as well not," grunted the patient.

Then, as the m.koddem turned to carry out his instructions, Ben Hassan thrust his face close to the Kaid's, and held wide open the streaming, blood-shot eye which was the seat of trouble.

"I must look very closely, lord; pardon the freedom."

"Grr'rr—freedom——"

"Huh!"

"By Allah!"

"How say ye, lord?"

"How say I?" The Kaid leaped to his feet. "Ih-yeh, by the hairs of the beard of the Prophet, Sidi, thou'rt on my head! My eye's free!" He bent and took Ben Hassan's hand in his, touching his lips then. "Art doctor and saint both, in very truth. One God, man, but how worked ye that marvel? I would that I had killed t'other villain now that I have seen what skill can do. I never even felt thy finger. One instant, and—pouf! And I suffering like any broken-boned poor devil in al Hotoma these ten long hours since!"

(Al Hotoma is one of the least pleasant apartments in hell, for its occupants spend eternity in having their bones broken.)

"Ah, lord," answered Ben Hassan—he had learned something of policy and diplomacy of late—"that is my poor skill thou knowest, as thine, in far greater measure, is ruling."

"By the Faith, I know not; but who should play the Kaid as thou the doctor would soon be no Kaid, but Sultan, methinks. Whence come ye?"

"Out of Ain Araish, lord."

"Say ye so? From Moulai Hassan's? Know ye the great Shareef?"

"Lord, I have served him. There is a distant relationship. I—I am called Shareef,[1] lord."

"And rightly, and rightly, by Allah! Art new landed and weary?"

"Very weary, lord, and somewhat faint, I and my companions."

"Ih-yeh! Ho, Hamadi! ho, m.koddem! So!" The m.koddem was at his side, obsequious attention in every curve of his flowing draperies. "Art no fool, m.koddem. Thy lord will not forget this show of thy discernment. Now, take me this learned Shareef and his following to the guest-chamber. See thou that all is at its best there. Put thine own hands to it, m.koddem; ye answer to me for this. My guest[2] must feast with his party this night, and afterward, an' if he will, we will talk together here. See to it, m.koddem."

[1] A Shareef is one who claims descent from some member of the Prophet's household. There are thousands in Morocco possessing nothing beyond this claim. The Sultans are the chiefs of all Shareefs; some others beg at city gates.

[2] Be it remembered that the Kaid would naturally suppose that he was offering his hospitality to a considerable number; perhaps a score or more, with a suitable number of animals.

Chapter XX

ONE WAY OF BREAD-WINNING

"LORD, lord," sighed Cassim from his place below the divan upon which Ben Hassan and his friend reclined in the principal guest-chamber of Tazigah—"lord, to be a true Shareef is, sure, to be greater than any Kaid and happy as a saint in Paradise."

Cassim had fed full, Ben Hassan and his friend had eaten as famished wayfarers will when they may, and there remained still in the great porcelain dishes with sugar-loaf basket-lids, which stood upon three round tables six inches high, enough of rich, fine food to feast a hungry family withal. A dozen candles burned near by in lanthorns and in cleft sticks. Two huge pear-shaped teapots, sprouting fresh mint, stood on trays, and between them the half of a great loaf of white sugar. The wanderers were in clover.

"How so, Cassim?" asked Ben Hassan, tucking his djellab under both bent knees, and reaching forward for his glass of tea.

"Lord, we hungered and were strangers; the Kaid was angered and sick, and of all things desired no strangers, and now"—Cassim heaved a deep sigh and placed one hand feelingly upon his sash—"we hunger no more, lord."

"Ih-yeh, that is so," Ben Hassan laughed cheerily.

"In truth, lord," said the Friend in his grave way, "I

would know how ye fared; how worked ye this magic cure?"

" Nay, 'tis a simple matter enough, once one knows it."

" Ih-yeh; but who but a Shareef would know it," gurgled Cassim, glass in hand, his lips a-wash in syrupy green tea.

" Do ye mind that day in Fás when the bark in mine eye kept me from the powder play?" asked Ben Hassan. The Friend nodded. " And how Haj Hamet gave me peace again just before the evening prayers?"

" Ih-yeh."

" But ye never knew how, nor I, till the good man told me—'twas so swiftly done. He looked; I waited for the finger's painful probing, and—whish! 'twas, done with just the softest, warmest touch of something—but an instant—in mine aching eye. *'Twas Haj Hamet's tongue*—and mine that freed the Kaid's eye this night. He thinks it magic—well. As Cassim sayeth, we have eaten. Bism 'Illah!"

" Ih-yeh! And, as Cassim sayeth, " 'tis well to be Ben Hassan. And—— Ah! here come they who will lead ye to the Kaid, methinks. I pray ye insure to us the continuance of his favour by—by continuing to be Ben Hassan lord; for in truth we have need of some rest in good quarters to recruit our strength withal, likewise the mule's. A clean tumni of washed barley, and brimming over, and good straw beside, they gave her ladyship in the fandak outside to-night."

But the gracious message bade Ben Hassan bring his Friend with him to share in the light of the Kaid's countenance. So the two wended their way together through shadowy corridors, under many fretted archways, and on to the Kaid's apartments, Cassim following, as the custom is in such cases, to take up his place among the other attendants at the room's lower end, and imbibe wisdom from the converse of his betters.

They found the great man squatting in high good-humour behind a tray which held teacups and kief-pipes. The Kaid's was a mood of beaming courtesy; he was all for the society and speech of Ben Hassan, it seemed. So, after some minutes devoted to salutations and the necessary exchange of compliments:

" Now, what is this of the Hûdi and his forty pieces, Shareef? " asked Abd es Selam.

The young man called to mind with some discomfort his boast of ability to amuse the great man—to beguile him with story and jest.

" Ih-yeh, lord; and have ye never heard of Ben Shudan and the Ain Araish water-carrier? But 'tis no story, lord "—Ben Hassan almost stammered in his embarrass-ment; for the life of him he could think of no stories with a laugh in them—" 'tis nothing but just a—a thing, lord, which fed the courtyard gossips in my native city for a day or so."

" And now shall feed one who loveth gossip and—and sound eyes, Shareef; so—prithee! "

" Nay, then, lord, 'twas just this: On a summer's morning a water-carrier—Hamman, they called him—came to my fa—came, that is, lord, to the Shareef of Ain Araish, with a most pitiful tale about the savings of his lifetime, the which he would sink in a certain hut he called house, standing in its patch of garden, and for sale at the price of two-and-fifty dollars. The man was known in Ain Araish for an honest, stupid, worthy fellow, hard-worked, and content with his one meal a day, so he could keep his old mother in comfort, and himself free of the Kaid his clutches—— Ah, I would say, lord, thou knowest that there be Kaids and Kaids, and few enough like him of Tazigah—the pity is!"

But Abd es Selam only laughed, and that with genuine amusement, over Ben Hassan's little slip. So that was an agreeable start for the man who had promised to earn his party's lodging by bringing laughter to one who found it seldom.

"Well, lord, the Shareef of Ain Araish pressed the weeping water-carrier as to the whereabouts of his savings. Whereupon the fellow counted out from his pouch, before our eyes, forty dollars; then he drew two from a knot in his sash, and would have the Shareef tell him how many that made. 'Why, forty-two,' says my—the Shareef, to be sure. 'And the price of the home mine eyes have been set on these years, lord, is fifty-two,' says Hamman. 'Well, then, by the Prophet, that's plain as thy face,' laughs our lord; 'thou'rt short by ten dollars, and must save a while yet.' And it may be the Shareef had given him the ten dollars then and there, for his heart was ever kind, as his hand open, before the white woman—— But, as I say, the water-carrier had more to tell. 'Lord,' says he, in much distress, 'I have known the price these ten years, and but four days since I reached it, less the two dollars here from my sash. I had saved forty dollars, and these two Salaam, the brass-worker, owed me, and paid me like a true man; and ten I had loaned to Ben Shudan, the Hûdi. So I took my forty pieces and placed them for safe keeping with the Hûdi, telling him I should come for it all, with the ten he owed me beside, this morning, when the aadool had made out his paper of the house.' And then the water-carrier fell to weeping again, till the Shareef stopped him with: 'Well, Allah be with us, man, and what ails

thee? Hath the Hûdi refused thee thy money, or—'
'Nay, lord,' cries Hamman, ''tis the counting, lord—it
must be the counting.' 'Why, what mean ye; how the
counting, man?' 'Lord, seven times this day have I returned to the Hûdi, and seven times most patiently hath
he counted over and paid me my money rightly enough,
as mine eyes saw and mine ears heard; yet—ya wâili!
here is all I have gotten from him, and thou, lord, like
the aadool, callest it but two-and-forty, and not two-and-
fifty dollars.'

"The Shareef of Ain Araish looked puzzled. Then
quoth he: 'Show us now just how the Hûdi counted
thee thy money, Hamman.' So the water-carrier, kneeling there before us, counted out the money piece by
piece, as the Jew had counted it to him. 'Ten, twenty,
thirty, forty—*and ten I owe ye makes fifty!* And ten
I owe ye,' repeats Hamman, like a sick parrot, 'makes
fifty.' And there was no driving it into the skull of him
what started my fa—the Shareef a-laughing."

And here, much to Ben Hassan's relief, the Kaid, being
in high good-humour over his relieved eye, fell to laughing himself, with far more show of heartiness than the
old tag of gossip told deserved.

"And what did the Shareef? What said Moulai Hassan el Gharbi?" he chuckled out.

"The Shareef he sent Hamet Arâf, his counsellor, to
bring him Ben Shudan the Hûdi," said Ben Hassan;
"and there in the courtyard before us all made him count
over poor Hamman's forty dollars. And when the Hûdi
came to 'forty': 'And an hundred I owe ye,' roars the
Shareef. 'Come, say, after me, Hûdi, and pay as ye say,
or by Allah His Prophet, there cometh for thee, and
presently, an hundred strokes for every dollar thou'rt
short!' But the Hûdi had liefer count out drops of his

blood, it seemed, for he waited for three strokes from the flogger's rod before dragging out his first dollar to add to Hamman's forty. But my fa—but Moulai Hassan was an ill man to deny then, and the Hûdi had to pay as well as say. And he did it, moaning afresh over every dollar, till his greasy pouch was empty and Hamman's store had grown to an hundred and thirteen pieces. And then, the pouch empty, the Shareef said he would remit the rest of the Hûdi's hundred, and sent two slaves and three snapping dogs to escort Ben Shudan on his way to the gates. So the Hûdi was loser after all, and the water-carrier gainer, by Hamman's thick head for figures."

" And by the great Shareef's head for the administra- tion of justice, b'Allah! forget ye not that. Such rulers are born, not made."

And while the Kaid spoke and laughed in best of spirits, Ben Hassan cursed his " sieve of a memory " for that he could recall no more proper and amusing sort of story with which to propitiate the Kaid: he who had spent hours past counting in listening to the story-tellers of Fás and Ain Araish. Yet he feared to recount any come by in that manner; " for sure so great a Kaid must have sickened ere this of every story I have seen taken from the pack of a professional." But there was little need for the young man to put himself about. The Shareef had been mightily tickled, it seemed, by one of the first stories he had ever heard from unprofessional lips. He laughed much and heartily, which in a Kaid means a good deal, since every one of his attendants and the companions of his right hand feel called upon to laugh twice at least for every one chuckle emitted by their lord. Thus the audience-room was filled with merri- ment to all seeming, and the travellers were bidden good-night and good rest with every show of courtesy and favour.

"To-morrow evening, Shareef," said the Kaid, " I have business of moment to transact with a messenger from Marrakish; but next evening, mind ye, I await ye here, with thy Friend, for I look to hear many another good tale from thy lips."

It tickled Ben Hassan to note the obsequious servility with which the Kaid's servants escorted him, with his friend, to the guest-chamber.

"Ih-yeh," murmured Cassim, stretching himself for the night below the divan of his lord; " 'tis honey in the mouth to be the slave of Ben Hassan, the favourite of Tazigah. Allah send repose like mine to the bones o' the old mule! Cassim is a person of consequence this night, and—ha—ee—hath a full belly, too!"

In the morning the m.koddem's own assistant brought snowy, fresh garments for the travellers, taking away the road-worn robes they had to be washed.

"Indeed, then, thy lord hath kindly eye for small matters," said Ben Hassan gratefully.

"Ih-yeh, when it is clear of that which filled our lord with pain and anger," agreed the underling.

So all that day and the next Ben Hassan, with his Friend, followed always in a swaggering gait by Cassim (for whom a clean kaftan, drawers, and djellab had been sent among the finer and more numerous garments which now adorned his masters) strolled, and rested, and chatted, in and about the Castle of Tazigah, discoursing pleasantly with officers of the household and visitors from far towns, and amply recompensing themselves for the hardships of the past few weeks.

And in the matter of those hardships, since it might be deemed ground for wonder that a little

journeying in their own country should have proved
so wearying to Believers, there fall to be offered
here one or two observations. Ben Hassan's little party
contained no single member whom experience had inured
to the shifts and rough polity of the open road in Morocco. Travelling Shareefs and great dignitaries who
have journeys to make in this or any other land learn
nothing of the vagabond, wandering life of the open
road, that kind of wayfaring which is not as second but
as first nature to many thousands of Believers, and which,
to judge by appearances, is not altogether unknown even
among the Christians and other more benighted infidels.
The journeys of the Saints of Ain Araish, in the shadow
of whose divans Cassim had been born and bred, had
partaken always of the nature of triumphal processions.
Money, food, tents, servants, and animals there had always been and to spare upon these travels. Such stately
marches are a most agreeable occupation, but belong not
at all to the primitive pursuit of wayfaring, in which
no man takes thought (or food) for the morrow, and
all things depend upon Kismet and Fate's ruling in the
matter of sunset happenings, chance meetings during the
mid-day halt, the tempers of village elders, favours given
and received by the roadside, and suchlike unmeasured
trifles. As for Ben Hassan's Friend, pious and even
saintly Believer as he might be, it had always been evi-
dent to those about him, judging alike by his speech, the
gentleness of his demeanour, and by various small pecul-
iarities in his habits, that the Friend had not been born
to the rough-and-ready wayfaring life of Sunset Land.
His knowledge of literary Arabic and the purity of his
speech alone served to connect him with lands nearer
Mekka than the Extreme West (so the name of Sunset
Land may be translated).

And so it was that our travellers, with their one beast and their empty purses, had not fared richly in their wanderings so far, but, contrariwise, had endured more of want, exposure, and discomfort than any migratory beggar in the land would dream of permitting himself to suffer. But no other such quick and thorough teaching exists as that given by necessity and experience. Ben Hassan and his companions had learned much that would be of service to them upon the open road during the week preceding their arrival at Tazigah.

On their third evening under his roof, the Kaid sent for his guests as soon as might be after supper, and, though he might well have prepared some entertainment for the occasion, Ben Hassan was disgusted to find himself again at a loss when the Kaid referred to his repute as a story-teller, and requested further demonstration of the same.

" Lord," he murmured, " I have been remiss. In truth the many interests of thy castle have absorbed me, and—we who were weary have been resting in the warmth of thy hospitality, and—behold thy servant, lord, as empty of entertainment as a date-stone is of meat. Then too, lord, in thy presence the listener's part were so greatly more profitable, more fitting, and more pleasant an one to play."

" Art too modest by half, Shareef, forgetting that we unsaintly jackals are apt to judge of a lion by his roar."

" My lord, the lion of Tazigah is pleased to be ironic to the pariah within his gates."

And so they trifled, tossing compliments and self-deprecation, and Ben Hassan the while cudgelled his drowsy fancy for recollection of some mirth-provoking incident or tale. At length:

" Ye have heard, belike," he said, " of Abd er Rahman and the Holy Man of Wad Srou?"

" Nay, Shareef. Your Ain Araish stories are all new to me," said the Kaid.

" But this, lord, is no story I fear, but—but just a thing that was, lord."

" Again the Shareef's modesty beclouds the story-teller. Pray thee what else should your story be but ' just a thing that was ' ? and so it be a merry thing, what better would ye have ? "

" Lord, thy question is for wiser heads than mine—thy learned scribe's there, belike."

" I have heard and read of much discussion round and about the same question in—in other lands," remarked Ben Hassan's Friend, speaking with an air of abstraction, the which had added greatly to his repute as a learned man, though it was not, like the most of the foundations of public repute, an affectation, but something which came naturally upon the man when he sat at his ease.

" Ah! "—there was the threat of a yawn in the Kaid's tone—" but I pray ye tell us of Abd er Rahman and his holy man, Shareef, for time flies, and——"

There came a distinct yawn now, and, with the interests of his following sincerely at heart, Ben Hassan plunged abruptly into his reminiscence.

" Thou seest, lord, this Abd er Rahman inherited his father's savings at a time at which Allah had not willed that he should have attained to the possession of any noteworthy amount of wisdom. And so, in the scattering of those savings, the young man walked a deal faster and less circumspectly than his father before him had travelled in the opposite direction. There were few courses of foolishness or dissipation which Abd er Rahman made no trial of, and, at the last of it, when the idlers and un-veiled women of his choice were beginning to shun him as they might a leper, the young man was not merely at an end of his little fortune, but found himself also considerably in debt.

" Who so blithe, then, as foolish Abd er Rahman when he heard that the Holy Man of Wad Srou, his own uncle and a man with no other blood-relation living than himself, lay sick unto death in his stone house beside the river. 'At worst the old hermit can but leave one part of his hoard to the woman who tends him,' thought Abd er Rahman. 'The rest must surely come to his poor nephew. I must go forthwith and pay my respects.' Accordingly, dressed in his soberest garb, his head new shaven, and a most pious gravity in his face, the young man hied him to the old man's door, whither he had not once thought to journey during his year-long dissipation of his father's hoard. But, alas for Abd er Rahman and his dutiful intent! the old man not merely would not see him, but gave word to the woman who cared for his house to set the dogs upon his visitor and bar the door. So Abd er Rahman went his ways again to his own empty house, and sat him down to smoke kief and ponder upon his debts.

" Now, on the morrow, when afternoon sunlight lay warm upon the roofs and men slept, a messenger came to Abd er Rahman from his uncle, the holy man, to bid him to the death-bed. The old man had relented, it seemed. Or it might be, thought the nephew, that he had never really refused to see his relative. The old woman had been acting in her own interests, belike. In any case, here was the word of peace—death at hand, money in sight. Abd er Rahman fared forth to the holy man's house, his ardour but thinly hidden behind a pretence at condolence.

" With mutterings and a scowl the old woman in charge admitted Abd er Rahman, and her malign expression pleased the young man in that it strengthened his theory regarding his uncle's real feelings and intentions toward himself. In an inner chamber Abd er Rahman found the holy man, or the mask of him, livid, and fighting for every breath he drew, crouched rather than reclining upon a mattress. Economizing his breath with great caution, the old man motioned his blear-eyed hand-maiden to be gone, and beckoned the hopeful Abd er Rahman to his side.

"'Take thou key—under my head—go—chest yonder —unlock drawer below—bring me here!' gasped the dying saint. Abd er Rahman obeyed promptly, and in a manner at once deft and subdued, as one overcome by grief. ''Tis for his papers,' was the young man's hot thought. 'Last instructions—his savings for his nephew, with an injunction that the old witch be cared for. By Allah, but she shall earn her bread!' He carried the drawer to the side of the holy man, and stood with head duteously bowed, awaiting instructions.

"'Now sit thee here beside me, Abd er Rahman, close as may be, for to a bargain words must go, and for them I have saved my breath.' The mourning nephew, a picture of the wild youth reformed, bent low over his uncle's head. 'Now for the conditions,' thought he. 'They must needs be curious if I cannot agree to them. He is a foxy old scrape-the-bowl to the last, this saintly uncle of mine.' And now, as he glanced at the old man's face, Abd er Rahman could not but marvel at what he saw there. Slowly, almost creepingly, so to say, a certain new expression took possession of the pinched features, and, coming so deliberately, it seemed to have come to stay. The look of the holy man, the saint, the f.keeh, which belonged to the old man's repute, gave place to something not properly human, and singularly lascivious. It was as though the temper and instincts of some chap-

licking, old, ruttish goat were to be instilled somehow
into the veins of a revered and holy saint. The grey lips
were puckered into a vile leer; the sunken right eye was
almost covered in an unmistakable and most libidinous
wink; the whole livid, ghastly face was overruled by a
look of senile and crapulous viciousness most unwhole-
some to look upon. Abd er Rahman was no prude, and
he sickened at the sight.

"'My nephew,' began the old saint, with something
resembling the ghost of a chuckle, and not unlike the
sound of the death rattle—a most revolting and indecent
sound—' I know thou hast been a wild fellow, a wild, gay
lad, pranking among the unveiled ones—huh! Oh, I
know,' 'Know! By the faith,' said Abd er Rahman
afterwards, 'his slimy old jaws gave you to understand
that nothing vicious ever had been ih this world but what
he knew thereof and had tasted, and his rheumy, ex-
piring eyes told you he'd exhausted all vices save the
one that held him miser to the end.' Aloud: 'Nay, uncle,'
quoth he; 'but indeed ye must have patience with the
hot blood of youth. Thy nephew is a reformed character
now, needing only a little money to start him soberly in
business withal.'

"'Ha! Ih-yeh! Business, business, that is the thing.
But in the leisure hours—hey? Name of Allah! the
Prophet himself had blood in his veins, not water, and
blood makes for—hey? Thou rascal! thy uncle knows;
he hath heard of these behind the curtain delights.' (The
old man's slavering excitement was hideous to see.
Thou'st seen, maybe, an old boar—ha? Too lustful to
die, too worn for gallantry.) 'Now haste we; I have
but little breath. In that drawer are four-and-twenty
pictures from the big city of the Fransáwi [1]—such pic-

---

[1] French.

tures, boy! each one painted by their devil-sent infidel machine, which harnesses the very sun to its services; taken from real flesh and blood, Abd er Rahman. Ah! such flesh and blood—white, and round, and fat! Ih-yeh, hachsheesh can never give a man such visions as these, Abd er Rahman. Thou hast heard of those the French Jew took to our lord the Sultan? Our lord was kept behind the curtain by them three moons long. And these, Abd er Rahman—by the Prophet's sacred beard I swear it—they *are more indecent by half!* And they are all for thee, my nephew, every one of them. Ih-yeh, I would not have them discovered in the holy man's house. Nay, thou shalt take them with thee this very day.' The young man overcame the access of real disgust which made him turn his face aside from the leering, loathly mask on the pillow. 'As thou sayest, uncle, that surely will I do. Nothing shall be discovered here. And now, uncle, regarding worldly matters, that I may start with decency in some——' 'Eh, eh! Wait, wait! Let me finish, boy; my breath is short. They cost me two dollars and a half each, my nephew, and at that no other man than me could have coaxed them out of the French-protected Hûdi, Benoliel, thou knowest. Now, Abd er Rahman, I know ye young bloods will pay great sums for your fancies; yet thou'rt o' my blood, young or no—and—take them with ye, Abd er Rahman, they are thine at a paltry two dollars a-piece, that *cost,* cost *me,* look ye, more than that. Come, then, eight-and-forty little dollars; count them out on my beside here.'

"And the holy man——"

"Mohammed's blood!" interjected the Kaid Tazigah. But Ben Hassan continued smoothly:

"The holy man fell back upon his couch exhausted, goatish lasciviousness and a miser's itch for money

struggling for first place in the ghoulish face of
him.

"'But, uncle, I have no need of these pictures,' began
Abd er Rahman, 'and am pressed for money now.' He
strove to hide his angry impatience in pretended solicitude.
'And indeed, uncle, you are in no health for the making
of bargains, but rather for rest and peace, and—and the
giving of instructions, the——'

"'The leaving of my poor handful o' money, eh,
nephew?' gasped the breathless patient. 'Ih-yeh, time
enough, time enough; but the dollars, my nephew, the
eight-and-forty pieces. B'Allah, I can decide nothing till
that is settled.' And the old ruin of a man shook and
quivered in so ghastly a manner under the influence of
his excitement that Abd er Rahman feared his dying then
and there, without arrangement made for the disposal of
his property.

"'Well, well, uncle,' said he, to humour his relative,
'it shall be as you say. I need them not, but sooner than
disoblige a holy man and my nearest of kin, uncle, I will
take them.'

"'The dollars, nephew; count them out.'

"'I have but two-and-forty, uncle.'

"The holy man groaned aloud. 'But two-and-forty,
and—and such pictures, too! Why, the Kadi would
order a man's public beating for the possession of any
one of them, and keep the picture for his own pleasure
to boot. Ah, me! but thou'rt kin to me. Take them,
Abd er Rahman; take them and count out the dollars.'

"Abd er Rahman ruefully counted the last of his
fortune, sighing as the holy man's talons closed on piece
after piece.

"'And now leave me, nephew, for a while. I must
rest. Take thou thy bargain with thee; 'tis a gift, no

less. I will send for thee. Ih-yeh, I know,' he continued, as the fuming young man endeavoured to put his case forward, 'I know, I know; but age and sickness know no haste. I will send for thee—perhaps—soon. Get thee gone with the cheapest bargain man ever bought, and—and send me hither old Zohrah.'

" So Abd er Rahman had no choice but to go forth with his bundle of—offal."

" Ih-yeh; and so?" put in the Kaid eagerly.

" And the holy man died before sunset that day, bequeathing all his belongings, under a notary's hand and seal, to the old witch Zohrah; and Abd er Rahman, with his parcel of shame, was left weeping and penniless, from which, lord, it is apparent that if, as I said t'other night, there be kaids and kaids, then very surely, b'Allah, there be also saints and saints in this our Al Maghreb!"

It seemed that this was quite the right sort of story for Kaid Tazigah, since he applauded its narration to the echo and parted with his guests with many flattering expressions of his favour and regard.

Chapter XXI

THE FORTUNE OF TRAVEL

THE events of the preceding chapter were set forth with some sort of particularity and show of detail, for the reason that they represent in miniature some hundreds of other events, the life of scores of weeks, in the two years of wandering which followed Ben Hassan's departure from out the gates of Ain Araish. It was a life remote enough from ordered ease, from stable regularity or dignity, and compact of ups and downs, swift and extreme. Not always by any means was Ben Hassan able to earn comfortable quarters for the party by the telling of a story. Not every day, or even every month, were the wanderers housed in spacious guest-chambers and made free of castles, though once again they did win three weeks of petted idleness and pleasure as the result of another famous cure performed by Ben Hassan.

It happened in this wise: A certain sheikh lived in a village among the Atlas foot-hills, where no prickly pears grew. A passing traveller left a bag of the succulent fruit as a gift to the sheikh. The sheikh ate of them greedily, and did not discover until some time afterwards that he had skinned the fruits unskilfully, and that scores of their minute, hair-like thorns were left imbedded in the skin of his lips and hands. Time passed, and the presence of these invisible spikes became a veritable torment to the sheikh, and no attempt made by his villagers to extract

190

them were of any avail. Then came Ben Hassan with his companions seeking shelter.

"Fetch me hither the old mule there," cried Ben Hassan, when he heard of the trouble. (Ain Araish country grows prickly pears in every hedge.)

Lifting the rope-like tail of the hammer-headed grey mule, Ben Hassan drew forth two or three brown horse-flies from among many that appeared to have their abode there. These he held delicately by their hind-quarters, and then applied their fore-quarters to the old sheikh's hands and lips. While pinched across their buttocks, the insects, of course, grappled valiantly with fore-feet and nippers. Smooth skin gave them no hold, but presently they found and gripped the hair-like prickly pear-spikes which man with his naked eye could not even see. Their strength was just sufficient to withdraw the tiny spikes they gripped. When one fly had thus drawn a dozen stings, Ben Hassan rewarded it with liberty, and chose a fresh one to fill its place. There was no bungling, no pain, no difficulty of any sort, and in ten minutes the sheikh, who had been brought near to madness from pain, impotence, and irritation, was as free of the pests as on the day of his birth. Ben Hassan's little party were the honoured and feasted guests of that village while a moon waxed full and waned again to vanishing point.

But no man, unless an "angel's favourite" or fool, looks for continuous favours from the hands of his destiny. So far from being feasted and petted, the party were once driven with sticks and stones from out the confines of a mountain village, where, if all the fighting men of the place had not been absent and busy over the conduct of a little inter-tribal war, they had been little likely to win clear with unbroken bones or even with their lives. Ben Hassan's Friend was the unwitting cause of this unfortunate incident, and that, in view of his repute for piety and learning, was singular, for your f.keeh is naturally supposed to be versed in the pious lore and rites of all sorts and conditions of Believers, and yet in this matter the Friend betrayed ignorance (it were unjust to accuse him of indifference) regarding no less fundamental a matter than the propitiation by sacrifice of Sidi Kenooz, our lord the ruler of all the Djinnoon—the Other People, or spirits of the air, that is—in southern Al Maghreb.

It fell in this wise: After three hungry days' journeying in a remote corner of the Ha-Ha, darkness overtook the little caravan from Ain Araish, while as yet they had seen no human habitation since noon, and were lacking any sup or bite to comfort them withal. Weary and faint, they tethered the grey mule to a palmetto clump, rigged the frayed and blackened little tent, and flung them down to forget hunger in sleep. Toward daylight Ben Hassan's Friend, after changing the mule's place, wandered toward the foot of a great lone argan-tree, and there performed his morning devotions, the which, no doubt, included a reminder to our Lord Mohammed of the parlous bodily estate of himself and his companions. Then he arose, and straightway stumbled upon a miracle wrought apparently in answer to his prayer. There before him, upon a splintered shelf of rock, lay a fresh-killed black cock, its head all newly bloody upon the earth beside it.

"Ihy' Allah, the good black fowl, the noble bird of good omen!" cried Cassim, when the Friend arrived at camp with his prize.

"How came ye by it?" asked Ben Hassan, with hungry eyes a-sparkle.

"From the One Who answereth prayer," was all the reply the Friend made; and less than two hours later the last of the ebon rooster's bones were being polished betwixt the teeth of three men with appetites fully half slaked.

And then came the payment.

Half a score of angry women, forgetting the use of their face-cloths, as many eager lads, carrying stout cudgels, with four or five village elders, who between them had mustered two wooden swords, a reaping-hook, and a battered Riff gun, nigh upon seven feet long and swathed in scarlet cloth—these were the members of a band which descended suddenly from the crest of a neighbouring ridge upon the three half-filled men of Ain Araish at their bone-picking. Hot-foot, the avengers had travelled from their village of Arbah Sôk, distant some three miles over hill and valley, and their leader was a girl—a slip of a girl—with great blazing eyes, the daughter of a but recently buried saint. This girl had roused the village at daybreak with a tale shrilled forth half hysterically, and telling of the desecration by a stranger of that sacred Fakeera,[1] the Father of Lightning, ten little minutes after the maiden's before-dawn sacrifice there of a black cock, offered with a petition for the cure of her widowed mother's dropsy. Ben Hassan and his companions were not merely proven guilty—guilty was hardly the word—they were discovered gnawing the bones of a creature forfeit to the spirit-world. They had grievously outraged a mortal girl, but—consider the

[1] Sacred trees are thus given half-personal, half-divine attributes in Morocco. The writer has seen his own Moorish servant dismount when passing such a tree on a journey, make humble obeisance, and deposit a pinch of snuff in a crevice of its trunk, by way of offering.

astounding heinousness of their crime against the Djinnoon! As well might men go shouting complaints [1] or
crying the numeral which indicates one and four! [2]

But the panting band from the village recked little of
the punishment that the Ain Araish party would surely
have to face at the hands of the Other People. They had
their own wrath to slake. The Fakeera was their particular shrine; the wronged maiden was their own late
Shareef's daughter.

" By Allah the One, O strangers! were thy forbears
sôk-dogs and without shame that ye sit licking foul lips
there?" shouted the ancient of the party, gasping and
puffing behind a large, fleshy woman with a gazelle-eyed
piccaninny swathed upon her back.

" Come, come! Come, come, ancient!" replied Ben
Hassan, wiping his mouth, and ready as usual with the
pleasant word of good-humour. " A little civility would
become thy beard better than talk of foul lips, and ease
thy way withal in the path thou must e'en travel shortly."

" Bare-faced child of the illegitimate!" spluttered the
elder. " Shalt fear my old hands, and if ye've not sense
enough to fear the wrath of Djinnoon outraged by thy
theft of the black cock."

" Lord, lord—the black cock! Ya waili! Why said
ye not 'twas taken from a shrine? Lord Mohammed
pity us—we're doomed men!"

But while Cassim wailed and the Friend was making
a shrewd guess as to the nature of his crime, the girl
he had wronged advanced and flung full in his face
a stone she carried. It took the Friend beside the
mouth that had been called " foul," and shattered the

[1] To complain aloud is to court the worst of ill fortune.
[2] Five is a deadly unlucky number, never even named more
directly than in the manner here indicated.

better part of two teeth after sorely cutting cheek and lip. But, as Ben Hassan thoughtfully remarked some hours later, "'Twas most marvellous well flung for a girl!"

Sticks and stones fell thickly now, though no further advance was made by the villagers.

"Is't true, Friend, what they say?" shouted Ben Hassan, shielding his head with bent forearm.

"Lord, I fear me it is true."

"Allah preserve us, then! Up there, Cassim! Don't sleep, man! Pack thou the mule swiftly! Here be mad-angry women, crazy old men, and mischievous boys—no place for fighting, but only for running, this. Haste ye!"

And within the briefest possible time the three men were retreating in the most undignified manner and with all haste, goading their beast before them, themselves goaded by a shower of taunts and missiles from the rear, and anxious only to put a substantial extent of open country betwixt themselves and the scene of their breakfast. Not one of them was free from visible wounds when the last of the shouts behind them died away; and, as has been said, if the fighting-men of Arbah Sôk had been within reach, it was odds the Ain Araish party had not escaped with their lives. Remained, however, certain far graver terrors for the three to face: the vengeance of the Djinnoon, to wit. The Other People, of the good sort and the bad sort alike, have long arms and memories never known to fail, as many a luckless wight in Sunset Land, maimed, halt, blind, beggared, and otherwise afflicted, could testify.

The Friend did not confess to ignorance or indifference in the matter of his unfortunate act, neither did he profess knowledge. He offered no explanation, and none was asked; but it may be assumed that, curious as such want of knowledge must be considered in so reputable and grave a man, ignorance was indeed at the root of the matter. For the Other People, as it were, allowed the incident to close, and did not visit the party with the condign punishment which had most surely been theirs as the result of any wilful offence against the sanctity of the argan of Arbah Sôk.

It was full nine months after the affair of the black cock, and the three wanderers were in a valley near Ed-dár el Kebeer, and distant some hundreds of miles from Arbah Sôk, when there befell them an adventure which bore every semblance of disaster, though in the end it did but prove the wondrous mercy of Allah, and the great kindness with which the steps of His saints are guarded.

The little caravan had halted for its noonday rest and refreshment beside a hillock which overlooked the great straggling highway betwixt beauteous, scholarly Fás, the Mekka of the West, and beauteous, but infidel-afflicted, Nazarene-polluted Tangier by the sea. To their right the straggling highway mounted abruptly a steep little ridge, to their left it wound away into the shimmering distance on a downward slope.

"To us will come presently men who ride upon borrowed or stolen horses," mumbled Cassim, who was burrowing in a huge pomegranate, the which, with a slab of black bread, formed his dinner. Nodding, Ben Hassan and his Friend paused in their eating the better to give ear to the faint, confused sounds of horses galloping, which came to them from beyond the ridge. A few moments passed, and then the need of listening was at an end, all the attention of the little caravan being concentrated in their eyes.

A big, raw-boned black stallion, of Zemouri breed by

the look of him, crested the ridge under a double burden
and, urged furiously by one of its riders, plunged on
down the stony incline below the men of Ain Araish.
The black horse was flecked from flank to shoulder with
blood and foam, and the man who so recklessly rode the
poor beast held before him on the scarlet saddle-peak the
figure of a woman, swathed and bundled in flowing white.
Three lengths behind the trio a score of swarthy, ragged
soldiers pounded thunderously over the stones, the blue
tassels of their high-peaked caps fluttering, selhams
streaming, guns athwart their horses' withers, triangular
stirrup corners drumming viciously the poorly-covered
barrels of the beasts they rode. The black stallion had
far more gallop left in him than had the horses of the
soldiery.

"Another hundred strides and he will begin to draw
clear," muttered Ben Hassan, instinctively siding with
the pursued.

"Ya waili, it is finished!" shouted Cassim, leaping to
his feet.

The heavy-laden black horse had poised his weight
one second too long on a rolling stone, and so had come
to earth with a terrible crash, and, as it seemed, a broken
neck. For a moment the spectators could make nothing
of the confusion below them; but, even as they stepped
forward to witness the outworking, a ring formed itself
about the fallen man and his burden, and one saw that
their flight was ended. The soldiers had jagged their
horses almost to earth in coming to a standstill, and now
were all dismounted and had closely surrounded their
quarry.

"Yá!" shouted one of the soldiers, suddenly bringing
his hand down upon the shoulder of a comrade.

"Aiwa?" (What then?) came the growling reply.

"Look up! look up! By Lord Mohammed! here be more of them—into our hand, b'Allah! Quick, man!"

And a dozen of the soldiers, their eyes directed toward the peaceful three from Ain Araish, came rushing at Ben Hassan.

"Es-salamu alaikum" (Peace be on you), "good soldiers!" cried Ben Hassan pleasantly.

"And upon thee," answered one of the men quite mechanically, as he and his immediate neighbour seized each an arm of the son of the Shareef of Ain Araish.

"Come, come! what make ye with my hands?" quoth Ben Hassan, still willing to credit his captors with honest intentions.

"What make we, M'amed—what make we?" echoed the rascal, addressing his hare-lipped and brutal-looking companion. "Methinks we do make but for pastime no more; a trifle scarce worth mention is the business of our lord the Sultan."

"But what concern hath our lord the Sultan with poor travellers?" asked Ben Hassan, as his Friend and his slave, both firmly pinioned in their own sashes, were drawn alongside of him.

"What concern, my sucking-lamb—another turn about the elbow there, M'amed. So! Now he is neatly trussed —what concern is it? Why, not much, truly; save that thy head on a city-gate spike is as good as another, and worth the same dollar to us who take it—eh, M'amed, eh?"

"Eh, verily," grunted the other.

"And when ' poor travellers ' fare forth hot-foot from a village just three minutes before our lord's poor soldiers arrive, in the course of duty, to eat up that village for arrears of taxes, why then——"

"That's our concern with thee, my suck:ng-f.keeh,"

interrupted the hare-lipped man of war, "so step out. We would join our khaleefah below there."

"But, good man——" began Ben Hassan.

"O, we be all good men here and poor talkers, so step out, I say, and save thy breath for the maghrib rik'ah" (for the sunset prayer, that is).

So the three men of Ain Araish, all securely bound as to their arms, walked down the rise among their captors to where the rest of the band were halted in the roadway. One man was sent back to untether and lead down the hammer-headed grey mule.

"Ya waili!" moaned poor Cassim. "Here, truly, cometh the Other People's recollection of the black cock of Arbah Sôk. May Allah the Pitiful have mercy upon us!"

As they drew near to the little knot of soldiers, who were gathered about the fallen black horse and the pair he had borne so gallantly, Ben Hassan could see that the woman had been put aside under guard, and that her companion in flight was lying at the feet of the other soldiers, still stunned and unconscious from his fall.

"But, this being the sheikh's son, O Absalam, it may be that er-Rais[1] hath a need of him alive."

"Stuff! Am I a magic-worker, then, that I should keep him alive? And will ye carry him, O head of mud, and so leave another in our camp this night to lop off his head, and take our lord's dollar therefor?"

"He is no more than stunned, O Absalam. See thou the woman there, barely scratched, and not hurt at all?"

"Ih-yeh, the woman; that is sense. She will bring us maybe fifty dollars or more in open market, and no man the wiser for that. But for men, thou knowest our orders were slay, burn, and spare not at all."

[1] The captain.

"But, O Absalam, this——"

"Oh, stand back, babbler!" And raising the point of his sword from where it rested in the sand at his feet, the first speaker whirled the blade on high and brought it whistling down then upon the neck of the unconscious wretch who had ridden the black stallion. Ben Hassan had involuntarily made to leap forward, but was held back firmly by his assássah [1]—his guards, that is—and so, with a groan, turned his head aside as the khaleefah stooped leisurely to complete the rather bungled task of severing his victim's head from its trunk, and tossing it into a palmetto saddle-bag. Then the khaleefah turned to inspect the latest addition to his haul.

"Well," said he, grimly staring at Ben Hassan, "heads are easier carried than men."

"But these are all unknown and able-bodied rascals," suggested the soldier, whose desire for greater rewards than the regular price for rebels' heads made him to appear humane.

"Ay, truly. They should fetch twenty apiece in Fás market," admitted the khaleefah. "But can we keep them out of sight of er-Rais?"

"Nay, that may hardly be, O Absalam; but we might offer him the half of their price in Fás. It should be worth more to us then than just the head o' them."

"Wakkha!" (that is, "Very good!") replied the lieutenant. "Hitch them to thy stirrups then, men, and ride we for the camp. I would not have evening find us thus far from shelter."

"And from cous-coosou," added Hamadi, the comrade of hare-lipped M'amed, with a grin, which he emphasized by a tug at the spare bridle which connected him with the elbows of Ben Hassan. "Come, O learned basheer,"

[1] Anglicé, assassin.

quoth he satirically. (A basheer is a preacher or expounder.)

Cassim had long since accepted the situation and its ills as the direct work of those spirits of the air whom his masters had offended in the matter of the black cock at Arbah Sôk. Ben Hassan, the first flush of his resentment cooled, shrugged his shoulders, as one who had already learned the folly of endeavouring to blot out or alter the writings of Destiny. But the Friend, the offender of the Other People, who, by that token, might have been the first to recognize the hopelessness of resistance, wheeled indignantly upon the khaleefah at this point, lifting his voice as one in authority and crying a halt.

" My men," said he to the astonished soldiery, " ye will spend years in regretting the hours ye give to performing, and if ye lead us bound as prisoners to your camp."

" What, two preachers among three poor travellers! Allah pity them! " laughed Ben Hassan's guard.

" Man," shouted the Friend, turning now upon the last speaker, " do you guess who it is your foul hands hold bound there? Do ye know that the holy——"

" Friend," put in Ben Hassan warningly, " thou hast surely forgotten a certain agreement."

" So the other learned basheer's holy, is he? " said the soldier, with good-humoured scorn. " Ah, well, I've an uncle that once sewed a pair of drawers for a khateeb [1] in Rabat, so the reverend gentleman shall run by my stirrup, and thus keep reverend company."

Checked by the reminder of their agreement in the matter of not disclosing his lord's identity, the Friend seemed about to resign himself to the inevitable. Then, addressing the khaleefah, he made further protest.

[1] A reader in the mosque.

"Khaleefah, mark well thy feet where they do lead thee. We be no villagers from hereabouts; neither enemies of thine or thy lord's, but true men from a far place, travelling, with as much right to freedom on the road as thou hast. Thy captain will not thank thee for thy day's work, and if we be brought prisoners to him, and for the market in Fás, ye would never leave it alive if ye led us there."

"What say ye, men?" growled the khaleefah. "Their tongues are long; 'twere easier far to carry their heads. Heads make no clatter, lacking bodies, and cannot make trouble for good soldiers."

Some of the men laughed at their leader's grim humour, but all of them were anxious for a share in the prices their prisoners might fetch in the slave-market, and so said as much plainly.

"Wakkha! Now, harkee, sir preacher, you and your companions. We be soldiers here, not women. A quiet tongue will leave ye whole skins; a wagging one will bring thee stick or steel to eat. Ye say ye come from far. Well, it matters not the half of a date-stone to me whence ye come. Ye go with us to our camp, and thence to the nearest market in which such ready-tongued knaves will fetch a price. There's a score or more of your kind escaped us this day, and when we do lay hands upon ye, it's little odds to us who ye be—or to our lord either, for that matter. So if ye care for whole skins, and heads to your shoulders withal, keep quiet and step out briskly—no hanging back on the stirrup, mind! Ho! M'amed! Bind ye the woman on the grey mule yonder. 'Tis lightly laden. By Allah, if the others were not all burned out, we shall have a harem in the camp this night!"

And so, amid hoarse laughter, the cavalcade made a start, and the three men of Ain Araish, who but an hour or two earlier had been free as the birds overhead, were dragged prisoners now at the blood-stained stirrups of men admittedly the basest in Al Maghreb.

Chapter XXII

THOU ART SHAREEF

DARKNESS had set in, and the men of Ain Araish were weary and aching in every limb, when at length their captors came to a halt beside the dense aloe and cactus-hedge of the village of the Father of Thorns. Here they were welcomed by a dozen cut-throat rascals of their kind who had been told off to wait for them and to remain on guard at this particular spot. The main body to which they all belonged (some thirteen hundred assassins of the Shareefian army under orders to " eat up " certain non-taxpaying villages of this country-side) had carried fire and the sword, it seemed, to a valley some twenty miles and more away. The twelve assassins had made good their reputations, and a plentiful supper awaited the captors of Ben Hassan in the houses of the Father of Thorns. The villagers themselves were for the most part camped in the open spaces between their huts, absolutely all that they possessed of food and shelter having been taken from them at the sword's point. It may be true that, as the pious always affirm, " Allah sends the locusts." It must be true that, as good and bad alike assert, " Shaïtán sends the soldiers."

When their excellencies the assassins had fed full, and had turned to gall within them the blood of the sons of the Father of Thorns by means of the lewd and brutal jests which they flung about them regarding their female prisoner and the crouching, frightened womenkind of the village, then only were some broken scraps of food flung contemptuously to Ben Hassan and his companions where they sat, fast bound to the trunk of an ancient olive. Stung more shrewdly by this last indignity than by the callousness of all that had gone before, the Friend leaned toward the shoulder of his lord, saying, as one from whom words were forced:

"Lord, lord, give me thy leave to name names; to show these dogs the thing they do. It is not meet, lord, that thy father's son should——"

"Should shame his father, thou would'st say, Friend? And that is most true. Fear not; I will never bid men look upon the Shareef's son forced to journey as a beggar among Believers."

The Friend sighed, and sheer hunger presently drove them both to follow the lead of Cassim, who was busily munching at scraps from the tables of the assassins. But even tyrannical hunger and most masterful weariness failed to force Cassim's example upon his masters to the extent of wrapping them in slumber. Indeed, there were not many within the shelter of the Father of Thorns who slept that night as did the good Cassim—peacefully, and without other disturbance than the shock of being occasionally roused for a moment by the resonance of his own snores. There was much singing, tea-drinking, drum-playing, and even dancing, among the cheerful ruffians of the Shareefian army. The heavy smoke of kief poisoned the purity of the night about them, and more than one father and brother lost his life that night in a brief scuffle following upon a woman's cry of distress among the huts of the Father of Thorns. It was a foul and ugly nightmare, and never perhaps had Ben Hassan welcomed so warmly or understood so clearly a call to prayer as when, with the earliest streak of coming dawn, there arose from the straw and tapia mosque of the village the weary muedhin's fejer chant:

"The night has departed with the darkness, and the day approaches with light and brightness!

"Praise God for securing His favour and kindness!

"God is most great! God is most great! I testify that there is no god but God!

"I testify that Mohammed is the Apostle of God!

"Come to prayer!

"Come to security!

"Prayer is better than sleep!

"God is most great!

"There is no god but God!

"Arise, make morning, and to God be the praise!"

As the last stately words of the magnificent chant echoed across the low stretches of the valley, the village dogs with one accord began to bark, a way-worn stranger, his slippers in his hand, entered the village from the highway without, fresh and dripping from his ablutions, and, his forehead turned toward the rising sun, placed both hands to his ears and began his morning prayer. A few minutes later, when all men might have been assumed to have concluded their fard, or obligatory devotions, the stranger rose from his last "two bow" prayer and looked searchingly about him in the village. His staff, thrust between shirt and body, protruded upon one side of a short, muscular neck. His djellab was girt tightly about his middle with a cord, and on his loins swung a basket or bag of palmetto. The stranger had the air of one who travelled light, fast, and upon urgent business.

"O true Believers!" he shouted, right hand raised to the side of his mouth, "hath any one among ye here seen aught of Sidi Hassan, the son of Moulai Hassan el Gharbi, our Lord the Shareef of Ain Araish?"

You may be sure that the men of Ain Araish, even including the newly and barely awakened Cassim, turned with one accord, and as far as their bonds allowed them, in the direction of the crier, and:

"Here, true Believer!" roared Cassim, as a lad in school answers when a rap of the f.keeh's stick accentuates the calling of his name. "Here be those who have seen and felt him, bound here like sheep before el Aïd el Kabeer!"[1]

"Askut! skut!" (hush! hush!) muttered Ben Hassan; and aloud then, as surprise in his recognition of the crier forced forgetfulness of diplomacy: "By Allah and His Prophet, 'tis one-eyed Haj Abd el Lateef! Ho, Abd el Lateef, Araishi!"

It was a great sight, a pleasant sight, to see the one-eyed stranger, after giving one piercing look in the direction of the old olive-tree, come bounding forward like a driven thing and fall to his knees at the feet of pinioned Ben Hassan and his companions.

"Lord, lord, Allah be praised! Abd el Lateef hath found thee!" he cried. "But three little days from Christian-cursed Tanjáh, and Lord Mohammed hath guided my feet to thee. The praise be to Him, the One. Thy father lieth sick unto death in Tanjáh, lord, and did send me to—— But, lord, lord, what dog, son of a dog, dared so to tie a holy Shareef? One God be merciful! What! Ho, ho, there! pigs and dogs, come out o' thy holes that a Shareef may spit upon thee and be gone! Ho—oh—ah!"

Words failed the one-eyed man. Horror, rage, wrath, choked him. One by one the villagers of the Father of Thorns and the assassins of the Shareefian horde gathered

[1] The great Feast, or Feast of the Sheep, by which Believers commemorate Abraham's sacrifice of a ram in place of his son.

round about the ancient olive and its prisoners. One by
one they edged behind each other, the soldiers calling in
murmurs upon the name of Allah, and again upon that of
their rascal khaleefah. At length, thrust forward by his
fearful comrades, the blustering chief of yesterday's
affray slouched before Ben Hassan, and was understood
to whiningly deliver himself thus:

"Lord, why wronged ye simple soldier men? How
could we know ye for Shareef of Ain Araish? Pardon,
lord—um-um-um!"

"Stop muttering, man, and cut me these ropes if ye
would talk with my father's son," quoth Ben Hassan in
his own pleasant way. "So I wronged ye, did I, by keeping a still tongue? But, my brave khaleefah, ye were
urgent in advising me to keep that tongue still but a few
hours since, and if I did place any value upon a whole
skin."

"O dog-begotten child of the illegitimate!"

"Nay, nay, Abd el Lateef, speak not so of the man we
have injured. He had no means of knowing that we
were true men. He took us, if you please, for wild
beasts, and so, and so——"

"Down, down on thy pig-bones and loose those cords!"
roared the one-eyed messenger. "But nay, that is not
for thy hands, either, but for mine, who being a true man,
may touch the Lord's anointed. Mind out, dog!"

They were hard names to swallow, these that Abd el
Lateef (the slave of the benevolent) flung from him into
the clean air of the dawn, and the assassins drew aside to
consider them and the matter from which they rose.[1] The

[1] The writer was once travelling with a Moorish servant of
saintly blood whose family or territorial name was, let us say,
Gharbi. There was a scuffle in a certain small fandak, or cara-
vanserai, in which Gharbi desired room for the writer's animals

khaleefah was ungenerously reminded that on the previous day he had been for carrying away only the heads of the prisoners.

"And then where should we have been?" he was asked. And the question found him at a disadvantage. In the upshot, the khaleefah was forced forward as spokesman to humbly sue for the young Shareef's pardon and make proffer of assistance.

"As for pardon, say no more," answered Ben Hassan, whom life on the open road had made tolerant. "Only I pray ye not only to be more careful in future whom ye take captive to your stirrup-thongs, but also to treat a little more gently even those whom duty casts in thy way. Now for assistance. I need some food. There be here four mouths with hungry bellies beneath them; and I need four horses, the swiftest here, and in return ye have my word for it ye shall not be losers."

The horses were immediately forthcoming (though, out of respect for truth, it must be stated that five were subsequently stolen by the assassins from the Father of Thorns to replace the four so promptly furnished to meet Ben Hassan's need), and within the hour the men of Ain Araish, with one-eyed Abd el Lateef, had fed full on good cous-coosou and cold kiftá, and were ready for

and himself. A dozen others scuffled to obtain this room for themselves. "Ah, would you?" the writer heard Gharbi exclaim, as a burly Riffian flung him backward on a bale of djellab cloth. "Would ye lay hands upon a Gharbi, ye dog, son of a dog?" The Riffian fell back instantly, making way, as did all the others, with a half-resentful, half-apologetic air, as he said: "*Why could ye not have told me so before* How could I know ye for a Gharbi?" Conceive, if you can, a man in a street row in England claiming precedence on the ground of kinship to the Cecils or to the Archbishop of Canterbury—*and getting it.*— A. J. D.

the road.   The Ain Araish mule, as well as Ben Hassan's saintly word, were left as surety for the return of the borrowed horses, and, amid the respectful salutations and good wishes alike of peasants and assassins ringing in their ears, the company of Sidi Ben Hassan set forth at a brisk amble for sea-girt Tangier and the bed of the great Shareef's decline.

The mind of Ben Hassan was occupied chiefly by thoughts of his father and natural anxiety as to the saint's welfare.   Abd el Lateef was divided betwixt wrath against those " children of the illegitimate," the Shareefian soldiers, and self-congratulation in and for that he had succeeded so well and speedily in his mission to discover Ben Hassan.   As for Cassim, that good slave could hardly be said to have any mental occupation as he jogged steadily along in the wake of his masters.   He was still, in gentle rumination fancy free, chewing the cud of the excellent repast with which his hunger had that morning been stayed at the Father of Thorns.   Among the little cavalcade but one mind was really actively employed, and that was the mind of the Friend of Ben Hassan, who rode beside his young lord upon a dull-bay Barb, and occasionally was heard to urge their leader, Abd el Lateef, to quicken the pace of the party.

If Ben Hassan was thinking of the imminent death of his father, the Friend was thinking of the imminent death of the Shareef of Ain Araish and of what that event might mean for Ben Hassan.   He was, of course, aware that Islam knows not the law of entail.   Any son of Moulai Hassan's must needs be a Shareef; but there could be only one Shareef of Ain Araish, even as there could be but one holder of the Shareefian Parasol, and he must needs receive the succession by his father's appointment.   In their first words of intercourse at the Father of Thorns the Friend had learned from Abd el Lateef that the shareefa and her boy were in Ain Araish, and not with the Shareef in Tangier. " But natheless in these days the most of those who are about the person of the Shareef are no doubt creatures of the shareefa," reflected Ben Hassan's Friend. " It is certain that the shareefa hath foreseen and arranged all these matters that the succession may pass to her son, and I—I should be the last among men to seek to interfere or to thwart el M'ra Sidi, and yet, and yet——"

But no definite end was reached in the Friend's reflections. Only he steadily urged on his bay horse, and now and again bade their leader to hasten. " For, look you, good Abd el Lateef, we ride not for pleasure this day, but in a race with the thing which is written."

And so the jangling bridle of the Slave of the Benevolent's horse clacked again in the poor beast's jaws, and the brisk pace was made brisker.

At high noon they splashed abreast through the river which encircles the city of Ed-dár el Kebeer, and here fresh horses were demanded and freely given in the name of the dying saint of Ain Araish. But, though the temptations to delay in this northern stronghold of the Shareef's influence were numerous, Ben Hassan and his Friend spared little time for the exchange of greetings, and none for the partaking of refreshment.

" Fresh horses are a feast for fast riders," quoth the young saint.

" We will eat riding, good friends, and if ye give us bread," added the Friend.

" And a city full of sweet-savoured cous-coosou a-crying out to be eaten!" moaned Cassim, as he mounted behind his lord.

Ben Hassan marvelled that his Friend should insist

upon riding out by the kasbah gate when their most direct route lay by the road of the " Gate of Sunrise."

" Lord, 'tis a feeling in me that tells me we shall gain by this half mile of loss."   And they did, too, for beside the Sunrise Gate sat Haj Cassim, as the Friend well knew, and it had scarcely been possible to pass that holy man with few words.

Now, from Ed-dár el Kebeer to Tanjáh, as rich men travel, easily, is accounted a three days' journey. Traders and those who hasten make it a longish two days. Ben Hassan and his company were in greater haste now than traders, and the horses they rode from Ed-dár were the horses of rich men, as also were those they exchanged these for in mid-Gharb.   From the ill-famed Red Hill, which they scaled in pitchy darkness, no rein was drawn, and es-Swaanee was crossed at a plunging gallop.   In Tangier men were but new-roused for the morning prayer when, sixteen hours after leaving Ed-dár, Ben Hassan, with his three followers, galloped their smoking horses across the outer Sôk, and broke into a hard-held trot over the greasy cobbles of the city's main street.

" Our lord liveth, and no more; may God be merciful to him!" exclaimed the guard, who stood without the curious old Spanish door by which one entered the court-yard of the great Shareef's Tangier house. " He asks for thee every hour, Sidi," added the man, as he held Ben Hassan's stirrup for the young man to dismount.

" Hush, hush, good people, our lord can see *no man!*"

This was Ben Hassan's greeting at the stair's foot, where he met the portly counsellor, Ben Hamet Aráf, descending with two holy men of great repute as healers of the sick.

" Yet will he see Ben Hassan and those with him,"

replied the young man, pausing not for ceremony, but pushing directly past the counsellor.

" Ih-yeh," stammered the man of affairs. " To be sure, I knew ye not. Ih-yeh, we are in God's hands!" And then he added in his beard: " But methinks the time for words is past."

It was a strange and gloomy scene which greeted Ben Hassan in the chamber where his father lay dying. When he reached the entrance archway his three followers were about him, and behind them, watchful and silent, hovered Ben Hamet Arâf, whose great power in Ain Araish had its root in his absolute subservience to the will of the real ruler there—Shareefa Margaret.

The chamber was a very long one, lofty, but not wide, and in the centre of it, upon a divan raised but a few inches from the floor, lay all that was left of the great Shareef Moulai Hassan el Gharbi. At the foot of the divan crouched two girls, their faces but half-veiled; at its head a boy sat, holding a great horse-hair whisk. As Ben Hassan removed his slippers at the entrance, two attendants, bearing a brass ewer and a cloth, were in the act of moistening the lips of the dying man.

" Withdraw the pillows, and may God have mercy upon our lord," said one of five holy men and f.keehs who sat upon cushions against the wall facing the couch.

Death was evidently very near to Moulai Hassan, and so, according to custom and tradition, his face was to be covered and his pillows removed. Already a slave had passed the word without, and presently the narrow city street would be blocked by mourners of all classes assembled there to offer prayers for mercy and for bliss for the departed.

" Sidi, I grieve with thee; thou'rt too late," whispered the counsellor in Ben Hassan's ear.

"Not so, to Allah the praise; my father seeth! Hands off those pillows!"

And with these words on his lips, Ben Hassan strode forward and dropped upon his knees beside the divan.

It was true. The Shareef had seen, and now his blurred and clouded eyes opened wide and rested for a moment, understandingly, upon the face of his son.

"Ben Hassan," he gasped, and lower still the young man bowed his head. "To Allah the praise! Bring hither—Arâf!"

Ben Hassan turned on his knees, and beckoned to him the counsellor, who, with the f.keehs, drew closely about the bed-head. The dying man's lips moved again, and the boy who sat above the pillows reached for a bottle and glass.

"T's this he asks for."

"Nay, nay; 'tis infidel-made—accursed!"

The f.keehs spread their hands in horror, and the dying saint without doubt understood them; for a faint smile flickered over his grey lips. Then for a moment the dull eyes were lighted up, blazed almost, as they had been wont to, and the Shareef spoke clearly, so that all men might hear and follow him.

"Ben Hassan, true Muslim—flesh of my flesh, blood o' my blood—none other—praise Allah!"

And here there fell a pregnant pause, in which the Shareef's eyes closed, the watchers held their breath suspended, and an end seemed to have come. But an instant more, and, with a great heave, the saint sat bolt upright, one hand outstretched, authority speaking in every line of his wasted form.

"There is but one God, and Mohammed is His Apostle! There is but one Shareef of Ain Araish, and from this day thou'rt he—Ben Hassan—my son—to Allah—the Merciful!"

And that was the last word spoken and the last breath drawn upon earth by Allah's anointed, Moulai Hassan el Gharbi, who thus ended a strange life, with the name and attribute of his God on his lips, having duly named his successor the greatest saint in all Al Maghreb.

Three minutes later the wail of mourners, the shrill cries of women, and the sonorous chanting of prayers by hundreds of the Faithful, echoed through the streets of Christian-influenced Tangier, bidding all men to know that the soul of Moulai Hassan had passed from earth to the borders of Paradise.

But, by the strict order of Ben Hamet Arâf, no man spoke of the succession.

Chapter XXIII

THE SHAREEF IN TANGIER

"LORD, would it not be well for thee, who art Shareef of Ain Araish, to order out men and horses and journey forthright to thine own place?"

Ben Hassan looked up indifferently at the speaker, Cassim, and the Friend, who sat beside Ben Hassan, looked troubled.

"What is thy haste, Cassim?" asked the young Shareef.

"Lord, where is the counsellor of thy dead father—may Allah have mercy upon him!" (This expression, as applied to the departed, is traditional, and suggests no sort of reflection upon his memory.)

"Nay, I know not, good Cassim; I am not his keeper."

"But he should be the keeper of thy seal and keys, lord, as of thy father's—may Allah—um—before thee. *And he started for Ain Araish with many followers before the sun rose yesterday.*"

"Gossip sayeth he went but to visit a shrine, and will return," put in the Friend, speaking as one who lacked conviction.

"And I say gossip lieth, master," replied Cassim.[1]

---

[1] Favoured slaves are accorded a freedom of speech and liberty of action which is unknown among mere hired dependents in Morocco, and most slaves lead easier and pleasanter lives than do the poorest sort of free men.

"Eh, eh; it hath that repute," admitted the Friend.

"And further, lord, I say that the slave, Mansûr Marrakshi, bearing a sealed letter from Ben Hamet Arâf, left here for Ain Araish three days ago, and no more than three hours after the death of our lord, thy father— may God pity him!—and as I know from Hamadi the egg-carrier, lord, Mansûr left his horse nearer dead than alive at Midouar; two days' journey covered by him in under ten hours. Thinking of these things, lord, thy slave dares to urge thee to put aside mourning and journey straightway to Ain Araish that we may see what things are toward there."

"Ah'm! How say ye, Friend?"

"Lord, I—I blame myself for that I have said nothing; but—though I desire peace and rest for thee, lord, I cannot say but what I think Cassim is in the right of it —by his lights."

"But ye would not have el M'ra Sidi in Ain Araish put about—eh, Friend?"

"Nay, speak not bitterly, lord. I would have peace and content for thee."

"Ah'm—ih-yeh—peace and content, peace and—— Go thou, Cassim, and make ready for the road. We start to-morrow."

The time was early afternoon, and the day the fourth after Moulai Hassan's death. The funeral—by far the most imposing ever seen in the neighbourhood of polluted Tangier—had taken place within four-and-twenty hours of the death. Six of the holiest men in the Gharb had borne Moulai Hassan's bier to the lofty plateau, midway betwixt Tangier and Cape Spartel, in which the dead saint had been laid to rest, the spot over which a band of workmen were now erecting a temporary mosque, to be presently replaced by a permanent tomb and receptacle for the devotions of the pious. Throughout the various ceremonies following upon the great man's end, Ben Hassan's had been the leading figure. Indeed, almost the whole of his time during those three days had been divided between attendance at the mosque and attendance at the grave-side. To be sure, this was no more than piety and tradition demanded of the son and heir of a Shareef; but there be many (though fewer far in mission-staked Morocco than in the lands the missionaries come from) who fall short of the demands made by piety, and, contrasting it with the hurried departure and scarce decent disregard of ceremony of Ben Hamet Arâf and his following, the Believers of Tangier were greatly impressed by Ben Hassan's demeanour and conduct, and yielded him tributes of allegiance, of sympathy, and respect upon the strength of it. Yet the young man had given never a thought to policy in the matter, but had simply followed the dictates of feeling and of his nature, the depths of which had been stirred by his meeting with and final parting from his father.

But now at length the practical significance of every-day life began to assert itself once more in Ben Hassan's mind; the meaning words of his trusted slave had fallen upon soil prepared to receive and profit by them; the young man was awakened from his absorption in the past to considerations of the present and the future.

" Friend," he said slowly, " I will not ask thee why thou hast not guided my thoughts in these days; but I would say, let us set about now the putting into order of our affairs."

" Ay, lord, I fear me we may not linger further. And —and I thank thee for not putting that question, lord; for, indeed, I know not how I could answer it. Mine is not a very easy or direct path in life betwixt——"

"Say no more, Friend. I was a witless clown to jibe at thee. Well, I know thou'rt truly Friend of me."

But for his generous interruption, Ben Hassan might have heard some interesting details regarding the difficulties which beset the path of his Friend, in whom two antithetical influences were for ever at war. But Ben Hassan, like most healthy young animals, was ruled mainly by feeling and instinct, and it may be that in friendship, which is not philosophy, trust is a higher thing than understanding.

"Well, now, Friend, what think ye of this talk of Cassim's?" asked the Shareef. "Ben Hamet Arâf hath departed, it seems. A man having great power and authority as counsellor, he was present and heard my father—upon whom may God send peace!—name me Shareef of Ain Araish. Bethink thee, Friend! He surely should have taken counsel with me as to his goings and comings. What means it all, think ye?"

"Lord, what thou hast said is most true, and I greatly fear me we have no friend in Ben Hamet. But if I pressed that point, men would tell thee that it was because I desired to stand in Ben Hamet's shoes. To be sure, lord, it might be that he simply fears to meet thee, well knowing that thou hast seen his lack of friendly duty and respect to thee in the past, and even here, before— before the end. And if that were so, the story of his visit to some shrine might well be true, as also his intention to return."

"Ah'm! And in any case, Friend, I think we do well to delay no further in setting out for my home in Ain Araish. A Shareef hath duties, look ye, friend—duties which I am little inclined to leave to a shareefa. And, beside——"

At this moment Cassim entered to them, his face full of news.

"Lord," he cried, "if Ben Hamet goeth to a shrine, he goeth as a great Shareef—no less. As Allah is merciful, he hath cleared the Shareef's fandak!"

"How? What mean ye, Cassim?"

"I mean, lord, that the following of the Shareef of Ain Araish here in Tangier is limited to those who are in this room, some half dozen of servants, and no more than a dozen animals. The man of fat hath stopped short of taking the great white horse of thy father, whom may God pity! but the most of his other horses are gone, every one of the pack-animals, save three or four, and well laden, and the whole of the slaves and soldiers to boot. Indeed, Ben Hamet goeth in state, thy banner before him, and thy holy seal in his pouch, no doubt."

"By Allah, this is to go from disrespect to robbery!" cried Ben Hassan.

"Is it true, lord, that he hath the seal?" asked the Friend anxiously.

"I make no doubt of it, Friend—I make no doubt of it. I have taken nothing."

"Then, lord——" began the Friend slowly.

"Ih-yeh, aïwá?" (Yes, what then?)

"Then thou'rt right, indeed, and we should be on the road to-morrow."

"Ay, verily. See to it, Cassim. Have all things prepared."

"As our lord sayeth—and may Allah prosper the going!" muttered Cassim, as he departed upon his affairs as m.koddem over a poor half dozen of men and beasts, who had looked to be directing many scores. It was the loss of dignity that wounded good Cassim. However, he soon brought about some stir and hum of activity in the

Shareef's fandak. The tail and mane of the late Shareef's favourite steed were presently being plaited in curling ribbons; the great gold and green breast-plate, which
men had always associated with the Shareef and his journeys, was made to gleam like crystal; guns were polished;
shwarries packed; slaves told off to this and that duty
in the little caravan; and all was made ready for immediate embarkation upon what is, after all, the main
business in the life of every great Arab chief—travel. It
went to Cassim's heart to find that the Shareef's great
green banner, with its gold-topped staff, and the burly
Ain Araish man who bore it, had actually accompanied
the astute Ben Hamet Arâf.

"As well travel as carriers or pedlars at once," reflected poor Cassim, "as without our lord's banner."

And so, with never a word to his betters, Cassim sallied
forth into the street behind the Legation of the French,
and, by the influence of bribery, set half a dozen men of
the needle to the task of preparing a new banner, to be
completed before sundown and nailed to a fitting staff.
During the next hour or so M.koddem Cassim might have
been seen visiting in a casual fashion each one of the city
mosques, its various little coffee-shops, and other centres
in which Believers are wont to congregate. In each little
circle thus honoured Cassim passed the time of day and
the peace of Allah, with a judiciously-planted hint as to
the plans of his lord of Ain Araish, and so home to the
great deserted house, with its crumbling, cream-coloured
outer walls and spacious, twilit cloisters, in which Ben
Hassan sat colloguing with his Friend, and wisely resting
by way of preparation for the road.

Long before the dawning of the next day Cassim was
tramping to and fro, with a candle stuck in a huge pewter
lanthorn having in it glass of many colours, in the vast,

shadowy fandak of the Shareef, where at this time but
a dozen beasts stood tethered in a space which had ere
this held two hundred. Cassim prodded the sleeping
grooms with a long stick, and presently the sounds of
munching issuing from one corner of the fandak indicated that horses and mules were being heartened for
their work by an unaccustomed feed of barley. One meal
a day, and that after sunset, was the rule in the Shareef's
as in most other Moorish fandaks.

By sun-up all was prepared, and his little caravan of
nine beasts and five men stood waiting in the courtyard
of the Shareef's house, under the watchful eye of M.kod-
dem Cassim. Then Ben Hassan, followed by his Friend,
walked out to the neighbouring mosque to seek a blessing
upon his journey. Meantime the streets near by were
slowly filling. Upon neighbouring roofs one saw lines of
huddled white figures, swathed and shapeless, and these,
by their shrill, persistent ululation, would presently pro-
claim themselves women interested in anything in the
nature of a function. " Yo, yo, yo, yo, yo!" they would
cry, that being their chosen and only method of giving
public expression to joy, sorrow, admiration, wrath, good
wishes, or defiance. A goodly number of holy men, some
carrying staffs or spears, were dotted here and there
among the throng, which now filled the street upon which
the door of the Shareef's courtyard opened. Some carried guns, and others, again, wore scarlet gun-covers
twisted about their foreheads, as though to indicate that
their ownership of guns was not improbable.

As Ben Hassan appeared with his Friend returning
from the mosque, pious ejaculations and deep-voiced
salutations filled the air. The young Shareef was a good
deal taken by surprise, the more so since of late men
had not been over eager to kiss the hem of his garments

as now they showed themselves to be. But early training
and habit had taught him to receive such tribute
graciously, and now he bestowed his blessing in right
shareefian fashion, and with all that unseeing blandness
which sits so well upon a dignitary of al-Islam.

Mounting within the courtyard the famous white
charger which had borne his father in every part of Al
Maghreb, the young Shareef rode slowly out into the
street, the snowy folds of his haiik turned well back upon
his fez and falling gracefully about the peaks of his
saddle, as arranged there, after mounting, by M.koddem
Cassim. Immediately behind his lord rode the Friend,
on a big grey horse of the Abda strain. Followed then,
with great dignity, and a banner-staff stuck in a leathern
bottle at his stirrup, M.koddem Cassim, in the shadow of
a new green flag of generous size. After him, in single
file, six pack-animals and five slaves, and they represented
the rear-guard of this most modest shareefian cortège.

But insignificant though the caravan was as to the
number of its members, its escort from the walls of
Tangier was of noteworthy strength, and showed considerable enthusiasm. In the Swaanee Valley, where this
following finally parted from the Shareef, there was a
deal of gunfiring, and among the gossips in Tangier that
day there was never a hint dropped showing any lack
of respect for Ben Hassan or want of recognition of his
true and proper succession to the Shareefate of Ain
Araish. All men were aware that any son of the late
Moulai Hassan's must needs be *a* Shareef, but no man
doubted for a moment that Ben Hassan, upon all counts,
was now *the* Shareef of Ain Araish, and, as such, the
most exalted saint in all the West. And so here, at all
events, in Northern Tangier, the curious white city which
is in, yet not wholly of, the land of the Setting Sun (by

reason of its proximity to Europe and its contamination by infidels) it was assumed that Ben Hassan el Gharbi had come into his kingdom.

And now, quitting hybrid Tangier, the young Shareef was entering upon the real Al Maghreb, home and stronghold of true Believers.

Chapter XXIV

PEACE UNDER THE OPEN SKY

OF the young Shareef Ben Hassan's journey to Ain Araish little need be said. It was naturally less in the way of vagabondage and wayfaring than had been his travels of the past two years, but it was exceedingly unlike the kind of progress through the country which Shareefs of Ain Araish had been wont to make. By the Friend's advice all important centres were avoided. Ben Hassan agreed that it would be unwise to court public attention to his little caravan whilst his position was still ill-defined and unsupported by material establishment.

"Let me be Shareef in Ain Araish before going among Believers as Shareef of Ain Araish," said he. And the Friend expressed cordial approval. Even Cassim, with his dark slave's blood and inborn love of display, felt the wisdom of this, and kept his new banner unobtrusively rolled and bound to a tent-pole in one of the shwarries.

"That was well enough to open their eyes with in Tanjáh," he told himself (and the contempt with which he even thought of the Christian-afflicted city's name was scathingly intolerant); but in Al Maghreb, among Believers, by Allah, the Shareef of Ain Araish may not parade like a common village f.keeh, with half a dozen followers, a flag, and a gourd for the coppers of the charitable. Nay, by the Prophet's true blood, but we of Ain Araish do not peddle!"

Ben Hassan's accession to the saintly rank of his dead father had not notably enriched the young man himself either in dignity or in the goods of this world. But with M.koddem Cassim the matter was far otherwise. His standing in life had absolutely changed, a fact which he had been at some pains to impress upon the thoughtless and reverence-lacking minds of sundry grooms and other persons of insignificant estate. Cassim's girth was increased by mere reflection upon his present dignity as M.koddem to the Shareef of Ain Araish, apart from the mundane fact that his meals were of more regular and sustaining character than they had been in the days of his comparative obscurity.

At sunset upon an evening which fell in early April, the little caravan was halted in that hollow among the hills which had sheltered its three principal members on the occasion of their first night of freedom from the dangerous rule of Shareefa Margaret. Ain Araish might have been reached that night, but:

" Methinks we seek light upon our affairs, Friend, and so had better enter fresh and by daylight to-morrow."

" Im sha'Allah ! " agreed the Friend devoutly.

Day by day he had postponed talk of this entry of theirs into the city where Shareefs had ruled as autocrats for centuries past, where by all the recognized laws and traditions of the country Ben Hassan should now be received as absolute lord and master. The Friend was perfectly aware of these things, and he was the loyal and devoted servant of his lord. But, withal, in the very bones of him he felt that Ben Hassan was not to be received as reigning Shareef in the city of his birth; he felt that the young man's mere presence in any capacity would be bitterly, and perhaps actively, resented by the shareefa, and that the formation of some definite policy for the young Shareef's guidance upon his return to Ain Araish was imperatively necessary. Yet day by day he had avoided mention of the subject, dreading Ben Hassan's reference to it, even as he dreaded the crucial event itself—their entry at the city.

Opposition to the powerful and ambitious woman who had now ruled Ain Araish for years meant to the Friend apostacy, the throwing up of the creed of his later life, the deliberate outraging of his fixed principles, which were in effect that, for the out-working of his own redemption, he must needs serve faithfully, support consistently, and protect at all hazards this English-born shareefa. As against this there strove in him the force of the companionship of years, his love of his lord, and his instinctive respect for purity of breeding and for racial integrity, an instinct more strongly developed in him than in the ordinary man of unmixed blood.

"There are two kinds of men," says the robust Britisher, "sportsmen and men who are not sportsmen." And the classification is less narrowly superficial than the casual observer of sedentary habit might suppose. Now, all that in Ben Hassan's Friend which represented the sportsman insistently demanded of him unwavering support of his lord. Again, even that same side of his character said: "Oppose, defeat, or injure in any way the English shareefa, knowing all that you do know—do this, and you place yourself beyond the pale, a pariah and despicable for all time, a creature irredeemable."

So being not another, but just the man he was, the Friend had postponed and again postponed the evil moment of discussion. But it had to be faced now, and their evening meal ended, and preparation for the night's rest completed, the Friend approached deviously the topic that held him in bondage.

"Ay, Friend," responded Ben Hassan encouragingly,
" we have to pass the gates to-morrow, quitting, I suppose, for good and all, privacy and—and our freedom of
the road, for the Shareef's place."

There was a ring of something that certainly was not
elation in the young man's voice. The note he struck
was one nearer to regret and sadness than to eagerness
or pride. It must be remembered that Ben Hassan was
no longer a lad. He had left youth finally behind him
on the day of his favourite hound's death by poison in
Ain Araish. The open road had taught him much, and,
among other things, had established fixedly in his mind
a loving trust in his Friend—a trust which was content
not to understand all, and which had finally removed
all desire to probe into the why and the wherefore
of certain restraining influences at work in Haj
Yûsef, whose devotion could not be doubted. In moments of impatience the young man might be led to
taunt his Friend somewhat in the matter of his attitude
toward the shareefa and her open enmity; but that attitude could no longer inspire distrust of his Friend's
loyalty in Ben Hassan's mind, nor yet a demand for
explanation.

"It is a part of him that is outside my understanding.
But what of that? The whole of him is my Friend," Ben
Hassan had told himself. And now he was by no means
blind to the reluctance with which his Friend approached
the subject of his entering into his kingdom. And, further, he was not without some sort of shrinking reluctance in the whole matter himself, having but little taste
for formalities and semi-official dignity, and loving above
all things his freedom and the unrestrained and adventurous life which gave him for seat his saddle and for roof
the open sky—as he said, in enlarging upon his preference:

"Es-samá, shemsi wa kamari" (The sky, sunny and moon-coloured).

"But fear not disappointment for me, Friend," the young man continued, as they lay wrapped in their travelling haiiks, and facing one another upon opposite sides of a tent which had sheltered the younger of them before ever Ain Araish had heard of its white shareefa. "I do not look to find the shareefa and her household on their knees without the gates to welcome me; I have a sharper eye for affairs than that."

"Ih-yeh, lord, that I know; but—but what do ye look to find?" asked the Friend.

"Well, sober truth to tell, Friend, I do not greatly care what things we may see or what dignities they assume for their part, so they leave us live in peace and plenty in one half the castle, and I am free to—to wed one, Friend, for whom methinks I've waited and wandered far enough."

"And ye would not seek in any way to belittle the shareefa and her son, or to interfere with their authority and standing in Ain Araish?"

"Now Allah forbid, good Friend! For why?"

"Nay, dear lord, I am but too glad to hear ye say it, and 'tis like thee. But not every young man hath equal freedom from malice."

"Oh, as to malice, Friend—pha! But, come to that, 'tis not every young man, look you, or any other young man, save just this most blessed one—to Allah the praise! —to be—to—how shall I say it?—to know Fatimah, O Friend of me!"

"And that is so, lord—that is so," said the Friend reflectively, "and being so, it doth insure peace and freedom from disappointment or ill-will to-morrow, or so it seemeth to my mind."

" It should do, Friend—assuredly it should do; and—and now are mine eyelids heavy upon my face, Friend. God make prosperous your evening.[1]

" And thine, lord, and thy morning blessed."

And so, each with his mind at rest (a state that one of them had known but little of late), the two turned snugly in their wraps and slept.

[1] The customary equivalent to the English " Good Night."

Chapter XXV

"MARHABBÂ BI-K-UM!" [1]

IN the very early dawning, when the hills were still mantled in mauve twilight, they rode away from the sheltered dell in which Ben Hassan had first tasted of real freedom. Leaving it, the young Shareef lingered a few paces in the rear of his little caravan, and gave way to an odd sentimental sort of sadness of parting, murmuring his farewell to the friendly hollow, as to the companion of his irresponsibility and his wayfaring.

"And so to claim that which I desire not," he murmured, " from those who do desire it, and—and not me." And then he lifted his great white horse into an ambling canter. "But also, by Allah's grace, I go to claim her whom my heart doth most thirstily desire, and whose little—little henna-coloured finger-tip is dearer far to me than all the rank and honours in wide Al Maghreb. So Allah smooth my path to her!"

"Our lord feels the Shareef's blood stirring in him this morning," quoth one slave to another, as the white charger curvetted past them to the fore-front of the little caravan. And presently, before dipping into the great Ain Araish valley (in the hollow of which their destination would be lost sight of again), the travellers drew rein simultaneously on the bend of a hill-track, and some murmured phrases left each man's lips as the crenulated walls, the vivid manarats, and the white roofs of Ain Araish

---

[1] " Welcome to thee!"

city came into clear view upon the plain, the birthplace of all save one of them, and the home and stronghold through many centuries of the forbears of their leader.

"Bism' Illah!"

"To Allah the praise!"

"We are come, by Allah's mercy!"

"Ain Araish, thanks be to the One!"

"By the Prophet! but there goeth one who loveth Ain Araish better than his horse!" cried M.koddem Cassim, pointing to the figure of a mounted man galloping at speed on the winding path beneath them, and in the direction of the city."

"Ih-yeh! Name of the One, what travelling! Ah, 'tis Ain Araish for fleet horses!" cried one of the followers.

Full five minutes later, when the flying horseman had raced across the valley into which the caravan now dipped, and was out of sight beyond it, Ben Hassan said thoughtfully:

"Now whence came that galloper, in Allah's name? No man hath passed us, and the hill hath no other road."

"Lord, it is the question I was but now putting to myself," replied the Friend gravely.

"And the answer, Friend?"

"Nay, I had not so far adventured, lord; but it may be that our coming hath been more thought upon than we fancy."

"And withal I like not the look of that."

"It hath not altogether a pleasant savour to me, lord."

Ben Hassan laughed, and the white charger's nose drew in to its chest.

"And so we are both croakers together," cried the Shareef. "Eh, eh! 'we are God's, and unto Him shall surely return.' But, taking it for all in all, 'tis less like a home-coming than a sally into the land of an enemy. Allah send my love to me, and a date-stone for the rest, say I!"

"The less my lord desires from Ain Araish the better am I pleased, and the more completely are we armoured against the assaults of unkind djinnoon," responded the friend sententiously.

"Ay, Fate cannot hurt me, Friend—in His name, and to Him the praise—saving only through one mortal, and the one is so sweet and fair that the harshest djinn that moves above or under the earth would feel his heart melt within him at sight of her."

"May Allah rule it so, lord! for all alike we are but as grains in the hollow of His hand."

"Bism' Illah! Ah! I see the gates, Friend."

Again there arose among the followers murmured ejaculations and pious calls upon sacred names; for now the little caravan had debouched upon the plateau outside Ain Araish, upon which powder-plays and other public ceremonies were performed, and from which the main gateway of the city and one side of the Shareef's great castle were clearly visible.

On rode the travellers at the measured, even gait which belongs to the ends of journeys on the road. Presently Cassim spoke:

"Lord, some hours have passed since the sun rose, and this is es-sbáh." (The morning, as distinguished from el fejer, the dawning; roughly, the hours between 8 A. M. and noon.)

"As thou sayest, O Cassim."

"Yet, if my eyes be not possessed of djinnoon, the gates of this thy Ain Araish are fast closed."

"And that is no more than I have been thinking, good m.koddem," replied the Shareef dubiously.

And then with a sudden shake of the head, as who should decline further dalliance in suspense, Ben Hassan spoke with bit and spur to the white charger, and broke into a swinging canter, followed closely by the other members of his party, and crying aloud: " Ohé, Ain Araish ! "

To the Moor, as to all Arabs, there is magic in a cry, whether used in war, in the chase, or in a mere access of high spirits. The blood stirring warmly in the veins of his followers answered swiftly to the Shareef's call, and from being a steadily marching little band of way-worn travellers the caravan was transformed in a moment of time into a quite dashing cavalcade, such as one meets and stands hurriedly aside for in narrow city streets when a young prince or a holy Shareef is returning from the bath or from an afternoon of dalliance in his favourite garden. Ben Hassan on his great white horse was the centre, his followers curvetted all round him upon hard-held, spur-fretted animals.

And so they drew near to the great gate which faces holy Mekka, with its twin watch-towers pierced by many narrow loopholes. Abdullah, the youngest member of Ben Hassan's guard, found himself unable any longer to restrain the ardour roused in all of them by the Shareef's cry. He was well mounted, and apart from that carried an aloe-head by way of spur. With a wild shout of " Ohé, Lord Ben Hassan, Allah's hand upon earth ! " he darted past his fellows at the gallop, bridle hanging, gun waving, haiik fluttering like a torn sail behind him, the peak of his crisp, black beard well-nigh in a line with his forehead with its fillet of camel-hair. So sped Abdullah, a gallant pursuivant, across the hoof-marked slope which separated his master from the gates.

And then the city's grim silence was ended; Ain Araish spoke. The welcome was short, sharp, and decisive, and having heard it Abdullah heard nothing else in this life; for he toppled forward over the scarlet fore-peak of his saddle with one thick cough of agony, and his Barb carried a dead Moor to the gates to announce the coming of the new Shareef, his master.

" By Allah and the Prophet, they have shot Abdullah dead!" cried M.koddem Cassim, as with one accord Ben Hassan's party reined in their beasts and drew together to a standstill.

A tell-tale film of white smoke still floated from a lower right-hand loophole of one of the great towers, while the echo of the report which announced Abdullah's start for Paradise yet rumbled faintly across the valley from the hills he had that morning scaled so blithely.

" This is welcome home in very sooth," muttered Ben Hassan, speaking between clenched teeth and with great bitterness. And then the Arab in him added: " By the blood of my fathers, that bone-faced dam of a bastard shall rue this day!"

The Friend of Ben Hassan shivered in his saddle at these words, his teeth closing on his lower lip till blood started there.

" Lord," he murmured, " forget not charity. Here be influences at work of which we know nothing. Dear lord, forget not our talk of last night. We want but the one thing here."

And at that, with a thought of the old sheikh's daughter, Ben Hassan's sombre face lightened, like a rainy sky riven by thunder to make way for sunshine.

" Ay, b'Allah!" he cried. " Thou'rt right as ever, Friend; we have little need of Ain Araish. But, natheless, we do not want to strew our bones before its gates. We must even sue as rebels for a parley, Friend. Send thou a herald to seek speech for me. Bid him go warily. Here, give him my selham to wave. Never heed its stains of travel; 'tis whiter than the hearts of them that sit within the tower yonder. O bloody-minded sheep—and driven by a Nazarene woman! Poor Abdullah's father hath his shop not thirty paces within the gates. Oh, shame! to fire upon a singing man seeking welcome!"

"Lord, we're to have patience, thou knowest, seeking but the one thing here," reminded the Friend.

And again his charm worked as oil upon the troubled sea of Ben Hassan's wrath. A herald was despatched afoot to the gates, waving the Shareef's selham, and charged to demand a parley for Ben Hassan and explanation of the strange and bloody reception with which he had been greeted. Meanwhile, that the Shareef might be seated and have some shelter from the sun, a small sleeping-tent was pitched over a couple of plain mats. So, denied entrance to the home of his fathers, Ben Hassan sat him down with his Friend on the plain without.

"Lord, they will not give Abd el Lateef entry"— the one-eyed man had been sent as herald—said a slave who, from his saddle, had followed eagerly the progress of the herald. "He stoops over fallen Abdullah, but—ah! he finds him dead. Nay, they will not give him entry at the gate."

"At least they give him speech, then?" questioned the Shareef.

"Ah! they have opened the wicket,[1] lord, and there cometh one from the city to speak with Abd 'Lateef. Nay,

---

[1] Doors in Morocco are, for the most part, very large and highly ornamental. Each flap (for they are invariably double) has within it a wicket or lesser gate for ordinary use.

they come this way. 'Tis a messenger sent to have speech with thee, lord, and he is clothed like a wazeer."[1]

" Ih-yeh," murmured the Shareef. " I doubt not there be many wazeers in Ain Araish, since a woman rules and no Shareef is there."

Upon his nearer approach the messenger was seen to be one Abd el Kareem, an officer of the castle who had stood high in the shareefa's favour even before Ben Hassan's departure from Ain Araish. This great man was ushered with due formality into the little travel-stained tent, where he looked about him in vain for a mat or seat in keeping with his quality. Upon entering, Abd el Kareem placed one hand upon his breast, and inclined his head very slightly (a salutation for equals) as he murmured : " Peace be upon ye."

" God's prophet, man ! see ye not the Shareef of Ain Araish ? " growled M.koddem Cassim, tugging at a silky fold of the messenger's fine-spun haiik.

" Our lord is in Ain Araish, slave," replied Abd el Kareem, in a tone which scarcely suited his name. (Abd el Kareem means Slave of the Generous, of the Deity, that is, here referred to by the name of one of His traditional attributes.)

" H'm ! we will not discuss that at present," interposed Ben Hassan with dignity. " Peace be upon—all true Believers who acknowledge Allah's saints upon earth. Ye may be seated, Abd el Kareem, for I would ask of thee what message is sent me from within my father's—may God show Him mercy !—gates yonder. Also I would ask the meaning of the shooting of an innocent man, who rode before me without thought of evil, a servant of the

[1] Rich men and those of high standing wear many garments, and these of many folds. Poor men wear few, and those of simple cut.

Shareef—of the Shareef, Abd el Kareem. Speak, then; let us hear thy message."

"O Ben Hassan, it——"

"Flesh of a dog! to whom speak ye?" snarled the attendant Cassim.

"Lord" had been Ben Hassan's title by right of immemorial usage from his birth.

"Silence, O Cassim; I await the message. And thou, Abd el Kareem, forget not altogether the teaching of thy youth. Art not addressing thine own kin, man."

Abashed, but very slightly, the messenger began again:

"Lord, my message concerns only thy coming to Ain Araish, and as regards the shooting of the slave, I know no more than thou, beyond that I am told he charged up to the gates of the sacred city, crying out that the Shareef of Ain Araish, whose blessed name we know as Moulai Mohammed, was some other person having another name. For that it was, I understood, some pious watcher shot him."

"H'm! And so the Shareef's name is Moulai Mohammed, is it?"

"Upon whom may Allah send peace!" Abd el Kareem bowed low, touching first his lips and then his forehead with the fingers of his right hand.

"May God shame liars before they be burnt!" murmured M.koddem Cassim, in a pleasant aside.

"Well, and well! 'We are God's, and unto Him we shall surely return.' He knoweth all things. And so let us hear thy message, O Abd el Kareem."

Ben Hassan bowed his head slightly in listening anticipation. The Friend looked the grateful satisfaction he felt regarding his lord's moderation and self-command.

"Lord, it is this: The holy Shareef and the wife of our dead lord (may God have mercy of his soul!) bid

me give greeting in their name to—to Sidi Ben Hassan,
and to say that there is one condition upon which he is
free to enter the sacred city. He must come afoot with
his followers, and he must kneel and swear his allegiance
to Sidi Moulai Mohammed, the lord's anointed and Shareef of Ain Araish, before passing the gates. Upon this
condition, and upon no other, need he look to enter in."

" To pigs, the spawn of pigs, and children of the illegitimate, the good God giveth no sense of shame," remarked M.koddem Cassim, conversationally addressing
the tent-pole.

Ben Hassan looked at his Friend, half gravely and with
half a smile. He was thinking of the daughter of Sheikh
Mohamet Tor, and wondering if in her place within the
walls she knew of his nearness. His half smile was born
of the reflection that to him all Ain Araish, the shareefate, and Al Maghreb itself, to boot, were less of
weight and import than this one maiden in her crumbling
old yellow-walled palace. His gravity arose from contemplation of the messenger before him, whose words, so
smoothly spoken, gave evidence of long and careful
scheming—successful scheming, the results of which
seemed fixed and accepted.

" Ye have heard, Friend: what say ye? " he asked.

" Lord, it is no more than I had thought to hear, after
—after the shooting."

" And thy counsel, Friend? "

" My counsel, lord, is ever for peace. The ways of
Allah's saints are ways of peace, and not of strife or
bitterness. Those who will not see must remain blind.
It is not the Shareef's part to force them into seeing. And,
lord "—the Friend lowered his voice and whispered now,
putting stress and meaning into each word—" The Shareef of Ain Araish may not wage war upon a woman."

" War, Friend ! Bethink thee ! We are six, or is it seven ? "

" Ay, lord, that is so; and in any case, what need have we of their city or their acknowledgments of thee as their Shareef? Allah knoweth all things. Al Maghreb is ours to wander and to live in. Peace and honour in thine own tent are preferable far to wrangling and intrigue in this thy city of Ain Araish. And again, lord, this place is not all Al Maghreb. In Nazarene-accursed Tangier thou'rt Shareef."

" Ay, or in Ed-dár el Kebeer, Friend; there in the house of my father (upon whom be peace!) is place for me and mine, methinks."

" That is true, lord; no better could be found—or desired."

" But, by Allah and the Prophet, Friend, I, too, have my one condition to make even as did the—these folk, yonder."

" And that, lord ? "

" Where is thy memory, Friend ? Think ye I would leave them "—the Shareef whispered low behind his hand —" the pearl of Ain Araish ? "

The Friend nodded, but the look of anxiety on his face deepened somewhat as he answered:

" I had not forgot, lord; but—but even in this, lord, we have a need of patience."

" Ih-yeh, thou'rt ever on the wise side, Friend; but methinks no man could say of us that we were puffed up or over-assertive of our rights and rank."

And now Ben Hassan turned, with the vigour of decision, to the messenger.

" Now, heed ye well, Abd el Kareem," said he, " and see ye bear my words aright to them that sent ye; for I would not have ye burned a second time, nor yet saddle your mistress with fresh invention."

The messenger scowled. To a Believer, freeborn, "mistress" is not a pleasant-sounding word.

"Never scowl at that, man," laughed Ben Hassan. "By the Faith, ye must look to pay something for the office that swells thy girth and gives thee these soft and flowing garments of thine. Why, man, ye were glad to hold my stirrup for me many a score of times, ere ever my head reached the height o' thy girdle."

"Say on, lord, and I will bear thy words truly," said Abd el Kareem, now for the first time lowering his head in something akin to real shame.

"It is well, O Abd el Kareem; keep thou thy heart still in the same place, whichsoever way thy cloak is turned."

Without a word the messenger bowed his head, and, touching Ben Hassan's worn haiik with one hand, raised the fingers thereof to his lips then.

"There!" said Ben Hassan, as one speaking indulgently to a child. "The true Shareef's blessing go with thee, and—we will say naught as whether 'tis mine or Moulai Mohammed's."

"There is a new follower for ye, and if ye will, lord," whispered the Friend.

And this was no more than the truth, and an instance, too, of the sway exercised by the personality of Ben Hassan.

"Nay," quoth he, and smiled in answer to his Friend, "there must be no converting done under the flag of truce and parley; and, withal, this Shareef of Ain Araish hath not where to lay his own head, leave alone that of highly-placed officers in his following. But leave me to send my message." He turned again to Abd el Kareem. "And so, good Abd el Kareem, thou'lt go straightway to them that sent ye and say that I, Ben Hassan, Shareef of Ain Araish, so named upon his death-bed in the presence of holy men, and of Ben Hamet Arâf, by my father —may God have pardoned him and received him into bliss!—that I kneel to no man, but only to Allah; that I make no vows, denials, or acknowledgments, save of the Faith; that I will go quietly hence, and bide in peace far from this my birthplace, vexing no he *or she* in Ain Araish, and making no claims whatsoever—upon one condition. Mark ye, the absolute condition, O Abd el Kareem! It is that Lalla Fatimah, the daughter of the Sheikh Mohamet Tor, be sent to me, with a suitable following, that we be wedded in due course, and as soon as may be. That is my message."

"Lord," said Abd el Kareem, speaking now with all deference and respect, "I will bear thy message faithfully, but thou knowest the sheikh is not here, but in his garden in the city of Ed-dár el Kebeer, where some learned conference is being held, and—and——"

"Ay, and?"

"And, lord, the talk of the city hath been that the wife of our dead lord (may God have pardoned him!) doth purpose wedding the Shareef—wedding her son to——"

"Heed ye not that, good, man," quoth Ben Hassan; "heed ye that not at all. Men, and especially women, will talk, and look ye: 'El abd iámmel wa er Rabb ikimmel.' "[1] The Shareef grasped his knees with both hands, and his voice rang loud and clear as he added: "One God, man, do ye know that if the woman so dared to do, I, Ben Hassan, my father's son, would bury her beneath

---

[1] The slave (mortal) designs, and God completes.

the ruins of the castle she holds from me yonder? Her son—by Allah's Prophet, man—take thought upon it! Her son—God strengthen his poor limbs!—marry Fatimah!"

"Lord, I but told thee of the gossip. Thou knowest that what the shareefa sayeth is law in Ain Araish; ay, and death the penalty for breaking that law. Thou'st asked me nought as to the establishment of her son, but——"

"Ih-yeh, I had forgot; tell us of that, good Abd el Kareem."

"Well, lord, ye must know that our lord Moulai Mohammed was, in a vision, appointed to succeed as Shareef."

"In a vision sayest thou? But the One! And I, O Abd el Kareem, in the flesh, by touch and voice."

"Lord, what could we know of that? And then, too, how knew our lord of the death of his father—may God have pardoned him!—five days before the counsellor, Ben Hamet Aráf, arrived here with the tidings?"

"Have I thy leave to put a question, lord?" interposed M.koddem Cassim. The Shareef nodded, and turning to the Ain Araish messenger: "Have ye seen aught of Mansûr Marrakshi, the slave?" he asked.

"May God have pity upon him, he is dead!" was the reply.

"Dead is he? God pardon him! When saw ye him?"

"Well, thou seest it was this way: Mansûr took ill months since now, when with our lord, the late Shareef—may God have pardoned him!—In Fás. So he never reached Tanjáh, but returned here from Fás direct. I myself saw him in the castle, on the very night of our lord Moulai Mohammed's miraculous vision, it was. But before morning Mansûr's sickness laid hold of him again, and within the day he was buried. May God pardon him and me! I mind me now that few gave heed to the poor fellow's death, being too full of the news of our lord's vision of the other greater death in Tanjáh there."

"Lord," whispered Cassim to Ben Hassan, " Mansûr stood without when thy father—God give him peace!—lay a-dying in Tangier. He was sent off, hot-foot, to Ain Araish with the tidings, as I told thee, and—and now thou hast heard of the reward of his speediness. Truly, lord, the shareefa hath a ready way with her in life and death."

The Shareef nodded gravely.

"And that same vision, lord," continued Abd el Kareem, " 'twas a most wondrous thing, and did fix firmly in the minds of all beholders our lord Moulai Mohammed's right of succession. It fell on the evening of Jumûah,[1] when the whole castle, free men and slaves, sups, as thou knowest, in the great hall. Our lord had touched the cous-coosou, when of a sudden a cry left him, and he rose to his feet, stretching forth both hands as one who would assist another, his eyes fixed and staring, yet seeming to see nought near at hand, but only much, as it were, beyond mortal sight.

" ' Ya waili!' he cried aloud, ' God sends me a vision. Behold I see, as through a mist, my father lying sick and in a far place. 'Tis in Tanjáh, the infidel-afflicted. My father, the Shareef, is dying; holy men are gathered about him. My step-brother, Ben Hassan, maketh unseemly noises in the chamber, and struggleth with the medicine men to reach my father. Hush! hush! our lord, my father, speaketh! Hear him! " O holy men," he saith, " hear thou my dying words. There is but one God, one

---

[1] Literally, congregation; actually Friday, the chief day for congregation in the mosques, the Sabbath of ab Islam.

Faith, one Prophet; there is but one Shareef of Ain Araish, and he is from this day my son, Moulai Mohammed, now in my castle of Ain Araish." He moveth his head wearily, for Ben Hassan curseth aloud and maketh riot in the chamber. " Thou hast disgraced me," sayest the Shareef, "and thou shalt know no peace, neither a home to shelter thee, or rank by which men can know thee. There is but one Shareef of Ain Araish, and he is in Ain Araish, my son, Moulai Mohammed, with the holy shareefa, his mother." Ah!' cries our lord, ' the end cometh, the end cometh! He dies! Allah be merciful unto him, my father hath passed, and I, his son, am Shareef!' And with that," concluded Abd el Kareem, " he fell forward upon his cushions, and lay like one dead for the more part of an hour. At length they brought him round, and by morning not a man in Ain Araish but had cried his name aloud, the new Shareef."

"And then poor Mansûr—may God have pardoned him!—having served his turn, was silenced for ever in the grave," quoth Ben Hassan slowly. " Truly we are here in deep waters. Natheless, good Abd el Kareem, we will send our message to these seers of visions and—and their teacher, and do thou thyself bring me hither the answer. May God guard thy ways, for thou hast dealings there in the castle with one possessed of Shaïtán!"

And so the messenger departed from that little tent, and walked slowly back to the city gates, leaving set, grave faces behind him.

Chapter XXVI

" B'ÍS-SALÁMAH ! "[1]

WHILE the half of an hour passed silence ruled in Ben Hassan's little tent, its occupants gazing occasionally at one another, but for the more part of the time at the ground before their knees.

"Ih-yeh, great is God," murmured the Friend, thus breaking this thoughtful silence; "and His wisdom hath spoken in thee this day, O lord."

"To Him the praise!" came Ben Hassan's inevitable response to this unwonted commendation. The Friend was little given to flattery. "And what think ye of it all, Friend—of the state of this our Ain Araish?"

"Lord, I think it is no wholesome place for thee, though thou'rt its Shareef."

"My very thought, Friend—mine own thought to a hair. I tell thee, Friend, that once I have won that which thou knowest I must win from Ain Araish, I desire not to set eyes upon its walls again while they shelter those that rule there now. Liefer would I live and end my days upon the road, liefer would I herd sheep upon the plains, than bide in state in the shadow cast by that woman's scheming."

"Ay, thou'rt right; we are far better away. But let us not judge her, the shareefa, lord, since of the workings of her mind we know nothing. Gossip may have maligned her; the event may yet prove her only misguided, and

[1] "Go in peace!"

246

not at all one harbouring designedly evil intentions against thee."

"Ah'm! There is but one God, the Judge of all mankind."

"Ay, verily."

And again they lapsed into thoughtful silence, while without, the sun, now riding high in a sky of flawless azure, poured out its gift of dazzling light and pervading heat over all the country's face, searching out crevices and worn spots alike in the traveller's flimsy shelter and in the ancient crenellated walls and roofs of lichen-covered Ain Araish.

Presently a slave who stood among the animals of the little caravan cried out:

"Lord, the gates open. There cometh out ten sheep and two laden mules, driven by two herd-boys. And one walketh behind them in rich garments, but it is not Abd el Kareem, lord."

"The witch-woman!" muttered M.koddem Cassim; "she hath read in the face of Abd el Kareem some understanding of her wickedness and some knowledge of the true Shareef, our lord Ben Hassan."

"It would seem, then, that my condition finds favour in her eyes, Friend, if these sheep be for us. Without a doubt 'tis a cheap price to pay for the shareefate of Ain Araish—a pair of mules and half a score of sheep. But we must bide our time. Gifts can in nowise alter my condition. Here is no litter or any women attendants. By Allah, but 'tis Absalaam Eraishi, the m.koddem of the castle! The shareefa must have great gifts if she hath given Absalaam belief in her fable of visions and the like. Absalaam knew my father—may God give him peace!— from his birth on, and me he taught to hold a gun ere ever the white shareefa came out of the Nazarene land.

Ih-yeh, times change indeed, but—'we are God's, and unto Him shall surely return.' "

There was no doubt but that the men of weight in Ain Araish, like their inferiors, had one and all accepted the evidence of Moulai Mohammed's vision. M.koddem Absalaam, whose negroid blood made his flat face to glisten in the sun like coal, approached the little tent which sheltered Ben Hassan with a mien of even greater hauteur and condescension than had been shown by Abd el Kareem before contact with the young Shareef's winning personality had softened that worthy's pride and shaken his convictions. From time immemorial the men of Ain Araish, like the most of their fellows south of Fez, had been guided in all the important issues of life by the decisions of holy men and students of Al-Koran, and by the heaven-sent wisdom of such as were blessed by Allah with visions. Shareefa Margaret had not spent years in Ain Araish without learning that the visionary utterances of even the least notable of hermits or f.keehs carried greater weight for good or evil than could any proclamation emanating from the shadow of the Parasol itself.

" Peace be upon all true Believers! " began the second messenger from Ain Araish solemnly, and as soon as his massive bulk cast its shadow athwart the fly of Ben Hassan's little tent. " Our lord Moulai Mohammed of Ain Araish and the holy shareefa are pleased to send words of gracious greeting unto Ben Hassan by the mouth of their slave Absalaam Eraishi——"

" Whose shadow hath swollen greatly since last he bore the slippers of Hassan, son of Moulai Hassan, the greatest of Shareefs, upon whose soul be the peace of Allah! Ih-yeh, come thee within, man; be seated; count thy gracious greetings all said, and let us straightway to the meat o' thy message."

Ben Hassan had laughed aloud, but not a muscle moved
in the ebon face of Absalaam. The m.koddem had his
dignity to consider, you see; a man of ponderous weight,
actual and metaphorical, and, it may be by reason of the
blood in him, a firmer believer in the magic of second
sight and visionary wisdom than was Abd el Kareem.

"My message is soon told," said he, still standing,
though scant of breath and greatly heated by his walk in
the noonday sun. "It is that thy wisdom is applauded
in seeking no entry here, that prosperity is wished thee
upon the road, that here be sheep and two mules laden
with wheat for thy better support on thy journey, and
that the daughter——"

"Yes, yes; be not so grudging o' thy speech, man!
What of the Sheikh's daughter?"

"This: that she cannot be sent thee, even though such
a course were fitting"—this addition was entirely Absalaam's own; his payment for what he deemed the slight
put upon his dignity by Ben Hassan—"by token that
she journeyed out of Ain Araish many days since with
the Sheikh, her father, to a house that he hath in Ed-dár
el Kebeer."

"Allah's Prophet!" cried Ben Hassan, turning to his
Friend. "And so, had we entered Ed-dár instead of
skirting it in our modesty—false pride!—we had been
saved a many miles of travel and—and the life of a faithful servant, b'Allah!"

"Lord, what has been was to be. Methinks thou'd
have journeyed to this thy birthplace none the less."

"Ah! It may be, Friend, it may be. In any case,
water spilled is spilt. We be whole men yet—the praise
to Allah!—and for us there's but one road, one bourne—
Ed-dár el Kebeer. But concerning these sheep, Friend,

and the rest, we will let them return whence they came. What say ye?"

"I would say nay to that, lord, and for two reasons: Sheep have no quarrel with any man, but do nourish and clothe his body, and for that purpose are gifts from Allah. That is one reason. Another is that nothing may be gained by returning insult for words of civil greeting and proffer of needed food. The sheep and the mules and all that cometh from the castle is thine, lord. We have a need of these things; wherefore spurn them, then?"

"Right; thou'rt right as ever, Friend. Then hark ye, O Absalaam of the growing shadow. Take my greeting to the shareefa, and tell her I go to my bride at Ed-dár el Kebeer; that I thank her for her thought of my welfare, for sending these sheep from the flocks of my father —may God have pardoned him!—and for the good wheat from out the granaries of my castle of Ain Araish, and that I say peace be upon—all true Believers! Bism 'Illah! Peace go with ye, and may thy girth continue to swell in all prosperity, O Absalaam!"

"I have no need of thy wishes," growled the m.koddem, turning in wrath to depart.

"Natheless, take them, and civilly, O Absalaam. Why, man, would'st have us think thee ashamed o' thy prospering girth? To be sure, there would be twice as much of thee to be beaten as there was that day, thou mindest, when my father caught thee handing out the loaves of sugar to—— Eh-yeh, now who'd have thought so great a vessel could prove so nimble? Ha! Good go with thee. Art far less a rascal than some o' thy betters, at the worst o' thee!"

But by this time the m.koddem, who had swept indignantly out of the tent, was striding along the sun-baked track toward the city gates, followed respectfully and at some distance by the half-naked lads, whose little drove of sheep and mules stood nozzling the earth now among the animals of Ben Hassan's caravan.

Chapter XXVII

IS IT PEACE?

IN their return journey along the road they had travelled to Ain Araish, the Shareef and his following
spared themselves and their beasts by making short
and easy stages and frequent rests; for, as his Friend
pointed out to Ben Hassan:

"If the Sheikh hath already despatched his business
and left Ed-dár el Kebeer, then needs must we meet or
hear of him by the way; and if, as is likely, he bides
still in his Ed-dár garden, we gain nothing and lose flesh
by haste."

So the little flock of sheep was driven behind them,
dwindling day by day in size, for usage and inclination
both demanded that whoever came within sight of the
evening camp should be offered a share in that day's
meat; and the wheat-laden mules grew daily fresher instead of more weary, as their shwarries were lightened
of wheat, ground for the Shareef's cous-coosou by the
women of wayside douars. Thus exactly, and not otherwise, journeyed the children of Israel two thousand years
earlier; and the garments worn and implements used by
those who ministered nightly to the needs of Ben Hassan
and his party were, as were their manners, habitations,
mode of life, and customs, precisely those of Abraham's
day to be seen here, as perhaps in no other corner of
the earth, and certainly not in Palestine, absolutely untouched by the passing of ages, by the influences of what

we call civilization, or by the events which have made
and unmade empires in the North and West. Exactly
who and what these people are, or whence they sprang,
we do not know. What we do know is that they were
there where they now are before the Roman Empire
existed. Conquering, they made a garden of palaces of
Spain. Conquered, they returned to their own land, their
daily life unruffled by the thunderous and epoch-marking
crises of European history. Words of theirs we find in
every European tongue. Peculiar ornaments in use
among them have been dug out of ruins in Ireland. In-
stitutions peculiar to them have lived and died out in
the Scottish Highlands. As they are to-day, they were
in the hey-day of a people whose end is obscured by the
mists of antiquity—the Phœnicians.

Even Ben Hassan, a by no means cold-blooded lover in
quest of his mistress, was, by daily contact with these
simple, prehistoric tent-dwellers, soothed into something
like aloofness or indifference to the passing of time and the
affairs of his life. The coming of daylight ended the
night's repose and fast, with prayer and a modest meal of
bread or dates and milk. Then came the burdening of
beasts, farewells to the hosts of the night, the exchange
of simple blessings and good wishes, and brief remarks
bearing upon earth, and sky, and air, and animals. And
then on, at a gentle, even pace, along the wide, winding
road of hoof-marks which linked one century with another
—to-day with the day before a thousand years ago. Hour
succeeded hour, till the downright strength of the sun's
rays told of the approach of noon, and then, in some dried
river-bed, beneath the thin shade of an argan-tree, or
beside a clump of giant aloes, the travellers would halt,
dismount, tether the fetlocks of their beasts, and, after a
few mouthfuls of some such elementary foods as milk and

wheat, or honey and fruit, or butter and eggs, with prayer, ablution, and a pull at the long-necked water-jar, they would stretch them in their folded haiiks upon the earth, and sleep till ed-dhohr, the time of the end of all mid-day prayers, or maybe until el âsár, the middle of the afternoon. But, whatever the period (there was no machine in that country to mete out the hours for them), they would arise, giving the praise and thanks to Allah, loose their horses, and proceed, until the sun behind them—they rode east and by north—nearing the bed of its decline, bade them also seek and choose their resting-place for the hours of darkness, the hours in which wandering djinnoon, or spirits of the air, are most active.

So the days slipped past them as they leisurely ate up the miles betwixt far Ain Araish and fabled, fountain-decked, scholarly Fás. And with the manarats of that Western Mekka glittering under his lee, Ben Hassan began to apply the spur, and to speak of a need he had of speed in their journeying to reach Ed-dár el Kebeer and the walls which sheltered his bride to be. So they left Fás, shining among its water-courses, a mile and more upon their right, while they pressed on toward Ed-dár, never dreaming that Sheikh Mahomet Tor was at that moment close to them, browsing genially upon musty folios in the vast cellars of the Karûeen Library. But he was, however, and the fact and its significance to our travellers was finely emblematic of the nomad life, of the exigencies and amenities of an age and society remote indeed from those of Christendom, though to be reached by a few days' journeying from the centres of Christendom.

Four days of more business-like travelling brought the Shareef and his following to the southern gates of Ed-dár el Kebeer, where, within five minutes, they learned of the departure for Fás, two weeks earlier, of Sheikh Mohamet Tor!"

"Body o' the Prophet, why slept we not in Fás?" cried Ben Hassan.

And then they dismounted for a night's rest before retracing their steps as far as the university city.

"Was all well with the Sheikh's house?" Ben Hassan inquired, as he sat that evening with the Basha of Ed-dár. (Any more direct inquiry, where a Believer's women-kind were concerned, had been indelicate.)

"Nay, lord, I know not," replied the Basha. "I believe the Sheikh travelled alone but for half a dozen men slaves."

Here was news of a chilling sort, yet not altogether the shock it might at first appear. "The Sheikh was never a man to trumpet his affairs in the ears of men," thought Ben Hassan. "Doubtless he left Fatimah quietly with her women in Fás whilst conducting his business here, and has returned there to join her. Well, and well, Fás is, after all, the pearl of cities—fit setting, by Allah, in which to find my pearl of damsels, my star among the gazelle-eyed beauties of the earth! Bism, Allah! In four little days, core of my heart's core—in four little days and nights Ben Hassan's sky shall be lighted gloriously by thy radiance."

And with this thought in his mind, Ben Hassan gave his followers but one night's rest in Ed-dár el Kebeer before taking to the road once more with Fás for his destination. Exactly how or where his Friend passed this "within-gates" night, as the slaves called it, Ben Hassan never knew. He did not think to seek enlightenment on the point, and, indeed, with the exception of holy Haj Cassim, the hermit of the city gate, it is doubtful if any man in all Ed-dár could have supplied such information.

And the hermit was not given to gossip. One thing the young Shareef did notice in connection with the first night he had spent within walls for several months now, and that was that it seemed to have exerted a very depressing influence upon his Friend. He rallied the Friend upon this point as they rode out from the city together in the morning.

" Nay, lord, Allah forbid that I should incline thee to the 'gloomy side o' the way,' but yet, lord—yet would I have thee to remember that the writings in the book of Destiny are never for long of the one colour. Allah hath ruled that the flesh of us should be purged by many falls in this world, and so——"

" And so, thou wouldst say, O grave and reverend Friend, that for us a long period of unbroken good fortune is in store, by token of our present not very princely estate, and our ill-luck in passing Fás when it sheltered my pearl, and our recent rebuffs in our own Ain Araish. Ih-yeh! art altogether in the right of it, Friend. But let us laugh and sing, therefore, rather than make our faces to cast shadows tall as trees upon the earth."

" Nay, lord, that was not at all my meaning. And if I saddened thee with a long face——"

" Be not perturbed, O Friend of me. It were indeed a great calamity that could sadden Ben Hassan upon this journey."

" But, lord, in despite the little ills that thou hast named, our fortune hath in truth been smooth and kindly enough of late. I look for certain disappointments in our future, and I would have thee prepared to face them calmly, strongly, as a Shareef should, and so to rob them of the better part o' their sting. That is all, lord."

" And enough, O grave, most trusty Raven, to set half

Al Maghreb a-croaking, and if 'twould listen to thee. Since when hath Ben Hassan forgot how to face the rough with the smooth? Was thy lord such a weakling, then, in all the months he journeyed with thee afoot? Art a little disturbed in thy stomach, Friend, that is all. I tell thee the world hath this morning a most rosy hue to a healthy eye. Ohé! My pearl's in Fás, where I'll be in three little days; and all's well wi' all Believers, under Allah's mercy—to Him the praise!"

"Ay, lord."

"Ay, Friend. Not but what I love thee, thou grave counsellor. Mistake me not, in Allah's name! Well I know the goodly meaning of all thy words, true Friend. But—the time of grass is on the earth, Heaven glitters through the sky—see else—and I go to the star and pearl of all that be women, Friend, and so my heart's a bird for soaring this day."

"Ih-yeh, God send it may be ever so, lord!" said the Friend, sighing over a grave smile, and adding then in a murmur that carried no farther than his beard: "And send we may find the Haj in the wrong of it, for, by Allah, no man may play peace and honesty against enmity and treachery for ever."

Now, being in just that frame of mind in which the departure from out Ed-dár found him, it will be understood that Ben Hassan by no means favoured easy stages on the road to Fás, and as his followers loved him to a man, and were as well posted in his affairs as he was himself, there were neither grumblings among them at the rate of travel nor vexatious delays to be faced, such as serve to madden at times the benighted Nazarene who ventures to take to the road in Sunset Land. No mules were lamed, no tent-pegs were forgot, no half-bound shwarries slid to earth and demanded new packing when Ben Hassan's little caravan set out by break of day. And being well and efficiently guarded from these mishaps of travel, it fell out that the young Shareef and his men came ambling briskly along the great northern wall of Fás early on the morning of their third day out from Ed-dár el Kebeer.

Ben Hassan's great white charger bore him nobly, and for his part the young man, riding upon air, felt in the bones of him that no ill hap could possibly creep between the world, its rosy fairness, and his nobility. So one hand upon the pommel of his dagger, and his thoughts in Paradise, rode Ben Hassan, Shareef of Ain Araish.

"Lord, lord, is not that the old grey horse of the Sheikh of Ain Araish? Look yonder, lord—led by a slave from the three tents there."

The speaker was M.koddem Cassim, and his eye for a horse was keen, as the event proved when, cantering up to the man who led the Barb in question, the Shareef's party found that it was indeed the Sheikh's.

"Whose be these tents, then, M.Barak?" asked Ben Hassan of the slave, whom he recognized.

"Sure, they are my master's, the Sheikh's, lord."

"Ah, then the women in attendance on the Sheikh's house are within the city, then?"

"Lord, I know nought of such matters," quoth the man slowly, a heavy-minded, flat-faced mountainéer. "My master brought us here from Ed-dár el Kebeer near twenty days since now, and we camped here without the walls, as he said, for the one night. My master had a book to look to, or some such learned mystery, in the Karûeen yonder. One night he said, and here we have lain these twenty days, and by the Faith, lord, if we drew him not nightly from his mysteries to the tent here, methinks my master would quit earth for Paradise for sheer lack o' food. But I am but a slave, lord, knowing nothing of these learned matters. God knoweth all things, and——"

" Ay, ay, as thou sayest. But tell me, man, where left the Sheikh his house and the women servants?"

" By the Prophet, lord, God pity me, but in Ain Araish, lord! Where else?"

" Allah grant me patience! When ye left Ain Araish, man, with the Sheikh and his following, who and how many were ye upon the road? Forget nothing, now!"

" Lord, be not angered against an unlearned man. These State affairs of noble men do 'wilder me most cruelly, and——"

" How many of ye were there?"

" Lord, there was me, and there was the Sheikh, and——"

" One God above, how many were ye?"

" Lord, there were ten and four of us; that is, lord, there were seven mules—the two that were heaviest laden no man rode—and the Sheikh's horse here, the Father of Fleet——"

" Yes, yes; never mind the beast's name, man. Get on, in God's name!"

" Well, lord, the Father of Fleet—pardon thy slave, lord; I did forget that thou hast said name not the horse, and in my——"

" Holy Prophet, what reckless speed in speech! what lightning flashes of wit, and—— Get on!"

" As thou sayest, lord. The horse, whose name thou knowest, made eight. Then the Sheikh, lord—may Allah prosper him!—made nine."

" Yes, yes."

"Well, and then lord, there were four and one [1]—all power is Allah's!—of us who be slaves—Fatah, Mansûr, Bellal, and——"

"Ih-yeh, God spare thee, I want no more o' thy slaves' names.[2] There were none among ye, or before or behind ye, or in any mortal sense belonging to ye, that were women?"

"Nay, lord, not to say women, for our master is aged, and we that be——"

"And the Sheikh, thy master, is now in the Karûeen?"

"If Allah wills it, lord, as thou sayest, the Sheikh is——"

"Peace go with ye! There are not years enough in one life to wait listening to thee, good man. Follow me ye that be of Ben Hassan's train."

And the white charger snorted under a jag of the spur, such as he had not felt for many a day, as Ben Hassan turned and galloped at speed toward the city gate, followed closely by his Friend, and at some distance by his men with the animals. Laden beasts and men that idled in the roadway had to bestir themselves to make way as Ben Hassan thundered past them on his way into Fás. An *iman* of the principal mosque in Tangier, riding quietly on an aged mule, looked up into the young man's face as he flew past and recognized the Shareef of Ain Araish, whose blessing by his dying father in Tangier had been witnessed by this holy man. The *iman* promptly gave the word to his neighbour. It flew from mouth to mouth in the mysterious fashion which men who know not the

[1] No man cares to name more directly the numeral thus indicated, unless he be fey; of all things it is the most unlucky, and even after mention of "four and one" it is rightly thought wise to interpose a prayer.

[2] In Morocco there is set apart a collection of names for bestowal upon all born in slavery.

East cannot realize, and it reached the streets of Fás before Ben Hassan did, in despite of the pace at which he rode.

"Ohé, Lord Ben Hassan! Way there, way, for the holy Shareef of Ain Araish!" shouted the beggars and idling students in the narrow street of the Karûeen, as, clattering past them over the slippery cobbles, Ben Hassan drew rein at length among the mouldering cloisters of one of the most ancient, and quite the most democratic and conservative, of all the homes of learning in the world.

The Shareef had no time to spare for contemplation of the hoary beauty of the three hundred and sixty square pillars of stone or the eight-and-twenty of marble among which he stood. (Those travellers mistake who speak of this collection of pillars as being all of marble and round.) During full eight centuries men of his race had frequented these vast cloisters, but upon quests quite other than that which gave Ben Hassan his eagerness. Six hundred years before students from as far afield as England had eagerly entered these shadowy courts in pursuit of the astronomical and other lore which gave to the Karûeen its world-wide repute for scholarship and learning. To-day Ben Hassan raised noisy echoes among the crumbling remains of all this magnificence in pursuit, not of wisdom, but, on the contrary, of a woman, of one whose name, but for the difference of a letter, was that of the wonder widow of Tunis, who, close upon a thousand years before Fatimah was born, founded the Karûeen.

A student in rags, who had many times stayed hunger at his table, sprang to the stirrup of Ben Hassan's horse, and, not without a hurried touch of his lips to the hem of the Shareefian garments, gave the desired information as to exact whereabouts in that murky labyrinth of arches, cells, and courts of Sheikh Mohamet Tor.

Three minutes later, a fold of his haiik streaming loose behind him, the Shareef came face to face with white, grave Sheikh Mohamet Tor, whose horn-set spectacles and over-hanging white eyebrows gave him a look of greater age and learning than were really his.

"Shareef, is it peace?" cried the old man, surprised into the stirring, questioning salutation which had belonged to the more active life of his early years.

"It is peace—upon thee the peace, Sheikh!" replied Ben Hassan, in tones by no means suggestive of placidity. "I pray ye, Sheikh, to attribute no churlish or evil intent to me if I do thrust an intimate question upon thee. I come hot-foot from Ed-dár el Kebeer, whither I was sent from Ain Araish, where they told me that the Sheikh, *with his house*—the companion of my childhood, Sheikh —was staying. Other men this day have told me other tales. Sheikh—ye may well pardon the son of my father; may God have pardoned him!—where, then is thy daughter?"

"By Allah and his Prophet, but I know no more than the stones at thy feet if she be not in the apartments of the wife of thy father—may God have pardoned him!— in whose loving care I left her by the shareefa's own request."

"Then, by the soul of my father, in Allah's merciful keeping, here is lying and treachery of the vilest, O Sheikh Mohamet!"

Chapter XXVIII

EL SULTÁN ET-TOLBAH

THE Moorish character being essentially and typically Oriental, it must needs be difficult for those unacquainted with the Eastern mind to realize clearly the bizarre effects which are at times produced by that basic combination of impassive phlegm and impassioned emotionality that is at the root of the Moorish temperament. The writer has seen a Moor seated under a tree blinking at the sunshine, crooning idly to himself, indifferent to the flies which swarmed about him, indifferent to all things, a veritable figure of fatalistic impassivity, of what you will that is imperturbable and placid. A wandering f.keeh of the mendicant order strolling that way gave vent, carelessly enough, to a cry, in which one caught the name of a great saint, a famous leader among the Faithful, long since dead and revered almost as a part of God. In one instant the somnolent figure of the lounger beneath the tree (a shoe-maker by trade, and by ordinary a common-place, sensible man enough) flashed into a picture of religious frenzy, of mad, fanatical excitement. His arms swung about him like the sails of a windmill, sweat and tears rained from his twitching face, his forehead smote stone as he flung himself upon the earth in stuttering, breathless adoration, and he tore the djellab from over his own head to bestow it upon the passing saint, who, nothing loth to profit by the storm he had raised, tucked the garment under his arm,

murmured a cheerful blessing, and went his ways chuck-
ling and praising God in the one breath. He left behind
him a man not merely bereft of his principal article of
attire, but physically, emotionally, and mentally prostrate,
who two minutes earlier had been a vegetable for placidity.

Would you know the explanation offered, and offered
casually, as though it were a sufficing reason? It was
said that a remote ancestor of the prostrated one had been
miraculously cured of a palsy by touching the djellab
hem of the saint whose name the mendicant had cried
aloud.

Now, while Ben Hassan, the legitimate Shareef of Ain
Araish, conversed in one of the vaults of the Karûeen
library with the Sheikh of Ain Araish (who, though as
scholar a man of peace, was yet a Moor of the Moors,
orthodox as any he of all the 'ulama [1] in Morocco, and
no lover of the Nazarene-born woman who for so long
now had queened it in Ain Araish), two things occurred
above them in the sunshine which, whilst not calculated
to have produced much stir in a European crowd, were
very rich in potential significance here in the Mekka of
the West.

M.koddem Cassim, bursting with indignation, had told
the story of his master's vain quest in Ed-dár and Fás
to Haj Abd er Rahman, the Tangier *iman* who had recognized Ben Hassan and had witnessed his deathbed appointment as Shareef. Haj Abd er Rahman had told all
this to Selam Ribati, the *Sultán et-Tolbah,* in his learned
majesty's camp on the river bank, below the gardens of
that other Sultan who ruled Morocco from beneath the
shareefian Parasol. And this involves another explanation.

---

[1] The learned, a class apart, and one deeply respected by all
others.

You must know that when in the middle of the seventeenth century the Lord's anointed, Moulai Rasheed II., was fighting hard for his throne, he found himself opposed by—of all creatures in the world of Islam—a Hûdi, who ruled in the stronghold of Táza. Now the scribes, or tolbah, of Táza, being gifted of Allah with learning, recognized the crying unfitness of this condition of affairs, rushed the kasbah of the ambitious Israelite, and slew him under his own fig-tree. In return for this yeoman service, Moulai Rasheed II. (may God have pardoned him!), and his shareefian successors to this day have permitted the students of Fás to choose each year a sultan of their own, who for one week may rule absolutely in the great camp which the Karûeen students and other men of the city form at the end of every grass-season on the banks of the river below the royal palace. Fines, free-will offerings (demanded at your door by young bloods who are ill to refuse), and the annual gifts of the occupant of the throne, provide the materials for a week of riotous feasting, throughout which the Sultán et-Tolbah's rule is really absolute—a benevolent despotism.[1]

This feast, Nozhat et-Tolbah, was drawing to its close when Imam Haj Abd er Rahman arrived at the riverside camp on his sorrel mule with the news of the presence in the Karûeen of the rightful Shareef of Ain Araish, then engaged on a fool's errand at the bidding of an infidel-born white woman, who had closed against him the gates of his own Ain Araish, in which she set up as Shareef her half-breed son, Moulai Mohammed.

---

[1] Nor is this the limit of the student sultan's privileges. The real Sultan of the Empire visits him during his brief reign, takes counsel with him upon matters of State, and grants him any one favour which he may ask. This one request generally involves the release of some prisoner, or the remitting of some tax, and has never yet been refused, whatever form it takes.

Like other bigots in other and more highly-civilized lands, the Moors are given to transgress here and there the spirit and the letter of their own codes; yet upon the whole it would not be easy to point out any people on earth more conservatively and consistently devoted to the principle of racial exclusiveness. And because of this they have endured, and endure, as an independent people in an age and in circumstances which make that endurance remarkable, and probably unique.

Among the assembled tolbah there were few who could not claim personal knowledge of Ben Hassan. Many there loved him. Some were there who had lived almost entirely upon his bounty (genuine charity this, for the young Shareef had not been lavishly supplied with funds) during the years he had devoted to learning in the university city. Here, clad in absolutely nothing beyond the one heavy djellab which came to them each year from the stores of the venerable foundation under whose shelter they studied, were hard-working students from every corner of Al Maghreb—youths who would become notaries, kadi's clerks,[1] official scribes, and the like, and who, beyond the price of their key at the Karûeen, had started out upon their academic career possessed of nothing in the world save a mudd of home-made cous-coosou and a bag of dried meat. Between the hours of study these hardy scholars groomed the mules and kept the accounts of traders for a living, finding that the one good loaf a day which the Karûeen m.koddem thrust into their cells

[1] All official positions, such as those of the kadis, bashas, kaids, and so forth, are purchased from the Government, and go almost invariably to the military class, members of which are never educated. Hence the Kadi, reverend seigneur though he may be, is obliged to employ an educated clerk to accomplish his reading and writing withal.

was not sufficient to keep their wiry young bodies in working order.

There, again, swathed voluminously in the most costly sort of garments, were the student sons of great sheikhs and wealthy merchants from the South (even from the Niger delta)—men who had paid as much as two hundred dollars for their keys in such favoured quarters as el-Attarin, who brought with them slaves and followers of every sort, married wives in Fás (to be divorced before student days were ended, and to be married again, and yet again, to successors of their first lords—a feature of the Karûeen life these bejewelled wives of successive generations of gilded youth, and an instance of Moorish fidelity to the letter at least of their moral codes), and lived in princely style, with but few thoughts to spare for learning—in books, at all events.

Shoulder to shoulder with such exquisites stood almost naked, and wholly unclean, probationers in the saintly craft—men who would neither wash, shave, nor change their garments for many years, who would harden their heads to withstand blows from an axe, their bodies to exist almost without nutriment and altogether without covering, and who, after a season spent in retirement or beside a gate or wall, would take up their abodes in a cave or beneath a tree, and be supported for the remainder of their days by villagers whom they chose to bless and honour by their proximity.

Not one man was there in the whole great throng— some nine hundred actual students, with at least two thousand men of learning and hangers-on to Learning's skirts, and several hundred unprofessional civilians—who would not at any time have run a mile to kiss the stirrup of the Shareef of Ain Araish, in whosoever's person that sacred office might be invested.

And to these came Imam Haj Abd er Rahman, with his tale of Ben Hassan, towards the riotous wind-up of the week's feasting, when the Sultán et-Tolbah's autocratic reign of a week was within measurable minutes of its end.

His Majesty the Sultán et-Tolbah bestowed a lingering glance upon the interior of his royal tent. His reign would be ended at sunset, and then his loyal courtiers of the present would, by all the laws of tradition, be free to trounce him and strip him of all the goods he had gathered about him during his little day of kingship if they were able. Certain valuables must be removed to a place of safety. He whispered directions to a favourite wazeer. And then, standing erect, one hand upon the shoulder of Abd er Rahman, the bearer of news, Sultan Selam shouted over the heads of his courtiers, as few save Moors and the mountaineers of the East can shout:

"God is great! great is God! There is but one God! But great also are God's chosen saints—His chosen upon earth! Great are the holy Shareefs—blood of our Lord, Mohammed, the Prophet of God!"

The many-throated roar which rose from that river-bank, started by the tolbah of the court, who had listened to Haj Abd er Rahman's story, and taken from them by ring after ring of excited men, even to the groups of casual idlers who sunned themselves beside the city walls, was an astounding, almost awe-inspiring example of the emotional receptivity and instant amenability to leadership, whatever the cause, which characterize the true Moor. When that great and pious shout—the wonderful jehad note which Arabs have been ready since the Hejira both to sound and to answer—died away among the hills encircling Fás, there was not a grown man within a radius of at least a mile who did not know the words which had inspired it. Within the minute men had also the information which had given rise to those words.[1]

" Ih-yeh, God is most great, and there is no other god but God," resumed the Sultán et-Tolbah, who now mounted upon the birda of a mule, the better to command and reach his audience. " And because there is no other than the great God His saints are great and holy. Only a fatherless dog, or an infidel begot of swine, could put an affront upon the holiest and greatest of the Shareefs, son of twice two thousand sons of the seed of our Lord Mohammed."

Again the hills echoed to a mighty roar of applause and adherence.

" Sons of Fás, hear me! The Nazarene woman who won to sanctity by wedding our Lord Moulai Hassan el Gharbi (may God have pardoned him!) hath so affronted our lord Moulai Ben Hassan, the present Shareef of Ain Araish. She hath shut him out from his own city, that the son of her womb might reign in his stead. She hath, by lying and treachery, sent him hither on an endless errand—Moulai Ben Hassan, who lived and learned and gave alms among us. He is even now among the pillars, there in our holy Karûeen."

Another earth-rocking shout boomed forth over Fás.

" True Believers, are we dogs and fatherless? Are we Jews, thus to be spat upon in the person of the holiest

[1] " Your London country with its devil-worked wires across the sky has lost, if it ever possessed, all knowledge of the thought-willed communication and the flame-like, mouth-to-mouth carriage of news which told us of ' The Seven Men ' and also good Senûsiyah of the Jerbûb in the desert behind Tripoli, and other believers the world over, all the details of your losses in South Africa. Ay, before your Shaïtán wires told you even the names of the battles " (*Extract from a letter written by a scribe in Marrakesh*).—A. J. D.

among us, whose feet-paring at the bath are of more worth, b'Allah, than all the infidels of the outlands, soul and body!"

Again the shout; hoarser now, and many times more threatening and purportful than before.

"O men of the Faith, am I yet a little longer your Sultán et-Tolbah?"

"Ih-yeh!"

Such an affirmative had satisfied an earless mute; it would have conveyed meaning to a mummy.

"Then hark ye, O men of the Karûeen, O students, O learned ones, O Believers, all and every one, follow ye me! Come to the Karûeen! Come to our Lord of Ain Araish!"

And lowering himself astride the patient beast whose pack had served him for platform, the Sultan of a week jerked at the creature's bit—"Ree! Ree! Arrahzee!"— and started at a fast amble for the Karûeen, escorted and cheered to the echo by every man in his feasted and highly-wrought following.

Chapter XXIX

"WILL YE FOLLOW ME TO AIN ARAISH?"

THE dramatic instinct, though not consciously responded to, is seldom lacking and generally powerful in the Moor. In Selam Ribati, at the head of three thousand followers, the instinct for effect had been fostered by a week's play at kingship. And so, as he headed his army into the Attarin, he despatched an advance runner with whispered instructions to the Karûeen.

"'Seek ye the Shareef, and bid him to the eastern doors of the mosque from within. Say friends await him in a matter of great import."

And then the Sultán et-Tolbah caused his mule to stumble and to sidle fractiously into food-laden shop covers. Thus he filled time, awaiting his cue. Simple Selam! Two years before, three parts naked, he had tended herds on a hill to the southward of Rabat. Evidently, then, the f.keehs of the Karûeen had taught something to this disciple of theirs.

"Lord, we are well met, by Allah's choosing! To God the praise! Behold those who will right thee—thy servants, lord. Ohé, Lord Moulai Ben Hassan, holy Shareef of Ain Araish! Great is God, and holy are the saints of God!"

Thus, at the last pitch of his great voice, thundered Selam Ribati (as one who had never hoped for so convenient a meeting) when, in the one moment of time,

Ben Hassan, followed by Sheikh Mohamet Tor and the Shareef's Friend, appeared at the great eastern doors of the greatest mosque in all Africa, and the Sultán et-Tolbah, his huge train well at heel, drew up his mule in the cobbled roadway facing that marvellous entrance. One may say marvellous. Of every stone and tile used scrupulously careful record has been kept. Every penny expended upon it was blessed and drawn from sacred sources. No infidel ever polluted that holy threshold since the day (more than eleven hundred years ago) upon which its first stones were laid. The vast copper doors, gloriously chased and fretted, open upon courts as spotlessly holy in their way to the world of Islam as the very Ka'abah; in truth a noble, an inspiring background for what was in a sense Ben Hassan's first public appearance as Shareef.

But it seemed he was not to be allowed to speak. Selam the Ribati had accomplished his self-appointed task to some purpose; his last act as Sultan was worthy the traditions of the exalted post. Wave after wave of sound echoed and re-echoed through the Attarin and along every arched and crannied thoroughfare in Fás. Unseen women jodelled shrilly from the house-tops. The throats of swart men fresh from remote mountain-sides were strained to bursting in the acclamation of Ben Hassan's name and holy station. Even exquisite Fásis, white and dainty as the women of their languid delight, raised their heads among gossamer folds of silken kseeyah,[1] and cried aloud their tribute to the one God's greatest saint upon earth.

Ben Hassan's Friend, plucking at his lord's djellab-sleeve, strove to make himself audible, not to the crowd, but to Ben Hassan. In vain he strove. The young man caught stray hints—"moderation," "no rash step,"

[1] The gauze-like outer garment of the aristocracy.

"nothing you will afterwards regret," "violent measures are ill measures," and the like—but he heard not much, and he was in no mood to hear that little to his profit if it contained counsel of further meekness. "The blood of the Shareef was a fire in him," as his men said. The roar of the great throng before him, the turbulent sea of white-hooded heads, the sense of power and leadership, pride of birth and rank, wrath that he should have been thwarted and out-witted in the dearest desire of his heart, all combined to thrill and inspire to action the man he was, and to justify the remark that his men passed upon him: "The blood of the Shareef was a fire in his veins!" And, indeed, even in the Friend's eyes, it did appear that the proper limits of meek endurance had been passed. The treachery which Sheikh Mohamet Tor's explanation had exposed was something not to be borne humbly and passively by any free man, to make no mention of shareefs of Ain Araish.

At length the rolling breakers of sound receded and dwindled somewhat; one began to follow their construction; the sequence, the rise and fall of distinct waves could be noted. Then the waves subsided into here and there a ripple, easily over-ridden. Ben Hassan's right hand was stretched in shareefian benediction. His eyes were alight from the exhilarating strength within, of his first draught of tangible, ostensible power. Never had saint a finer audience; seldom had saint a more strikingly handsome presence, or a richer, more decorative frame and background withal. The people knew him, and as to his powers, imagination and traditional teaching proved these to be greater far than any actual knowledge could have shown them. His sacred rank, the blood in him, had earned their pious devotion in any circumstances. His present appearance before them in the sanctified doorway of the Karûeen as one wronged, affronted, ousted, and by the woman of hated infidel origin, this made of the feasted tolbah his eager slaves, and of every man in Fás his loyal adherent.

"O children of the Karûeen!" he cried, and to be sure a most partial djinn must have placed the words in his mouth, for they were as honey and hachsheesh to the people, touching as they did upon the base of his most intimate and personal hold upon his hearers. "O learned tolbah! O men of Fás, accept ye the loving blessing of the Shareef of Ain Araish!"

"To Allah the praise; His saints are very holy!"

There were many such grateful ejaculations to assure Ben Hassan that his blessing was appreciated.

"O men of Fás, it doth appear that ye are informed as to the nature of the fool's errand that brought me among ye this day."

"We are here to do thy bidding and to right the wrong done," cried Sultan Selam er-Ribati, and a roar from the crowd at his back endorsed the tilmid's words.

The Shareef's eyes flashed out his thanks and his pride.

"But, O my friends, our Ain Araish is a far cry from the Karûeen, rough and long the road is."

"We are no sucklings or Nazarenes to fear the roughness of the road, O Lord. 'Twill serve us in place of the summer pilgrimage.[1] The most of us have guns, and all of us have hands, and, by our Lord Mohammed, father of all Shareefs, we will open thy Ain Araish gates for

---

[1] It is the custom of some of the professors of the Karûeen to go upon summer pilgrimages with their pupils, to whom ready hospitality is accorded by the peasantry through whose villages they pass, in return for a nightly sermon from the learned leader. In no other country in the world, perhaps, is more respect paid to learning than in unlearned Morocco.

thee—ay, and win thy way to thy bride for thee, though all the West stood in the way!"

Selam was the speaker, but the crowd punctuated his every sentence with its thousand-voiced approval.

"Ah, friends, I see ye know the way my mind sets," said the Shareef. "Well, I need not deny it. I do but desire that my forbears before me desired.[1] We—we were playmates together as children. I journeyed here hot-foot, content to relinquish my rights at Ain Araish, and, behold——"

"Lead on; lead us there, Lord! By Allah, but the Ain Araish usurpers cannot defy the tolbah!"

"But, O friends, many of ye are students here, and I would not that ye should lose——"

"Our summer pilgrimage, lord. Thou canst not deny thine old comrades, lord."

"Nay, that would I never; but neither would I wrong any one among ye by a grain of cous-coosou, and so I must tell ye that, Shareef of Ain Araish or no, I am now as poor as any wight among ye, lacking all things save——"

"The holy blood of a thousand Shareefs in thy veins, lord. We want no pay. Some of us have money, and will help those who have none. Have no fear for thy army, lord. The cause is Lord Mohammed's own—in Him our trust. 'Tis a jehad, lord. Ohé! The holy war of our Lord Moulai Ben Hassan of Ain Araish! Ohé! Great is God, and holy are His chosen saints!"

"O men of Fás, I cannot pit my will against thine, for, by my father—may God give him peace!—'tis all with thee where my heart is! Only I would say, for the sake

[1] This was an historical fact, and no mere figure of speech. For many generations the Shareefs of Ain Araish had taken wives from the families of the sheikhs of Ain Araish.

of the love ye show me, let not any poor student's greater hardship be upon my conscience. Do those among ye who have fixed tasks to perform serve me by remaining here, and so earn my gratitude for a goodwill as kindly as any deed. For the rest, if those among ye who have guns, horses, a little food, and the time to afford, will follow me to Ain Araish, and there help me to—to teach certain lessons, and to win—to win my quest, why, friends, the Shareef of Ain Araish will never show himself an ingrate, and—there is bread and meat for all comers if I am master in my father's castle—may God have pardoned him!—and so to you I would say, Will ye follow me to Ain Araish?"

From mouth to mouth the question passed, and along the road the answer swept, an ever-increasing volume of sound and assurance. There was no room for doubt, and could not have been in the mind of the most dubious.

"Then, O friends of me, I ask ye to send a dozen of your leaders to talk with me in the great court of the Karûeen, and to-morrow, by God's mercy, with the passing of night and the first coming of day, we ride out from Fás for Ain Araish, and God prosper the journey!"

"Allah isahhel tareek-kum! Fí ámán I'llah! Allah iwassal-ek alá khaìr!"[1]

And that was the end of Shareef Ben Hassan's speech to the men of Fás, spoken upon the glorious and holy threshold of the Karûeen mosque, and treasured to-day in the minds of the faithful of Fás as warmly as it was listened to and applauded in the making.

Within the hour eleven of the most prominent members of the great crowd which had blocked el-Attarin sat with Ben Hassan, his Friend, and M.koddem Cassim in one of

[1] "May God make thy way easy! May ye go in the safe keeping of Allah! May God cause thee to arrive in safety!"

the inner halls of the Karûeen sipping tea and discussing
the order of the morrow's journey.

Later in the evening, when the meeting of leaders had
dispersed, when Ben Hassan slept after his excitement,
and in preparation for his out-setting, when M.koddem
Cassim and many hundreds of other Believers were looking carefully to girths and stirrups, horses' feet and pack-
lines, the Friend of Ben Hassan, wrapped closely in his
travelling haiik, arose from the niche beside the city gates
in which he had been crouched with a hermit, or " pivot "
(kot'b), as Moors say, new-landed from the city of Ed-
dár el Kebeer.

" And so may Allah have thee ever in His closest
keeping, old friend and master. Rest thou assured that
in all these matters thy disciple will do thy bidding
loyally, and with gratitude for thy wise counsel, the which
hath guided him in all the years since that night of clear
moonlight and great weariness which brought him first
to thy mat. May good be with thee! Peace!"

" B'ís-salámah!" (Go in peace!), quoth the holy man.
" And may ye have come to your good fortune! May
God take thee through! Peace!"

And then the favoured counsellor and friend of the
greatest Shareef in Sunset Land departed from the
beggar's seat, his white-swathed figure melting away
among the shadows of the narrow, overarched street.

Presently he stopped before a low, old door of olive-
wood, studded over with great bolts and nails, and having
above its lock a pendant ring, a bangle for an elephant,
by way of knocker. This was in a poor quarter of the
city.

A patter of bare feet on the flags within, and the shrill
voice of a slave-girl crying through the keyhole, " Who's
there?" came in answer to the Friend's knock.

" The companion of Haj Cassim of Ed-dár el Kebeer
would speak with Abd el Kader er-rakkas." [1]

Again the pattering of naked feet, and then the slip-
slap of a man's heelless shoes, as the master of the house,
crying " Make way! make way!" so that his one wife
might be warned of the approach of a male visitor, paid
tribute to his guest by himself flinging wide the cumbrous
door, with words of welcome on his lips, and " All that is
in this house is thine!"

" Nay, O Abd el Kader, 'tis more than thy house: 'tis
thyself I come seeking this night," said the Friend, as
the door closed, and they walked along the sharply-turn-
ing little passage, past the wooden tray, on which shoes
were left behind, and so by a narrow stair from the court
to the guest-chamber opening upon the gallery above.
The one doorway passed by them was completely covered
by its hanging sheet, for again the courier had cried
" Make way!" as his guest mounted the little paved stair-
case, and the wife of Abd el Kader was no ill-bred gossip
such as are those who draw aside curtain edges and show
a peering eye to the incoming visitor.

Seated upon the bed, in the place of honour facing the
doorway, the Friend made haste over the customary inquiries and salutations, and begged his host to excuse
him from taking refreshment and for proceeding
without complimentary dalliance to the matter he had
in mind.

" Sidi, thou knowest that I am as the slave of thy right
hand. My debt to thee is not one to be easily discharged,
but Abd el Kader is ever ready to attempt a moiety
thereof."

" I take no account of debts, O Abd el Kader; but now
I have a favour to ask of thee, as one true man of another,

[1] The courier.

to go a journey and carry a paper for me. Can ye so far serve me?"

"Sidi, such a task is no greater to me than the task of sleeping or eating. To that was I born. See else the runner's leg, Sidi, and eke the seared toe of him that hath often slept by the wayside." [1]

And, indeed, a very casual glance at the man sufficed to assure one that he belonged to that order of Moors whose members are born to run, whose long, loping strides eat up the miles by night and day, outstripping easily the traveller who journeys a-horseback or by mule.

"Good! Take thou this paper, then, O Abd el Kader, and with it this money." The Friend handed two packets to his host, both bearing upon their covers Nazarene names writ in the curious backwards way of the infidel. "Thou knowest the station of the devil-wires in Christian-afflicted Tanjáh?"

"I know it well, Sidi, and have carried letters there to be flashed under the seas by the devil-machines of the Nazarenes to London country."

"As thou sayest; and that, O Abd el Kader, is the destination of this letter. But its purpose, a very urgent one, concerns the welfare of true Believers, and is a matter to which a good Muslim may with confidence put his hand."

"Sidi, it is enough for Abd el Kader that thy hand hath touched it. What thy left hand hath rested upon it is an honour for my right hand to touch.[2] When would ye, Sidi, that I should depart?"

[1] The courier who travels on urgent affairs rests but seldom by the way, and then with a cord steeped in saltpetre attached to his great toe, and lighted; a sort of slow-match alarum well calculated to rouse the very weariest wight who uses it.

[2] Among Believers the left hand is reserved for all menial and ignoble tasks, the right for salutation, and for use in prayer and in eating.

"If it could be before morning, O Abd el Kader, I——"

" Sidi, I asked only that I might know if time were left for me to bid my house farewell. Within the hour I start, in any case."

" I thank thee, true man," said the Friend, rising from his seat of honour. " And so I will leave thee to the ordering of thy house."

And as, after many parting blessings and good wishes, the Friend thridded his way from the rakkas' doors, along murky alleys to the house beside the Karûeen in which his lord slept, he muttered:

" God willing, they should be on their way out from England within a week, and then Tanjáh should prove sanctuary. May it be so. 'Tis but my bare duty to make it so—Bism 'Illah!"

Chapter XXX

"COME TO PARDON!"

"MAKE morning, and to God be the praise! Make morning, and to God be the praise! Make morning, and to God be the praise!"[1]
When these last familiar words of the muedhdhin's summons from the pinnacle of the Karûeen manarat informed Believers that, to him at all events, a faint streak of light was visible in the East, men were stirring by the light of many coloured lanthorns, in every fandak in Fás. But some few of them, for that matter, had been astir all night and many women, after a long evening at the grinding-stones, had devoted the night watches to the preparation of scores of bushels of cous-coosou.

Before broad daylight came Ben Hassan with his Friend, Sheikh Mohamet Tor, and a dozen or more of the principal members of his new following were standing erect, outstretched hands to their ears, in prayer before the most sacred shrine of Moulai Idrees, the holy founder of the kingdom in whose capital they were. But an even more impressive sight was the morning praying of the great concourse which had already assembled without the gates. Thousands of men and thousands of animals were

---

[1] This concluding phrase in the morning call to prayer is not known in the East, and is peculiar to Morocco. According to Mr. Budgett Meakin (see " The Moors," p. 268) it was added by Abd el Mûm-in, the Mumahhadi, in 1150, and though sternly forbidden a century later, has been held to ever since.

there, many for the purpose of making the journey to Ain Araish, and others to wish God-speed to the travellers.

As the lower rim of the sun cleared the horizon a shout, rising along the walls, turned the eyes of all men toward the city gate. There, seated upon his great white charger, and surrounded by his chiefs and advisers, was Moulai Ben Hassan, Shareef of Ain Araish, his right hand extended in benediction, the raised arm disclosing a strip of pale green kaftan beneath the snowy whiteness of his haiik, the breast-plate of his horse ablaze with green and gold in the sun's very eye, his own eyes alight with pride and gladness; the whole picture, framed by the great fretted Moorish arch of the gateway, one to strike into the most casual observer's mind, and there remain, when common sights and common happenings had been forgotten.

Slowly the Shareef marched his charger along the irregular line of waiting men and horse outside the walls. Hundreds succeeded in kissing his horse, his stirrup, or his draperies; thousands made their endeavour, and so were doubtless included in the scope of his blessing. Fás women, exposing each no more than the half of one eye, lined the walls and hailed the lordly young Shareef with shrill, strange ululation. At length the head of his mile-long caravan was reached, and Ben Hassan turned his horse to pronounce again the shareefian benediction upon his following, and to invoke a blessing upon the journey before them.

This he did in dead silence, his outstretched hand giving the signal to the great throng. And then, wheeling the white horse once again, the Shareef faced toward their destination, and a mighty shout of farewell and blessing arose from the walls and gates of Fás.

So the journey was begun, and when the first camping-place was reached that evening, it was found that no less than two thousand men and five thousand animals were contained in this great caravan. Their tents formed a considerable settlement. Their fires and cooking-braziers lit up the calm night for miles around them. And from every village, and from every tiny wayside douar, recruits —possessed in some cases of little beyond a waist-cloth, and in other cases of long, scarlet-covered guns, raw-boned steeds, and laden pack-mares—flocked to the green standard of the Shareef of Ain Araish.

One of Ben Hassan's lieutenants, Abd el Ghani, the son of a great Kaid in the Atlas, was himself at the head of eighteen slaves, twelve hired men, a score of mules and ten horses. For these—and five-and-twenty guns and good store of food and ammunition the young man was personally responsible. Indirectly, he and a few other wealthy students of the Karûeen were responsible for the attendance and up-keep of one-half the great following. These youths maintained harems and a princely style of living in Fás, yet, personal and pious devotion to a shareefian mission aside, they had hailed with delight this adventurous departure from the smooth gaieties of their student life.

The happenings of the journey were numerous past all count, as is ever the case in journeys upon the road, and deeply interesting—to those concerned, and at the time. Indeed, the present recorder has been sufficiently absorbed by story-tellers' accounts of them in more than one marketplace. But that was when the events described were but a few months old, and there is a limit to the patience of Christian readers, and it is one that is not hard to overstep. Suffice it, then, to say that there were no ill happenings of any serious note, and that, so ready was the tribute paid by the tent-dwellers of the south-west to the cause of the Shareef that, not only were the Fás supplies of food practically preserved intact throughout the journey, but the animals of the caravan put on flesh as they travelled and the muster of men who rode and drove them rose to close upon four thousand strong by the morning of the day preceding that of arrival at Ain Araish.

And on that morning the Shareef overtook a traveller who upon inspection, proved to be no less a personage than Abd el Kareem, the officer of the castle who had brought word to Ben Hassan's tent from the shareefa. Now the Khulafá and advisers of the Shareef's following, including even the gentle-minded Sheikh Mohamet Tor, would have had him take Abd el Kareem in his train, perforce as prisoner, or as pressed man. But Ben Hassan, knowing his man, ordered otherwise.

" Nay, I will coerce no man," said he. " Serve thou thine own master. He who rides alone rides quickly ; and ye, Abd el Kareem, must have slept in the saddle to have allowed us to overtake thee. Spur on then, my friend, and do thou to me as I to thee. Tell no man in Ain Araish of our coming. What say ye ? "

" Lord, give me thy leave," began Abd el Kareem, " and my gun is at thy——"

" Nay, ride thou on, friend, to Ain Araish, and, arrived there, keep thine eyes open and thy tongue still. B'íssalámah ! "

So Abd el Kareem went on his way, and was soon out of sight ahead of the Shareef.

" Our lord is too generous to be wise," quoth the lieutenants.

But the Shareef's own personal following, under M.koddem Cassim, held their peace, believing as they did that wisdom and the Shareef's decision upon a given point were synonymous.

Within ten miles of Ain Araish the Shareef came in sight, here and there, of a mounted man. They faded out of sight more quickly, as inferior insects flee before the locusts at top speed.

"It seems our Ain Araish is well guarded. News travels faster than men; we are to be welcomed," said Ben Hassan. And his lieutenants, hitching up the dagger-cords about their shoulders, smiled as sportsmen who draw near their quarry.

Within an hour of noon the great caravan (an army now keening action like hounds about a covert) halted, and broke bread, and looked to arms, in the hollow of the valley two miles from the gates of Ain Araish. Here all pack-animals were left in charge of such men as were without guns, a hard, wiry, fearless band from the smaller wayside douars. The rest of the army, horse and foot, advanced now in battle array, primed for bloody war, upon the gates of Ain Araish.

On they went, the Shareef at their head, his personal body-guard about him—on and on to within five hundred yards of the gates. Then for a moment they halted. The hoary walls and gates of the city gleaming before them in noonday sunshine had spoken from a hundred mouths, and every spoken word was a bullet. And yet not one bullet reached its mark by a good hundred yards. Shareefa Margaret had failed as a general in one particular, even as her sex are apt to fail as hostesses in the matter of wine; she had purchased no European built guns, and well it was for the Shareef and his following that she had not.

Ben Hassan took hurried counsel among his chiefs, and as a result thereof the whole of his mounted men drew forward in loose, spreading formation, sheltering the foot-men and awaiting orders.

"Great is God!" shouted the Shareef, pressing spurs to his charger.

"And holy are His chosen saints!" roared the Khulafá, giving rein to their Barbs.

And with that the whole line of two thousand mounted men swept forward at the gallop, some with guns, but most with swords waving, whilst behind them a line of footmen advanced, waiting the given word to drop to their knees and fire, for of these everyone carried a gun, and most a gun of European make.

There was no generalship, no knowledge of tactics displayed, and when the line of horsemen, scarred and broken here and there by the home-made bullets of Ain Araish, drew under the shadow of the lichen-covered walls, they had not among them so much as a ladder, or any other means of effecting an entrance.

"Open in the name of Allah and the true Shareef of Ain——" cried Abd el Ghani, smiting with the pommel of his sword upon the iron-studded great doors. And then he fell, choking in his own blood, taken fairly in the throat by a jagged slug fired from twenty paces distant by a marksman in the right-hand gate tower.

"In blood shall ye pay for that, by Allah and His holy Prophet!" swore the Shareef. "Follow me, men!" he shouted, wheeling his charger and galloping back by the road of the advance. As the horsemen passed their comrades afoot the latter poured in a careful volley from weapons of some precision, and whenever a head had shown above the parapets or a gun-barrel at a loop-hole there was now blood to staunch within the walls.

"We have made one mistake—a bad one," said the Shareef, when he took counsel with his leaders out of gunshot, "and now we will set that right."

Blood had been spilt. Men's eyes rolled. They were

by with considerations of policy now. The men behind
those slug-filled guns in Ain Araish had got to die. Two
scaling ladders were produced, fifty men were told off to
construct roughly some other ladders, fifty more set out
to fell and fetch a young tree on the valley's far side.
This was to be used as a battering-ram.

"Lord," said Abd el Ghani's seventeen-year-old brother,
Abd el Malik, "have I thy leave to speak?"

The words were meek enough, but the young man's
face was a revelation of bloody wrath and savage, venge-
ful rage. He had seen his brother fall dead. His own
djellab-sleeve was dark with that brother's blood.

"Ay, that is the right of all men here," said the Shareef.

"Then, lord, I have on my pack-mule yonder a better
battering-ram than any tree—the twelve-throated rifle
that the Alemáni [1] Bashador gave to my brother—may
God have pardoned him! I pray ye let me give my
horse to a slave, and go forward under cover of some
footmen with guns. Then I will fire at the locks of their
gates, lord, twelve explosive bullets to the minute; and
when I have done, lord, our men will force those gates
as the wind carries straw."

"Good! Shalt have thy chance when we go forward,
Abd el Malik."

The Shareef and Abd el Malik were the only men there
who had ever seen a magazine rifle at work, and even
their ideas as to the powers of the explosive bullet were
vague. Either would far rather have ridden into action
with a sword than used the rifle, but a man may not
ride over city walls, and so the rifle was to be given its
chance.

All was made ready now for a second advance—for the
final advance, men said. Abd el Malik carried his rifle, a

---

[1] German.

lad attended him with ammunition, and ten of his servants with out-of-date Remingtons surrounded him by way of cover. Fifty footmen, surrounded by gun-bearers, bore the ram, slung from their shoulders by palmetto-cords. Others carried six ladders, and the mounted men gathered on either flank of the line.

The word was given and the advance began slowly.

" There is to be no return," cried Abd el Malik, his young face stern and set. And " no return " was the word sent down the line from mouth to mouth. It was arranged that the firing line, and especially the holder of the magazine rifle, should be given free play for a while before the main body entered upon the narrow zone which had marked the limits of Ain Araish gun-shot range. At six hundred yards Abd el Malik, whose aim anger seemed to steady, began to pump lead into the great gates of the city. A few stray shots reached the earth about his little bodyguard, but no man was struck, and his twentieth bullet let daylight through the right-hand gate of Ain Araish. The impulsive young Khulafá recognized this with an exultant roar, and, against his better judgment (for there was nothing to prevent the continuance of these tactics, which involved practically no risk or loss to the attacking party), Ben Hassan yielded to their petition and gave the word for the whole body of mounted men to charge from either flank of the still busy firing line.

At once the bullets of the Ain Araish men began to tell with some effect. Many were wounded in that charge, and more than a score were slain outright. But when the walls themselves were reached—loop-holes being care-fully avoided—the Ain Araish bullets became harmless again, and went singing in all directions over the heads of the attacking force. Ladders were rushed into position now, and the Shareef, dismounting from his charger, had set foot upon the first of them, sword in hand, when his Friend, using small ceremony, thrust him back, crying:

"Lord, the Shareef hath duties as well as rights. Men fight here for the Shareef, not the Shareef for men."

And even as the Friend spoke, Selam er-Ribati, the erstwhile Sultán et-Tolbah, who had sprung into the place vacated by Ben Hassan, toppled down and backward at the Shareef's feet, the curved sword of an Ain Araish man skewered through his chest.

"May peace in bliss be his!" quoth the Friend reverently. "He died that his lord might live and rule. Come, lord, thy men swarm like ants now at the gates. Mount ye, and let the sight o' their lord give weight to their arms. But, prythee, ride close to the wall, lord!"

There came a groaning, tearing sound not fifty yards in their rear.

"One God, what thing is this?" cried the Friend. And then, as he looked: "See, lord; come quickly! 'Tis good Abd el Kareem—may Allah reward him!—letting down the drawbridge, the Shareef's own entrance to the castle. Lord, the day is ours! Enter we by this way— the Shareef coming down upon his people from out his own castle—not one man in Ain Araish would dare to raise hand to thee. Ohé, Sheikh Mohamet Tor! Ho, Abd el Malik! Ali Glawi! Moulai Hamed! Sidi Achmet! Follow there! Guard ye our lord! Here is entry for all! Ho, M.koddem Cassim! Ho, Absalaam! Ho, Abd el Lateef! Haste ye! haste ye! Ho, rally there! To our lord, to the lord Moulai Ben Hassan! On, lord; I am at thy stirrup!" (The Friend's horse had fallen under him. riddled by a chance volley of slugs, not one of which had struck another horse or man.)

And so, seated upon his white charger, and surrounded by five-and-twenty of his leaders, also mounted, with fifty running footmen bearing guns, his Friend at his stirrup, and renegade Abd el Kareem (the convert to a personality rather than a cause) at his bridle, the Shareef of Ain Araish entered in all deliberation the inner court of his own castle, whilst his army thundered at the city gates, within which assembled Ain Araish, directed by the shareefa in person from a low litter, stood to its guns and piled barricades across the gateway.

The castle gates communicating with the city street were hurriedly closed.

" But, lord, lord, in pity's name let us take them from the rear, and slay, slay, slay!" cried Abd el Malik, a-tremble with passion. " My brother's blood cries out to me, lord!"

But the Shareef was sufficiently a leader of men to know that the conduct of an army must not be directed by the feelings of an individual.

" Nay, we must give them their chance, O Abd el Malik," he said; and then, noting the bitter wrath in the young man's face, he added: " But one chance, O Abd el Malik, and if they come not to heel, I promise thee to lead a sally against them with thee, and to spare none within reach of our blades."

And now messengers were sent racing across the draw-bridge for drummers and horn-blowers from the Shareef's following. Ben Hassan, his Friend, the Sheikh, and his Khulafá mounted the terraced roof of the castle guard-house, having sent orders for the withdrawal of the at-tacking party at the gates. In a few minutes the castle courtyard was filled to overflowing by members of Ben Hassan's train, and half a dozen of his standards fluttered over the walls.

Crash went the drums of the Shareef, and the sudden
blaring of his ghaitahs drowned all other sound in Aïn
Araish. A Fási muedhdhin and four leaders gave tongue
then in tones which had served to assemble the Faithful
to prayer from the remotest corners of the city.

"Ohé! Come to security! Come to peace! O foolish
men of Aïn Araish, come to the feet of thy true Shareef!
Come to thy lord, Moulai Ben Hassan, Allah's chosen
upon earth! Come to pardon! Come to peace! Lay
down your arms, misguided ones! Thy lord, uplifted by
the hand of God, hath entered again into his castle! Come
to peace! Come to pardon! Holy are God's true saints!
Áshahadu, lá ílaha ill Allah; wa áshahadu ínna Sey-
yidiná Mohammed er-rasûl Allah!" (I testify that there
is no god but God, and I testify that our lord Mohammed
is the Apostle of God!)

"Lord," cried Abd el Malik on the instant, his sword
half drawn, "they come not! I have thy word, lord!"

"Ay, thou hast my word, and—— Come!"

The Shareef drew his sword, a score of blades flashed
out about him, and the Khulafá prepared to descend with
their lord into the city. The gates were flung wide.

"By Allah, the true Shareef himself cometh with a
sword of fire for traitors!"

Men said afterwards that it was the Friend of Ben
Hassan who, his garments kilted about him, rushed, unarmed, ahead of his lord and the Khulafá to convey that
message to the gates, and so enforce surrender. This
may well have been so, for the Friend had heard that
the shareefa was at the city gate, and death was written
on the faces of those about Ben Hassan as they left the
castle. But whoever gave the word, it is certain it reached
the city gates, and in the form here given, and that its
effect was magical. It forced the Shareef's sword back

into its scabbard, and the Shareef and his party back to their position at the castle gate.

Every soul employed at the city gate dropped his task and turned in response to the first word of the cry.

"Come! Come to pardon! Come to security! Come to thy true lord, Shareef Moulai Ben Hassan!"

Again the sonorous voices spoke. Every soul at the city gate (save two) was moved to complete, unquestioning resignation, and conviction to boot, before the last resonant words of command had died away in the still heat of the afternoon air. Many fell upon their knees. Others, heads drooping, hands open, moved like chidden hounds toward the men whose words had smitten them. None showed any thought of further resistance.

"Fools! Sheep! Slaves driven by a word! Will ye go to your death with open hands, then?" snarled the shareefa from her litter beside the gates.

"Come, thou fools—come to security! Come to pardon while pardon may be had! Come to thy true lord, ye misled men of Ain Araish!"

Once again the booming voices from the castle yard had spoken, and their words fell among Ain Araish men with more telling effect than cannon-balls. Men pressed together like frightened children on their submissive way to the castle. The scene was an intensely dramatic one, impressive as a storied scene of Scriptural history. But its background and the character of the men concerned were essential features of its dramatic impressiveness. The same forces could not conceivably have produced the same effect outside the world of Islam. The philosophy which Western observers, who are constitutionally incapable of comprehending it, call fatalism, served dramatic fitness and Ben Hassan well upon this occasion.

Of a sudden, and just as the first surrendering band of
Ain Araish men reached the gate above which Ben Hassan stood once more among his Khulafá, a cry arose from
the streets and again from the castle drawbridge, where
Fási sentinels were posted.

"The white woman escapes! The shareefa escapes!"
Ben Hassan's Friend sprang from his lord's side.

"Give the word that she be not injured, lord!" he
cried, and raced then for the drawbridge, shouting to
M.koddem Cassim to follow. The first horse to hand was
the Shareef's great charger, its right shoulder clotted
darkly with blood from a gunshot flesh wound. The act
verged upon sacrilege, but the Friend gave no thought to
that. Springing into the high-peaked green saddle, which
careened far over as it caught his weight, the Friend
smote the noble brute over its flank with a trailing fathom
of green bridle, and started at a furious gallop toward
the road beyond the gates.

He had not far to go. Unable to keep her seat upon
the loose-girthed Moorish saddle of the horse she had
mounted, Shareefa Margaret had fallen when no more
than half a mile from the gates. Her not too gallant son,
Moulai Mohammed, to whom she had given a far fleeter
mount than her own, paid no heed to his mother's poor
plight, but galloped on alone in advance of the frightened
beast from which the shareefa had fallen.

"Lalla, I pray ye not to give hostages to fortune by
tempting the tempers of fighting men!" cried the Friend,
as he dismounted before her.

"Man, pester me not with thy wagging tongue! I
have no need of thy counsel!"

There was not much submissiveness about Shareefa
Margaret.

"Lalla, I thought only to serve thee."

The Friend's eyes were upon the ground. He spoke as men never heard him speak.

" Serve me? " she echoed, her dark eyes blazing.

" Ih-yeh, Lalla! What can ye do alone in the desert? "

" Fool! Oh, God, give me patience to bear with fools, for I am surrounded by them! Oh, God, curse them all —the Moors! Serve me, would ye? Mount, then— mount, man, and ride to guard my son—the Shareef! "

At that moment galloping men of Ben Hassan's train reined their horses on their haunches, scattering sand and dust in a cloud about the twain.

" That may I not do, Lalla, whilst thou'rt unprotected; but he shall not be harmed." He turned to the followers: " Ride, men—ride hard," he shouted, " and bring the young man back to the castle. Hurt him not, for your lives! The Shareef's honour is pledged not to harm him. See, I ride the Shareef's horse—on his errand! He is pledged. On your heads the care of Moulai Moham-med! On with ye! " They sprang to the gallop, M.kod-dem Cassim at their head. " Lalla, thy son will stand before thee safe and unharmed within the hour. Escap-ing, your lives were forfeit. Be advised. Return with me to—to thy women, and no man will harm thee."

The shareefa, calm again now, seemed to weigh these words carefully, coldly, and to find reason in them.

" Ay," she said slowly, " it is true I can do more there than here. Give me thy hand, then, and I will ride on this horse to the castle."

" Lalla, it is the Shareef's own horse! his father's be-fore him—may God have pardoned him! "

" Thy hand, man, not thy tongue! "

" Lalla, I dare not. The Shareef's very slaves would tear thee down."

" Thy hand! "

"Lalla, think of it—of what has gone before. Beyond a certain limit I could not protect thee. It is too——"

"Thy hand—slave!"

"Lalla, for thine own sake I cannot."

Without a word she sank down upon the ground, veiled among her draperies, and there sat, a woman indomitable.

The Friend fretted and fumed. The woman never moved so much as a fold of her silken haiik. He had been right and wise, and very possibly she knew it. Her plan of riding into Ain Araish on the Shareef's famous white charger was one which no Moor, man or woman, would have given a moment's thought to in similar circumstances. Much, very much, might be forgiven her at a nod from Ben Hassan. This little piece of half theatrical display would have roused the populace to frenzy and cost the author of it her life.

So there sat the shareefa, and there beside the bloodstained white horse of his lord stood the Friend, whilst the hot sun dipped low for evening, and many picturesque happenings were toward in Ain Araish, not least among which were the preparations beside a thousand fires for the feasting that night of close on 4,000 fighting men.

At last the troop under M.koddem Cassim arrived, walking their horses after a long gallop; and in their midst rode the puny, peevish-faced lad in whose interests the walls of an ancient and venerable city had that day been subjected to the shock and assault of a siege, whilst the lives of close upon a hundred better men than himself had been sacrificed.

"If thou hadst not fallen, mother, we should have won clear."

"Ay, as thou sayest, my son; but—I did fall."

The young man dismounted beside her, facing the Friend. One half caste faced another, and spoke.

" I believe this man is at the root of it, curse him! "

" Ay, curse him if ye will, my son, but help me to a horse."

The Friend stepped forward with bowed head.

" Ho, rájál! " cried he to one of the troopers; " dismount and bring hither thy horse."

And so as the sun set they all rode at a foot-pace into Ain Araish, the Friend leading his lord's white horse at the head of them, with its empty saddle of the Prophet's own green.

Chapter XXXI

THE QUESTION

"LORD, I am an old man, and my child was very
dear to me."

The speaker was Sheikh Mohamet Tor, and
he addressed Ben Hassan at the entrance to the great
banqueting hall of the castle, where 400 of the principals
among his Fási following were to feast with the Shareef.

"Allah, forbid that I should cast a stain upon thy hospitality, lord. Thy followers must be feasted. But for
me, I cannot to the feasting, lord, still ignorant of my
child's whereabouts. See, lord, I bled for thee this day."
The old man pushed aside his great white beard, and
showed the hem of a kaftan deeply blood-stained. "Have
out the woman, lord, I pray ye, and set my old heart at
rest."

"That will I, Sheikh, gladly. Only my duty to our
guests hath delayed me. O lords, counsellors, and
friends!" He turned to the throng of guests behind him.
(Moorish etiquette demands that a host shall precede his
guests in all things. It is regarded as a proof of good
faith.) "Will ye bear with me for yet a few minutes? I
would question the widow of my father—may God have
pardoned him!—and set two uneasy minds at peace."

"Ih-yeh, let us hear the woman!" they cried, and
trooped behind Shareef and Sheikh to the great main hall
of the castle. There Ben Hassan sat him down upon his

father's raised divan, and his supporters clustered about his feet, Sheikh Mohamet being invited to a cushion beside the Shareef, whilst the Friend sent slaves to bid the shareefa's women bring her to the hall.

She came with little delay, a tall, defiant figure of a woman, her white face naked to all beholders, two slave women walking behind her.

" What would ye with me ? " she said, naming no names, but addressing the Shareef, with head erect.

" A shameless breed ! "

" A bitch-wolf at bay ! "

" By Allah, the Shareef's too soft i' th' heart ! "

" She would never wag that shameless tongue again were I Shareef."

" The dam hath a kind of courage that passed not out from her dugs; but, to be sure, the whelp's a mongrel ! "

Of such like were the muttered comments passed upon Shareefa Margaret by the leaders among the Shareef's following.

" Nay, shareefa, I would liefer listen than speak with thee," answered the Shareef in measured tones. " Answer thou, I pray thee, the Sheikh here, who is, like thee, a parent."

" Now, that is very kindly said," quoth the old Sheikh; and, turning then to the woman before them, he said gravely: " Forgive me if I look upon thy face; it lacks a cover, and I am seeking truth. Why sent ye the Shareef here to Ed-dár el Kebeer seeking my daughter ? "

" I thought she was there."

The words were lamely spoken. It was not a well-told lie. The woman's pose was made less defiant by the weakness of it. Her eyes were lowered.

" That is a lie," said the old Sheikh very quietly. Anyone who knew him well would have feared him at that moment. A stranger had seen little cause for uneasiness in his demeanour. "And I seek truth, being, like thee, a parent. So I put aside that question, and thy lie, and ask another. Where is now my daughter, whom I left in thy care as a mother?"

"She is in the house of her uncle, thy brother, in Tanjáh."

"And what does she there?"

"I sent her there because—to be out of danger, since trouble threatened here."

"Have ye any more to tell me?"

"No."

"Lord," said the Sheikh, turning slowly to Ben Hassan, "I am an old man for this restless life, but by break of day, God willing, I start for Tanjáh."

"I also, O Sheikh."

"As I see these things, lord, her first words were without truth, her second words were true, her third, again, were a lie. But as to reasons, we have little concern with them, and as to counsel, in taking that, lord, we are better, I believe, without those that wear the veil—or should wear it. I have no more to say."

"Surely, lord, ye would not allow this woman to go free?" asked one of the older leaders from Fás.

"Lord, on my head be it; I will answer for the shareefa's safe keeping," said the Friend of Ben Hassan.

The woman flashed a curious glance upon him; in part grateful it was, yet more wondering.

"And the son?" asked Abd el Malik.

"Ay, and the son," answered the Friend.

"From here to Tanjáh, look ye, till the truth of her words be tested!" exclaimed the old Sheikh, looking up suddenly.

"Ay." The Friend paused thoughtfully. "That is

best," he murmured. "Ay, from here to Tanjáh, O
Sheikh," he repeated aloud.

And so the shareefa was led away to her own apartments, and Shareef and Sheikh led their great company
in to the banqueting hall, where the first dish to be discussed comprised some seven-and-twenty fat young sheep.

Chapter XXXII

THE OPEN ROAD AGAIN

IT might reasonably be thought that Shareef Ben Hassan pledged himself to a course of some risk and danger when he said that the morrow should see him on his way toward Tangier with the father of Fatimah. But a few hours before and the gates of his own stronghold had been closed to him by a force of his own people acting offensively as well as defensively. But, as the Basha of the city affirmed, when brought before his lord that night with the city elders:

"Lord, Allah, who knoweth all things, knoweth also that ye had but the one enemy in all Ain Araish, or, at the most, if ye will pardon the liberty, but one and a half. So long as men can mind, thy city of Ain Araish hath been ruled from the castle here. So it is and hath ever been. Lord, I would ask thee who hath ruled in the castle these several years past?"

The Shareef nodded brusquely.

"By the greatest misfortune of our time, lord, Ain Araish was ruled by the only enemy thou hadst within its walls. Thus were we ruled who are of Ain Araish by, as I said, the greatest misfortune of our time, which this day hath proved a most bloody misfortune to boot, and one as grievous to us whole men, lord, within the walls as to thy noble following without the walls."

The plea of the Basha was felt to be sound and truthful, and after due consideration had been given to the whole matter, and all the principal residents had made humble submission to their lord in person, the Shareef's pardon was given fully and freely to all the men of Ain Araish with one exception. Hamet ben Hamet Arâf was ordered to the prison of the kasbah, there to await his lord's pleasure.

"For thou," said the young Shareef judicially, "art no fit man to be abroad among my people, since, whilst acting under no compulsion save that of thine own evil heart, thou didst very basely betray thy lord the true Shareef by leaving him in Tanjáh, by stealing his property, and by spreading lies concerning the words spoken from the death-bed of my father, upon whose soul may Allah send unending peace! I believe I am no more than just in saying that for a lesser thing than this any one of my forbears sitting now in Paradise—may God have pardoned them one and all!—had ordered thy treacherous tongue to be cut out. For the present I propose to leave thee in prison, where, if thou'rt wise, thou'lt seek to make peace with thy conscience. For thy face, I never wish to see it again."

So that, for the time, was the last men saw of the portly counsellor, who in truth was not a good man, nor yet a wholly bad one, and withal, as sundry written histories have proved, a very gifted scribe. And that reminds one of the wise words of Abd el Mukhtar: "Who hath a ready pen hath ever also a mind ready, for good and for evil; and in this life evil predominates. Wherefore, teach not letters to thy little daughter, neither let her to live upon the housetops."

To the Basha the Shareef said:

"Now, Basha, do thou consider in the next few months that thou hast the repute of the Shareef of Ain Araish in thy hands. Thine the part of justifying my decision regarding thyself and the elders of the city. Fail me, and you show the Shareef to have been mistaken—apparently. Play thy part loyally and honourably, as guardian of this, my Ain Araish, and ye demonstrate to all men the truth of my judgment of ye, and bid fair to end thy days prosperously, Basha of the dearest city in Al Maghreb. B'ís-salámah!"

Be sure the Basha bowed low as he withdrew, and, like many another important person in Ain Araish, knew not sleep that night for self-gratulation and gossip. But, indeed, few of the residents of the sacred town took any rest that night, for there was much to be done. Their lord's guests were every one to be treated as visiting princes, no less. Their animals were to be most carefully tended, and, if road-weary, replaced by fresh and better steeds. Their stores were to be replenished amply and well. Themselves were to rest after feasting, and perform no tasks whatever that other hands might carry out for them. This was their lord the Shareef's good pleasure, and here was M.koddem Cassim to see it carried out—M.koddem Cassim, a new power in the land, once every official's berated slave, but to-day a most imposing magnate, bearing about his neck upon a rope of green silk, sundry keys of shareefian storehouses, and ruffling it among the servants, himself a veritable prince of dependents. One thing the m.koddem did with his own worshipful hands, and that was the dressing of the shallow wound upon the shoulder of the Shareef's white charger, and the plaiting in silk of the tail and mane of the same exalted creature. Two other magnificent Abda-bred chargers, favourites of the late Shareef's, were similarly tired and bedight for the morrow's journey, in order that the famous white stallion might march for a few days with no other burden than a saddle. Busied among such weighty matters, the good Cassim began to feel that this, at last, was in very truth to be the m.koddem of a great Shareef.

Before dawn this same m.koddem had every pack-animal of the whole great caravan outside the bullet-riven gates, and on its way in charge of its respective driver.

"It is in my mind that this will not be a long day's march," quoth he, to the kaid of the band, "so halt ye below the hill of the five tombs, and I will see that ye have word in good time that the tents may be pitched, and the various matters ye wot of in train before our lord shall arrive. B'îs-salámah!"

And then the busy m.koddem returned to the castle fandak, to snatch a hurried meal, and to see that the horses of his lord, and those of his worshipful lieutenants, were as the steeds of a notable should be, curled and oiled, and full of the bit-champing pride of good living.

Many that morning found it hard in practice to realize the truth of the muedhdhin's announcement that prayer was "better than sleep." But all were astir by break of day, and, after prayer, fared sumptuously at the kind of breakfast which only sybarites or honoured guests enjoy in Sunset Land : thick soup, stewed chicken, and green tea with mint in hundreds of diminutive glasses.

The sun was high in the heavens and the third hour after daybreak well advanced when Ben Hassan, upon a crimson-girt black horse, rode out from Ain Araish, with the Sheikh and his Friend, at the head of a great company, among whom—surrounded by her women, a score of her own slaves, and another score of armed footmen—was Shareefa Margaret in a litter of green and gold. Her son, Moulai Mohammed, rode before his mother upon a tall red mule; this, the young man's own choice of a mount, being, as he said, the easiest pacer in Ain Araish.

It was noted that some few officers of the castle who had been the most completely and submissively her tools kept close even now to the person of the shareefa. Their choice in this matter was not interfered with, though two of his lieutenants spoke warningly to Ben Hassan thereon.

"Ih-yeh," laughed the young Shareef, "to deny that she had wit and ambition, and power to bend men to the same, withal, were childish and a folly. Some of the old thraldom remains. Bismfi 'Illah! It may remain for me. I love a loyal servant. They will learn in time. Meanwhile, if she hath spoken truly this time, touching the Pearl of Ain Araish, why Allah forbid that I should irk her with pricks and nips of humiliation such as she visited on me. If she hath again lied—— Eh, eh! but we will not speak of that."

And the listening Khaleefah felt that, though not to be spoken of, the events pertaining to that contingency would be of a stirring sort. In fact, so strongly was he interested by reflection upon the possibilities of which the Shareef had said he would not speak that, when the company drew near to Fás, he proved the leader of the handful of young aristocrats who declined to part company with Ben Hassan for the present, and elected instead to journey on with him to the port at which Islam in the West touches Christendom, in a state of armed neutrality and veiled hostility—to Tangier, of the many tongues, diverse faiths, and innumerable desecrations. The name of the young man was Abd el Malik, and his personal following was comprised of the slaves of his dead brother as well as his own men.

For the rest, arrival at Fás transformed the Shareef's train from an army into a still sufficiently imposing caravan. There remained with him Abd el Malik, with his forty men and twice that number of animals; four other bright particular stars of the tolbah, with their slaves; Sheikh Mohamet Tor, with a dozen personal attendants and several women slaves; some fifty armed footmen from Ain Araish, with an hundred animals; the shareefa and her son and attendants; and the Shareef, his Friend, his m.koddem, his body-guard, and fifty horsemen.

One night only was spent at Fás, and that was a night of feasting in the halls of the Karûeen, ushered in by an hour of solemn thanksgiving and prayer among the great square pillars of the Karûeen mosque. More than 7,000 men are said to have simultaneously testified in the rear of Moulai Ben Hassan among the pillars that evening. It was a marvel such as had stirred Christendom to its depths could Christendom have heard and seen it. And in the morning the Shareef publicly gave thanks to the tolbah and people of Fás, speaking from the mosque doors as he had spoken on the eve of his outsetting for his own territory. And bearded men wept to see and hear him, standing there in his pride and his gratitude, a hand upon the bowed shoulder of aged Sheikh Mohamet Tor, whose wound irked him sorely, even as his anxiety as a father had of late made him to appear ancient. Men wept, so the speech and figure of the tall young Shareef reached and played upon their heart-strings; but theirs was of the good sort of weeping, in which wet eyes are seen above laughing lips.

"He is a man made after God's own heart!" cried a ripe and towardly-looking young Jewess who stood near the Salted Place, or abode of Jews, as Ben Hassan rode out of the city that morning, bowing and smiling gravely, at the head of his company. And a greasy-gaberdined and rheumy-eyed ancient with her chid the young Rebecca for that she had thoughtlessly applied to a Mohammedan the words used by the chronicler of David, the greatest Prince in Israel.

"I know nought of the Chronicle," protested Rebecca stoutly; "but I know a goodly young man when I do look upon him, and if this one were not made after God's heart, then, my faith, but he was made after mine!"

She meant no evil, this comely slip of the ancient stock contemned in Morocco, but the venerable and orthodox elder with her tore his filthy skull-cap from his love-locks and trampled upon it in impotent wrath. For the girl, she ran, laughing noisily, into the Mellah, and plucked the petals of a flower, murmuring gibberish the while regarding the affections of some young male bird of her feather.

There was no doubt whatever but that Moulai Ben Hassan, by Allah's grace Shareef of Ain Araish, possessed in rich measure that wondrous electric gift by means of which some men can draw down to themselves, like stringed kites, the hearts of most other men, and especially women.

Chapter XXXIII

OUTSIDE TANGIER

THE Shareef was in high good humour. His affairs had prospered exceedingly, and he had reached the last stage of his journey, was upon the verge of winning his quest, and was camped for the last time before reaching Tangier—Tangier, which, despite its blemishes and foul spots innumerable, was yet for the time the most radiantly blessed city upon earth, by token that it sheltered Fatimah, the Pearl of Ain Araish. Men spoke and thought well of Ben Hassan. He had of late played a royal hand in the game of life, and he himself was inclined to think tolerably well of (as he would have said) his father's son.

"Ih-yeh, Friend," said he, as they sat together before retiring for the night, "and what think ye of things? Art pleased with thy poor lord and his doings?"

"Lord," replied the Friend, in a tone which notably lacked the light complaisance of the question, "no man here hath a right to be displeased with the Shareef of Ain Araish; and, indeed, thou hast in all things done well and honourably—as befits thee."

"Ah! But—ih-yeh, there is a 'but' in thy mind, Friend. 'Twere better spoken."

"Lord, it is no qualification of a bare acknowledgment of the truth; yet I will admit to thee, lord, I am somewhat anxious in mine own mind regarding the fate of the shareefa and her son and thy ultimate disposition of them."

" Wherefore, Friend?"

" Lord, she was the wife of thy father—may God have pardoned him!"

" Truly; and the most unwifely, unwomanly leader and director in her own person of those who sought not alone to usurp all rights of mine, but to slay me and mine outright."

" That is true, lord, and lamentable; but I would say firstly that all our teaching shows we must not judge women as men are judged, and, again, that a mother fighting for the welfare of her offspring knows no other law than the yearning of the breasts that suckled her child and the stirring of the blood which he shares. If one may not excuse one may well understand, lord, and a prince more than most men, a Shareef before men and princes, should temper his judgment with mercy, lord."

" Ay, ay; all that thou sayest, as ever, Friend, is just and true. But, I ask ye, how have I shown myself lacking in mercy? Friend, I tell thee I have never a thought of revenge, but only desire to so overcome the shareefa's scheming that I win my Pearl. That done, Friend, she and her son are free as air for me, to go whithersoever they list, and in all things to consult only their own wishes."

" And that is kindly spoken, lord, and like thee. Yet I would ask more. Now that thou hast stepped into thine own, lord, whither would ye have them go? Of what use to them will be their freedom, having lost their home?"

. " Nay, Friend, but ye do me less than justice. God forbid that I should make the widow homeless, howsoever much she may have striven to rob me of a home. They shall be free to come and go as ever in Ain Araish. I would never deny her as she denied me in the old days."

" It is of that that I would speak, lord. It is in my mind that, for thy sake as well as hers, Ain Araish is no place for the shareefa, neither for Moulai Mohammed, her son; and so, lord, I would say to thee, the Shareef, be more than merciful—be generous, as becomes the great."

" But how, Friend?"

" If it please thee, lord, take the house of thy father—upon whose soul be peace!—in Tangier, and settle it, with the other Tangier property, upon the shareefa and her son. Let him live there as a Shareef should—in dignity—with her. Though not, as she hath claimed, the Shareef of Ain Araish, he is yet a Shareef, lord, since thy father—whom may God have pardoned!—was his father. Tanjáh is a far cry from thy Ain Araish, and it may be better suited for—for a young man of—of his mixed parentage. Will ye do that, lord?"

" Why Friend, I have never given it a thought, but—but thy counsel was ever wise counsel. Yes, if she desireth that, and strives no longer to thwart and injure me, I will do the thing as thou hast said it, Friend. And —and if it eases her and him that he should play Shareef of Ain Araish in Tanjáh, why, I care nought for Tanjáh, Friend, once my Pearl is in my hand and out of it. So I pass ye my word, Friend. Is thy mind at rest now?"

" Lord, I have nothing left to desire."

" Good. Then, if that be thy pleasure, Friend, we will sleep."

In the morning Mohammed er-Raishi, the chief among the castle officials whom the shareefa had honoured, and who still lingered half-heartedly about her person, came to the Shareef with word that his mistress was indisposed and desired to remain in camp with her attendants while the company entered Tangier and transacted its affairs there. The Shareef nodded indifferently, but Sheikh Mohamet Tor looked up sharply over his snuff-tube.

"Nay, by Allah!" he swore. "With thy good leave, lord, she shall do no such thing. Her litter is as good a sick-couch as any other, methinks, and I stir no step without the shareefa till mine eyes have seen my child safe and sound."

Again the Shareef nodded, but more thoughtfully this time.

"Thou'rt wiser than I, Sheikh," said he. And then, turning to the messenger: "Tell thou the shareefa that the stage is an easy one, and the pace shall be easy; but we desire her presence in her litter, according to the terms decided in Ain Araish."

The messenger departed, and, a good deal to his surprise, as well as somewhat to his discomfiture (for the young man had a tender conscience), Ben Hassan heard nothing further regarding the shareefa's indisposition until the day was far advanced, and the hill which Tangier folk call their mountain had come plainly into view. And now, in the undulating valley which lies between the Tetouan and the Fás roads, the caravan was halted at the instance of the occupant of the great green and gold litter.

"Lord Ben Hassan was now in Tangier," said her messenger, "and the shareefa begged that she be not forced into the city itself that day. The Shareef was asked to be generous in the hour of his triumph, and not to demand the public humiliation in a city's streets of the widow of his father, to whom Allah had doubtless awarded bliss in Paradise." It was the final suggestion—the claim upon him as his father's son—that decided the Shareef.

"She is but a woman, when all is said," he pointed out to the aged Sheikh, "and here indubitably at our hands is Tanjáh, and—and thy daughter. Let her await us here, then. Thou hast no more stomach for this Tanjáh of pollution than I have; the more reason for us to hasten from it, with—with our quest ended. There is Ed-dár el Kebeer, Sheikh. What better spot could ye desire for——"

"For thy wedding, lord, thou wouldst say? Ah, well! be it as thou hast said. But leave her with her guards, and some trusted——"

"Let me bide here, lord," said the Friend of Ben Hassan.

And so it fell out.

"Of what country is he, thy Friend, lord?" asked the old Sheikh thoughtfully, as he rode beside the Shareef.

"Now, Allah make us wiser!" cried Ben Hassan, "in all my years I never thought nor sought to know. There is but the one Faith, O Sheikh, and its sons are all brothers, let their birth hap where it will. But, now that ye do speak of it, I believe 'twas holy land, Al Madinah methinks, that gave my Friend birth. But——"

"And why did thy Friend of holy birth go to speak with the shareefa's attendants late last night, lord, when all slept, save him and me?"

"Nay, I know not, Sheikh—I know not at all, unless it was to tell her of a matter regarding which we had some talk together last night. But, see! Here is Tanjáh. How Nazarene-like their windowed houses, agape upon the open road, like the dens of the daughters of the illegitimate."

And now, as the company entered the surroundings of the port, riding between the residences of foreigners, the hearts of the two leaders, the lover and the father, were too full to admit of speech or casual thought. The main body of the caravan came to a halt in the great outer Sôk, whilst its leaders, with a score of attendants, rode in through Bab el Fás, and so, walking their horses slowly, by the cobbled and crowded main street, to the house of the Sheikh's brother, escorted by a gaping crowd of idlers.

The words spoken in the courtyard of that house between Sheikh Mohamet Tor and the brother whom he scarcely knew were very, very few. Yet their meaning and consequences were far-reaching, and, incidentally, they caused a panic in Tangier, which led presently to the closing of the city gates, and the hurried drawing together of the Basha's ragged and disreputable soldiers, the town " assassins."

" Why—may God pardon us!—where should she be, my brother, save in the house of her husband, whom she went forth with her women to join, but two days since, with the escort who bore the Shareef's sealed authority— may Allah have him in——"

" She left here—left thee—two days since, to go to—to——"

" To her lord and husband, the holy Shareef of——"

" Way there!" roared Ben Hassan, wheeling his great charger on its own ground in the little paved courtyard. " Bál-ak! bál-ak!¹ Come, Sheikh! Bál-ak!"

And, followed closely by the old Sheikh, the Shareef of Ain Araish went thundering through the gates, on by an alley to the main street, and up that greasy, break-neck incline at a pace which tried even the famous white horse, stung to madness as it was by reckless spurring and a slashing rein upon its flank.

" Bál-ak! bál-ak!" screamed the affrighted loiterers of

¹ Literally, Thy mind! By usage, Look out! Attention!

the street; and "way! way! Way there for the Shareef! Way for thy life!" bellowed the followers, who urged their beasts with curb and spur behind the streaming tail of the white horse. The shouts of the populace warned the rest of the caravan in the outer Sôk. Guns were fired in the air, as guns must always be fired upon occasions of any kind of stress or excitement in which Moors are concerned. Wondering Nazarenes hurried to the shelter of walls and doors, and the gates of the British and German Legations were slammed to by their respective guards and securely bolted.

But between Moulai Ben Hassan and the people of Tangier could be no question of any sort. The young Shareef saw but the one picture as he galloped—and that through a ruddy mist, as of blood—the woman who had fooled him a second time, and, as it seemed, fatally, out there in the green valley, with her son, this bastard Shareef—the "lord and husband."

"God give me wings, and a strong hand to strike withal!" he snarled, between tightly-clenched teeth.

And he smote the gallant beast that strained every muscle beneath him with his flying green rein.

The valley was empty. Not a living creature could be seen in it, though some scattered articles of dress, and the prints of many hoofs and feet, showed clearly where the shareefa's party had been.

The old Sheikh, unmanned, and utterly exhausted by his furious ride, bowed low over the peak of his saddle.

"Lord, I asked thee whence came thy Friend," he moaned.

"One God, it cannot be!" exclaimed the Shareef in the tone of one who falters. But, an instant more, and he was bitter and firm as before. "Bide ye with the Sheikh here, some two or three o' ye!" he shouted to those of his followers who had come so far. "On with me the rest o' ye, while the track is warm!"

And so he galloped on again, a hard-breathing figure of vengeance, his princely robes a-flutter and his naked sword aloft. So an Arab would depict remorseless Azrael.

Retailers of the story have greatly magnified the event, for, when all is said, the Shareef's furious hunt was a short one. Within four miles of the valley he overtook the shareefa's following, and brought it to a standstill. This (the story-teller's versions to the contrary notwithstanding) the writer can affirm with the more confidence by token that himself stood, not many days afterward, with his feet planted in the self-same furrows that were gouged out of the earth by the hoofs of the Shareef's white charger when the animal was jerked to its haunches by Ben Hassan on that eventful day.

The true matter for marvel, the which even Sôk storytellers could scarcely exaggerate, was that the Shareef could have brought the whole of that armed caravan to the halt himself, absolutely unaided and alone, his gleaming sword, the bloody fire of his eyes, and the thunder of wrath in his voice the only visible forces at his command. (Few horses could live beside the famous white stallion at the gallop; few men had dared to ride over that broken ground at the pace Ben Hassan had made. The foremost of his followers lost three-quarters of a mile in the four miles covered.) Many there be who point to supernatural agencies for an explanation of the event, urging what, of course, is beyond denial—that the Shareefs of Ain Araish are not as other men, and that God's saints, walking in the light of God's eye, may execute God's will, be it upon a thousand or upon a single little child.

But these be rather points for the ulamá than for the lay observer, and do not at all lend themselves to the

story-teller's use, though many a one in the market-places
has made the mistake of forcing them into his service.
The remarkable and not disputed fact is that the fleeing
company, whose leader and director was Shareefa Margaret, halted in a formless body, as herded sheep will
halt, when the roar of Ben Hassan's voice smote upon
them, and opened out among themselves a clear pathway
to where the shareefa stood, dismounted, in their midst,
as the thud of the white stallion's feet shook the earth in
their rear.

Stories differ as to the exact words of the Shareef's
awe-compelling cry, but the most generally accepted ver-
sion is that he shouted first: "Halt, ye traitorous dogs!
Halt, I say, ye bitch-led sons of dogs!" And that, as
he dismounted and strode among them—"breathing aloud
as a winded horse"—he flashed out upon the throng with:
"Be ye all accursed, and be the seed of ye all accursed!"

Sober men have affirmed that the sword in his hand
turned to lambent flame, and played over their heads till
those on the edge of his path fell upon their knees, crying
out upon their lord for mercy. It is more likely that
slanting sun-rays upon a weapon held passionately in play
suggested this notion of a sword of flame.

"As the Shareef drew near to the white-faced woman
of infidel birth," says a subsequently imprisoned eye-
witness named Mohammed er-Raishi, "the man they called
his Friend eluded in some mysterious manner the half-
dozen of slaves who had been set about him"—the probable fact is that this "half-dozen of slaves" were slavishly
terrorized, like many of their betters—"and rushed forward to where the shareefa stood alone, facing vengeance,
advancing in the sacred person of our lord. One or two
rash spirits were stirred by this sight (it being obvious
hat the Friend acted thus as protector of the shareefa),

and stepped forward with weapons raised to intercept their rightful lord. As we hope for mercy our lord literally clove them, three of them—spilt them in sunder, as God's my judge, and scarcely broke his stride. And here cometh the greatest marvel of all.

"As our lord raised his flame-like sword to the third of those reckless ones who blocked his way, the Friend of our lord reached the woman he purposed shielding from the bloody vengeance of the thrice-betrayed Shareef. 'Stand ye behind me,' were the words the Friend spake to the shareefa, and at that moment, acting either deliberately out of the evil in her, or upon a misunderstanding of the Friend's intent, she drew a dagger from under her haiik, swiftly as a vulture pounces, and flashed it to the very hilt into the side of him who sought to protect her. He fell with a moan, huddled at her feet, and gasping out some words in a foreign tongue as he fell. The shareefa had slain her protector, it seemed, and yet, by Allah and his Prophet, the deed unquestionably saved her life.

"These be matters which no common man may explain; indeed, they are not fitting subjects for gossip. This is certain, that our lord, having strode over three slain men, had again raised his sword to smite even his Friend if need be, that he might reach the naked-faced object of his wrath. Then he saw the hated hand smite his long-beloved Friend to earth; and in the self-same moment he saw emerge from out of the shareefa's great litter (in her flight the shareefa had ridden a horse) Fatimah, the daughter of Sheikh Mohamet Tor, full half her beauteous face unveiled, and tears streaming from her midnight eyes upon her dawn-like cheeks. For years now our lord had been travelling, starving, fighting, and striving for no other thing upon earth but the winning of this Pearl

among virgins. Yet be it recorded here, that all men
may know, our lord gave but one glance in her direction
when she stepped from out the litter, and then, flinging
from him his sword of flame, dropped moaning upon his
knees beside the Friend, whom men say he loved even as
Dáwûd [1] loved his friend, and whose blood now fed the
earth. Greater love than this hath no friend known, methinks. And, be it noted of all men, while the holy
Shareef strove mightily to stanch the bleeding of his
Friend's wound, and nursed him most tenderly there upon
the ground, no move was made toward him by any one
among the company he had cursed, neither the four hundred paid tribesmen from beyond Tetouan, who had come
with the maiden Fatimah to the appointed place for the
rescue of the shareefa, nor yet the more miserable wights,
who, like myself, had known our lord's favour and mercy,
and yet were led to countenance and assist the mad attempt at flight. I say mad, for who but a woman—and
a desperate woman—could have conceived so hopeless a
scheme and drawn grown men to aid her in it?

" But the wonders of that most wonderful of days were
not yet ended, for, as our lord tended his dying Friend
upon the earth, there came riding among us to his very
side a company of the Shareef's men, headed by one Absalaam, (a slave whom the Friend had managed at the
beginning of the shareefa's flight, while he had wrestled
with her in speech, striving to change her desperate purpose, to despatch in haste to Tanjáh) with Sheikh Mohamet Tor, M.koddem Cassim, Abd el Malik, and two
Nazarenes—a man and a woman—with a town Moor.
Fed full upon surprises, we stood as trees, but watching
it all. The company dismounted; Sheikh Mohamet Tor,
spitting upon the ground as he passed the shareefa, strode,

---

[1] David.

as a young man strides, to his daughter, drawing her haiik over her face, calling her women about her, and leading her to the litter. The male Nazarene walked straightway to the shareefa, saluting her in the speech of the English; and as he did so, Moulai Mohammed, the shareefa's son, came forward from his hiding-place behind the litter, and spoke also in the English tongue to the Nazarene, whom he called by the name of ' Dunn.'

" Come we now to the more remarkable event. The female Nazarene, whose face was more kindly seeming and less brazen than those of the most of her unveiled countrywomen, stepped forward with her man as though. to speak with the shareefa. As she passed the fallen Friend of our lord he groaned aloud, and we who were by distinctly heard him call upon the Nazarene woman by the name of Maryam,[1] the Mother of Seed-ná Aïsà. The Nazarene woman gave a cry and fell, even as the Shareef had fallen, upon her knees beside the Friend. But mark ye this mystery: She called out upon the fallen man by name, in grief and anguish for him, and the name she called was that of Yûsef,[2] the husband of the Mother of Seed-ná Aïsà. The name of the Friend, as some but not all knew, was Haj Yûsef, but few had ever used it."

Of the close of that scene it is easier to tell without the assistance of Mohammed er-Raishi, who understood little that he saw of it and nothing that he heard.

The central figures crowded about the fallen Friend of Ben Hassan. His head lay upon the knees of his lord the Shareef, his hands were in those of Mary Dunn, his wife, who called him husband while she wept. And Dick Dunn, who called her wife, he, too, bent over Haj Yûsef.

[1] Mary, the mother of our Lord Jesus.
[2] Europeans will probably detect nothing miraculous in a man being called Joseph and a woman Mary.

And the shareefa, by whose hand he had fallen, she also peered down upon him, crying as she did so, with a curious broken ring in her voice of some emotion that was neither pity or remorse.

"Joseph Khassan! I thought it once—the day I first saw you in this country. And then I thought——" But this singular woman never told her after-thought. "And I killed you," she said brokenly, yet not with sorrow; "I killed you!"

"No," murmured the dying man, "don't think of that. My time had come. Only—forgive me. Because of—of all the wrong I did, I tried to serve you and—and my lord here" (this in Arabic), "because of the love I bore him." He turned his misty eyes upon the woman who held his hands. "Mary, forgive me." She bathed his hands with her tears, murmuring incoherently and calling him by name. "Sidi"—his eyes shifted again to his lord —"forgive thy Friend for that he failed thee to-day. I have always loved thee, but—was ever a divided thing."

The Shareef cried aloud upon Allah to save him his Friend, for whom he knew love passing the love of women.

"Dick!"

Dick Dunn bent lower over the fallen man, saying: "Old friend, don't try to talk; we all——"

But the Friend knew best, and made no mistake about the period of his end.

"Dick," he gasped again, "I wronged you first and last and all along, yet—I have tried in these late years. I had grown cleaner, Dick. The nearest thing to cleanness in me was the savage in me. I was working clear— here—on the earth, Dick. Forgive me, Dick. At the end I failed, you see—but—cleaner—cleaner!"

The Friend sat erect for a moment. He stretched forth his hands. The Shareef caught one of them and

laid it to his breast. Mary Dunn took the other most lov-
ingly. Dick Dunn threw a strong arm behind him.

"But at the end, with it all—there was the blood. So
I was divided—torn—failed—half-caste."

And that was his last breath.

*   *   *   *   *

The following passage is extracted, with the recipient's
permission, from a letter headed "Villa de France Hotel,
Tangier," signed "Yours always affectionately, Dick
Dunn," and directed to a well-known black-and-white
artist in London.

"And so that was the end of him. You said he was
dramatically impressive in life. I tell you, Harry, his
end was the most awfully impressive thing I ever saw.
Picture it—that gorgeous young Shareef, Solomon in his
dress and David in his grief, striding off into the desert
at the head of the curious bier they'd sent for to Tangier
to carry the dead man in, his bride riding behind in a
litter, her ancient patriarch of a father behind her again.
That's the picture I see whenever I shut my eyes now—
the Shareef striding out into the desert, with the bride of
his sword and the body of his Friend, we insignificants
remaining behind with the woman who had caused it all
and her son, half-bred like the dead man, but a far lesser
creature. The procession stretched across an entire valley,
and the dhikr they wailed, "Lá á-lá-ha íl' Al-lah, wa
Mo-ham-med er-ra-sûl Al-lah!" an antiphonal chant from
a thousand hoarse throats, by heavens, it was superb!
And think of what the scene must have been between
Khassan and Margaret before she started upon her flight,
he torn between the protection he felt he owed her and
his loyal love of the Shareef. He felt he had failed, divided to the last—but I don't know. A tremendous busi-

ness, remote as Deuteronomy from the age we know and live in. They call these Moors a hopelessly decadent people, and I suppose they are, but, my faith, they have the roots of things and peoples in them. They are Homeric. We may be the finished and surviving article; they are the raw material, the seed we sprang from.

"They said the Shareef was going on foot the whole way, some forty miles, to a sacred spot in which the dead man was to be buried. He absolutely claimed the body—swept me aside with a word:

"'He is ours when all is said. Let him lie among us, and may Allah send peace to his soul!'

"So his speech was translated to me. And you know it was perfectly true, too. As for Margaret, we are going to leave her with that boy of hers in Tangier. She declined to come to England, and is well provided for, it seems. She will always be a person of note here, of course, particularly in Tangier—a most extraordinary woman! It appears she had actually married her son to the old Sheikh's daughter. But, in their high-handed fashion, the Sheikh declared the whole thing null and void; and, to be sure, it had never been consummated. So the Shareef is to marry Fatimah, at a city called Ed-dár el Kebeer, where he has a castle of some note. For the legal aspect of the tragedy—don't ask me! It's a queer country. I feel somehow, despite regrets, that the end was fitting. The savage side of him worked out his redemption. (The other side—the higher side, as I suppose we Europeans would call it—was hopeless—all black streak.) And that way he has gone in death. The end, the death, was a wonderful picture; but, lord, what a life was his! God save us all from mixed marriages, I say!"

Lightning Source UK Ltd.
Milton Keynes UK
UKOW06f2234250913

217968UK00011B/527/P